I0651448

Edmund Spenser, George William Kitchin

Book II of the Faery Queene

Edited by G.W. Kitchin

Edmund Spenser, George William Kitchin

Book II of the Faery Queene
Edited by G.W. Kitchin

ISBN/EAN: 9783337001278

Printed in Europe, USA, Canada, Australia, Japan

Cover: Foto ©Andreas Hilbeck / pixelio.de

More available books at **www.hansebooks.com**

Clarendon Press Series

H. C. B

3: Pa

SPENSER

FAERY QUEENE, BOOK II

KITCHIN

London

HENRY FROWDE

Oxford University Press Warehouse

Amen Corner, E.C.

(Clarendon Press Series)

Edmund
SPENSER

BOOK II

OF

THE FAERY QUEENE

EDITED BY

G. W. KITCHIN, D.D.

DEAN OF WINCHESTER

SEVENTH EDITION

354325

7. 9. 38.

Oxford

AT THE CLARENDON PRESS

M DCCC LXXXVIII

INTRODUCTION.

THE First Book of the Faery Queene pourtrays the struggles
and final victory of Truth, intellectual and spiritual, under the
name of Holiness. The Second Book sets forth the temptations
and triumphs of Moral Purity, under the name of Temperance.
The two, between them, contain the substance of man's faith
and duty. In the First Book the Christian comes out firmly
assured in his belief, and that, not as a mere effort of the imagination, or as a devotional sentiment, but as a severe intellectual
enquiry and sifting of the truth, a " proving all things" in order
to " hold fast that which is good." For this combination of
reason with religion was deemed not only allowable but essential
in the sixteenth century, and bore fruit in the appeals to men's
judgment and personal reason as against authority, to common
sense as against the iron rules and quibbles of the later Scholastics,
to the personal study of the Bible as against a blind reliance on a
traditional and sacerdotal system. In the Second Book we have
the Christian working out, with many lets and slips, the moral
ends of his existence, moderate and manly, the true ' gentleman '
in the right sense of the word. The Book expresses, in fact, the
profound belief of the age in morality as the natural sequel of
a true and enlightened faith : and Duessa and Archimago are
introduced at the opening of the " pageant," as Spenser calls it,
not merely to act as artistic links, binding Book with Book, but
more especially to indicate this close connection of religion with
morality. For falsehood and the false Church, said the age,
fight against purity of life as well as against truth of doctrine,
and the magician and the witch go on " deceiving and deceived "
to the end.

It follows that Spenser, having risen to this high conception

of the purpose of these Books, is obliged to break away from
the plan he laid down for himself in his well-known Letter to
Sir Walter Raleigh. To have worked out the twelve Books as
representing " the twelve moral virtues," each with its own
knight and its own adventures, would have demanded a far
narrower treatment of these two opening Books. Instead of
ranging over the whole extent of human life and interests as they
do, pourtraying Holiness and Temperance, we should have had
the adventures of the liberal soul struggling against extravagance
or stinginess, or the brave man attacked by temptations of rashness or of cowardice. The genius of the poet happily delivered
him from his own bonds, and enabled him to deal with his
subject with a dignity and completeness which makes each Book
a work by itself, and a commentary on the whole breadth of
human life.

But though we may look on each of these Books as a whole,
still the author is mindful to link the different " gests " together,
by likeness of structure, by reference to the original design, by
the introduction of the old actors at the beginning of the new
piece, and especially by the grander figures of Arthur and the
Faery Queene, who appear dimly throughout. The image of
the Queen looking down on the action is never absent from the
Books: in a veiled form she actually enters on the stage, the
divine huntress, chaste and beautiful as Artemis herself, and
ennobles the work with her presence and her high-souled words.
The Prince, in quest of her through the world, full of a mysterious love and allegiance to her, appears in each Book to help
the labouring knights. This link is so artfully contrived, that
while it carries on the mysterious undercurrent of the action, it
does not diminish the interest felt in the main actors. Prince
Arthur comes as a deliverer when the heroes are reduced to
helplessness: he delivers them, but he does not do their work
for them His work is noble and perfect; but it only tends
in these Books to restore the knights to themselves, and so to
enable them to work out their proper ends for themselves.

In this respect, and in many others, the two Books run upon
parallel lines. It may be worth while to notice some of these
similarities.

While Error's hateful figure forms a very striking introduction to the treatment of the subject of the search after Truth, the sad picture of the fall of Mordant and the consequent miseries of Amavia give us, in the same way, the key-note of the Second Book, pourtraying the terrible power of moral evil, if not resisted; it gives Sir Guyon the clue to his path in life, as avenger of their innocent babe. Acrasia is thus brought before us, the central figure of evil, foreseen in the effects of her poisonous fascinations: " Sin, when it hath conceived, bringeth forth death."

The House of Pride may be contrasted with Alma's Castle; the description of the Cave of Despair, and the discussion on suicide which follows it, stand over against the account of Mammon's Cave, and the disquisition held in it respecting the use and value of riches, and man's proper aim in life.

Again, as in Canto VIII of the First Book we have the overthrow of Orgoglio (that most formidable enemy of the religious character, Pride) by the hand of Arthur; so in Canto VIII of the Second Book we meet the same Prince doing to death the various forms of angry passion and fiery temper, which had all but undone the weakened and prostrate Sir Guyon.

Una corresponds, in a sort, to the Black Palmer; though we may rank the religious purity of the snow-white maiden higher than the moral equanimity of the sad-robed sober Mentor. Una guides the Red Cross Knight, the Palmer Sir Guyon: they are parted from one another under circumstances suitable to the character of each Book. The Red Cross Knight loses his companion through false illusions: Sir Guyon parts with his Palmer in order that he may pass with Idleness, in the boat that goes without an oar, across the Idle Lake.

And, lastly, the tenth Canto of each book is dedicated to the preparation of the hero of each for the crowning work of his calling. When the Red Cross Knight is taken to the House of Mercy, it is that his mind may be enlightened, and that his soul may obtain glimpses of heavenly truth before his last struggle with the Old Serpent, the Father of Lies. When Guyon reaches the Castle of Alma, he betakes himself to the study of the " Antiquities of Faery Land," in order that he may prepare himself by high example and the tranquil study of the great actions of the past to discern the difference between the glitter and allurement of Acrasia and the true greatness of a temperate and upright life.

There are also, on the other hand, special characteristics and points of difference between the two Books, arising from the different themes treated in them. The Second Book stands quite alone in English literature for its melodious diction and beautiful descriptions of a false Fairyland; while the First Book is full of fighting and grim pictures, some of them revolting rather than terrible. The Dragon, laid low over acres of land, horrible even in death, fills the mind with painful images: on the other hand, Acrasia, fair and frail, carried away in bonds, not tormented nor slain, her slaves released, and restored to human form; her bower broken down, her garden defaced, may be sad, but is not horrible. Again, the First Book is naturally far fuller of historical allusions to the time in which it was written than the Second: for the latter dealt simply with the development of each man's moral nature, while the former treated of the great religious and political questions which were agitating the world. For the same reason the allegorical character of the First Book is more strongly marked than that of the Second, though we have the general similitude of the struggle against temptation, and the detailed and interpolated allegories of the House of Moderation and of the Castle of the Soul.

It may be well to trace the way in which this allegory is worked out.

We have already noticed how the episode of Mordant and Amavia, with their bloody-handed babe, sets the action of the story into its right course. They save us from forgetting that all the struggles of the earlier Books are only preparatory to the main issue yet to come. It seems that Spenser originally intended to have given this key-note even earlier; for in the Letter to Sir Walter Raleigh he describes the Palmer as coming in (at the very outset) to the Queen's presence, bearing the babe in his arms, and seeking redress for him; he goes on to say that the task was assigned to Sir Guyon, who went forth at once to fulfil it. But the poet has happily deviated from his plan: otherwise we must have waited till the never-written

Twelfth Book for the history of the babe and the grievance against Acrasia. The hero of the Book is drawn as an honest, manly gentleman, tried as man is, but (fortified by the wise counsels of his calmer comrade) finally victorious over all temptations. And just as the episode of the bloody-handed babe brings before us the evil to be overcome, so does the Castle of Medina, in the second Canto, lay out the general principle which is to run through all morality, the Aristotelian principle that Virtue lies in the mean between the extremes of excess and defect. Yet even here the poet deviates from the philosopher. His 'defect,' the frowning Elissa, is not merely too little of the quality of which 'excess,' the gay Perissa, is too much; but each of them is a definite and independent obliquity. The one is too fond of pleasure; the other is too morose and gloomy. The knight, devoting himself to moderation, will be called on to contend now against the one, now against the other; for Spenser tacitly divides the moral trials of the knight into those of pleasure and those of pain; those of anger and spite, and those of idleness and license. The earlier Cantos deal with painful struggles against the passions of wrath and malignity, the latter ones with the passions of desire. We may say, in passing, that the episode of Braggadocchio and Trompart, in the third Canto, is intended both to be quasi-comic, as a foil to the grave nobleness of the hero, and also to complete the general treatment of the subject by adding a picture of cowardice and low knavery. It would have been impossible to have subjected Sir Guyon himself to temptations to that moral deficiency, the merest suspicion of which would have damaged the dignity of the knightly character. Braggadocchio is, therefore, drawn and left alone, after being contrasted with the splendid vision of the Virgin Queen.

The serious business of the Book begins with the fourth Canto. There Guyon encounters and overcomes Fury and the hag Occasion; and we have in the episode of Phedon a pleasing if not original illustration of the evils against which the knight is now struggling—the evils of unbridled anger and revenge. The Book continues in the same strain: to Fury and Occasion succeed the varlet Strife and the fiery Pyrocles. But in the sixth Canto the transition to the other series of temptations begins in the introduction of Phaedria, the spirit of idleness. The Knight, after these toilsome struggles, falls into her hands, and is parted from the wise Palmer. This incident relieves the action, and also prepares the way for what is to come. The loose merriment of Phaedria, the love-song in praise of idleness, the floating island, the idle lake, the little gliding skippet,—all foreshadow the yet more soft and alluring beauties of the Bower of Bliss.

With the sight of the agony and burning wounds of Pyrocles, the utter misery and pain of ungoverned wrath, this division of the Book comes to an end.

Thus far Passion (τὸ θυμικόν); now Desire (τὸ ἐπιθυμητικόν). And first the temptations of wealth and ambition in Mammon's Cave, overcome by Guyon, but with so much stress on him that he lies senseless and as dead on his return to the upper air. In this condition he is attacked by the fiery brothers. Cymocles and Pyrocles, and would have perished had not Prince Arthur appeared to rescue him and to overthrow them finally.

Then we have the Castle of the Soul, and the venomous assaults of its myriad foes, the twelve troops of temptation— five attacking the five senses, and seven representing the seven deadly sins—led by their gaunt captain Maleger. The curious and very dull episode of the British annals delays the action through a long Canto, and mars its unity and forward movement. But in the last two Cantos the struggle draws to its end. Arthur delivers the beleaguered soul, destroying the devilish captain and scattering the villains away; and Guyon, passing undismayed through many marvellous risks, reaches at last his goal the Bower of Bliss, and (thanks to a power guiding him stronger than himself) resists all the most subtle temptations of the flesh, and destroys for ever the charmed domains of luxury and intemperance.

Thus in Mammon's Cave, the World is overcome; in the person of Maleger, Arthur resists the Devil; in Acrasia's bower, Guyon wrestles with the flesh, and prevails against it. So the three great enemies are smitten down, and the task is done.

If the First Book drew the portrait of the English Christian, this Book may be said to draw that of the English gentleman, as Spenser conceived it. He says as much in the opening stanzas of the third Canto, where Braggadocchio cannot manage the steed. The thought also runs through the Book : on it are based the principles, the actions, even the temptations of the knight. Spenser draws with a loving hand the picture of a true Englishman doing his duty to God and his Queen, in the noble lines in which Belphoebe covers Braggadocchio with scorn. Those words may be regarded as the utterance of Queen Elizabeth herself, speaking for the re-awakened national life of this country. They are her protest against all lowness of aim, idleness, worldliness, self-indulgence. To be simple, industrious, truthful, pure—this is the ideal set before the Englishman, this is the moral teaching of the Book.

Let this then be our excuse for laying this little volume before the students of English history and literature. It is essentially an ennobling book, giving us a full and admirable conception of the ideal of man's best estate as a moral agent, as it was understood in those days of the young life of this country. Add to this a nobility of tone and aim, a splendour of imagery never excelled, exquisite beauty of language, dignity of thought, ever-varied incident, graphic touches of character, ceaseless variety of illustration and accessories, and we have a book well worthy to be ranked, forgotten though it has been, among the masterpieces of that age of masters.

One word as to this edition. As before, the text is founded on the editions of 1590 and 1596, collated afresh by the Rev. W. H. Bliss, M.A., of the Bodleian Library. My best thanks are due to him for his valuable help, and for the extreme care with which he has secured the accuracy of the text. The natural rule in the case of two editions issued in an author's lifetime and under his eye, is to trust almost entirely to the later. But unfortunately this rule does not hold here. The edition of 1596 shows throughout signs of great carelessness and haste. It is full of misprints and errors : when it does make corrections they are often for the worse; and one is almost tempted to think that the edition of 1590, with its page of " Faults Escaped " at the end, would have been a safer guide by itself alone. It is possible that Spenser (who was far busier, probably, in 1596 than in 1590) confined his attention almost entirely to the Fourth, Fifth, and Sixth Books, then for the first time appearing[a].

The Notes to this Book are bulkier than those to the First, in consequence of the very large amount of historical allusion, especially in the tenth Canto. I have tried to shorten them by omitting most of the explanations of idiomatic and peculiar phrases; thinking that many of them have been already given in the First Book; and also, indeed, believing that the student is not the better for being over-helped.

The Notes of this volume have had the very great advantage of the oversight of Professor Cowell, to whom this little book and I owe much.

[a] The editio princeps, 1590, contains only the first three Books.

A NEW and enlarged Glossary was compiled for the Sixth edition by the Rev. A. L. Mayhew, M.A., of Wadham College, and has been carefully revised by him for the present edition.

OXFORD, 1887.

THE FAERY QUEENE

CONTAYNING

The Legend of Sir Guyon,

or of Temperaunce.

1 RIGHT well I wote, most mighty soveraine,
That all this famous antique history,
Of some th' aboundance of an idle braine
Will judged be, and painted forgery,
Rather then matter of just memory,
Sith none, that breatheth living aire, does know
Where is that happy land of Faery,
Which I so much doe vaunt, yet no where show,
But vouch antiquities, which nobody can know.

2 But let that man with better sence advize,
That of the world least part of us is red:
And daily how through hardy enterprize
Many great regions are discovered,
Which to late age were never mentioned.
Who ever heard of th' Indian Peru?
Or who in venturous vessell measured
The Amazons huge river, now found trew?
Or fruitfullest Virginia who did ever vew?

B

3 Yet all these were, when no man did them know;
　　Yet have from wisest ages hidden beene;
　　And later times thinges more unknowne shall show.
　　Why then should witlesse man so much misweene,
　　That nothing is, but that which he hath seene?
　　What if within the moones fayre shining spheare?
　　What if in every other starre unseene
　　Of other worldes he happily should heare?
He wonder would much more: yet such to some appeare.

4 Of Faerie lond yet if he more inquire,
　　By certaine signes, here sett in sundry place,
　　He may it find: ne let him then admire,
　　But yield his sence to bee too blunt and bace,
　　That no'te without an hound fine footing trace.
　　And thou, O fairest princesse under sky,
　　In this fayre mirrhour maist behold thy face,
　　And thine own realmes in lond of Faery,
And in this antique image thy great auncestry.

5 The which, O pardon me thus to enfold
　　In covert vele, and wrap in shadowes light,
　　That feeble eyes your glory may behold,
　　Which else could not endure those beames bright,
　　But would bee dazled with exceeding light.
　　O pardon, and vouchsafe with patient eare
　　The brave adventures of this Faery knight,
　　The good Sir Guyon, gratiously to heare,
In whom great rule of Temp'raunce goodly doth appeare.

CANTO I.

Guyon, by Archimage abusd,
The Redcrosse knight awaytes;
Fyndes Mordant and Amavia slaine
With pleasures poisoned baytes.

1 THAT cunning architect of cancred guile,
  Whom princes late displeasure left in bands,
  For falsed letters, and suborned wile,
  Soone as the Redcrosse knight he understands
  To beene departed out of Eden landes,
  To serve againe his soveraine Elfin Queene;
  His artes he moves, and out of caytives hands
  Himselfe he frees by secret meanes unseene;
His shackles emptie lefte, him selfe escaped cleene.

2 And forth he fares, full of malicious mynd,
  To worken mischiefe and avenging woe,
  Whereever he that godly knight may fynd,
  His onely hart sore and his onely foe;
  Sith Una now he algates must forgoe,
  Whom his victorious handes did earst restore
  To native crowne and kingdom late ygoe:
  Where she enjoyes sure peace for evermore,
As wether-beaten ship arriv'd on happie shore.

3 Him therefore now the object of his spight
  And deadly food he makes: him to offend
  By forged treason, or by open fight,
  He seekes, of all his drifte the aymed end:
  Thereto his subtile engins he does bend,
  His practick wit and his fayre filed tong,
  With thousand other sleights: for well he kend
  His credit now in doubtfull ballaunce hong;
For hardly could be hurt, who was already stong.

4 Still as he went, he craftie stales did lay
  With cunning traynes him to entrap unwares,
  And privie spials plast in all his way,
  To weete what course he takes, and how he fares;
  To ketch him at a vantage in his snares.
  But now so wise and warie was the knight
  By tryall of his former harmes and cares,
  . That he descride, and shonned still, his slight:
The fish, that once was caught, new bait will hardly bite.

5 Nath'lesse th' enchaunter would not spare his payne,
  In hope to win occasion to his will;
  Which when he long awaited had in vaine,
  He chaunged his mind from one to other ill:
  For to all good he enimy was still.
  Upon the way him fortuned to meet,
  Faire marching underneath a shady hill,
  A goodly knight, all armd in harnesse meete,
That from his head no place appeared to his feete.

6 His carriage was full comely and upright;
  His countenance demure and temperate;
  But yet so sterne and terrible in sight,
  That cheard his friendes, and did his foes amate:
  He was an Elfin borne, of noble state
  And mickle worship in his native land;
  Well could he tourney, and in lists debate,
  And knighthood tooke of good Sir Huons hand,
When with king Oberon he came to Faerie land.

7 Him als accompanyd upon the way
  A comely palmer, clad in black attire,
  Of ripest yeares, and haires all hoarie gray,
  That with a staffe his feeble steps did stire,
  Least his long way his aged limbes should tire:
  And, if by lookes one may the mind aread,
  He seemed to be a sage and sober sire,
  And ever with slow pace the knight did lead,
Who taught his trampling steed with equall steps to tread.

8 Such whenas Archimago them did view,
   He weened well to worke some uncouth wile:
   Eftsoones, untwisting his deceiptfull clew,
   He gan to weave a web of wicked guile;
   And with a faire countenance and flattring stile
   To them approching, thus the knight bespake;
   Fayre sonne of Mars, that seeke with warlike spoile,
   And great atchiev'ments, great your self to make,
Vouchsafe to stay your steed for humble misers sake.

9 He stayd his steed for humble misers sake,
   And bad tell on the tenor of his plaint;
   Who feigning then in every limb to quake
   Through inward feare, and seeming pale and faint,
   With piteous moan his percing speach gan paint:
   Deare lady how shall I declare thy cace,
   Whom late I left in languorous constraynt?
   Would God thyselfe now present were in place
To tell this ruefull tale; thy sight could win thee grace.

10 Or rather would, O would it so had chaunst,
   That you, most noble Sir, had present beene
   When that lewd ribauld, with vile lust advaunst,
   Laid first his filthy hands on virgin cleene,
   To spoyle her dainty corse, so faire and sheene,
   As on the earth, great mother of us all,
   With living eye more faire was never seene
   Of chastitie and honour virginall:
Witnes ye heavens, whom she in vaine to help did call.

11 How may it be, (sayd then the knight halfe wroth,)
   That knight should knighthood ever so have shent?
   None but that saw, (quoth he,) would weene for troth,
   How shamefully that mayd he did torment:
   Her looser golden lockes he rudely rent,
   And drew her on the ground, and his sharpe sword
   Against her snowy brest he fiercely bent,
   And threatned death with many a bloudie word;
Toung hates to tell the rest, that eye to see abhord.

12 Therewith amoved from his sober mood,
   And lives he yet, (said he,) that wrought this act,
   And doen the heavens afford him vitall food?
   He lives, (quoth he,) and boasteth of the fact,
   Ne yet hath any knight his courage crackt.
   Where may that treachour then, (said he,) be found,
   Or by what meanes may I his footing tract?
   That shall I shew, (said he,) as sure as hound
The stricken deare doth chalenge by the bleeding wound.

13 He staid not lenger talke, but with fierce ire
   And zealous hast away is quickly gone
   To seeke that knight, where him that craftie squire
   Supposed to be. They do arrive anone
   Where sate a gentle lady all alone,
   With garments rent, and haire discheveled,
   Wringing her hands, and making piteous mone;
   Her swollen eyes were much disfigured,
And her faire face with teares was fowly blubbered.

14 The knight, approching nigh, thus to her said,
   Faire lady, through fowle sorrow ill bedight,
   Great pittie is to see you thus dismaid,
   And marre the blossome of your beautie bright:
   Forthy appease your griefe and heavie plight,
   And tell the cause of your conceived payne.
   For if he live, that hath you doen despight;
   He shall you doe dew recompence againe,
Or else his wrong with greater puissance maintaine.

15 Which when she heard, as in despightfull wise
   She wilfully her sorrow did augment,
   And offred hope of comfort did despise:
   Her golden lockes most cruelly she rent,
   And scratcht her face with ghastly dreriment;
   Ne would she speake, ne see, ne yet be seene,
   But hid her visage, and her head downe bent,
   Either for grievous shame, or for great teene,
As if her hart with sorrow had transfixed beene.

16 Till her that squire bespake, Madame my liefe,
   For Gods deare love be not so wilfull bent,
   But doe vouchsafe now to receive reliefe,
   The which good fortune doth to you present.
   For what bootes it to weepe and to wayment,
   When ill is chaunst, but doth the ill increase,
   And the weake minde with double woe torment?
   When she her squire heard speake, she gan appease
Her voluntarie paine, and feele some secret ease.

17 Eftsoone she said, Ah gentle trustie squire,
   What comfort can I wofull wretch conceave,
   Or why should ever I henceforth desire
   To see faire heavens face, and life not leave,
   Sith that false traytour did my honour reave?
   False traytour certes, (saide the Faerie knight)
   I read the man, that ever would deceave
   A gentle ladie, or her wrong through might:
Death were too little paine for such a fowle despight.

18 But now, faire ladie, comfort to you make,
   And read, who hath ye wrought this shamefull plight,
   That short revenge the man may overtake,
   Where so he be, and soone upon him light.
   Certes, (said she,) I wote not how he hight,
   But under him a gray steede he did wield,
   Whose sides with dapled circles weren dight;
   Upright he rode, and in his silver shield
He bore a bloodie crosse, that quartred all the field.

19 Now by my head, (saide Guyon,) much I muse,
   How that same knight should doe so foule amis,
   Or ever gentle damzell so abuse:
   For may I boldly say, he surely is
   A right good knight, and trew of word ywis:
   I present was, and can it witnesse well,
   When armes he swore, and streight did enterpris
   Th' adventure of the errant damozell;
In which he hath great glorie wonne, as I heare tel.

20 Nathlesse he shortly shall againe be trydc,
   And fairely quite him of th' imputed blame,
   Else be ye sure he dearely shall abyde,
   Or make you good amendment for the same:
   All wrongs have mends, but no amends of shame.
   Now therefore ladie rise out of your paine,
   And see the salving of your blotted name.
   Full loth she seemd thereto, but yet did faine;
For she was inly glad her purpose so to gaine.

21 Her purpose was not such, as she did faine,
   Ne yet her person such, as it was seene,
   But under simple shew and semblant plaine,
   Lurckt false Duessa secretly unseene,
   As a chast virgin, that had wronged beene:
   So had false Archimago her disguisd,
   To cloke her guile with sorrow and sad teene;
   And eke himselfe had craftily devisd
To be her squire, and do her service well aguisd.

22 Her late forlorne and naked he had found,
   Where she did wander in waste wildernesse,
   Lurking in rockes and caves farre under ground,
   And with greene mosse cov'ring her nakednesse
   To hide her shame and loathly filthinesse,
   Sith her Prince Arthur of proud ornaments
   And borrow'd beautie spoyld. Her nathelesse
   Th' enchanter finding fit for his intents
Did thus revest, and deckt with due habiliments.

23 For all he did, was to deceive good knights,
   And draw them from pursuit of praise and fame
   To slug in slouth and sensuall delights,
   And end their daies with irrenowmed shame.
   And now exceeding griefe him overcame,
   To see the Redcrosse thus advaunced hye;
   Therefore this craftie engine he did frame,
   Against his praise to stirre up enmitye
Of such, as vertues like mote unto him allye.

24 So now he Guyon guydes an uncouth way
    Through woods and mountaines, till they came at last
    Into a pleasant dale, that lowly lay
    Betwixt two hils, whose high heads overplast.
    The valley did with coole shade overcast;
    Through midst thereof a little river rold,
    By which there sate a knight with helme unlast,
    Himselfe refreshing with the liquid cold,
After his travell long and labours manifold.

25 Lo yonder he, cryde Archimage alowd,
    That wrought the shameful fact, which I did shew;
    And now he doth himselfe in secret shrowd,
    To fly the vengeance for his outrage dew;
    But vaine: for ye shall dearely do him rew,
    So God ye speed, and send you good successe
    Which we farre off will here abide to vew.
    So they him left, inflam'd with wrathfulnesse,
That streight against that knight his speare he did addresse.

26 Who seeing him from farre so fierce to pricke,
    His warlike armes about him gan embrace,
    And in the rest his readie speare did sticke;
    Tho when as still he saw him towards pace,
    He gan rencounter him in equall race.
    They bene ymet, both readie to affrap,
    When suddenly that warriour gan abace
    His threatned speare, as if some new mishap
Had him betidde, or hidden daunger did entrap.

27 And cryde, Mercie, sir knight, and mercie, lord,
    For mine offence and heedelesse hardiment,
    That had almost committed crime abhord,
    And with reprochfull shame mine honour shent,
    Whiles cursed steele against that badge I bent,
    The sacred badge of my Redeemers death,
    Which on your shield is set for ornament:
    But his fierce foe his steed could stay uneath,
Who, prickt with courage kene, did cruell battell breath,

28 But when he heard him speake, streight way he knew
His errour, and himselfe inclyning, sayd;
Ah deare Sir Guyon, well becommeth you,
  But me behoveth rather to upbrayd,
Whose hastie hand so far from reason strayd,
That almost it did haynous violence
On that fayre image of that heavenly mayd,
That decks and armes your shield with faire defence:
Your court'sie takes on you anothers due offence.

29 So bene they both attone, and doen upreare
Their bevers bright, each other for to greete;
Goodly comportance each to other beare,
And entertaine themselves with court'sies meet.
Then said the Redcrosse knight, Now mote I weet,
Sir Guyon, why with so fierce saliaunce,
And fell intent ye did at earst me meet;
For sith I know your goodly gouvernaunce,
Great cause, I weene, you guided, or some uncouth chaunce.

30 Certes, (said he,) well mote I shame to tell
The fond encheason, that me hether led.
A false infamous faitour late befell
Me for to meet, that seemed ill bested,
And playnd of grievous outrage, which he red
A knight had wrought against a ladie gent;
Which to avenge, he to this place me led,
Where you he made the marke of his intent,
And now is fled: foule shame him follow, where he went.

31 So can he turne his earnest unto game,
Through goodly handling and wise temperaunce.
By this his aged guide in presence came;
Who soone as on that knight his eye did glance,
Eft soones of him had perfect cognizance,
Sith him in Faerie court he late avizd;
And said, Fayre sonne, God give you happie chaunce,
And that deare Crosse uppon your shield devizd,
Wherewith above all knights ye goodly seeme aguizd.

32 Joy may you have, and everlasting fame,
Of late most hard atchiev'ment by you donne,
For which enrolled is your glorious name
In heavenly registers above the sunne,
Where you a saint with saints your seat have wonne:
But wretched we, where ye have left your marke,
Must now anew begin like race to runne.
God guide thee, Guyon, well to end thy warke,
And to the wished haven bring thy weary barke.

33 Palmer, (him answered the Redcrosse knight,)
His be the praise, that this atchiev'ment wrought,
Who made my hand the organ of His might;
More then goodwill to me attribute nought;
For all I did, I did but as I ought.
But you, faire sir, whose pageant next ensewes,
Well mote yee thee, as well can wish your thought,
That home ye may report thrise happy newes;
For well ye worthy bene for worth and gentle thewes.

34 So courteous congé both did give and take,
With right hands plighted, pledges of good will.
Then Guyon forward gan his voyage make,
With his blacke palmer, that him guided still.
Still he him guided over dale and hill,
And with his steadie staffe did point his way;
His race with reason, and with words his will,
From fowle intemperance he oft did stay,
And suffred not in wrath his hastie steps to stray.

35 In this faire wize they traveild long yfere,
Through many hard assayes, which did betide;
Of which he honour still away did beare,
And spred his glorie through all countries wide.
At last as chaunst them by a forest side
To passe, for succour from the scorching ray,
They heard a ruefull voice, that dearnly cride
With percing shriekes and many a dolefull lay;
Which to attend, a while their forward steps they stay.

36 But if that carelesse hevens, (quoth she,) despise
   The doome of just revenge, and take delight
   To see sad pageaunts of mens miseries,
   As bownd by them to live in lives despight,
   Yet can they not warne death from wretched wight.
   Come then, come soone, come sweetest death to mee,
   And take away this long lent loathed light:
   Sharpe be thy wounds, but sweete the medicines be,
That long captived soules from wearie thraldome free.

37 But thou, sweete babe, whom frowning froward fate
   Hath made sad witnesse of thy fathers fall,
   Sith heven thee deignes to hold in living state,
   Long maist thou live, and better thrive withall
   Then to thy lucklesse parents did befall:
   Live thou, and to thy mother dead attest,
   That cleare she dide from blemish criminall:
   Thy litle hands embrewd in bleeding brest
Loe I for pledges leave. So give me leave to rest.

38 With that a deadly shrieke she forth did throw,
   That through the wood reechoed againe,
   And after gave a grone so deepe and low,
   That seemd her tender hart was rent in twaine,
   Or thrild with point of thorough-piercing paine ;
   As gentle hynd, whose sides with cruell steele
   Through launched, forth her bleeding life does raine,
   Whiles the sad pang approching shee does feele,
Brayes out her latest breath, and up her eyes doth seele.

39 Which when that warriour heard, dismounting straict
   From his tall steed, he rusht into the thicke,
   And soone arrived where that sad pourtraict
   Of death and dolour lay, halfe dead, halfe quick,
   In whose white alabaster brest did stick
   A cruell knife, that made a griesly wownd,
   From which forth gusht a stream of gore blood thick,
   That all her goodly garments staind arownd,
And into a deep sanguine dide the grassie grownd.

40 Pitifull spectacle of deadly smart,
  Beside a bubbling fountaine low she lay,
  Which she increased with her bleeding hart,
  And the cleane waves with purple gore did ray;
  Als in her lap a lovely babe did play
  His cruell sport, in stead of sorrow dew;
  For in her streaming blood he did embay
  His litle hands, and tender joints embrew;
Pitifull spectacle, as ever eye did vew.

41 Besides them both, upon the soiled gras
  The dead corse of an armed knight was spred,
  Whose armour all with bloud besprinckled was;
  His ruddie lips did smile, and rosy red
  Did paint his chearefull cheekes, yet being ded;
  Seemd to have beene a goodly personage,
  Now in his freshest flowre of lustie hed,
  Fit to. inflame faire ladie with loves rage,
But, that fiers fate did crop the blossome of his age.

42 Whom when the good Sir Guyon did behold,
  His hart gan wexe as starke as marble stone,
  And his fresh bloud did frieze with fearefull cold,
  That all his sences seemd bereft attone:
  At last his mightie ghost gan deepe to grone,
  As lion, grudging in his great disdaine,
  Mournes inwardly, and makes to himselfe mone;
  Till ruth and fraile affection did constraine
His stout courage to stoupe, and shew his inward paine.

43 Out of her gored wound the cruell steel
  He lightly snatcht, and did the floudgate stop
  With his faire garment: then gan softly feel
  Her feeble pulse, to prove if any drop
  Of living blood yet in her veynes did hop:
  Which when he felt to move, he hoped faire
  To call backe life to her forsaken shop:
  So well he did her deadly wounds repaire,
That at the last she gan to breath out aire

44 Which he perceiving, greatly gan rejoice,
   And goodly counsell, that for wounded hart
   Is meetest med'cine, tempred with sweet voice;
   Ay me, deare lady, which the image art
   Of ruefull pitie, and impatient smart,
   What direfull chance, armd with avenging fate,
   Or cursed hand hath plaid this cruell part,
   Thus fowle to hasten your untimely date?
Speake, O dear lady, speake: help never comes to late.

45 Therewith her dim cie-lids she up gan reare,
   On which the drery death did sit, as sad
   As lump of lead, and made darke clouds appeare;
   But when as him all in bright armour clad
   Before her standing she espied had,
   As one out of a deadly dreame affright,
   She weakely started, yet she nothing drad:
   Streight downe againe her selfe in great despight
She groveling threw to ground, as hating life and light.

46 The gentle knight her soone with carefull paine
   Uplifted light, and softly did uphold:
   Thrise he her reard, and thrise she sunke againe,
   Till he his armes about her sides gan fold,
   And to her said; Yet, if the stony cold
   Have not all seized on your frozen hart,
   Let one word fall that may your grief unfold,
   And tell the secrete of your mortall smart;
He oft finds present helpe, who does his griefe impart.

47 Then casting up a deadly looke, full low
   She sight from bottome of her wounded brest.
   And after, many bitter throbs did throw
   With lips full pale and foltring tongue opprest,
   These words she breathed forth from riven chest;
   Leave, ah leave off, whatever wight thou bee,
   To let a weary wretch from her dew rest,
   And trouble dying soules tranquilitee.
Take not away now got, which none would give to me.

40 Ah far be it, (said he,) dear dame, fro mee,
   To hinder soule from her desired rest,
   Or hold sad life in long captivitee:
   For, all I seeke, is but to have redrest
   The bitter pangs that doth your heart infest.
   Tell then, O lady tell, what fatall priefe
   Hath with so huge misfortune you opprest?
   That I may cast to compas your reliefe,
Or die with you in sorrow, and partake your griefe.

49 With feeble hands then stretched forth on hye,
   As heaven accusing guiltie of her death,
   And with dry drops congealed in her eye,
   In these sad wordes she spent her utmost breath;
   Heare then, O man, the sorrowes that uneath
   My tongue can tell, so far all sense they pas:
   Loe this dead corpse, that lies here underneath,
   The gentlest knight, that ever on greene gras
Gay steed with spurs did pricke, the good Sir Mordant was.

50 Was, (ay the while, that he is not so now)
   My lord, my love; my deare lord, my deare love,
   So long as heavens just with equall brow
   Vouchsafed to behold us from above.
   One day, when him high courage did emmove,
   As wont ye knights to seeke adventures wilde,
   He pricked forth, his puissant force to prove,
   Me then he left enwombed of this child,
This lucklesse child, whom thus ye see with bloud defild.

51 Him fortuned (hard fortune ye may ghesse)
   To come, where vile Acrasia does wonne,
   Acrasia a false enchaunteresse,
   That many errant knightes hath fowle fordonne:
   Within a wandring island, that doth ronne
   And stray in perilous gulfe, her dwelling is,
   Fayre sir, if ever there ye travell, shonne
   The cursed land where many wend amis.
And know it by the name; it hight the *Bowre of blis.*

52 Her blisse is all in pleasure and delight,
  Wherewith she makes her lovers drunken mad,
  And then with words, and weedes of wondrous might,
  On them she workes her will to uses bad:
  My liefest lord she thus beguiled had;
  For he was flesh: (all flesh doth frailtie breed.)
  Whom when I heard to beene so ill bestad,
  Weake wretch I wrapt myselfe in palmers weed,
And cast to seek him forth through daunger and great dreed.

      *   *   .*   *   *   *

54 Him so I sought, and so at last I found,
  Where him that witch had thralled to her will,
  In chaines of lust and lewde desires ybound,
  And so transformed from his former skill,
  That me he knew not, neither his owne ill;
  Till through wise handling and faire governaunce,
  I him recured to a better will,   .
  Purged from drugs of foule intemperance:
Then meanes I gan devise for his deliverance.

55 Which when the vile enchaunteresse perceiv'd,
  How that my lord from her I would reprive,
  With cup thus charmd, him parting she deceivd;
  Sad verse, give death to him that death does give,
  And losse of love, to her that loves to live,
  So soone as Bacchus with the Nymphe does lincke.
  So parted we, and on our journey drive,
  Till coming to this well, he stoupt to drincke:
The charme fulfild, dead suddenly he downe did sincke.

56 Which when I wretch,—Not one word more she sayd,
  But breaking off the end for want of breath,
  And slyding soft, as downe to sleepe her layd,
  And ended all her woe in quiet death.
  That seeing good Sir Guyon, could uneath
  From teares abstayne, for griefe his hart did grate,
  And from so heavie sight his head did wreath,
  Accusing fortune, and too cruell fate,
Which plonged had faire ladie in so wretched state.

57 Then turning to his palmer said, Old syre
   Behold the image of mortalitie,
   And feeble nature cloth'd with fleshly tyre,
   When raging Passion with fierce tyrannie
   Robs reason of her due regalitie,
   And makes it servaunt to her basest part;
   The strong it weakens with infirmitie,
   And with bold furie armes the weakest hart; [sm
The strong through pleasure soonest falles, the weake thro

58 But Temperance (said he) with golden squire
   Betwixt them both can measure out a meane;
   Nether to melt in pleasures whot desire,
   Nor fry in hartlesse griefe and dolefull tene.
   Thrise happy man, who fares them both atweene:
   But sith this wretched woman overcome
   Of anguish, rather then of crime hath beene,
   Reserve her cause to her eternall doome,
And, in the meane vouchsafe her honorable toombe.

59 Palmer (quoth he) death is an equall doome
   To good and bad, the common inne of rest;
   But after death the tryall is to come,
   When best shall bee to them, that lived best:
   But both alike, when death hath both supprest,
   Religious reverence doth burial teene,
   Which whoso wants, wants so much of his rest:
   For all so great shame after death I weene,
As selfe to dyen bad, unburied bad to beene,

60 So both agree their bodies to engrave;
   The great earthes wombe they open to the sky,
   And with sad cypresse seemely it embrave,
   Then covering with a clod their closed eye,
   They lay therein those corses tenderly,
   And bid them sleepe in everlasting peace.
   But ere they did their utmost obsequy,
   Sir Guyon more affection to increace,
Bynempt a sacred vow, which none should aye releace.

C

61 The dead knights sword out of his sheath he drew,
　　With which he cut a lock of all their heare,
　　Which medling with their blood and earth, he threw
　　Into the grave, and gan devoutly sweare;
　　Such and such evil God on Guyon reare,
　　And worse and worse young orphane be thy paine,
　　If I or thou dew vengeance doe forbeare,
　　Till guiltie bloud her guerdon doe obtayne:
So, shedding many teares, they closd the earth againe.

CANTO II.

Babes bloudie handes may not be clensd,
The face of Golden Meane,
Her sisters Two Extremities
Strive her to banish cleane.

1 THUS when Sir Guyon with his faithful guide
Had with due rites and dolorous lament
The end of their sad tragedie uptyde,
The litle babe up in his armes he hent;
Who with sweet pleasance, and bold blandishment,
Gan smyle on them, that rather ought to weepe,
As carelesse of his woe, or innocent
Of that was doen, that ruth emperced deepe   [steepe:
In that knightes heart, and wordes with bitter teares did

2 Ah lucklesse babe, borne under cruell starre,
And in dead parents balefull ashes bred,
Full litle weenest thou, what sorrowes are
Left thee for portion of thy livelihed,
Poore orphane in the wide world scattered,
As budding braunch rent from the native tree,
And throwen forth, till it be withered;
Such is the state of men: thus enter wee
Into this life with woe, and end with miseree.

3 Then, soft himselfe inclyning on his knee
Downe to that well, did in the water weene
(So love does loathe disdainefull nicitee)
His guiltie handes from bloodie gore to cleene.
He washt them oft and oft, yet nought they beene
For all his washing cleaner. Still he strove,
Yet still the litle hands were bloodie seene;
The which him into great amaz'ment drove,
And into diverse doubt his wavering wonder clove.

4 He wist not whether blot of foule offence
Might not be purged with water nor with bath;
Or that high God, in lieu of innocence,
Imprinted had that token of His wrath,
To shew how sore bloudguiltinesse He hat'th;
Or that the charme and venim, which they drunck,
Their blood with secret filth infected hath,
Being diffused through the senselesse truncke
That through the great contagion direfull deadly stunck.

5 Whom thus at gaze the palmer gan to bord
With goodly reason, and thus faire bespake;
Ye bene right hard amated, gratious lord,
And of your ignorance great marveill make
Whiles cause not well conceived ye mistake.
But know, that secret vertues are infusd
In every fountaine, and in every lake,
Which, who hath skill them rightly to have chusd,
To proofe of passing wonders hath full often usd.

6 Of those, some were so from their sourse indewd
By great dame Nature, from whose fruitfull pap
Their welheads spring, and are with moisture deawd;
Which feeds each living plant with liquid sap,
And fills with flowres fayre Floraes painted lap:
But other some by gifte of later grace,
Or by good prayers, or by other hap,
Had vertue pourd into their waters bace,   [place.
And thenceforth were renowmd, and sought from place to

7 Such is this well, wrought by occasion straunge,
Which to her nymph befell. Upon a day,
As she the woodes with bow and shaftes did raunge,
The heartlesse hind and robucke to dismay,
Dan Faunus chaunst to meet her by the way,
And kindling fire at her faire-burning eye,
Inflamed was to follow beauties chace,
And chaced her, that fast from him did fly:
As hind from her, so she fled from her enimy.

8 At last, when fayling breath began to faint,
  And saw no meanes to scape, of shame affrayd,
  She set her downe to weepe for sore constraint,
  And, to Diana calling lowd for ayde,
  Her deare besought, to let her die a mayd.
  The goddesse heard, and suddeine, where she sate
  Welling out streames of teares, and quite dismayd
  With stony feare of that rude rustick mate,
Transformd her to a stone from stedfast virgins state.

9 Lo now she is that stone, from whose two heads,
  As from two weeping eyes, fresh streames do flow,
  Yet colde through feare and old conceived dreads;
  And yet the stone her semblance seemes to show,
  Shapt like a maid, that such ye may her know;
  And yet her vertues in her water byde:
  For it is chast and pure, as purest snow,
  Ne lets her waves with any filth be dyde,
But ever like herselfe unstayned hath beene tryde.

10 From thence it comes, that this babes bloudy hand
  May not be clensd with water of this well:
  Ne certes Sir strive you it to withstand,
  But let them still be bloudy, as befell,
  That they his mothers innocence may tell,
  As she bequeathd in her last testament;
  That as a sacred symbole, it may dwell
  In her sonnes flesh, to mind revengement,
And be for all chast dames an endlesse moniment.

11 He hearkned to his reason; and the childe
  Uptaking, to the palmer gave to beare;
  But his sad fathers armes with bloud defilde,
  An heavie load, himselfe did lightly reare;
  And turning to that place, in which whyleare
  He left his loftie steed with golden sell
  And goodly gorgeous barbes, him found not theare.
  By other accident, that earst befell,
He is convaide, but how or where, here fits not tell.

12 Which when Sir Guyon saw, all were he wroth,
  Yet algates mote he soft himselfe appease,
  And fairely_fare on foot, however loth;
  His double burden did him sore disease.
  So long they traveiled with litle ease,
  Till that at last they to a castle came,
  Built on a rocke adjoyning to the seas,
  It was an auncient worke of antique fame,
And wondrous strong by nature, and by skilfull frame.

13 Therein three sisters dwelt of sundry sort,
  The children of one syre by mothers three;
  Who dying whylome did divide this fort
  To them by equall shares in equall fee:
  But strifull minde and diverse qualitee
  Drew them in partes, and each made others foe:
  Still did they strive and dayly disagree;
  The eldest did against the youngest goe,
And both against the middest meant to worken woe.

14 Where when the knight arriv'd, he was right well
  Receiv'd, as knight of so much worth became,
  Of second sister, who did far excell
  The other two; Medina was her name,
  A sober sad, and comely curteous dame:
  Who rich arayd, and yet in modest guize,
  In goodly garments that her well became,
  Faire marching forth in honorable wize,
Him at the threshold met and well did enterprize.

15 She led him up into a goodly bowre,
  And comely courted with meet modestie,
  Ne in her speach, ne in her haviour,
  Was lightnesse seene, or looser vanitie,
  But gratious womanhood, and gravitie,
  Above the reason of her youthly yeares:
  Her golden lockes she roundly did uptye
  In breaded tramels, that no looser heares
Did out of order stray about her daintie eares.

16 Whilst she her selfe thus busily did frame
　　Seemely to entertaine her new-come guest,
　　Newes hereof to her other sisters came,
　　Who all this while were at their wanton rest,
　　Accourting each her frend with lavish fest:
　　They were two knights of perelesse puissaunce,
　　And famous far abroad for warlike gest,
　　Which to these ladies love did countenaunce,
And to his mistresse each himselfe strove to advaunce.

17 He, that made love unto the eldest dame,
　　Was hight Sir Huddibras, a hardy man; *lo h·, tithe·*
　　Yet not so good of deedes as great of name,
　　Which he by many rash adventures wan,
　　Since errant armes to sew he first began.
　　More huge in strength, then wise in workes he was, *euphuis*
　　And reason with fool-hardize over-ran;
　　Sterne melancholy did his courage pas,
And was for terrour more, all armd in shyning bras.

18 But he, that lov'd the youngest, was Sans-loy;
　　He that faire Una late fowle outraged, *cunery trigger*
　　The most unruly, and the boldest boy,
　　That ever warlike weapons menaged,
　　And to all lawlesse lust encouraged,
　　Through strong opinion of his matchlesse might:
　　Ne ought he car'd, whom he endamaged
　　By tortious wrong, or whom bereav'd of right.
He now this ladies champion chose for love to fight.

19 These two gay knights, vowd to so diverse loves,
　　Each other does envie with deadly hate,
　　And dayly warre against his foeman moves,
　　In hope to win more favour with his mate,
　　And th' others pleasing service to abate,
　　To magnifie his owne. But when they heard
　　How in that place straunge knight arrived late,
　　Both knights and ladies forth right angry far'd,
And fiercely unto battell sterne themselves prepar'd.

20 But ere they could proceede unto the place
  Where he abode, themselves at discord fell,
  .And cruell combat joyn'd in middle space:
  With horrible assault, and fury fell,
  They heapt huge strokes, the scorned life to quell,
  That all on uprore from her settled seat
  The house was raysd, and all that in did dwell;
  Seemd that lowd thunder with amazement great
Did rend the ratling skyes with flames of fouldring heat.

21 The noyse thereof cald forth that straunger knight,
  To weet, what dreadfull thing was there in hand;
  Where when as two brave knights in bloudy fight
  With deadly rancour he enraunged fond,
  His sunbroad shield about his wrest he bond,
  And shyning blade unsheathd, with which he ran
  Unto that stead, their strife to understond;
  And, at his first arrivall, them began
With goodly meanes to pacifie, well as he can.

22 But they him spying, both with greedy forse
  Attonce upon him ran, and him beset
  With strokes of mortall steele without remorse,
  And on his shield like yron sledges bet:
  As when a beare and tygre being met
  In cruell fight on lybicke ocean wide,
  Espye a traveiler with feet surbet,
  Whom they in equall pray hope to devide,
They stint their strife, and him assaile on every side.

23 But he, not like a wearie traveilere,
  Their sharp assault right boldly did rebut,
  And suffred not their blowes to byte him nere,
  But with redoubled buffes them backe did put:
  Whose grieved mindes, which choler did englut,
  Against themselves turning their wrathfull spight,
  Gan with new rage their shieldes to hew and cut,
  But still, when Guyon came to part their fight,
With heavie load on him they freshly gan to smight.

24 As a tall ship tossed in troublous seas,
  Whom raging windes, threatning to make the pray
  Of the rough rockes, doe diversly disease,
  Meetes two contrary billowes by the way,
  That her on either side doe sore assay,
  And boast to swallow her in greedy grave;
  She scorning both their spights, does make wide way,
  And with her brest breaking the fomy wave,
Does ride on both their backs, and faire herself does save.

25 So boldly he him beares, and rusheth forth
  Betweene them both, by conduct of his blade.
  Wondrous great prowesse and heroick worth
  He shewd that day, and rare ensample made,
  When two so mighty warriours he dismade:
  Attonce he wards and strikes, he takes and paies,
  Now forst to yield, now forcing to invade,
  Before, behind, and round about him layes:
So double was his paines, so double be his prayse.

26 Straunge sort of fight, three valiant knights to see
  Three combates joyne in one, and to darraine
  A triple warre with triple enmitee,
  All for their ladies froward love to gaine,
  Which, gotten, was but hate. So Love does raine
  In stoutest minds, and maketh monstrous warre;
  He maketh warre, he maketh peace againe,
  And yett his peace is but continual jarre:
O miserable men, that to him subject arre.

27 Whilst thus they mingled were in furious armes,
  The faire Medina with her tresses torne,
  And naked brest, in pitty of their harmes,
  Emongst them ran, and falling them beforne,
  Besought them by the womb, which them had borne,
  And by the loves, which were to them most deare,
  And by the knighthood, which they sure had sworne,
  Their deadly cruell discord to forbeare,
And to her just conditions of faire peace to heare.

28 But her two other sisters standing by,
   Her lowd gainsaid, and both their champions bad
   Pursew the end of their strong enmity,
   As ever of their loves they would be glad.
   Yet she with pitthy words and counsell sad,
   Still strove their stubborne rages to revoke,
   That at the last suppressing fury mad,
   They gan abstaine from dint of direfull stroke,
And harken to the sober speaches, which she spoke.

29 Ah puissant lords, what cursed evill spright,
   Or fell Erinnys in your noble harts
   Her hellish brond hath kindled with despight,
   And stird you up to worke your wilfull smarts?
   Is this the joy of armes? be these the parts
   Of glorious knighthood, after blood to thrust,
   And not regard dew right and just desarts?
   Vaine is the vaunt, and victory unjust,
That more to mighty hands, then rightfull cause both trust.

30 And were there rightfull cause of difference,
   Yet were not better, faire it to accord,
   Then with blood guiltinesse to heape offence
   And mortal vengeaunce joyne to crime abhord?
   O fly from wrath, fly, O my liefest lord:
   Sad be the sights, and bitter fruits of warre,
   And thousand furies wait on wrathfull sword;
   Ne ought the prayse of prowesse more doth marre
Then fowle revenging rage, and base contentious jarre.

31 But lovely concord, and most sacred peace,
   Doth nourish vertue, and fast friendship breeds;
   Weake she makes strong, and strong thing doth increace,
   Till it the pitch of highest prayse exceeds:
   Brave be her warres, and honorable deeds,
   By which she triumphs over ire and pride,
   And winnes an olive girlond for her meeds:
   Be therefore, O my deare lords, pacifide,
And this misseeming discord meekely lay aside.

32 Her gracious words their rancour did appall,
    And suncke so deepe into their boyling brests,
    That downe they lett their cruell weapons fall,
    And lowly did abase their loftie crests
    To her faire presence and discrete behests.
    Then she began a treaty to procure,
    And stablish terms betwixt both their requests,
    That as a law for ever should endure;
Which to observe in word of knights they did assure.

33 Which to confirme and fast to bind their league,
    After their weary sweat and bloudy toile,
    She then besought, during their quiet treague,
    Into her lodging to repair a while,
    To rest themselves, and grace to reconcile,
    They soone consent: so forth with her they fare,
    Where they are well receivd and made to spoile
    Themselves of soiled armes, and to prepare
Their minds to pleasure, and their mouths to dainty fare.

34 And those two froward sisters, their faire loves
    Came with them eke, all were they wondrous loth,
    And fained cheare, as for the time behoves,
    But could not colour yet so well the troth,
    But that their natures bad appeard in both:
    For both did at their second sister grutch,
    And inly grieve, as doth an hidden moth
    The inner garment fret, not th' utter touch;
One thought her cheare too litle, th' other thought too mutch.

35 Elissa (so the eldest hight) did deeme
    Such entertainment base, ne ought would eat,
    Ne ought would speake, but evermore did seeme
    As discontent for want of merth or meat;
    No solace could her paramour intreat
    Her once to show, ne court, nor dalliance,
    But with bent lowring browes, as she would threat,
    She scould, and frownd with froward countenaunce,
Unworthy of faire ladies comely governaunce.

Excess

36 But young Perissa was of other mind,
  Full of disport, still laughing, loosely light,
  And quite contrary to her sisters kind;
  No measure in her mood, no rule of right,
  But poured out in pleasure and delight;
  In wine and meats she flowd above the bancke,
  And in excesse exceeded her owne might;
  In sumptuous tire she joyd her self to pranck,
But of her love too lavish (little have she thancke)!

37 Fast by her side did sitt the bold Sans-loy,
  Fit mate for such a mincing mineon,
  Who in her loosenesse tooke exceeding joy;
  Might not be found a franker franion,
  Of her lewd parts to make companion;
  But Huddibras, more like a malecontent,
  Did see and grieve at his bold fashion;
  Hardly could he endure his hardiment,
Yett still he sat, and inly did him selfe torment.

Golden mean

38 Betwixt them both the faire Medina sate
  With sober grace and goodly carriage:
  With equall measure she did moderate
  The strong extremities of their outrage;
  That forward paire she ever would asswage,
  When they would strive dew reason to exceed;
  But that same froward twaine would accourage,
  And of her plenty add unto their need:
So kept she them in order, and her selfe in heed.

39 Thus fairely she attempered her feast,
  And pleasd them all with meete satiety:
  At last when lust of meat and drinke was ceast,
  She Guyon deare besought of curtesie
  To tell from whence he came through jeopardie,
  And whether now on new adventure bound.
  Who with bold grace, and comely gravitie,
  Drawing to him the eies of all around,
From lofty siege began these words aloud to sound.

40 This thy demaund, O lady, doth revive
  Fresh memory in me of that great queene,
  Great and most glorious virgin queene alive,
  That with her soveraigne. powre, and scepter shene,
  All Faery lond does peaceably sustene.
  In widest ocean she her throne does reare,
  That over all the earth it may be seene;
  As morning sunne her beams dispredden cleare,
And in her face faire peace, and mercy doth appeare.

41 In her the richesse of all heavenly grace
  In chiefe degree are heaped up on hye:
  And all that els this worlds enclosure bace,
  Hath great or glorious in mortall eye
  Adornes the person of her majestie;
  That men beholding so great excellence,
  And rare perfection in mortalitie;
  Do her adore with sacred reverence,
As th' idole of her makers great magnificence.

42 To her I homage and my service owe,
  In number of the noblest knights on ground,
  Mongst whom on me she deigned to bestowe
  Order of maydenhead, the most renownd,
  That may this day in all the world be found:
  An yearely solemne feast she wontes to make,
  The day that first doth lead the yeare around;
  To which all knights of worth and courage bold
Resort, to heare of straunge adventures to be told.

43 There this old palmer shewd himselfe that day,
  And to that mighty princesse did complaine
  Of grievous mischiefes, which a wicked Fay
  Had wrought, and many whelmd in deadly paine,
  Whereof he crav'd redresse. My soveraine,
  Whose glory is in gracious deeds, and joyes
  Throughout the world her mercy to maintaine,
  Eftsoones devisd redresse for such annoyes;
Me all unfitt for so great purpose she employes.

44 Now hath faire Phebe with her silver face
   Thrise seene the shadowes of the neather world,
   Sith last I left that honorable place,
   In which her royall presence is enrold;
   Ne ever shall I rest in house nor hold,
   Till I that false Acrasia have wonne;
   Of whose fowle deedes, too hideous to be told,
   I witnesse am, and this their wretched sonne
Whose wofull parents she hath wickedly fordonne.

45 Tell on, fayre sir, said she, that dolefull tale,
   From which sad ruth does seeme you to restraine,
   That we may pitty such unhappy bale,
   And learne from pleasures poyson to abstaine:
   Ill by ensample good doth often gayne.
   Then forward he his purpose gan pursew,
   And told the story of the mortall payne,
   Which Mordant and Amavia did rew;
As with lamenting eyes himselfe did lately vew.

46 Night was far spent, and now in ocean deepe
   Orion, flying fast from hissing snake,
   His flaming head did hasten for to steepe,
   When of his pitteous tale he end did make;
   Whilest with delight of that he wisely spake
   Those guestes beguiled did beguile their eyes
   Of kindly sleepe, that did them overtake.
   At last when they had markt the chaunged skyes,
They wist their houre was spent; then each to rest him hyes.

CANTO III.

Vaine Braggadoccbio, getting Guyons
borse is made tbe scorne
Of knigbtbood trew, and is of fayre
Belpboebe fowle forlorne.

1 SOONE as the morrow faire with purple beames
Disperst the shadowes of the mistie night,
And Titan playing on the eastern streames,
Gan cleare the deawy ayre with springing light,
Sir Guyon mindfull of his vow yplight,
Uprose from drowsie couch, and him addrest
Unto the journey which he had behight:
His puissant armes about his noble brest,
And many-folded shield he bound about his wrest.

2 Then, taking congé of that virgin pure,
The bloudy-handed babe unto her truth
Did earnestly commit, and her conjure
In vertuous lore to traine his tender youth,
And all that gentle noriture ensu'th;
And that so soone as ryper yeares he raught,
He might, for memory of that dayes ruth,
Be called Ruddymane, and thereby taught
T' avenge his parents death on them, that had it wrought.

3 So forth he far'd, as now befell, on foot,
Sith his good steed is lately from him gone;
Patience perforce; helplesse what may it boot
To fret for anger, or for griefe to mone?
His palmer now shall foot no more alone:
So fortune wrought, as under greene woods syde
He lately heard that dying lady grone,
He left his steed without, and speare besyde,
And rushed in on foot to ayd her, ere she dyde.

4 The whyles a losell wandring by the way,
   One that to bountie never cast his mind,
   Ne thought of honour ever did assay
   His baser brest, but in his kestrell kind
   A pleasing vaine of glory did he fynd,
   To which his flowing toung and troublous spright
   Gave him great ayd, and made him more inclind:
   He that brave steed there finding ready dight,
Purloynd both steed and speare, and ran away full light.

5 Now gan his hart all swell in jollitie,
   And of himselfe great hope and help conceiv'd,
   That puffed up with smoke of vanitie,
   And with selfe-loved personage deceiv'd,
   He gan to hope, of men to be receiv'd
   For such, as he him thought, or faine would bee:
   But for in court gay portaunce he perceiv'd,
   And gallant shew to be in greatest gree,
Eftsoones to court he cast t' advaunce his first degree.

6 And by the way he chaunced to espy
   One sitting idle on a sunny bancke,
   To whom avaunting in great bravery,
   As peacocke, that his painted plumes doth prancke,
   He smote his courser in the trembling flancke,
   And to him threatned his hart-thrilling speare:
   The seely man, seeing him ryde so rancke,
   And ayme at him, fell flat to ground for feare,
And crying Mercy lowd, his pitious handes gan reare.

7 Thereat the scarcrow wexed wondrous prowd,
   Through fortune of his first adventure faire,
   And with big thundring voyce revyld him lowd;
   Vile caytive, vassal of dread and despayre,
   Unworthie of the commune breathed aire,
   Why livest thou, dead dog, a lenger day,
   And doest not unto death thyselfe prepaire?
   Dye, or thyselfe my captive yield for ay;
Great favour I thee graunt, for aunswere thus to stay.

8 Hold, O deare lord, hold your dead-doing hand,
   Then loud he cryde, I am your humble thrall.
   Ah wretch, (quoth he) thy destinies withstand
   My wrathfull will, and do for mercy call.
   I give thee life: therefore prostrated fall,
   And kisse my stirrup; that thy homage bee.
   The miser threw himselfe, as an offall,
   Streight at his foot in base humilitee,   ˙
And cleeped him his liege, to hold of him in fee.

9 So happy peace they made and faire accord.
   Eftsoones this liegeman gan to wexe more bold,
   And when he felt the folly of his lord,
   In his owne kind he gan him selfe unfold:
   For he was wylie witted, and growne old
   In cunning sleights and practick knavery.
   From that day forth he cast for to uphold
   His idle humour with fine flattery,
And blow the bellowes to his swelling vanity.

10 Trompart fitt man for Braggadocchio,
   To serve at court in view of vaunting eye:
   Vaine-glorious man, when fluttring wind does blow
   In his light wings is lifted up to skye:
   The scorne of knighthood and trew chevalrye,
   To thinke, without desert of gentle deed,
   And noble worth, to be advaunced hye:
   Such prayse is shame; but honour vertues meed
Doth beare the fayrest flowre in honourable seed.

11 So forth they pass, a well consorted paire,
   Till that at length with Archimage they meet:
   Who seeing one, that shone in armour fayre,
   On goodly courser thondring with his feet,
   Eftsoones supposed him a person meet,
   Of his revenge to make the instrument:
   For since the Redcrosse knight he earst did weet
   To beene with Guyon knit in one consent,
The ill, which earst to him, he now to Guyon ment.

12 And comming close to Trompart gan inquere
   Of him, what mightie warriour that mote bee,
   That rode in golden sell with single spere,
   But wanted sword to wreake his enmitee.
   He is a great adventurer (said he)
   That hath his sword through hard assay forgone,
   And now hath vowd, till he avenged bee
   Of that despight, never to wearen none;
That speare is him enough to doen a thousand grone.

13 Th' enchaunter greatly joyed in the vaunt,
   And weened well ere long his will to win,
   And both his foen with equall foyle to daunt.
   Tho to him louting lowly did begin
   To plaine of wrongs, which had committed bin
   By Guyon, and by that false Redcrosse knight,
   Which two, through treason and deceiptfull gin,
   Had slaine Sir Mordant and his lady bright:
That mote him honour win, to wreak so foule despight.

14 Therewith all suddeinly he seemd enraged,
   And threatned death with dreadfull countenaunce,
   As if their lives had in his hand beene gaged;
   And with stiffe force shaking his mortall launce,
   To let him weet his doughtie valiaunce,
   Thus said; Old man, great sure shalbe thy meed,
   If where those knights for feare of dew vengeaunce
   Doe lurke, thou certeinly to mee areed,
That I may wreake on them their hainous hateful deed.

15 Certes, my lord, (said he) that shall I soone,
   And give you eke good helpe to their decay,
   But mote I wisely you advise to doon;
   Give no ods to your foes, but doe purvay
   Yourselfe of sword before that bloudy day;
   For they be two the prowest knights on grownd,
   And oft approv'd in many hard assay,
   And eke of surest steele, that may be found,
Do arme yourselfe against that day. them to confound.

16 Dotard, (saide he) let be thy deepe advise;
   Seemes that through many yeares thy wits thee faile,
   And that weake eld hath left thee nothing wise,
   Els never should thy judgement be so fraile
   To measure manhood by the sword or maile.
   Is not enough foure quarters of a man,
   Withouten sword or shield, an hoste to quaile?
   Thou litle wotest what this right hand can:
Speake they, which have beheld the battailes which it wan.

17 The man was much abashed at his boast;
   Yet well he wist that whoso would contend
   With either of those knightes on even coast,
   Should neede of all his armes, him to defend;
   Yet feared lest his boldnesse should offend:
   When Braggadocchio saide, Once I did sweare,
   When with one sword seven knightes I brought to end,
   Thenceforth in battell never sword to beare,
But it were that, which noblest knight on earth doth weare.

18 Perdie sir knight, saide then th' enchaunter blive,
   That shall I shortly purchase to your hond:
   For now the best and noblest knight alive
   Prince Arthur is, that wonnes in Faerie lond;
   He hath a sword, that flames like burning brond.
   The same by my device I undertake
   Shall by to-morrow by thy side be fond.
   At which bold word that boaster gan to quake,
And wondred in his minde what mote that monster make.

19 He stayd not for more bidding, but away
   Was suddein vanished out of his sight:
   The northerne wind his wings did broad display
   At his commaund, and reared him up light
   From off the earth to take his aerie flight.
   They lookt about, but no where could espie
   Tract of his foot: then dead through great affright
   They both nigh were, and each bad other flie:
Both fled attonce, ne ever backe retourned eie;

D 2

20 Till that they come unto a forrest greene,
   In which they shrowd themselves from causelesse feare;
   Yet feare them followes still, where so they beene:
   Each trembling leafe, and whistling wind they heare,
   As ghastly bug their haire on end does reare;
   Yet both doe strive their fearfulnesse to faine.
   At last they heard a horne, that shrilled cleare
   Throughout the wood, that ecchoed againe,
And made the forrest ring, as it would rive in twaine.

21 Eft through the thicke they heard one rudely rush:
   With noyse whereof he from his loftie steed
   Downe fell to ground, and crept into a bush,
   To hide his coward head from dying dreed.
   But Trompart stoutly stayd to taken heed
   Of what might hap. Eftsoone there stepped foorth
   A goodly ladie clad in hunters weed,
   That seemd to be a woman of great worth,
And by her stately portance borne of heavenly birth.

22 Her face so faire, as flesh it seemed not,
   But heavenly pourtraict of bright angels hew,
   Cleare as the skie, withouten blame or blot,
   Through goodly mixture of complexions dew;
   And in her cheekes the vermeill red did shew
   Like roses in a bed of lillies shed,
   The which ambrosiall odours from them threw,
   And gazers sence with double pleasure fed,
Hable to heale the sicke, and to revive the ded.

23 In her faire eyes two living lamps did flame,
   Kindled above at th' heavenly makers light,
   And darted fyrie beames out of the same,
   So passing persant, and so wondrous bright,
   That quite bereav'd the rash beholders sight:
   In them the blinded god his lustfull fire
   To kindle oft assayd, but had no might;
   For, with dredd majestie, and awfull ire,
She broke his wanton darts, and quenched base desire.

24 Her ivorie forhead full of bountie brave,
　　Like a broad table did itselfe dispred,
　　For Love his loftie triumphes to engrave,
　　And write the battels of his great godhead:
　　All good and honour might therein be red:
　　For there their dwelling was. And when she spake,
　　Sweet wordes, like dropping honny, she did shed,
　　And twixt the perles and rubins softly brake
A silver sound, that heavenly musicke seemd to make.

25 Upon her eyelids many graces sate,
　　Under the shadow of her even browes,
　　Working belgards and amorous retrate,
　　And every one her with a grace endowes:
　　And everie one with meekenesse to her bowes.
　　So glorious mirrhour of celestiall grace,
　　And soveraine moniment of mortall vowes,
　　How shall fraile pen descrive her heavenly face,
For feare through want of skill her beauty to disgrace?

26 So faire, and thousand thousand times more faire
　　She seemd, when she presented was to sight,
　　And was yclad, for heat of scorching aire,
　　All in a silken Camus lylly whight,
　　Purfled upon with many a folded plight,
　　Which all above besprinckled was throughout,
　　With golden aygulets, that glistred bright,
　　Like twinckling starres, and all the skirt about
Was hemd with golden fringe.

27 Below her ham her weed did somewhat traine,
　　And her streight legs most bravely were embayld
　　In gilden buskins of costly cordwaine,
　　All bard with golden bendes, which were entayld
　　With curious antickes, and full faire aumayld:
　　Before, they fastned were under her knee
　　In a rich jewell, and therein entrayld
　　The ends of all the knots, that none might see
How they within their fouldings close enwrapped bee.

28 Like two faire marble pillours they were seene,
 Which doe the temple of the gods support,
 Whom all the people decke with girlands greene,
 And honour in their festivall resort;
 Those same with stately grace and princely port
 She taught to tread, when she herselfe would grace,
 But with the wooddie nymphes when she did play,
 Or when the flying libbard she did chace,
She could them nimbly move, and after fly apace.

29 And in her hand a sharp bore-speare she held,
 And at her backe a bow and quiver gay,
 Stuft with steel-headed dartes wherewith she queld
 The salvage beastes in her victorious play,
 Knit with a golden bauldricke which forelay
 Athwart her snowy brest,

   *   *   *   *   *
    *   *   *   *   *
    *   *   *   *   *

30 Her yellow lockes, crisped like golden wyre,
 About her shoulders weren loosely shed,
 And when the wind emongst them did inspyre,
 They waved like a penon wyde dispred,
 And low behinde her backe were scattered:
 And whether art it were, or heedlesse hap,
 As through the flouring forrest rash she fled,
 In her rude haires sweet flowres themselves did lap,
And flourishing fresh leaves and blossoms did enwrap.

31 Such as Diana by the sandie shore
 Of swift Eurotas, or on Cynthus greene,
 Where all the nymphes have her unwares forlore,
 Wandreth alone with bow and arrowes keene,
 To seeke her game: or as that famous queene
 Of Amazons, whom Pyrrhus did destroy,
 The day that first of Priame she was seene,
 Did shew herselfe in great triumphant joy,
To succour the weake state of sad afflicted Troy.

32 Such when as hartlesse Trompart her did vew,
He was dismayed in his coward mind,
And doubted, whether he himselfe should shew,
Or fly away, or bide alone behinde:
Both feare and hope he in her face did finde,
When she at last him spying thus bespake;
Hayle, groome; didst not thou see a bleeding hind,
Whose right haunch earst my stedfast arrow strake?
If thou didst, tell me, that I may her overtake.

33 Wherewith reviv'd, this answere forth he threw;
O goddesse, (for such I thee take to bee)
For neither doth thy face terrestriall shew,
Nor voyce sound mortall; I avow to thee,
Such wounded beast, as that, I did not see,
Sith earst into this forrest wild I came.
But mote thy goodlyhed forgive it mee,
To weete, which of the gods I shall thee name,
That unto thee due worship I may rightly frame.

34 To whom she thus; But ere her words ensewed,
Unto the bush her eye did suddein glaunce,
In which vaine Braggadocchio was mewed,
And saw it stirre: she lefte her piercing launce,
And towards gan a deadly shaft advaunce,
In mind to mark the beast. At which sad stowre,
Trompart forth stept, to stay the mortall chaunce,
Out crying, O whatever hevenly powre,
Or earthly wight thou be, withhold this deadly howre.

35 O stay thy hand, for yonder is no game
For thy fierce arrowes, them to exercize,
But loe my lord, my liege, whose warlike name
Is farre renowmd through many bold emprize;
And now in shade he shrowded yonder lies.
She staid: with that he crauld out of his nest,
Forth creeping on his caitive hands and thies,
And standing stoutly up, his loftie crest
Did fiercely shake, and rowze, as comming late from rest.

36 As fearfull fowle, that long in secret cave
　　For dread of soring hauke herselfe hath hid,
　　Not caring how, her silly life to save,
　　She her gay painted plumes disorderid,
　　Seeing at last herselfe from daunger rid,
　　Peeps foorth, and soone renewes her native pride;
　　She gins her feathers fowle disfigured
　　Prowdly to prune, and sett on every side,
So shakes off shame, ne thinks how erst she did her hide.

37 So when her goodly visage he beheld,
　　He gan himselfe to vaunt: but when he vewed
　　Those deadly tooles, which in her hand she held,
　　Soone into other fits he was transmewed,
　　Till she to him her gratious speach renewed;
　　All haile, sir knight, and well may thee befall,
　　As all the like, which honor have persewed
　　Through deeds of armes and prowesse martiall :
All vertue merits praise, but such the most of all.

38 To whom he thus; O fairest under skie,
　　True be thy words, and worthy of thy praise,
　　That warlike feats doest highest glorifie.
　　Therein I have spent all my youthly daies,
　　And many battailes fought and many fraies
　　Throughout the world, wherso they might be found,
　　Endevoring my dreadded name to raise
　　Above the moone, that fame may it resound
In her eternall trompe with laurell girland cround.

39 But what art thou, O ladie, which doest raunge
　　In this wilde forest, where no pleasure is,
　　And doest not it for joyous court exchaunge,
　　Emongst thine equall peres, where happy blis
　　And all delight does rainge much more then this?
　　There thou maist love, and dearely loved bee,
　　And swim in pleasure, which thou here doest mis;
　　There maist thou best be seene, and best maist see:
The wood is fit for beasts, the court is fit for thee.

40 Whoso in pompe of prowd estate (quoth she)
    Does swim, and bathes himselfe in courtly blis,
    Does waste his daies in darke obscuritee,
    And in oblivion ever buried is:
    Where ease abounds, yt's eath to do amis;
    But who his limbs with labours, and his mind
    Behaves with cares, cannot so easie mis.
    Abroad in armes, at home in studious kind
Who seekes with painfull toile, shall honor soonest find.

41 In woods, in waves, in warres she wonts to dwell,
    And wil be found with perill and with paine;
    Ne can the man, that moulds in idle cell,
    Unto her happie mansion attaine:
    Before her gate high God did sweat ordaine,
    And wakefull watches ever to abide:
    But easie is the way and passage plaine
    To Pleasures pallace; it may soone be spide,
And day and night her dores to all stand open wide.

42 In Princes Court,—The rest she would have sayd,
    But that the foolish man, fild with delight
    Of her sweet words that all his sence dismaid,
    And with her wondrous beautie ravisht quight,
    Thought in his bastard armes her to embrace.
    With that she swarving backe, her javelin bright
    Against him bent, and fiercely did menace:
So turned her about, and fled away apace.

43 Which when the pesaunt saw, amazd he stood,
    And grieved at her flight; yet durst he not
    Pursew her steps through wild unknowen wood;
    Besides he feard her wrath, and threatned shot,
    Whiles in the bush he lay, not yet forgot:
    Ne car'd he greatly for her presence vaine,
    But turning said to Trompart, What fowle blot
    Is this to knight, that lady should againe
Depart to woods untoucht, and leave so proud disdayne?

44 Perdie, (said Trompart) lett her passe at will,
   Least by her presence daunger mote befall.
   For who can tell (and sure I feare it ill)
   But that she is some powre celestiall?
   For, whiles she spake, her great words did apall
   My feeble courage, and my hart oppresse,
   That yet I quake and tremble over all.
   And I, (said Braggadocchio) thought no lesse,
When first I heard her horn sound with such ghastlinesse.

45 For from my mothers wombe this grace I have
   Me given by eternall destinie,
   That earthly thing may not my corage brave
   Dismay with feare, or cause on foote to flie,
   But either hellish feends, or powres on hie:
   Which was the cause, when earst that horn I heard,
   Weening it had been thunder in the skie,.
   I hid my selfe from it as one affeard;
But when I other knew, my self I boldly reard.

46 But now, for feare of worse that may betide,
   Let us soone hence depart. They soone agree;
   So to his steed he got, and gan to ride,
   As one unfit therefore, that all might see
   He had not trayned bene in chevalree,
   Which well that valiaunt courser did discerne;
   For he despysd to tread in dew degree,
   But chaufd and fom'd with courage fierce and sterne,
And to be easd of that base burden still did erne.

CANTO IV.

Guyon does Furor bind in chaines,
And stops Occasion:
Delivers Phedon, and therefore
By Strife is rayld upon.

1 IN brave pursuit of honorable deed,
There is I know not what great difference
Betweene the vulgar and the noble seed,
Which unto things of valorous pretence
Seemes to be borne by native influence;
As feates of armes, and love to entertaine,
But chiefly skill to ride seemes a science
Proper to gentle blood; some others faine
To menage steeds, as did this vaunter; but in vaine.

2 But he the rightfull owner of that steed,
Who well could menage and subdew his pride,
The whiles on foot was forced for to yeed,
With that blacke palmer, his most trusty guide;
Who suffred not his wandring feet to slide.
But when strong passion, or weake fleshlinesse,
Would from the right way seeke to draw him wide,
He would through temperance and stedfastnesse,
Teach him the weak to strengthen, and the strong suppresse.

3 It fortuned forth faring on his way,
He saw from farre, or seemed for to see,
Some troublous uprore or contentious fray,
Whereto he drew in haste it to agree.
A mad man, or that feigned mad to bee,
Drew by the haire along upon the grownd
A handsom stripling with great crueltee,
Whom sore he bett, and gor'd with many a wownd,
That cheekes with teares, and sides with blood, did all abound.

4 And him behynd, a wicked hag did stalke
　　In ragged robes, and filthy disaray,
　　Her other leg was lame, that she no'te walke,
　　But on a staffe her feeble steps did stay;
　　Her lockes, that loathly were and hoarie gray,
　　Grew all afore, and loosly hong unrold, —
　　But all behinde was bald, and worne away,
　　That none thereof could ever taken hold,
And eke her face ill favourd, full of wrinckles old.

5 And, ever as she went, her toung did walke
　　In foule reproch, and termes of vile despight,
　　Provoking him, by her outrageous talke,
　　To heape more vengeance on that wretched wight;
　　Sometimes she raught him stones, wherewith to smite,
　　Sometimes her staffe, though it her one leg were,
　　Withouten which she could not goe upright;
　　Ne any evil meanes she did forbeare,
That might him move to wrath, and indignation reare.

6 The noble Guyon, mov'd with great remorse
　　Approching, first the hag did thrust away;
　　And after adding more impetuous forse,
　　His mightie hands did on the madman lay,
　　And pluckt him backe; who, all on fire streight way
　　Against him turning all his fell intent,
　　With beastly brutish rage gan him assay,
　　And smot, and bit, and kickt, and scratcht, and rent,
And did he wist not what in his avengement.

7 And sure he was a man of mickle might,
　　Had he had governance, it well to guide:
　　But when the franticke fitt inflamd his spright,
　　His force was vaine, and strooke more often wide
　　Then at the aymed marke, which he had eide:
　　And oft himselfe he chaunst to hurt unwares,
　　Whilst reason blent through passion, nought descride,
　　But as a blindfold bull at randon fares,　[nought cares.
And where he hits, nought knowes, and whom he hurts,

8 His rude assault and rugged handeling
  Straunge seemed to the knight, that aye with foe
  In fayre defence and goodly menaging
  Of armes was wont to fight, yet nathemoe
  Was he abashed now not· fighting so,   ·
  But more enfierced through his currish play,
  Him sternly grypt, and hayling to and fro,
  To overthrow him strongly did assay,
But overthrew himselfe unwares, and lower lay.

9 And being downe the villein sore did beat,
  And bruze with clownish fistes his manly face:
  And eke the hag with many a bitter threat,
  Still cald upon to kill him in the place.
  With whose reproch, and odious menace,
  The knight emboyling in his haughtie hart
  Knit all his forces, and gan soone unbrace
  His grasping hold: so lightly did upstart,
And drew his deadly weapon, to maintaine his part.

10 Which when the palmer saw, he loudly cryde,
   Not so, O Guyon, never thinke that so
   That monster can be maistred or destroyd:
   He is not, ah, he is not such a foe,
   As steele can wounde, or strength can overthroe.
   That same is Furor, cursed cruel ,wight,
   That unto knighthood workes much shame and woe;
   And that same hag, his aged mother, hight
Occasion, the root of all wrath and despight.

11 With her, whoso will raging Furor tame,
   Must first begin, and well her amenage:
   First her restraine from her reprochfull blame,
   And evill meanes, with which she doth enrage
   Her franticke sonne, and kindles his courage;
   Then when she is withdrawen, or strong withstood,
   It's eath his idle fury to asswage,
   And calme the tempest of his passion wood;
The bankes are overflowen, when stopped is the flood.

12 Therewith Sir Guyon left his first emprise,
And, turning to that woman, fast her hent
By the hoare lockes that hong before her eyes,
And to the ground her threw: yet n'ould she stent
Her bitter rayling and foule revilement;
But still provokt her sonne to wreake her wrong;
But nathelesse he did her still torment,
And, catching hold of her ungratious tong,
Thereon an yron lock did fasten firme and strong.

13 Then whenas use of speach was from her reft,
With her two crooked handes she signes did make,
And beckned him, the last help she had left:
But he that last left helpe away did take,
And both her handes fast bound unto a stake,
That she note stirre. Then gan her sonne to flie
Full fast away, and did her quite forsake :
But Guyon after him in hast did hie,
And soone him overtooke in sad perplexitie. ,

14 In his strong armes he stiffely him embraste,
Who him gain striving nought at all prevaild :
For all his power was utterly defaste,
And furious fits at earst quite weren quaild :
Oft he re'nforst, and oft his forces fayld,
Yet yield he would not, nor his rancor slacke.
Then him to ground he cast, and rudely hayld,
And both his hands fast bound behind his backe,
And both his feet in fetters to an yron racke.

15 With hundred yron chaines he did him bind,
And hundred knots, that did him sore constraine:
Yet his great yron teeth he still did grind,
And grimly gnash, threatning revenge in vaine:
His burning eyen, whom bloudie strakes did staine,
Stared full wide, and threw forth sparkes of fire,
And more for ranck despight, then for great paine,
Shakt his long lockes colourd like copper-wire,
And bit his tawny beard to shew his raging ire.

16 Thus when as Guyon Furor had captivd,
 Turning about he saw that wretched squire,
 Whom that mad man of life nigh late depriv'd,
 Lying on ground, all soild with bloud and mire:
 Whom when as he perceived to respire,
 He gan to comfort, and his woundes to dresse.
 Being at last recured, he gan inquire,
 What hard mishap him brought to such distresse,
And made that caytives thral, the thral of wretchednesse.

17 With hart then throbbing, and with watry eyes,
 Fayre sir, (quoth he) what man can shun the hap
 That hidden lyes unwares him to surpryse?
 Misfortune waites advantage to entrap
 The man most warie in her whelming lap.
 So me weake wretch, of many weakest one,
 Unweeting, and unware of such mishap,
 She brought to mischiefe through Occasion,
Where this same wicked villein did me light upon.

18 It was a faithelesse squire, that was the sourse
 Of all my sorrow, and of these sad teares,
 With whom from tender dug of commune nourse
 Attonce I was upbrought, and eft when yeares
 More rype us reason lent to chose our peares,
 Ourselves in league of vowed love we knit:
 In which we long time without gealous feares ·
 Or faultie thoughts, continewd as was fit;
And for my part I vow, dissembled not a whit.

19 It was my fortune, commune to that age,
 To love a lady faire of great degree,
 The which was borne of noble parentage,
 And set in highest seat of dignitee,
 Yet seemd no lesse to love, then lovd to bee:
 Long I her serv'd, and found her faithfull still,
 Ne ever thing could cause us disagree:
 Love that two hartes makes one, makes eke one will:
Each strove to please, and others pleasure to fulfill.

20 My friend, hight Philemon, I did partake
　　Of all my love and all my privitie;
　　Who greatly joyous seemed for my sake,
　　And gratious to that ladie, as to mee;
　　Ne ever wight, that mote so welcome bee
　　As he to her, withouten blot or blame,
　　Ne ever thing, that she could thinke or see,
　　But unto him she would impart the same:
O wretched man, that would abuse so gentle dame.

21 At last such grace I found, and meanes I wrought,
　　That I that lady to my spouse had wonne;
　　Accord of friends, consent of parents sought,
　　Affiance made, my happinesse begonne,
　　There wanted nought but few rites to be donne,
　　Which marriage make; that day too farre did seeme:
　　Most joyous man, on whome the shining sunne
　　Did shew his face, myself I did esteeme,
And that my falser friend did no lesse joyous deeme.

22 But ere that wished day his beame disclosd,
　　He either envying my toward good,
　　Or of himselfe to treason ill disposd,
　　One day unto me came in friendly mood,
　　And told for secret how he understood
　　That ladie whom I had to me assynd,
　　Had both distaind her honorable blood,
　　And eke the faith which she to me did bynd;
And therefore wisht me stay, till I more truth should fynd.

23 The gnawing anguish, and sharp gelosy,
　　Which his sad speach infixed in my brest,
　　Ranckled so sore, and festred inwardly,
　　That my engreeved mind could find no rest,
　　Till that the truth thereof I did outwrest;
　　And him besought, by that same sacred band
　　Betwixt us both, to counsell me the best.
　　He then with solemne oath and plighted hand
Assur'd, ere long the truth to let me understand.

24 Ere long with like againe he boorded mee,
 Saying, he now had boulted all the floure,
 And that it was a groome of base degree,
 Which of my love was partner paramoure:
 Who used in a darksome inner bowre
 Her oft to meete: which better to approve,
 He promised to bring me at that howre,
 When I should see that would me nearer move,
And drive me to withdraw my blind abused love.

25 This gracelesse man for furtherance of his guile,·
 Did court the handmayd of my lady deare,
 Who glad t'embosome his affection vile,
 Did all she might more pleasing to appeare.
 One day to worke her to his will more neare,
 He woo'd her thus; Pryene, (so she hight)
 What great despight does fortune to thee beare,
 Thus lowly to abase thy beautie bright,
That it should not deface all others lesser light?

26 But if she had her least helpe to thee lent,
 T' adorne thy forme according thy desart,
 Their blazing pride thou wouldest soone have blent,
 And staynd their prayses with thy least good part;
 Ne should faire Claribell with all her art,
 Though she thy lady be, approch thee neare:
 For proofe thereof, this evening, as thou art,
 Aray thyselfe in her most gorgeous geare,
That I may more delight in thy embracement deare.

27 The mayden proud through prayse, and mad through love,
 Him hearkned to, and soone herselfe arayd;
 The whiles to me the treachour did remove
 His craftie engin, and as he had sayd, ·
 Me leading, in a secret corner layd,
 The sad spectatour of my tragedie;
 Where left, he went, and his owne false part playd, ·
 Disguised like that groome of base degree,
Whom he had feignd th' abuser of my love to bee.

E

28 Eftsoones he came unto th'appointed place,
   And with him brought Pryene, rich arayd,
   In Claribellaes clothes. Her proper. face
   I not descerned in that darkesome shade,
   But weend it was my love, with whom he playd.
   Ah God, what horrour and tormenting griefe
   My hart, my handes, mine eies, and all assayd:
   Me liefer were ten thousand deathes priefe
Then wound of gealous worme, and shame of such repriefe.

29 I home returning, fraught with fowle despight,
   And chawing vengeaunce all the way I went,
   Soone as my loathed love appeard in sight,
   With wrathfull hand I slew her innocent;
   That after soone I dearely did lament:
   For when the cause of that outrageous deede
   Demaunded, I made plaine and evident,
   Her faultie handmayd, which that bale did breede,
Confest how Philemon her wrought to chaunge her weede.

30 Which when I heard, with horrible afrright
   And hellish fury all enragd, I sought
   Upon myselfe that vengeable despight
   To punish: yet it better first I thought
   To wreake my wrath on him, that first it wrought.
   To Philemon, false faytour Philemon,
   I cast to pay that I so dearely bought;
   Of deadly drugs I gave him drinke anon,
And washt away his guilt with guiltie potion.

31 Thus heaping crime on crime, and griefe on griefe,
   To losse of love adjoyning losse of frend,
   I meant to purge both with a third mischiefe,
   And in my woes beginner it to end:
   That was Pryene; she did first offend,
   She last should smart: with which cruell intent,
   When I at her my murdrous blade did bend,
   She fled away with ghastly dreriment,
And I, pursewing my fell purpose, after went.

32 Feare gave her wings, and rage enforst my flight;
　Through woods and plaines so long I did her chace,
　Till this mad man, whom your victorious might
　Hath now fast bound, me met in middle space:
　As I her, so he me pursewd apace,
　And shortly overtooke: I breathing yre,
　Sore chauffed at my stay in such a cace,
　And with my heat kindled his cruell fyre;
Which kindled once, his mother did more rage inspyre.

33 Betwixt them both, they have me doen to dye,
　Through wounds, and strokes, and stubborne handeling,
　That death were better then such agony,
　As griefe and furie unto me did bring;
　Of which in me yet stickes the mortall sting,
　That during life will never be appeasd.
　When he thus ended had his sorrowing,
　Said Guyon, Squire, sore have ye beene diseasd;
But all your hurts may soone through temperance be easd.

34 Then gan the palmer thus, Most wretched man,
　That to affections does the bridle lend;
　In their beginning they are weake and wan,
　But soone through suff'rance growe to fearefull end;
　Whiles they are weake betimes with them contend:
　For when they once to perfect strength do grow,
　Strong warres they make, and cruell battry bend
　Gainst fort of reason, it to overthrow:
Wrath, gelosie, griefe, love this squire have laide thus low.

35 Wrath, gealosie, griefe, love do thus expell:
　Wrath is a fire, and gealosie a weede,
　Griefe is a flood, and love a monster fell;
　The 'fire of sparkes, the weede of little seede,
　The flood of drops, the monster filth did breede:
　But sparks, seed, drops, and filth, do thus delay;
　The sparks soone quench, the springing seed outweed,
　The drops dry up, the filth wipe cleane away:
So shall Wrath, gealosie, griefe, love, dye and decay.

36 Unlucky squire, (saide Guyon) sith thou hast
   Falne into mischiefe through intemperaunce,
   Henceforth take heede of that thou now hast past.
   And guide thy wayes with warie governaunce,
   Least worse betide thee by some later chaunce.
   But read how art thou nam'd, and of what kin.
   Phedon I hight, (quoth he) and do advaunce
   Mine auncestry from famous Coradin,
Who first to rayse our house to honour did begin.

37 Thus as he spake, lo far away they spyde
   A varlet ronning towards hastily,
   Whose flying feet so fast their way applyde,
   That round about a cloud of dust did fly,
   Which, mingled all with sweate, did dim his eye.
   He soone approched, panting, breathlesse, whot,
   And all so soyld, that none could him descry;
   His countenaunce was bold, and bashed not
For Guyons lookes, but scornefull ey glaunce at him shot.

38 Behinde his backe he bore a brasen shield,
   On which was drawen faire, in colours fit,
   A flaming fire in midst of bloudy field,
   And round about the wreath this word was writ,
   Burnt I doe burne. Right well beseemed it
   To be the shield of some redoubted knight;
   And in his hand two dartes exceeding flit,
   And deadly sharpe he held, whose heads were dight
In poyson and in bloud, of malice and despight.

39 When he in presence came, to Guyon first
   He boldly spake, Sir knight, if knight thou bee,
   Abandon this forestalled place at erst,
   For feare of further harme, I counsell thee,
   Or bide the chaunce at thine owne jeoperdie.
   The knight at his great boldnesse wondered,
   And though he scornd his idle vanitie,
   Yet mildly him to purpose answered;
For not to grow of nought he it conjectured.

40 Varlet, this place most dew to me I deeme,
Yielded by him, that held it forcibly.
But whence shold come that harme, which thou dost seeme
To threat to him, that mindes his chaunce t'abye?
Perdy, (sayd he) here comes, and is hard by
A knight of wondrous powre and great assay,
That never yet encountred enemy,
But did him deadly daunt, or fowle dismay;
Ne thou for better hope, if thou his presence stay.

41 How hight he then (said Guyon) and from whence?
Pyrochles is his name, renowmed farre
For his bold feats and hardy confidence,
Full oft approvd in many a cruell warre,
The brother of Cymochles, both which arre
The sonnes of old Acrates and Despight,—
Acrates sonne of Phlegeton and Jarre;
But Phlegeton is sonne of Herebus and Night;
But Herebus sonne of Aeternitie is hight.

42 So from immortall race he does proceede,
That mortall hands may not withstand his might,
Drad for his derring do, and bloudy deed;
For all in bloud and spoile is his delight.
His am I Atin, his in wrong and right,
That matter make for him to worke upon,
And stirre him up to strife and cruell fight.
Fly therefore, fly this fearefull stead anon,
Least thy foolhardize worke thy sad confusion.

43 His be that care, whom most it doth concerne,
(Sayd he) but whither with such hasty flight
Art thou now bound? for well mote I discerne
Great cause, that carries thee so swift and light.
My lord, (quoth he) me sent, and streight behight
To seeke Occasion, where so she bee:
For he is all disposd to bloudy fight,
And breathes out wrath and hainous crueltie;
Hard is his hap, that first fals in his jeopardie.

44 Mad man, (said then the palmer) that does seeke
Occasion to wrath, and cause of strife ;
She comes unsought, and shonned followes eke.
Happy, who can abstaine, when rancour rife
Kindles revenge, and threats his rusty knife ;
Woe never wants, where every cause is caught,
And rash Occasion makes unquiet life.
Then loe, where bound she sits, whom thou hast sought,
(Said Guyon) let that message to thy lord be brought.

45 That when the varlet heard and saw, streight way
He wexed wondrous wroth, and said, Vile knight,
That knights and knighthood doest with shame upbray,
And shewst th' ensample of thy childish might,
With silly weake old woman thus to fight.
Great glory and gay spoile sure hast thou got,
And stoutly prov'd thy puissaunce here in sight ;
That shall Pyrochles well requite, I wot,
And with thy blood abolish so reprochfull blot.

46 With that one of his thrillant darts he threw,
Headed with ire and vengeable despight :
The quivering steele his aymed end well knew,
And to his brest itselfe intended right :
But he was warie, and, ere it empight
In the meant marke, advaunst his shield atweenc, '
On which it seizing, no way enter might,
But backe rebounding left the forckhead keene ;
Eftsoones he fled away, and might no where be seene.

CANTO V.

1 WHOEVER doth to temperaunce apply
His stedfast life, and all his actions frame,
Trust me, shall find no greater enimy,
Then stubborne perturbation, to the same;
To which right well the wise do give that name,
For it the goodly peace of stayed mindes
Does overthrow, and troublous warre proclame :
His owne woes authour, who so bound it findes,
As did Pyrochles, and it wilfully unbindes.

2 After that varlets flight, it was not long,
Ere on the plaine fast pricking Guyon spide
One in bright armes embatteiled full strong,
That, as the sunny beames do glaunce and glide
Upon the trembling wave, so shined bright,
And round about him threw forth sparkling fire,
That seemd him to enflame on every side :
His steed was bloudy red, and fomed ire,
When with the maistring spur he did him roughly stire.

3 Approching nigh, he never staid to greete,
Ne chaffar words, prowd corage to provoke,
But prickt so fiers, that underneath his feete
The smouldring dust did rownd about him smoke,
Both horse and man nigh able for to choke;
And fayrly couching his steele-headed speare,
Him first saluted with a sturdy stroke;
It booted nought sir Guyon comming neare
To thinke such hideous puissaunce on foot to beare;

4 But lightly shunned it, and passing by,
  With his bright blade did smite at him so fell,
  That the sharpe steele arriving forcibly
  On his broad shield, bit not, but glauncing fell
  On his horse necke before the quilted sell,
  And from the head the body sundred quight.
  So him dismounted low, he did compell
  On foot with him to matchen equall fight;
The truncked beast fast bleeding did him fowly dight.

5 Sore bruzed with the fall, he slow uprose,
  And all enraged, thus him loudly shent;
  Disleall knight, whose coward courage chose
  To wreake it selfe on beast all innocent,
  And shund the marke, at which it should be ment,
  Therby thine armes seem strong, but manhood fraile;
  So hast thou oft with guile thine honor blent;
  But litle may such guile thee now availe,
If wonted force and fortune doe me not much faile.

6 With that he drew his flaming sword, and strooke
  At him so fiercely, that the upper marge
  Of his sevenfolded shield away it tooke,
  And glauncing on his helmet, made a large
  And open gash therein: were not his targe,
  That broke the violence of his intent,
  The weary soule from thence it would discharge;
  Nathelesse so sore a buff to him it lent,
That made him reele, and to his brest his beyer bent.

7 Exceeding wroth was Guyon at that blow,
  And much ashamd, that stroke of living arme
  Should him dismay, and make him stoup so low,
  Though otherwise it did him litle harme:
  Tho hurling high his yron braced arme,
  He smote so manly on his shoulder plate,
  That all his left side it did quite disarme;
  Yet there the steel stayd not, but inly bate
Deepe in his flesh, and opened wide a red floodgate.

8 Deadly dismayd with horror of that dint
　Pyrochles was, and grieved eke entyre;
　Yet nathemore did it his fury stint,
　But added flame unto his former fire,
　That welnigh molt his hart in raging yre,
　Ne thenceforth his approved skill, to ward,
　Or strike, or hurtle rownd in warlike gyre, *circle*
　Remembred he, ne car'd for his saufgard,
But rudely rag'd, and like a cruell tygre far'd.

9 He hewd, and lasht, and foynd, and thundred blowes,
　And every way did seeke into his life,
　Ne plate, ne male could ward so mighty throwes,
　But yielded passage to his cruell knife.
　But Guyon, in the heat of all his strife,
　Was warie wise, and closely did awayt
　Avauntage, whilest his foe did rage most rife;
　Sometimes athwart, sometimes he strooke him strayt,
And falsed oft his blowes, t'illude him with such bayt.

10 Like as a lyon whose imperiall powre
　A prowd rebellious unicorn defyes,
　T' avoide the rash assault and wrathful stowre *battle*
　Of his fiers foe, him to a tree applies,
　And when him running in full course he spies,
　He slips aside; the whiles that furious beast
　His precious horne, sought of his enimies,
　Strikes in the stocke, ne thence can be releast,
But to the mighty victour yields a bounteous feast.

11 With such faire sleight him Guyon often faild,
　Till at the last all breathlesse, wearie, faint,
　Him spying, with fresh onset he assaild,
　And, kindling new his courage seeming queint,
　Strooke him so hugely, that through great constraint
　He made him stoup perforce unto his knee,
　And do unwilling worship to the saint,
　That on his shield depainted he did see;
Such homage till that instant never learned hee.

12 Whom Guyon seeing stoup, pursewed fast
The present offer of faire victory,
And soone his dreadfull blade about he cast,
Wherewith he smote his haughty crest so hye,
That streight on grownd made him full low to lye;
Then on his brest his victour foote he thrust :
With that he cryde; Mercy, doe me not dye,
Ne deeme thy force by fortunes doome unjust,
That hath (maugre her spight) thus low me laid in dust.

13 Eftsoones his cruell hand Sir Guyon stayd,
Tempring the passion with advizement slow
And maistring might on enimy dismayd;
For th' equall dye of warre he well did know;
Then to him said, Live, and allegaunce owe
To him, that gives thee life and libertie,
And henceforth by this dayes ensample trow,
That hasty wroth, and heedlesse hazardie,
Do breede repentaunce late, and lasting infamie.

14 So up he let him rise, who with grim looke
And count'naunce sterne upstanding, gan to grind
His grated teeth for great disdeigne, and shooke
His sandy lockes, long hanging downe behind,
Knotted in bloud and dust, for griefe of mind
That he in ods of armes was conquered;
Yet in himselfe some comfort he did find,
That him so noble knight had maistered,
Whose bounty more then might, yet both he wondered.

15 Which Guyon marking said, Be nought agriev'd,
Sir knight, that thus ye now subdewed arre:
Was never man, who most conquestes atchiev'd
But sometimes had the worse, and lost by warre,
Yet shortly gaynd, that losse exceeded farre;
Losse is no shame, nor to bee lesse then foe,
But to bee lesser, then himselfe, doth marre
Both loosers lot, and victour's prayse alsoe :
Vaine others overthrowes, who selfe doth overthrowe.

16 Fly, O Pyrochles, fly the dreadfull warre,
　　That in thyselfe thy lesser parts do move,
　　Outrageous anger, and woe working jarre,
　　Direfull impatience, and hart murdring love;
　　Those, those thy foes, those warriours far remove,
　　Which thee to endlesse bale captived lead.
　　But sith in might thou didst my mercy prove,
　　Of curtesie to me the cause aread
That thee against me drew with so impetuous dread.

17 Dreadlesse, (said he) that I shall soone declare:
　　It was complaind that thou hadst done great tort
　　Unto an aged woman, poore and bare,
　　And thralled her in chaines with strong effort,
　　Voide of all succour and needfull comfort:
　　That ill beseemes thee, such as I thee see,
　　To worke such shame. Therefore I thee exhort
　　To chaunge thy will, and set Occasion free,
And to her captive sonne yield his first libertee.

18 Thereat Sir Guyon smilde, And is that all
　　(Said he) that thee so sore displeased hath?
　　Great mercy sure, for to enlarge a thrall,
　　Whose freedom shall thee turne to greatest scath.
　　Nath'lesse now quench thy whot emboyling wrath:
　　Loe there they be; to thee I yield them free.
　　Thereat he wondrous glad, out of the path
　　Did lightly leape, where he them bound did see,
And gan to breake the bands of their captivitee.

19 Soone as Occasion felt her selfe untyde,
　　Before her sonne could well assoyled bee,
　　She to her use returnd, and streight defyde
　　Both Guyon and Pyrochles: th' one (said shee)
　　Bycause he wonne; the other, because hee
　　Was wonne: So matter did she make of nought,
　　To stirre up strife, and garre them disagree:
　　But soone as Furor was enlargd, she sought
To kindle his quencht fire, and thousand causes wrought.

20 It was not long, ere she inflam'd him so,
   That he would <u>algates</u> with Pyrochles fight,
   And his redeemer chalengd for his foe,
   Because he had not well mainteind his right,
   But yielded had to that same straunger knight.
   Now gan Pyrochles wex as wood as hee,
   And him affronted with impatient might :
   So both together fiers engrasped bee,
Whiles Guyon standing by their uncouth strife does see.

21 Him all that while Occasion did provoke
   Against Pyrochles, and new matter framed
   Upon the old, him stirring to be wroke
   Of his late wrongs, in which she oft him blamed
   For suffering such abuse as knighthood sham'd,
   And him <u>dishabled</u> quyte. But he was wise,
   Ne would with vaine occasions be inflamed;
   Yet others she more urgent did devise :
Yet nothing could him to impatience entise.

22 Their fell contention still increased more,
   And more thereby increased Furors might,
   That <u>he</u> <u>his</u> foe has hurt and wounded sore
   And him in bloud and durt deformed quight.
   His mother eke, more to augment his spight,
   Now brought to him a flaming fier brond,
   Which she in Stygian lake, ay burning bright
   Had kindled : that she gave into his hond,
That armd with fire, more hardly he mote him withstond.

23 Tho gan that villein wex so fiers and strong,
   That nothing might sustaine his furious forse ;
   He cast him downe to ground, and all along
   Drew him through durt and myre without remorse,
   And fowly battered his comely corse,
   That Guyon much disdeignd so loathly sight.
   At last he was compeld to cry perforse,
   Help, O Sir Guyon, helpe most noble knight,
To rid a wretched man from hands of hellish wight.

24 The knight was greatly moved at his plaint,
And gan him dight to succour his distresse,
Till that the palmer, by his grave restraint,
Him stayd from yielding pittifull redresse,
And said, Deare sonne, thy causelesse ruth represse,
Ne let thy stout hart melt in pitty vayne:
He that his sorrow sought through wilfulnesse,
And his foe fettred would release agayne,
Deserves to taste his follies fruit, repented payne.

25 Guyon obayd; so him away he drew
From needlesse trouble of renewing fight
Already fought, his voyage to pursew.
But rash Pyrochles varlet, Atin hight,
When late he saw his lord in heavy plight,
Under Sir Guyons puissaunt stroke to fall,
Him deeming dead, as then he seemd in sight,
Fled fast away, to tell his funerall
Unto his brother, whom Cymochles men did call.

26 He was a man of rare redoubted might,
Famous throughout the world for warlike prayse,
And glorious spoiles, purchast in perilous fight:
Full many doughtie knights he in his dayes
Had doen to death, subdewde in equall frayes;
Whose carkases, for terrour of his name,
Of fowles and beastes he made the piteous prayes,
And hong their conquered armes for more defame
On gallow trees, in honour of his dearest dame.

27 His dearest dame is that enchaunteresse,
The vile Acrasia, that with vaine delightes,
And idle pleasures, in her bowre of blisse,
Does charme her lovers, and the feeble sprightes
·Can call out of the bodies of fraile wightes;
Whom then she does transforme to monstrous hewes
And horribly misshapes with ugly sightes,
Captiv'd eternally in yron mewes
And darksom dens, where Titan his face never shewes.

      *   *   *   *   *   *

29 And over him, art striving to compaire
    With nature, did an arber greene dispred.
    Framed of wanton yvie, flouring faire,
    Through which the fragrant eglantine did spred
    His pricking armes, entrayld with roses red,
    Which daintie odours round about them threw,
    And all within with flowres was garnished,
    That, when myld Zephyrus emongst them blew,
Did breath out bounteous smels, and painted colors shew.

30 And fast beside there trickled softly downe
    A gentle streame, whose murmuring wave did play
    Emongst the pumy stones, and made a sowne,
    To lull him soft a sleepe, that by it lay:
    The wearie traveiler, wandring that way,
    Therein did often quench his thirsty heat,
    And then by it his wearie limbes display,
    Whiles creeping slomber made him to forget
His former paine, and wypt away his toylsom sweat.

31 And on the other side a pleasaunt grove
    Was shot up high, full of the stately tree
    That dedicated is t' Olympick Jove,
    And to his sonne Alcides, whenas hee
    Gaynd in Nemea goodly victoree:
    Therein the mery birdes of every sort
    Chaunted alowd their chearefull harmonie,
    And made emongst themselves a sweet consort,
That quickned the dull spright with musicall comfort.
          *   *   *   *   *   *

35 Atin arriving there, when him he spide
    Thus in still waves of deepe delight to wade,
    Fiercely approching to him lowdly cride
    Cymochles; oh no, but Cymochles shade,
    In which that manly person late did fade,
    What is become of great Acrates sonne?
    Or where hath he hong up his mortall blade,
    That hath so many haughtie conquests wonne?
Is all his force forlorne, and all his glory donne?

36 Then pricking him with his sharpe-pointed dart,
  He said; Up, up, thou womanish weake knight,
  That here in ladies lap entombed art,
  Unmindfull of thy praise and prowest might,
  And weetlesse eke of lately wrought despight;
  Whiles sad Pyrochles lies on senselesse ground,
  And groneth out his utmost grudging spright,
  Through many a stroke and many a streaming wound,
Calling thy help in vaine, that here in joyes art dround.

37 Suddeinly out of his delightfull dreame
  The man awoke, and would have questiond more;
  But he would not endure that wofull theame
  For to dilate at large, but urged sore,
  With percing words, and pittifull implore,
  Him hastie to arise. As one affright
  With hellish feends, or furies mad uprore,
  He then uprose, inflamd with fell despight,
And called for his armes: for he would algates fight

38 They bene ybrought; he quickly does him dight,
  And lightly mounted passeth on his way;
  Ne ladies loves, ne sweete entreaties, might
  Appease his heat, or hastie passage stay;
  For he has vowd to beene avengd that day
  (That day itselfe him seemed all too long)
  On him, that did Pyrochles deare dismay:
  So proudly pricketh on his courser strong,
And Atin aie him pricks with spurs of shame and wrong.

CANTO VI.

Guyon is of immodest Merth
Led into loose desire;
Fights with Cymocbles, whiles his bro-
ther burnes in furious fire.

1 A HARDER lesson, to learne continence
In joyous pleasure then in grievous paine:
For sweetnesse doth allure the weaker sence
So strongly, that uneathes it can refraine
From that, which feeble nature covets faine:
But griefe and wrath, that be her enemies,
And foes of life, she better can restraine:
Yet Vertue vaunts in both her victories;
And Guyon in them all shewes goodly maisteries.

2 Whom bold Cymochles travelling to finde,
With cruell purpose bent to wreake on him
The wrath, which Atin kindled in his mind,
Came to a river, by whose utmost brim
Wayting to passe, he saw whereas did swim
Along the shore, as swift as glaunce of eye,
A little gondelay, bedecked trim
With boughes and arbours woven cunningly,
That like a litle forrest seemed outwardly.

3 And therein sate a lady fresh and faire,
Making sweet solace to her selfe alone:
Sometimes she sung as loud as larke in aire,
Sometimes she laught, that nigh her breth was gone;
Yet was there not with her else any one,
That to her might move cause of meriment:
Matter of merth enough, though there were none,
She could devize, and thousand waies invent
To feede her foolish humour, and vaine jolliment.

4 Which when far off Cymochles heard, and saw,
　He loudly cald to such as were a bord
　The little barke unto the shore to draw,
　And him to ferrie over that deepe ford.
　The merry mariner unto his word
　Soone hearkned, and her painted bote streightway
　Turnd to the shore, where that same warlike lord
　She in receiv'd; but Atin by no way
She would admit, albe the knïght her much did pray.

5 Eftsoones her shallow ship away did slide,
　More swift than swallow sheres the liquid skie,
　Withouten oare or pilot it to guide,
　Or winged canvas with the wind to flie:
　Onely she turned a pin, and by and by
　It cut away upon the yielding wave,
　Ne cared she her course for to apply;
　For it was taught the way, which she would have,
And both from rocks and flats it selfe could wisely save.

6 And all the way the wanton damsell found
　New merth, her passenger to entertaine;
　For she in pleasant purpose did abound,
　And greatly joyed merry tales to faine,
　Of which a store-house did with her remaine;
　Yet seemed, nothing well they her became;
　For all her wordes she drownd with laughter vaine,
　And wanted grace in utt'ring of the same,
That turned all her pleasance to a scoffing game.

7 And other whiles vaine toyes she would devize,
　As her fantasticke wit did most delight;
　Sometimes her head she fondly would aguize
　With gaudie girlonds, or fresh flowrets dight
　About her necke, or rings of rushes plight:
　Sometimes, to do him laugh, she would assay
　To laugh at shaking of the leaves light,
　Or to behold the water worke, and play
About her little frigot, therein making way.

F

8 Her light behaviour, and loose dalliaunce
  Gave wondrous great contentment to the knight,
  That of his way he had no sovenaunce,
  Nor care of vow'd revenge and cruell fight,
  But to weake wench did yeeld his martiall might.
  So easie was to quench his flamed mind
  With one sweet drop of sensuall delight,
  So easie is t' appease the stormy wind
Of malice in the calme of pleasant womankind.

9 Diverse discourses in their way they spent;
  Mongst which Cymochles of her questioned
  Both what she was, and what that usage ment,
  Which in her cot she daily practized:
  Vaine man (said she) thou wouldest be reckoned
  A straunger in thy home, and ignoraunt
  Of Phaedria (for so my name is red)
  Of Phaedria, thine owne fellow servaunt
For thou to serve Acrasia thy selfe doest vaunt.

10 In this wide inland sea, that hight by name
  The Idle Lake, my wandring ship I row,
  That knowes her port, and thither sailes by ayme,
  Ne care, ne feare I how the wind do blow,
  Or whether swift I wend, or whether slow:
  Both slow and swift a like do serve my tournc;
  Ne swelling Neptune ne loud thundring Jove
  Can chaunge my cheare, or make me ever mourne:
My litle boat can safely passe this perilous bourne.

11 Whiles thus she talked, and whiles thus she toyd,
  They were far past the passage, which he spake,
  And come unto an island waste and voyd,
  That floted in the midst of that great lake;
  There her small gondelay her port did make,
  And that gay paire issuing on the shore
  Disburdned her. Their way they forward take
  Into the land, that lay them faire before,
Whose pleasaunce she him shew'd and plentifull great store.

12 It was a chosen plot of fertile land,
Emongst wide waves set, like a litle nest,
As if it had by Natures cunning hand
Bene choisely picked out from all the rest,
And laid forth for ensample of the best:
No daintie flowre or herbe, that growes on ground,
No arboret with painted blossomes drest
And smelling sweet, but there it might be found
To bud out faire, and her sweet smels throw all around

13 No tree, whose braunches did not bravely spring;
No braunch, whereon a fine bird did not sit:
No bird, but did her shrill notes sweetly sing;
No song but did containe a lovely dit.
Trees, braunches, birds, and songs, were framed fit
For to allure fraile mind to carelesse ease.
Carelesse the man soone woxe, and his weake wit
Was overcome of thing, that did him please:
So pleased, did his wrathfull purpose faire appease.

14 Thus when shee had his eyes and senses fed
With false delights, and fild with pleasures vaine,
Into a shadie dale she soft him led,
And layd him downe upon a grassie plaine:
And her sweet selfe without dread or disdain
She set beside, laying his head disarmd
In her loose lap, it softly to sustaine,
Where soone he slumbred, fearing not be harm'd,
The whiles with a love lay she thus him sweetly charmd:

15 Behold, O man, that toilesome paines doest take,
The flowres, the fields, and all that pleasant growes,
How they themselves doe thine ensample make,
Whiles nothing envious nature them forth throwes
Out of her fruitfull lap: how, no man knowes,
They spring, they bud, they blossome fresh and faire,
And decke the world with their rich pompous showes;
Yet no man for them taketh paines or care,
Yet no man to them can his carefull paines compare.

16 The lilly, ladie of the flowring field,
    The Flowre-deluce, her lovely paramoure,
    Bid thee to them thy fruitlesse labours yield,
    And soone leave off this toylsome wearie stoure :
    Loe loe, how brave she decks her bounteous boure,
    With silken curtens and gold coverlets,
    Therein to shrowd her sumptuous Belamoure,
    Yet nether spinnes nor cardes, ne cares nor fretts,
But to her mother Nature all her care she lets.

17 Why then dost thou, O man, that of them all
    Art lord, and eke of nature soveraine,
    Wilfully make thy selfe a wretched thrall,
    And waste thy joyous houres in needelese paine,
    Seeking for daunger and adventures vaine ?
    What bootes it all to have, and nothing use ?
    Who shall him rew, that swimming in the maine,
    Will die for thirst, and water doth refuse ?
Refuse such fruitlesse toile, and present pleasures chuse.

18 By this she had him lulled fast a sleepe,
    That of no wordly thing he care did take :
    Then she with liquors strong his eyes did steepe,
    That nothing should him hastily awake.
    So she him left, and did her selfe betake
    Unto her boat againe, with which she cleft
    The slouthfull wave of that great griesly lake :
    Soone she that island far behind her lefte,
And now is come to that same place where first she wefte.

19 By this time was the worthy Guyon brought
    Unto the other side of that wide strond
    Where she was rowing, and for passage sought :
    Him needed not long call, she soone to hond
    Her ferry brought, where him she byding fond
    With his sad guide : him selfe shee tooke aboord,
    But his black palmer suffred still to stond,
    Ne would for price or prayers once affoord
To ferry that old man over the perlous foord.

20 Guyon was loath to leave his guide behind,
  Yet being entred might not backe retyre;
  For the flit barke, obaying to her mind,
  Forth launched quickly as she did desire,
  Ne gave him leave to bid that aged sire
  Adieu, but nimbly ran her wonted course
  Through the dull billowes thicke as troubled mire,
  Whom neither wind out pf their seat could forse,
Nor timely tides did drive out of their sluggish sourse.

21 And by the way, as was her wonted guize,
  Her mery fitt she freshly gan to reare,
  And did of joy and jollity devize
  Her selfe to cherish, and her guest to cheare.
  The knight was courteous, and did not forbeare
  Her honest merth and pleasaunce to partake:
  But when he saw her toy, and gibe, and geare,
  And passe the bonds of modest merimake,
Her dalliaunce he despisd and follies did forsake.

22 Yet she still followed her former style,
  And said, and did all that mote him delight,
  Till they arrived in that pleasaunt ile,
  Where sleeping late she lefte her other knight.
  But, whenas Guyon of that land had sight,
  He wist himselfe amisse, and angry said:
  Ah dame, perdie ye have not doen me right,
  Thus to mislead me, whiles I you obaid:
Mee litle needed from my right way to have straid.

23 Faire sir (quoth she) be not displeasd at all;
  Who fares on sea may not commaund his way,
  Ne wind and weather at his pleasure call:
  The sea is wide, and easie for to stray;
  The wind unstable, and doth never stay.
  But here a while ye may in safety rest,
  Till season serve new passage to assay;
  Better safe port then be in seas distrest.
Therewith she laught, and did her earnest end in jest.

24 But he halfe discontent, mote nathelesse
   Himselfe appease, and issewd forth on shore :
   The joyes whereof, and happie fruitfulnesse,
   Such as he saw, she gan him lay before,
   And all though pleasaunt, yet she made much more :
   The fields did laugh, the flowres did freshly spring,
   The trees did bud, and earely blossomes bore ;
   And all the quire of birds did sweetly sing,
And told that gardins pleasures in their caroling.

25 And she more sweete, than any bird on bough,
   Would oftentimes emongst them beare a part,
 . And strive to passe (as she could well enough)
   Their native musicke by her skilful art :
   So did she all, that might his constant hart
   Withdraw from thought of warlike enterprize,
   And drowne in dissolute delights apart,
   Where noyse of armes, or vew of martiall guize,
Might not revive desire of knightly exercize.

26 But he was wise, and warie of her will,
   And ever held his hand upon his hart ;
   Yet would not seeme so rude, and thewed ill,
   As to despise so courteous seeming part
   That gentle ladie did to him impart ;
   But fairly tempring fond desire subdewd,
   And ever her desired to depart.
   She list not heare, but her disports poursewd,
And ever bad him stay till time the tide renewd.

27 And now by this, Cymochles howre was spent,
   That he awoke out of his idle dreme ;
   And shaking off his drowsie dreriment,
   Gan him avize, how ill did him beseme,
   In slouthfull sleepe his molten hart to steme,
   And quench the brond of his conceived ire.
   Tho up he started, stird with shame extreme,
   Ne staied for his damsell to inquire,
But marched to the strond, their passage to require.

28 And in the way he with Sir Guyon met,
   Accompanyde with Phaedria the faire:
   Eftsoones he gan to rage, and inly fret,
   Crying, Let be that ladie debonaire,
   Thou recreaunt knight, and soone thyselfe prepaire
   To battell, if thou meane her love to gaine:
   Loe, loe alreadie how the fowles in aire
   Doe flocke, awaiting shortly to obtaine
Thy carcasse for their pray, the guerdon of thy paine.

29 And there withall he fiersly at him flew,
   And with importune outrage him assayld; ·
   Who soone prepard to field, his sword forth drew,
   And him with equall value countervayld:
   Their mightie strokes their haberjeons dismayld,
   And naked made each others manly spalles;
   The mortall steele despiteously entayld
   Deepe in their flesh, quite through the yron walles,
That a large purple streme adowne their giambeux falles.

30 Cymochles, that had never mett before
   So puissant foe, with envious despight
   His prowd presumed force increased more,
   Disdeigning to bee held so long in fight.
   Sir Guyon grudging not so much his might
   As those unknightly raylings which he spoke,
   With wrathfull fire his courage kindled bright,
   Thereof devising shoitly to be wroke,
And doubling all his powres, redoubled every stroke.

31 Both of them high attonce their hands enhaunst,
   And both attonce their huge blowes down did sway:
   Cymochles sword on Guyons shield yglaunst,
   And thereof nigh one quarter sheard away:
   But Guyons angry blade so fierce did play
   Or th' others helmet, which as Titan shone,
   That quite it clove his plumed crest in tway,
   And bared all his head unto the bone;
Where with astonisht, still he stood, as senselesse stone.

32 Still as he stood, fayre Phaedria, that beheld
   That deadly daunger, soone atweene them ran;
   And at their feet her selfe most humbly feld,
   Crying with pitteous voice, and count'nance wan,
   Ah well away, most noble lords, how can
   Your cruell eyes endure so pitteous sight,
   To shed your lives on ground? Wo worth the man,
   That first did teach the cursed steele to bight
In his owne flesh, and make way to the living spright.

33 If ever love of lady did empierce
   Your yron brestes, or pittie could find place,
   Withhold your bloudie handes from battell fierce;
   And, sith for me ye fight, to me this grace
   Both yeeld, to stay your deadly strife a space.
   They stayd a while: and forth she gan proceed:
   Most wretched woman and of wicked race,
   That am the authour of this hainous deed,   [breed.
And cause of death betweene two doughtie knights do

34 But if for me ye fight, or me will serve,
   Not this rude kind of battell, nor these armes
   Are meet, the which doe men in bale to sterve,
   And dolefull sorrow heape with deadly harmes:
   Such cruell game my scarmoges disarmes.
   Another warre, and other weapons, I
   Doe love, where love does give his sweete alarmes
   Without bloudshed, and where the enemy
Does yeeld unto his foe a pleasant victory.

35 Debatefull strife and cruell enmitie
   The famous name of knighthood fowly shend;
   But lovely peace, and gentle amitie,
   And in amours the passing houres to spend,
   The mightie martiall hands doe most commend;
   Of love they ever greater glory bore
   Then of their armes: Mars is Cupidoes frend,
   And is for Venus loves renowmed more
Then all his wars and spoiles, the which he did of yore.

36 Therewith she sweetly smyld. They though full bent
   To prove extremities of bloudie fight,
   Yet at her speach their rages gan relent,
   And calme the sea of their tempestuous spight;
   Such powre have pleasing wordes: such is the might
   Of courteous clemency in gentle hart.
   Now after all was ceast, the Faery knight
   Besought that damzell suffer him depart,
And yield him readie passage to that other part.

37 She no lesse glad then he desirous was
   Of his departure thence: for of her joy
   And vaine delight she saw he light did pas,
   A foe of folly and immodest toy,
   Still solemne sad, or still disdainfull coy,
   Delighting all in armes and cruell warre,
   That her sweete peace and pleasures did annoy,
   Troubled with terrour and unquiet jarre,
That she well pleased was thence to amove him farre.

38 Tho him she brought abord, and her swift bote
   Forthwith directed to that further strand;
   The which on the dull waves did lightly flote,
   And soone arrived on the shallow sand,
   Where gladsome Guyon salied forth to land,
   And to that damzell thankes gave for reward.
   Upon that shore he spied Atin stand,
   There by his maister left, when late he far'd
In Phaedrias flitt barke over that perlous shard.

39 Well could he him remember, sith of late
   He with Pyrochles sharp debatement made:
   Streight gan he him revile, and bitter rate,
   As shepheardes curre, that in darke evenings shade
   Hath tracted forth some salvage beastes trade:
   Vile miscreant, (said he) whither dost thou flie
   The shame and death, which will thee soon invade?
   What coward hand shall doe thee next to die,
That art thus fouly fled from famous enemie?

40 With that he stiffely shooke his steelhead dart:
　But sober Guyon, hearing him so raile,
　Though somewhat moved in his mightie hart,
　Yet with strong reason maistred passion fraile,
　And passed fairely forth.　He turning taile,
　Backe to the strond retyrd, and there still stayd,
　Awaiting passage, which him late did faile;
　The whiles Cymochles with that wanton mayd
The hastie heat of his avowd revenge delayd.

41 Whylest there the varlet stood, he saw from farre
　An armed knight, that towards him fast ran;
　He ran on foot, as if in lucklesse warre
　His forlorne steed from him the victour wan;
　He seemed breathlesse, hartlesse, faint, and wan,
　And all his armour sprinckled was with bloud,
　And soyld with durtie gore, that no man can
　Discerne the hew thereof.　He never stood,
But bent his hastie course towardes the idle flood.

42 The varlet saw, when to the flood he came
　How without stop or stay he fiercely lept,
　And deepe him selfe beduked in the same,
　That in the lake his loftie crest was steept,
　Ne of his safetie seemed care he kept,
　But with his raging armes he rudely flasht
　The waves about, and all his armour swept,
　That all the blood and filth away was washt;
Yet still he bet the water, and the billowes dasht.

43 Atin drew nigh to weet what it mote bee;
　For much he wondred at that uncouth sight:
　Whom should he, but his own deare lord, there see,
　His owne deare lord Pyrochles, in sad plight,
　Readie to drowne himselfe for fell despight:
　Harrow now out, and well away, he cryde,
　What dismall day hath lent this cursed light,
　To see my lord so deadly damnifyde;
Pyrochles, O Pyrochles, what is thee betyde?

44 I burne, I burne, I burne, then loud he cryde,
   O how I burne with implacable fire,
   Yet nought can quench mine inly flaming syde,
   Nor sea of licour cold, nor lake of mire;
   Nothing but death can doe me to respire.
   Ah be it, (said he) from Pyrochles farre
   After pursewing death once to require,
   Or think, that ought those puissant hands may marre:
Death is for wretches borne under unhappie starre

45 Perdie, then is it fit for me, (said he)
   That am, I weene, most wretched man alive;
   Burning in flames, yet no flames can I see,
   And, dying daily, daily yet revive:
   O Atin, helpe to me last death to give.
   The varlet at his plaint was grievd so sore,
   That his deepe wounded hart in two did rive,
   And his owne health remembring now no more.
Did follow that ensample, which he blam'd afore.

46 Into the lake he lept, his lord to ayd,
   (So love the dread of daunger doth despise)
   And of him catching hold him strongly stayd
   From drowning. But more happie he, then wise,
   Of that seas nature did him not avise.
   The waves thereof so slow and sluggish were,
   Engrost with mud, which did them foule agrise,
   That every weightie thing they did upbeare,
Ne ought mote ever sinke downe to the bottome there.

47 Whiles thus they strugled in that idle wave,
   And strove in vaine, the one himselfe to drowne,
   The other both from drowning for to save,
   Lo, to that shore one in an aunlient gowne,
   Whose hoarie locks great gravitie did crowne,
   Holding in hand a goodly arming sword,
   By fortune came, led with the troublous sowne:
   Where drenched deepe he found in that dull ford
The carefull servaunt striving with his raging lord.

48 Him Atin spying knew right well of yore,
   And loudly cald; Helpe helpe, O Archimage,
   To save my lord in wretched plight forlore;
   Helpe with thy hand, or with thy counsell sage:
   Weake handes, but counsell is most strong in age.
   Him when the old man saw, he wondred sore
   To see Pyrochles there so rudely rage:
   Yet sithens helpe, he saw, he needed more
Then pittie, he in hast approched to the shore.

49 And cald, Pyrochles, what is this I see?
   What hellish furie hath at earst thee hent?
   Furious ever I thee knew to bee,
   Yet never in this straunge astonishment.
   These flames, these flames (he cryde) doe me torment.
   What flames (quoth he) when I thee present see
   In daunger rather to be drent, then brent?
   Harrow, the flames, which me consume (said he)
Ne can be quencht, within my secret bowels be.

50 That cursed man, that cruell feend of hell,
   Furor, oh Furor hath me thus bedight:
   His deadly wounds within my liver swell,
   And his whot fire burnes in mine entrails bright,
   Kindled through his infernall brond of spight,
   Sith late with him I batteil vaine would boste;
   That now I weene Joves dreaded thunder light
   Does scorch not halfe so sore, nor damned ghoste
In flaming Phlegeton does not so felly roste.

51 Which when as Archimago heard, his griefe
   He knew right well, and him attonce disarmd:
   Then searcht his secret wounds, and made a priefe
   Of every place, that was with brusing harmd,
   Or with the hidden fire too inly warmd.
   Which done, he balmes and herbes thereto applyde,
   And evermore with mighty spels them charmd,
   That in short space he has them qualifyde,
And him restor'd to health, that would have algates dyde.

CANTO VII.

Guyon findes Mammon in a delve,
Sunning his threasure bore;
Is by him tempted, and led downe
To see his secret store.

1 As pilot well expert in perilous wave,
   That to a stedfast starre his course hath bent,
   When foggy mistes, or cloudy tempests have
   The faithfull light of that faire lampe yblent,
   And cover'd heaven with hideous dreriment,
   Upon his card and compas firmes his eye,
   The maisters of his long experiment,
   And to them does the steddy helme apply,
Bidding his winged vessell fairely forward fly:

2 So Guyon having lost his trusty guide,
   Late left beyond that Ydle Lake, proceedes
   Yet on his way, of none accompanide;
   And evermore himselfe with comfort feedes
   Of his owne vertues and prayse-worthy deedes.
   So, long he yode, yet no adventure found,
   Which Fame of her shrill trompet worthy reedes:
   For still he traveild through wide wastfull ground,
That nought but desert wildernesse shew'd all around.

3 At last he came unto a gloomy glade,
   Cover'd with boughes and shrubs from heavens light;
   Whereas he sitting found in secret shade
   An uncouth, salvage, and uncivile wight,
   Of griesly hew and fowle ill favour'd sight;
   His face with smoke was tand, and eyes were bleard,
   His head and beard with sout were ill bedight,
   His cole-blacke hands did seeme to have ben seard
In smithes fire-spitting forge, and nayles like clawes appeard.

4 His yron coate, all overgrowne with rust,
 Was underneath enveloped with gold,
 Whose glistring glosse, darkned with filthy dust,
 Well yet appeared to have beene of old
 A worke of rich entayle and curious mould,
 Woven with antickes and wild imagery:
 And in his lap a masse of coyne he told,
 And turned upsidowne, to feede his eye
And covetous desire with his huge threasury.

5 And round about him lay on every side
 Great heapes of gold, that never could be spent;
 Of which some were rude owre, not purifide
 Of Mulcibers devouring element;
 Some others were new driven, and distent
 Into great ingoes and to wedges square;
 Some in round plates withouten moniment:
 But most were stampt, and in their metal bare
The antique shapes of kings and kesars straunge and rare.

6 Soone as he Guyon saw, in great affright
 And haste he rose, for to remove aside
 Those pretious hils from straungers envious sight,
 And downe them poured through an hole full wide
 Into the hollow earth, them there to hide.
 But Guyon, lightly to him leaping, stayd
 His hand, that trembled as one terrifyde;
 And though him selfe were at the sight dismayd,
Yet him perforce restraynd, and to him doubtfull sayd;

7 What art thou, man, (if man at all thou art,)
 That here in desert hast thine habitaunce,
 And these rich heapes of wealth doest hide apart
 From the worldes eye, and from her right usaunce?
 Thereat with staring eyes fixed askaunce,
 In great disdaine, he answerd; Hardy Elfe,
 That darest view my direfull countenaunce,
 I read thee rash, and heedlesse of thy selfe,
To trouble my still seate, and heapes of pretious pelfe.

8 God of the world and worldlings I me call,
Great Mammon, greatest god below the skye,
That of my plenty poure out unto all,
And unto none my graces do envye:
Riches, renowme, and principality,
Honour, estate, and all this worldes good,
For which men swinck and sweat incessantly,
Fro me do flow into an ample flood,
And in the hollow earth have their eternall brood.

9 Wherefore if me thou deigne to serve and sew,
At thy commaund lo all these mountaines bee:
Or if to thy great mind, or greedy vew,
All these may not suffise, there shall to thee
Ten times so much be nombred francke and free.
Mammon (said he) thy godheades vaunt is vaine,
And idle offers of thy golden fee;
To them that covet such eye-glutting gaine
Proffer thy giftes, and fitter servaunts entertaine.

10 Me ill besits, that in der-doing armes
And honours suit my vowed dayes do spend,
Unto thy bounteous baytes and pleasing charmes,
With which weake men thou witchest, to attend;
Regard of worldly mucke doth fowly blend
And low abase the high heroicke spright,
That joyes for crownes and kingdomes to contend:
Faire shields, gay steedes, bright armes, be my delight;
Those be the riches fit for an advent'rous knight.

11 Vaine glorious Elfe (saide he) doest not thou weet,
That money can thy wantes at will supply?
Shields, steeds, and armes, and all things for thee meet,
It can purvay in twinckling of an eye;
And crownes and kingdomes to thee multiply.
Do not I kings create, and throw the crowne
Sometimes to him, that low in dust doth ly?
And him that raighd into his rowme thrust downe,
And whom I lust, do heape with glory and renowne?

12 All otherwise (saide he) I riches read,
   And deeme them roote of all disquietnesse;
   First got with guile, and then preserv'd with dreàd,
   And after spent with pride and lavishnesse,
   Leaving behind them griefe and heavinesse:
   Infinite mischiefes of them doe arize;
   Strife, and debate, bloodshed, and bitternesse,
   Outrageous wrong, and hellish covetize,
That noble heart as great dishonour doth despize.

13 Ne thine be kingdomes, ne the scepters thine;
   But realmes and rulers thou doest both confound,
   And loyall truth to treason doest incline:
   Witnesse the guiltlesse bloud pourd oft on ground,
   The crowned often slaine, the slayer crouned,
   The sacred diademe in peeces rent,
   And purple robe gored with many a wound;
   Castles surprizd, great cities sackt and brent:
So mak'st thou kings, and gaynest wrongfull government

14 Long were to tell the troublous stormes, that tosse
   The private state, and make the life unsweet:
   Who swelling sayles in Caspian sea doth crosse,
   And in frayle wood on Adrian gulf doth fleet,
   Doth not, I weene, so many evils meet.
   Then Mammon wexing wroth, And why then, sayd,
   Are mortall men so fond and undiscreet,
   So evill thing to seeke unto their ayd;
And having not complaine, and having it upbrayd?

15 Indeede (quoth he) through fowle intemperaunce,
   Frayle men are oft captiv'd to covetise:
   But would they thinke, with how small allowaunce
   Untroubled nature doth herselfe suffise,
   Such superfluities they would despise,
   Which with sad cares empeach our native joyes.
   At the well-head the purest streames arise;
   But mucky filth his braunching armes annoyes,
And with uncomely weedes the gentle wave accloyes.

16 The antique world, in his first flowring youth,
 Found no defect in his Creatours grace;
 But with glad thankes, and unreproved truth,
 The giftes of soveraigne bounty did embrace:
 Like angels life was then mens happy cace;
 But later ages pride, like corn-fed steed,
 Abusd her plenty, and fat-swolne encreace
 To all licentious lust, and gan exceed
The measure of her meane, and naturall first need.

17 Then gan a cursed hand the quiet wombe
 Of his great grandmother with steele to wound,
 And the hid treasures in her sacred tombe
 With sacriledge to dig. Therein he found
 Fountaines of gold and silver to abound,
 Of which the matter of his huge desire
 And pompous pride eftsoones he did compound;
 Then Avarice gan through his veines inspire
His greedy flames, and kindled life-devouring fire.

18 Sonne (said he then) let be thy bitter scorne,
 And leave the rudenesse of that antique age
 To them, that liv'd therein in state forlorne:
 Thou that doest live in later times must wage
 Thy workes for wealth, and life for gold engage.
 If then thee list my offred grace to use,
 Take what thou please of all this surplusage;
 If thee list not, leave have thou to refuse:
But thing refused do not afterward accuse.

19 Me list not (said the Elfin knight) receave
 Thing offred, till I know it well be got;
 Ne wote I, but thou didst these goods bereave
 From rightfull owner by unrighteous lot,
 Or that bloud guiltinesse or guile them blot.
 Perdy (quoth he) yet never eye did vew,
 Ne toung did tell, ne hand these handled not;
 But safe I have them kept in secret mew
From hevens sight, and powre of all which them pursew.

G

20 What secret place (quoth he) can safely hold
  So huge a masse, and hide from heavens eye?
  Or where hast thou thy wonne, that so much gold
  Thou canst preserve from wrong and robbery?
  Come thou (quoth he) and see. So by and by
  Through that thicke covert he him led, and found
  A darksome way, which no man could descry,
  That deepe descended through the hollow ground,
And was with dread and horrour compassed around.

21 At length they came into a larger space,
  That stretcht it selfe into an ample plaine,
  Through which a beaten broad high way did trace,
  That streight did lead to Plutoes griesly raine:
  By that wayes side there sate infernall Payne,
  And fast beside him sate tumultuous Strife:
  The one in hand an yron whip did straine,
  The other brandished a bloudy knife,
And both did gnash their teeth, and both did threaten life.

22 On thother side in one consort there sate
  Cruell Revenge, and rancorous Despight,
  Disloyall Treason, and hart-burning Hate;
  But gnawing Gealosie out of their sight
  Sitting alone, his bitter lips did bight;
  And trembling Feare still to and fro did fly,
  And found no place where safe he shroud him might;
  Lamenting Sorrow did in darknes lye;
And Shame his ugly face did hide from living eye.

23 And over them sad Horror with grim hew
  Did alwayes sore, beating his yron wings;
  And after him owles and night-ravens flew,
  The hatefull messengers of heavy things,
  Of death and dolor telling sad tidings;
  Whiles sad Celeno, sitting on a clift,
  A song of bale and bitter sorrow sings,
  That hart of flint a sunder could have rifte;
Which having ended after him she flyeth swift.

24 All these before the gates of Pluto lay,
   By whom they passing spake unto them nought.
   But th' Elfin knight with wonder all the way
   Did feed his eyes, and fild his inner thought.
   At last him to a litle dore he brought,
   That to the gate of hell, which gaped wide,
   Was next adjoyning, ne them parted ought:
   Betwixt them both was but a little stride,
That did the house of Richesse from hell-mouth divide.

25 Before the dore sat selfe-consuming Care,
   Day and night keeping wary watch and ward,
   For feare lest Force or Fraud should unaware
   Break in, and spoile the treasure there in gard:
   Ne would he suffer Sleepe once thither-ward
   Approch, albe his drowsy den were next;
   For next to death is Sleepe to be compard;
   Therefore his house is unto his annext:
Here Sleep, there Richesse, and Hel-gate them both betwex'.

26 So soon as Mammon there arriv'd, the dore
   To him did open, and affoorded way:
   Him followed eke Sir Guyon evermore,
   Ne darknesse him, ne daunger might dismay.
   Soone as he entred was, the dore streightway
   Did shut, and from behind it forth there lept
   An ugly feend, more fowle then dismall day,
   The which with monstrous stalke behind him stept,
And ever as he went dew watch upon him kept.

27 Well hoped he, ere long that hardy guest,
   If ever covetous hand, or lustfull eye,
   Or lips he layd on thing, that likt him best,
   Or ever sleepe his eye-strings did untye,
   Should be his pray: and therefore still on hye
   He over him did hold his cruell clawes,
   Threatning with greedy gripe to doe him dye,
   And rend in peeces with his ravenous pawes,
If ever he transgrest the fatall Stygian lawes.

G 2

28 That houses forme within was rude and strong,
    Like an huge cave, hewne out of rocky clifte,
    From whose rough vaut the ragged breaches hong
    Embost with massy gold of glorious gift,
    And with rich metal loaded every rifte,
    That heavy ruine they did seeme to threat:
    And over them Arachne high did lifte
    Her cunning web, and spred her subtile nett,
Enwrapped in fowle smoke and clouds more black then jet.

29 Both roofe, and floore, and wals, were all of gold,
    But overgrowne with dust and old decay,
    And hid in darknesse, that none could behold
    The hew thereof: for vew of cheareful day
    Did never in that house it selfe display,
    But a faint shadow of uncertain light;
    Such as a lamp, whose life does fade away;
    Or as the moone, cloathed with clowdy night,
Does shew to him, that walkes in feare and sad affright.

30 In all that rowme was nothing to be seene
    But huge great yron chests, and coffers strong,
    All bard with double bends, that none could weene
    Them to efforce by violence or wrong;
    On every side they placed were along.
    But all the ground with sculs was scattered
    And dead mens bones, which round about were flong;
    Whose lives, it seemed, whilome there were shed,
And their vile carcases now left unburied.

31 They forward passe; ne Guyon yet spoke word,
    Till that they came unto an yron dore,
    Which to them opened of his owne accord,
    And shewd of richesse such exceeding store,
    As eye of man did never see before,
    Ne ever could within one place be found,
    Though all the wealth, which is, or was of yore,
    Could gatherd be through all the world around,
And that above were added to that under ground.

32 The charge thereof unto a covetous spright
Commaunded was, who thereby did attend,
And warily awaited day and night,
From other covetous feends it to defend,
Who it to rob and ransacke did intend.
Then Mammon, turning to that warriour, said;
Loe here the worldes blis, loe here the end,
To which al men do ayme, rich to be made:
Such grace now to be happy is before thee laid.

33 Certes (sayd he) I n'ill thine offred grace,
Ne to be made so happy doe intend:
Another blis before mine eyes I place,
Another happines, another end.
To them, that list, these base regardes I lend:
But I in armes, and in atchievements brave,
Do rather choose my flitting houres to spend,
And to be lord of those, that riches have,
Then them to have my selfe, and be their servile sclave.

34 Thereat the feend his gnashing teeth did grate,
And griev'd, so long to lacke his greedy pray;
For well he weened, that so glorious bayte
Would tempt his guest to take thereof assay:
Had he so doen, he had him snatcht away,
More light than culver in the faulcons fist:
Eternall God thee save from such decay.
But whenas Mammon saw his purpose mist,
Him to entrap unwares another way he wist.

35 Thence forward he him led, and shortly brought
Unto another rowme, whose dore forthright
To him did open, as it had beene taught:
Therein an hundred raunges weren pight,
And hundred fornaces all burning bright:
By every fornace many feends did bide,
Deformed creatures, horrible in sight;
And every feend his busie paines applide
To melt the golden metall, ready to be tride.

36 One with great bellowes gathered filling aire,
  And with forst wind the fewell did inflame;
  Another did the dying bronds repaire
  With yron toungs, and sprinckled oft the same
  With liquid waves, fiers Vulcans rage to tame,
  Who maystring them, renewd his former heat:
  Some scumd the drosse, that from the metall came;
  Some stird the molten owre with ladles great:
And every one did swincke, and every one did sweat.

37 But, when an earthly wight they present saw,
  Glistring in armes and battailous aray,
  From their whot worke they did themselves withdraw
  To wonder at the sight; for till that day,
  They never creature saw, that came that way:
  Their staring eyes sparckling with fervent fire
  And ugly shapes did nigh the man dismay,
  That, were it not for shame, he would retire;
Till that him thus bespake their soveraigne lord and sire:

38 Behold, thou Faeries sonne, with mortall eye,
  That living eye before did never see:
  The thing, that thou didst crave so earnestly,
  To weet whence all the wealth late shewd by mee
  Proceeded, lo now is reveald to thee.
  Here is the fountaine of the worldes good:
  Now therefore, if thou wilt enriched bee,
  Avise thee well, and chaunge thy wilfull mood,
Least thou perhaps hereafter wish, and be withstood.

39 Suffise it then, thou money god (quoth he)
  That all thine idle offers I refuse.
  All that I need I have; what needeth mee
  To covet more then I have cause to use?
  With such vaine shewes thy worldlinges vile abuse:
  But give me leave to follow mine emprise.
  Mammon was much displeasd, yet no'te he chuse
  But beare the rigour of his bold mesprise:
And thence him forward ledd, him further to entise.

40 He brought him through a darksom narrow strait,
  To a broad gate all built of beaten gold:
  The gate was open, but therein did wait
  A sturdy villein, striding stiffe and bold,
  As if the highest God defie he would:
  In his right hand an yron club he held,
  But he himselfe was all of golden mould,
  Yet had both life and sence, and well could weld
That cursed weapon, when his cruell foes he queld.

41 Disdayne he called was, and did disdaine
  To be so cald, and who so did him call:
  Sterne was his looke, and full of stomacke vaine;
  His portaunce terrible, and stature tall,
  Far passing th' hight of men terrestriall;
  Like an huge gyant of the Titans race;
  That made him scorne all creatures great and small,
  And with his pride all others powre deface:
More fitt emonst black fiendes then men to have his place.

42 Soone as those glitterand armes he did espye,
  That with their brightnesse made that darknes light,
  His harmefull club he gan to hurtle hye,
  And threaten batteill to the Faery knight;
  Who likewise gan himselfe to batteill dight,
  Till Mammon did his hasty hand withhold,
  And counseld him abstaine from perilous fight:
  For nothing might abash the villein bold,
Ne mortall steele emperce his miscreated mould.

43 So having him with reason pacifide,
  And that fiers carle commaunding to forbeare,
  He brought him in. The rowme was large and wide,
  As it some gyeld or solemne temple weare:
  Many great golden pillours did upbeare
  The massy roofe, and riches huge sustayne;
  And every pillour decked was full deare
  With crownes, and diademes, and titles vaine,
Which mortall princes wore whiles they on earth did rayne.

44 A route of people there assembled were,
Of every sort and nation under skye,
Which with great uprore preaced to draw nere
To th' upper part, where was advaunced hye
A stately siege of soveraine majestye;
And thereon satt a woman gorgeous gay,
And richly clad in robes of royaltye,
That never earthly prince in such aray
His glory did enhaunce, and pompous pride display.

45 Her face right wondrous faire did seeme to bee,
That her broad beauties beam great brightnes threw
Through the dim shade, that all men might it see;
Yet was not that same her owne native hew,
But wrpught by art and counterfetted shew,
Thereby more lovers unto her to call;
Nath'lesse most heavenly faire in deed and vew
She by creation was, till she did fall;
Thenceforth she sought for helps, to cloke her crime withall.

46 There, as in glistring glory she did sit,
She held a great gold chaine ylincked well,
Whose upper end to highest heaven was knit,
And lower part did reach to lowest hell;
And all that preace did rownd about her swell
To catchen hold of that long chaine, thereby
To climbe aloft, and others to excell:
That was Ambition, rash desire to sty,
And every linck thereof a step of dignity.

47 Some thought to raise themselves to high degree
By riches and unrighteous reward,
Some by close shouldring, some by flatteree,
Others through friendes, others for base regard;
And all by wrong wayes, for themselves prepard.
Those that were up themselves, kept others low;
Those that were low themselves, held others hard,
Ne suffred them to rise or greater grow;
But every one did strive his fellow downe to throw.

48 Which whenas Guyon saw, he gan inquire,
   What meant that preace about that ladies throne.
   And what she was that did so high aspire.
   Him Mammon answered; That goodly one,
   Whom all that folke with such contention
   Do flock about, my deare my daughter is:
   Honour and dignitie from her alone
   Derived are, and all this worldes blis,
For which ye men do strive; few get, but many mis:

49 And faire Philotime she rightly hight,
   The fairest wight that wonneth under skye,
   But that this darksome neather world her light
   Doth dim with horrour and deformitie,
   Worthie of heaven and hye felicitie,
   From whence the gods have her for envy thrust:
   But sith thou hast found favour in mine eye,
   Thy spouse I will her make, if that thou lust;
That she may thee advance for workes and merites just.

50 Gramercy Mammon (said the gentle knight)
   For so great grace and offred high estate;
   But I, that am fraile flesh and earthly wight,
   Unworthy match for such immortall mate
   Myselfe well wote, and mine unequall fate:
   And were I not, yet is my trouth yplight,
   And love avowd to other lady late,
   That to remove the same I have no might:
To chaunge love causelesse is reproch to warlike knight.

51 Mammon emmoved was with inward wrath;
   Yet forcing it to faine, him forth thence led
   Through griesly shadowes by a beaten path,
   Into a gardin goodly garnished
   With hearbs and fruits, whose kinds mote not be red:
   Not such, as earth out of her fruitfull woomb
   Throwes forth to men, sweet and well savored,
   But direfull deadly blacke both leafe and bloom,
Fitt to adorne the dead, and decke the drery toombe.

52 There mournfull cypresse grew in greatest store,
   And trees of bitter gall, and heben sad,
   Dead sleeping poppy, and black hellebore,
   Cold coloquintida, and tetra mad,
   Mortall samnitis, and cicuta bad,
   With which th' unjust Atheniens made to dy
   Wise Socrates, who thereof quaffing glad
   Pourd out his life and last philosophy
To the faire Critias, his dearest belamy.

53 The gardin of Proserpina this hight;
   And in the midst thereof a silver seat,
   With a thicke arber goodly over dight,
   In which she often usd from open heat
   Her selfe to shroud, and pleasures to entreat:
   Next thereunto did grow a goodly tree,
   With braunches broad dispred and body great,
   Clothed with leaves, that none the wood mote see,
And loaden all with fruit as thick as it might bee.

54 Their fruit were golden apples glistring bright,
   That goodly was their glory to behold,
   On earth like never grew, ne living wight
   Like ever saw, but they from hence were sold;
   For those, which Hercules with conquest bold
   Got from great Atlas daughters, hence began,
   And planted there, did bring forth fruit of gold;
   And those, with which th' Euboean young man wan
Swift Atalanta, when through craft he her out ran.

55 Here also sprong that goodly golden fruit,
   With which Acontius got his lover trew,
   Whom he had long time sought with fruitlesse suit:
   Here eke that famous golden apple grew,
   The which emongst the gods false Ate threw;
   For which th' Idaean ladies disagreed,
   Till partiall Paris dempt it Venus dew,
   And had of her faire Helen for his meed,
That many noble Greekes and Trojans made to bleed.

56 The warlike Elfe much wondred at this tree,
  So faire and great, that shadowed all the ground,
  And his broad braunches, laden with rich fee,
  Did stretch themselves without the utmost bound
  Of this great gardin, compast with a mound:
  Which over-hanging, they themselves did steepe
  In a blacke flood, which flow'd about it round;
  That is the river of Cocytus deepe,
In which full many soules do endlesse waile and weepe.

57 Which to behold he clomb up to the bancke;
  And looking downe, saw many damned wights
  In those sad waves, which direfull deadly stanke,
  Plonged continually of cruell sprightes,
  That with their pitteous cryes, and yelling shrightes,
  They made the further shore resounden wide:
  Emongst the rest of those same ruefull sights,
  One cursed creature he by chaunce espide,
That drenched lay full deepe under the garden side.

58 Deepe was he drenched to the upmost chin,
  Yet gaped still, as coveting to drinke
  Of the cold liquor, which he waded in;
  And stretching forth his hand, did often thinke
  To reach the fruit which grew upon the brincke:
  But both the fruit from hand, and floud from mouth
  Did fly abacke, and made him vainely swinke;
  The whiles he sterv'd with hunger, and with drouth
He daily dyde, yet never throughly dyen couth.

59 The knight him seeing labour so in vaine,
  Askt who he was, and what he meant thereby:
  Who groning deepe, thus answerd him againe;
  Most cursed of all creatures under skye,
  Lo Tantalus I here tormented lye:
  Of whom high Jove wont whylome feasted bee;
  Lo, here I now for want of food doe dye:
  But if that thou be such, as I thee see,
Of grace I pray thee, give to eat and drinke to mee.

60 Nay, nay, thou greedie Tantalus (quoth he)
   Abide the fortune of thy present fate,
   And unto all that live in high degree,
   Ensample be of mind intemperate.
   To teach them how to use their present state.
   Then gan the cursed wretch aloud to cry,
   Accusing highest Jove and gods ingrate;
   And eke blaspheming heaven bitterly,
As author of unjustice, there to let him dye.

61 He lookt a little further, and espyde
   Another wretch, whose carcasse deepe was drent
   Within the river, which the same did hyde:
   But both his handes most filthy feculent,
   Above the water were on high extent,
   And faynd to wash themselves incessantly,
   Yet nothing cleaner were for such intent,
   But rather fowler seemed to the eye;
So lost his labour vaine and idle industry.

62 The knight him calling, asked who he was,
   Who lifting up his head, him answerd thus;
   I Pilate am the falsest judge, alas,
   And most unjust, that by unrighteous
   And wicked doome, to Jewes despiteous
   Delivered up the Lord of life to die,
   And did acquite a murdrer felonous;
   The whiles my handes I washt in puritie,
The whiles my soule was soyld with foule iniquitie.

63 Infinite moe, tormented in like paine
   He there beheld, too long here to be told:
   Ne Mammon would there let him long remaine,
   For terrour of the tortures manifold,
   In which the damned soules he did behold,
   But roughly him bespake: Thou fearefull foole,
   Why takest not of that same fruite of gold,
   Ne sittest downe on that same silver stoole,
To rest thy wearie person in the shadow coole.

64 All which he did, to do him deadly fall
   In frayle intemperance through sinfull bayt;
   To which if he inclined had at all,
   That dreadfull feend, which did behinde him wayt,
   Would him have rent in thousand peeces strayt:
   But he was warie wise in all his way,
   And wel perceived his deceiptfull sleight,
   Ne suffred lust his safetie to betray;
So goodly did beguile the guyler of his pray.

65 And now he has so long remained there,
   That vitall powres gan wexe both weake and wan,
   For want of food, and sleepe, which two upbeare,
   Like mightie pillours, this fraile life of man,
   That none without the same enduren can.
   For now three dayes of men were full outwrought,
   Since he this hardie enterprize began:
   Forthy great Mammon fairely he besought
Into the world to guide him backe, as he him brought.

66 The god, though loth, yet was constraind t' obay;
   For lenger time, then that, no living wight
   Below the earth might suffred be to stay:
   So backe againe him brought to living light.
   But all so soone as his enfeebled spright
   Gan sucke this vitall aire into his brest,
   As overcome with too exceeding might,
   The life did flit away out of her nest,
And all his senses were with deadly fit opprest.

CANTO VIII.

Sir Guyon, layd in swowne is by
Acrates sonnes despoyld,
Whom Arthur soone hath reskewed,
And Paynim brethren foyld.

1 AND is there care in heaven? And is there love
  In heavenly spirits to these creatures bace,
  That may compassion of their evils move?
  There is: else much more wretched were the cace
  Of men then beasts. But O th' exceeding grace
  Of highest God, that loves his creatures so,
  And all his workes with mercy doth embrace,
  That blessed angels he sends to and fro,
To serve to wicked man, to serve his wicked foe.

2 How oft do they their silver bowers leave
  To come to succour us, that succour want,
  How oft do they with golden pineons cleave
  The flitting skyes, like flying pursuivant,
  Against foule feendes to aide us militant:
  They for us fight, they watch and dewly ward,
  And their bright squadrons round about us plant;
  And all for love, and nothing for reward:
O, why should heavenly God to men have such regard?

3 During the while, that Guyon did abide
  In Mammons house, the palmer, whom whyleare
  That wanton mayd of passage had denide,
  By further search had passage found elsewhere,
  And being on his way, approched neare
  Where Guyon lay in traunce; when suddenly
  He heard a voice that called loud and cleare,
  Come hither, hither, O come hastily;
That all the fields resounded with the ruefull cry.

4 The palmer lent his eare unto the noyce,
  To weet who called so importunely:
  Againe he heard a more efforced voyce,
  That bad him come in haste. He by and by
  His feeble feet directed to the cry;
  Which to that shady delve him brought at last,
  Where Mammon earst did sunne his threasury:
  There the good Guyon he found slumbring fast
In senselesse dreame; which sight at first him sore aghast.

5 Beside his head there sate a faire young man,
  Of wondrous beautie and of freshest yeares,
  Whose tender bud to blossome new began,
  And flourish faire above his equall peares:
  His snowy front curled with golden heares,
  Like Phoebus face adornd with sunny rayes,
  Divinely shone; and two sharpe winged sheares,
  Decked with diverse plumes, like painted jayes,
Were fixed at his backe to cut his ayerie wayes.

6 Like as Cupido on Idaean hill,
  When having laid his cruell bow away,
  And mortall arrowes, wherewith he doth fill
  The world with murdrous spoiles and bloudie pray,
  With his faire mother he him dights to play,
  And with his goodly sisters, Graces three;
  The goddess pleased with his wanton play,
  Suffers her selfe through sleepe beguild to bee,
The whiles the other ladies mind their merry glee.

7 Whom when the palmer saw, abasht he was
  Through fear and wonder, that he nought could say,
  Till him the childe bespoke, Long lackt, alas,
  Hath bene thy faithfull aide in hard assay,
  Whiles deadly fit thy pupill doth dismay,
  Behold this heavie sight, thou reverend sire,
  But dread of death and dolor doe away;
  For life ere long shall to her home retire,
And he that breathlesse seems shal corage bold respire.

8 The charge, which God doth unto me arret,
  Of his deare safetie I to thee commend;
  Yet will I not forgoe, ne yet forget
  The care thereof my selfe unto the end,
  But evermore him succour, and defend
  Against his foe and mine: watch thou I pray;
  For evill is at hand him to offend.
  So having said, eftsoones he gan display
His painted nimble wings, and vanisht quite away.

9 The palmer seeing his left empty place,
  And his slow eyes beguiled of their sight,
  Woxe sore affraid, and standing still a space
  Gaz'd after him, as fowle escapt by flight:
  At last him turning to his charge behight,
  With trembling hand his troubled pulse gan try;
  Where finding life not yet dislodged quight,
  He much rejoyst, and courd it tenderly,
As chicken newly hacht, from dreaded destiny.

10 At last he spide where towards him did pace
  Two Paynim knights, all armd as bright as skie,
  And them beside an aged sire did trace,
  And farre before a light-foot page did flie,
  That breathed strife and troublous enmitie.
  Those were the two sonnes of Acrates old,
  Who meeting earst with Archimago slie,
  Foreby that idle strond, of him were told,
That he, which earst them combatted, was Guyon bold.

11 Which to avenge on him they dearly vowd,
  Whereever that on ground they mote him find:
  False Archimage provokt their courage prowd,
  And stryfull Atin in their stubborne mind
  Coles of contention and whot vengeaunce tind.
  Now bene they come whereas the palmer sate,
  Keeping that slombred corse to him assind:
  Well knew they both his person, sith of late
With him in bloudie armes they rashly did debate.

12 Whom when Pyrochles saw, inflam'd with rage
That sire he foule bespake, Thou dotard vile,
That with thy brutenesse shendst thy comely age,
Abandon soone, I read, the caitive spoile
Of that same outcast carcasse, that erewhile
Made it selfe famous through false trechery,
And crownd his coward crest with knightly stile:
Loe where he now inglorious doth lye,
To proove he lived ill, that did thus foully dye.

13 To whom the palmer fearlesse answered;
Certes, sir knight, ye bene too much to blame,
Thus for to blot the honour of the dead,
And with foule cowardize his carcasse shame
Whose living handes immortalizd his name.
Vile is the vengeance on the ashes cold,
And envie base, to barke at sleeping fame:
Was never wight, that treason of him told;
Your selfe his prowesse prov'd, and found him fiers and bold.

14 Then sayd Cymochles; Palmer, thou doest dote,
Ne canst of prowesse, ne of knighthood deeme,
Save as thou seest or hearst. But well I wote,
That of his puissance tryall made extreeme:
Yet gold all is not, that doth golden seeme;
Ne all good knights, that shake well speare and shield:
The worth of all men by their end esteeme;
And then due praise or due reproch them yield:
Bad therefore I him deeme, that thus lies dead on field.

15 Good or bad (gan his brother fierce reply)
What doe I recke, sith that he dyde entire?
Or what doth his bad death now satisfy
The greedy hunger of revenging ire,
Sith wrathfull hand wrought not her owne desire?
Yet since no way is left to wreake my spight,
I will him reave of armes, the victors hire,
And of that shield, more worthy of good knight;
For why should a dead dog be deckt in armour bright?

H

16 Faire sir, said then the palmer suppliaunt,
   For knighthoods love, do not so foule a deed,
   Ne blame your honour with so shamefull vaunt
   Of vile revenge. To spoile the dead of weed
   Is sacrilege, and doth all sinnes exceed:
   But leave these relicks of his living might
   To deck his herce, and trap his tomb-blacke steed.
   What herce or steede (said he) should he have dight,
But be entombed in the raven or the kight?

17 With that, rude hand upon his shield he laid,
   And th'other brother gan his helme unlace;
   Both fiercely bent to have him disaraid:
   Till that they spide where towards them did pace
   An armed knight, of bold and bounteous grace,
   Whose squire bore after him an heben launce,
   And coverd shield. Well kend him so farre space
   Th' enchaunter by his armes and amenaunce,
When under him he saw his Lyþian steed to praunce:

18 And to those brethren said, Rise, rise bylive,
   And unto battell doe yourselves addresse;
   For yonder comes the prowest knight alive,
   Prince Arthur, flowre of grace and nobilesse,
   That hath to Paynim knights wrought great distresse,
   And thousand Sar'zins foully donne to dye.
   That word so deepe did in their harts impresse,
   That both eftsoones upstarted furiously,
And gan themselves prepare to battell greedily.

19 But fierce Pyrochles, lacking his owne sword,
   The want thereof now greatly gan to plaine,
   And Archimage besought him that afford
   Which he had brought for Braggadochio vaine.
   So would I (said th' enchaunter) glad and faine
   Beteeme to you this sword, you to defend,
   Or ought that els your honour might maintaine,
   But that this weapons powre I well have kend
To be contrarie to the worke, which ye intend:

20 For that same knights owne sword this is of yore,
    Which Merlin made by his almightie art
    For this his noursling, when he knighthood swore,
    Therewith to doen his foes eternall smart.
    The metall first he mixt with Medaewart,
    That no enchauntment from his dint might save;
    Then it in flames of Aetna wrought apart,
    And seven times dipped in the bitter wave
Of hellish Styx, which hidden vertue to it gave.

21 The vertue is, that neither steele nor stone
    The stroke thereof from entrance may defend;
    Ne ever may be used by his fone;
    Ne forst his rightfull owner to offend;
    Ne ever will it breake, ne ever bend.
    Wherefore *Morddure* it rightfully is hight.
    In vaine therefore, Pyrochles, should I lend
    The same to thee, against his lord to fight;
For sure it would deceive thy labour and thy might.

22 Foolish old man, said then the Pagan wroth,
    That weenest words or charms may force withstond:
    Soone shalt thou see, and then beleeve for troth,
    That I can carve with this inchaunted brond
    His lords owne flesh. Therewith out of his hond
    That vertuous steele he rudely snatcht away;
    And Guyons shield about his wrest he bond:
    So readie dight, fierce battaile to assaye,
And match his brother proud in battailous aray.

23 By this that straunger knight in presence came,
    And goodly salved them; who nought againe
    Him answered, as courtesie became,
    But with sterne lookes, and stomachous disdaine,
    Gave signes of grudge and discontentment vaine:
    Then turning to the palmer, he gan spy
    Where at his feet, with sorrowfull demaine
    And deadly hew, an armed corse did lye,
In whose dead face he red great magnanimity.

24 Said he then to the palmer; Reverend syre,
What great misfortune hath betidd this knight?
Or did his life her fatall date expyre,
Or did he fall by treason, or by fight?
However, sure I rew his pitteous plight.
Not one, nor other, (sayd the palmer grave)
Hath him befalne, but cloudes of deadly night
Awhile his heavie eylids cover'd have,
And all his senses drowned in deep senselesse wave:

25 Which those same cruell foes, that stand hereby,
Making advantage, to revenge their spight,
Would him disarme and treaten shamefully;
Unworthy usage of redoubted knight.
But you, faire sir, whose honourable sight
Doth promise hope of helpe, and timely grace,
Mote I beseech to succour his sad plight,
And by your powre protect his feeble cace.
First praise of knighthood is, foule outrage to deface.

26 Palmer, (said he) no knight so rude, I weene,
As to doen outrage to a sleeping ghost:
Ne was there ever noble courage seene,
That in advauntage would his puissance bost:
Honour is least, where oddes appeareth most.
May be, that better reason will aswage
The rash revengers heat. Words well dispost
Have secret powre t' appease inflamed rage:
If not, leave unto me thy knights last patronage.

27 Tho turning to those brethren, thus bespoke,
Ye warlike payre, whose valorous great might,
It seemes, just wrongs to vengeance doe provoke,
To wreake your wrath on this dead seeming knight,
Mote ought allay the storme of your despight,
And settle patience in so furious heat?
Not to debate the chalenge of your right,
But for his carkasse pardon I entreat,
Whom fortune hath alreadie laid in lowest seat.

28 To whom Cymochles said; For what art thou,
   That mak'st thyselfe his dayes-man, to prolong
   The vengeance prest? Or who shall let me now
   On this vile body from to wreake my wrong,
   And make his carkasse as the outcast dong? .
   Why should not that dead carrion satisfie
   The guilt, which, if he lived had thus long,
   His life for due revenge should deare abie?
The trespasse still doth live, albe the person die.

29 Indeed (then said the prince) the evill donne
   Dyes not, when breath the bodie first doth leave,
   But from the grandsyre to the nephewes sonne,
   And all his seed the curse doth often cleave,
   Till vengeance utterly the guilt bereave:
   So streightly God doth judge. But gentle knight,
   That doth against the dead his hand upreare,
   His honour staines with rancour and despight,
And great disparagment makes to his former might.

30 Pyrochles gan reply the second tyme,
   And to him said, Now felon sure I read,
   How that thou art partaker of his crime:
   Therefore by Termagaunt thou shalt be dead.
   With that his hand, more sad than lomp of lead,
   Uplifting high, he weened with Morddure,
   His owne good sword Morddure, to cleave his head.
   The faithfull steele such treason no'uld endure,
But swarving from the marke, his lords life did assure.

31 Yet was the force so furious and so fell,
   That horse and man it made to reele aside:
   Nath'lesse the prince would not forsake his sell;
   For well of yore he learned had to ride,
   But full of anger fiercely to him cride;
   False traitour miscreant, thou broken hast
   The law of armes, to strike foe undefide;
   But thou thy treasons fruit, I hope, shalt taste
Right sowre, and feele the law, the which thou hast defast.

32 With that his balefull speare he fiercely bent
   Against the Pagans brest, and therewith thought
   His cursed life out of her lodge have rent:
   But ere the point arrived where it ought,
   That seven-fold shield, which he from Guyon brought,
   He cast betwene to ward the bitter stound:
   Through all those foldes the steelehead passage wrought,
   And through his shoulder pierst; wherwith to ground
He groveling fell, all gored in his gushing wound.

33 Which when his brother saw, fraught with great griefe
   And wrath, he to him leaped furiously,
   And fowly saide, By Mahoune, cursed thiefe,
   That direfull stroke thou dearely shalt aby.
   Then hurling up his harmefull blade on hye,
   Smote him so hugely on his haughtie crest,
   That from his saddle forced him to fly:
   Else mote it needes downe to his manly brest
Have cleft his head in twaine, and life thence dispossest.

34 Now was the prince in daungerous distresse,
   Wanting his sword, when he on foot should fight:
   His single speare could doe him small redresse
   Against two foes of so exceeding might,
   The least of which was match for any knight.
   And now the other, whom he earst did daunt,
   Had reard himselfe againe to cruell fight,
   Three times more furious and more puissaunt,
Unmindfull of his wound, of his fate ignoraunt.

35 So both attonce him charge on either side
   With hideous strokes, and importable powre,
   That forced him his ground to traverse wide,
   And wisely watch to ward that deadly stowre:
   For on his shield, as thicke as stormie showre,
   Their strokes did raine; yet did he never quaile,
   Ne backward shrinke; but as a stedfast towre,
   Whom foe with double battry doth assaile,
Them on her bulwarke beares, and bids them nought availe.

36 So stoutly he withstood their strong assay;
    Till that at last, when he advantage spyde,
    His poinant speare he thrust with puissant sway
    At proud Cymochles, whiles his shield was wyde,
    That through his thigh the mortall steele did gryde :
    He, swarving with the force, within his flesh
    Did breake the launce, and let the head abyde:
    Out of the wound the red blood flowed fresh,
That underneath his feet soone made a purple plesh.

37 Horribly then he gan to rage, and rayle,
    Cursing his gods, and him selfe damning deepe:
    Als when his brother saw the red blood rayle
    Adowne so fast, and all his armour steepe,
    For very felnesse lowd he gan to weepe,
    And said; Caytive, cursse on thy cruell hond,
    That twise hath sped; yet shall it not thee keepe
    From the third brunt of this my fatall brond:
Loe where the dreadfull Death behind thy backe doth stond.

38 With that he strooke, and th' other strooke withall,
    That nothing seem'd mote beare so monstrous might:
    The one upon his covered shield did fall,
    And glauncing downe would not his owner byte:
    But th' other did upon his troncheon smyte;
    Which hewing quite a sunder, further way
    It made, and on his hacqueton did lyte,
    The which dividing with importune sway,
It seizd in his right side, and there the dint did stay.

39 Wyde was the wound, and a large lukewarme flood,
    Red as the rose, thence gushed grievously;
    That when the Paynym spyde the streaming blood,
    Gave him great hart, and hope of victory.
    On th' other side, in huge perplexity
    The prince now stood, having his weapon broke;
    Nought could he hurt, but still at warde did ly:
    Yet with his troncheon he so rudely stroke
Cymochles twise, that twise him forst his foot revoke.

40 Whom when the palmer saw in such distresse,
  Sir Guyons sword he lightly to him raught,
  And said; Faire sonne, great God thy right hand blesse,
  To use that sword so wisely as he ought.
  Glad was the knight, and with fresh courage fraught,
  When as againe he armed felt his hond:
  Then like a lion, which had long time saught
  His robbed whelpes, and at the last them fond
Emongst the shepheard swaynes, then wexeth wood and yond:

41 So fierce he laid about him, and dealt blowes
  On either side, that neither mayle could hold,
  Ne shield defend the thunder of his throwes:
  Now to Pyrochles many strokes he told;
  Eft to Cymochles twise so many fold;
  Then backe againe turning his busie hond,
  Them both attonce compled with courage bold
  To yield wide way to his hart-thrilling brond;   [stond.
And though they both stood stiffe, yet could not both with-

42 As salvage bull, whom two fierce mastives bayt,
  When rancour doth with rage him once engore,
  Forgets with warie ward them to awayt,
  But with his dreadfull hornes them drives afore,
  Or flings aloft, or treades downe in the flore,
  Breathing out wrath, and bellowing disdaine,
  That all the forest quakes to heare him rore:
  So rag'd Prince Arthur twixt his foemen twaine,
That neither could his mightie puissaunce sustaine.

43 But ever at Pyrochles when he smit,
  Who Guyons shield cast ever him before,
  Whereon the Faery Queenes pourtract was writ,
  His hand relented and the stroke forbore,
  And his deare hart the picture gan adore;
  Which oft the Paynim sav'd from deadly stowre:
  But him henceforth the same can save no more;
  For now arrived is his fatall howre,
That no'te avoyded be by earthly skill or powre.

44 For when Cymochles saw the fowle reproch,
  Which them appeached, prickt with guiltie shame *eure*.
  And inward griefe, he fiercely gan approch,
  Resolv'd to put away that loathly blame,
  Or dye with honour and desert of fame;
  And on the hauberk stroke the prince so sore,
  That quite disparted all the linked frame,
  And pierced to the skin, but bit no more,
Yet made him twise to reele, that never moov'd afore.

45 Whereat renfierst with wrath and sharpe regret,
  He stroke so hugely with his borrowd blade,
  That it empierst the Pagans burganet, *helmet*
  And, cleaving the hard steele, did deepe invade
  Into his head, and cruell passage made
  Quite through his braine: he tombling downe on ground,
  Breathd out his ghost, which to th' infernall shade
  Fast flying, there eternall torment found
For all the sinnes wherewith his lewd life did abound.

46 Which when his german saw, the stony feare,
  Ran to his hart, and all his sence dismayd,
  Ne thenceforth life ne courage did appeare;
  But as a man, whom hellish feendes have frayd,
  Long trembling still he stoode; at last thus sayd;
  Traytour, what hast thou doen? How ever may
  Thy cursed hand so cruelly have swayd
  Against that knight. Harrow and well away,
After so wicked deed why liv'st thou lenger day?

47 With that all desperate, as loathing light,
  And with revenge desiring soone to dye,
  Assembling all his force and utmost might,
  With his owne sword he fierce at him did flye,
  And strooke, and foynd, and lasht outrageously,
  Withouten reason or regard. Well knew
  The prince, with patience and sufferaunce sly,
  So hasty heat soone cooled to subdew:
Tho when this breathlesse woxe, that batteil gan renew.

48 As when a windy tempest bloweth hye,
   That nothing may withstand his stormy stowre,
   The cloudes, as thinges affrayd, before him flye;
   But, all so soone as his outrageous powre
   Is layd, they fiercely then begin to shoure,
   And as in scorne of his spent stormy spight,
   Now all attonce their malice forth do poure;
   So did Prince Arthur beare himselfe in fight,
And suffred rash Pyrochles wast his idle might.

49 At last whenas the Sarazin perceiv'd
   How that straunge sword refusd to serve his need,
   But when he stroke most strong, the dint deceiv'd,
   He flong it from him, and devoyd of dreed,
   Upon him lightly leaping without heed,
   Twixt his two mighty armes engrasped fast,
   Thinking to overthrowe and downe him tred:
   But him in strength and skill the prince surpast,
And through his nimble sleight did under him down cast.

50 Nought booted it the Paynim then to strive;
   For as a bittur in the eagles claw,
   That may not hope by flight to scape alive,
   Still waites for death with dread and trembling aw;
   So he, now subject to the victours law,
   Did not once move, nor upward cast his eye,
   For vile disdaine and rancour, which did gnaw
   His hart in twaine with sad melancholy;
As one that loathed life, and yet despised to dye.

51 But full of princely bounty and great mind,
   The conquerour nought cared him to slay;
   But, casting wrongs and all revenge behind,
   More glory thought to give life, then decay,
   And said, Paynim, this is thy dismall day;
   Yet if thou wilt renounce thy miscreaunce.
   And my trew liegeman yield thyselfe for ay,
   Life will I graunt thee for thy valiaunce,
And all thy wrongs will wipe out of my sovenaunce.

52 Foole (said the pagan) I thy gift defye,
But use thy fortune, as it doth befall;
And say, that I not overcome doe dye,
But in despight of life for death doe call.
Wroth was the prince, and sory yet withall,
That he so wilfully refused grace;
Yet sith his fate so cruelly did fall,
His shining helmet he gan soone unlace,
And lefte his headlesse body bleeding all the place.

53 By this Sir Guyon from his traunce awakt,
Life having maistered her senceless foe;
And looking up, when as his shield he lakt,
And sword saw not, he wexed wondrous woe:
But when the palmer, whom he long ygoe
Had lost, he by him spide, right glad he grew,
And saide, Deare sir, whom wandring to and fro
I long have lackt, I joy thy face to vew;
Firme is thy faith, whom daunger never fro me drew.

54 But read what wicked hand hath robbed mee
Of my good sword and shield? The palmer, glad
With so fresh hew uprysing him to see,
Him answered; Faire sonne, be no whit sad
For want of weapons, they shall soone be had.
So gan he to discourse the whole debate,
Which that straunge knight for him sustained had,
And those two Sarazins confounded late,
Whose carcases on ground were horribly prostrate.

55 Which when he heard, and saw the tokens trew,
His hart with great affection was embayd,
And to the prince with bowing reverence dew,
As to the patrone of his life, thus sayd;
My lord, my liege, by whose most gratious ayd
I live this day, and see my foes subdewd,
What may suffise to be for meede repayd
Of so great graces as ye have me shewd,
But to be ever bound—

56 To whom the Infant thus, Faire sir, what need
   Good turnes be counted, as a servile bond,
   To bind their doers to receive their meede?
   Are not all knightes by oath bound to withstond
   Oppressours powre by armes and puissant hond?
   Suffise, that I have done my dew in place.
   So goodly purpose they together fond
   Of kindnesse and of courteous aggrace;
The whiles false Archimage and Atin fled apace.

CANTO IX.

The House of Temperance, in which
Doth sober Alma dwell,
Besiegd of many foes, whom straunger
knightes to flight compell.

1 OF all Gods workes, which do this worlde adorne,
There is no one more faire and excellent
Then is mans body both for powre and forme,
Whiles it is kept in·sober government;
But none then it more fowle and indecent,
Distempred through misrule and passions bace;
It grows a monster, and incontinent
Doth lose his dignitie and native grace:
Behold, who list, both one and other in this place.

2 After the Paynim brethren conquer'd were,
The Briton prince recov'ring his stolne sword,
And Guyon his lost shield, they both yfere
Forth passed on their way in faire accord,
Till him the prince with gentle court did bord;
Sir knight, mote I of you this curt'sie read,
To weet why on your shield, so goodly scord,
Beare ye the picture of that ladies head?
Full lively is the semblaunt, though the substance dead.

3 Faire sir (sayd he) if in that picture dead
Such life ye read, and vertue in vaine shew;
What mote ye weene, if the trew lively-head
Of that most glorious visage ye did vew?
But if the beautie of her mind ye knew,
That is, her bountie, and imperiall powre,
Thousand times fairer then her mortall hew,
O how great wonder would your thoughts devoure,
And infinite desire into your spirite poure.

4 She is the mighty Queene of Faerie,
  Whose faire retrait I in my shield doe beare;
  Shee is the flowre of grace and chastitie,
  Throughout the world renowmed far and neare,
  My life, my liege, my soveraigne, my deare,
  Whose glory shineth as the morning starre,
  And with her light the earth enlumines cleare;
  Far reach her mercies, and her prayses farre,
As well in state of peace, as puissaunce in warre.

5 Thrise happy man, (said then the Briton knight)
  Whom gracious lot and thy great valiaunce
  Have made thee souldier of that princesse bright,
  Which with her bounty and glad countenance
  Doth blesse her servaunts, and them high advaunce.
  How may straunge knight hope ever to aspire,
  By faithfull service and meete amenance
  Unto such blisse? sufficient were that hire
For losse of thousand lives, to dye at her desire.

6 Said Guyon, Noble lord, what meed so great,
  Or grace of earthly prince so soveraine,
  But by your wondrous worth and warlike feat
  Ye well may hope, and easely attaine?
  But were your will her sold to entertaine,
  And numbred be mongst knights of Maydenhed,
  Great guerdon, well I wote, should you remaine,
  And in her favor high bee reckoned,
As Arthegall and Sophy now beene honored.

7 Certes (then said the prince) I God avow,
  That sith I armes and knighthood first did plight,
  My whole desire hath beene, and yet is now,
  To serve that Queene with all my powre and might.
  Now hath the sunne with his lamp-burning light
  Walkt round about the world, and I no lesse,
  Sith of that goddesse I have sought the sight,
  Yet no where can her find: such happinesse
Heven doth to me envy and fortune favourlesse.

8 Fortune, the foe of famous chevisaunce,
　Seldome (said Guyon) yields to vertue aide,
　But in her way throwes mischiefe and mischaunce,
　Whereby her course is stopt, and passage staid.
　But you, faire sir, be not herewith dismaid,
　But constant keepe the way, in which ye stand;
　Which were it not that I am else delaid
　With hard adventure, which I have in hand,
I labour would to guide you through all Faery land.

9 Gramercy sir (said he) but mote I weete
　What straunge adventure doe ye now pursew?
　Perhaps my succour or advizement meete
　Mote stead you much your purpose to subdew.
　Then gan Sir Guyon all the story shew
　Of false Acrasia, and her wicked wiles;
　Which to avenge, the palmer him forth drew
　From Faery court. So talked they, the whiles
They wasted had much way, and measurd many miles.

10 And now faire Phoebus gan decline in hast
　His weary wagon to the westerne vale,
　Whenas they spide a goodly castle, plast
　Foreby a river in a pleasaunt dale,
　Which choosing for that evenings hospitale,
　They thither marcht: but when they came in sight,
　And from their sweaty coursers did avale,
　They found the gates fast barred long ere night,
And every loup fast lockt, as fearing foes despight.

11 Which when they saw, they weened fowle reproch
　Was to them doen, their entrance to forstall;
　Till that the squire gan nigher to approch,
　And wind his horne under the castle wall,
　That with the noise it shooke, as it would fall.
　Eftsoones forth looked from the highest spire
　The watch, and lowd unto the knights did call,
　To weete what they so rudely did require:
Who gently answered, they entrance did desire.

12 Fly fly, good knights, (said he) fly fast away,
    If that your lives ye love, as meete ye should;
    Fly fast, and save yourselves from neare decay;
    Here may ye not have entraunce, though we would:
    We would and would againe, if that we could;
    But thousand enemies about us rave,
    And with long siege us in this castle hould:
    Seven yeares this wize they us besieged have,
And many good knights slaine that have us sought to save.

13 Thus as he spoke, loe with outragious cry
    A thousand villeins round about them swarmd
    Out of the rockes and caves adjoyning nye;
    Vile caitive wretches, ragged, rude, deformd,
    All threatning death, all in straunge manner armd;
    Some with unweldy clubs, some with long speares,
    Some rusty knives, some staves in fire warmd.
    Sterne was their looke, like wild amazed steares,
Staring with hollow eyes, and stiff upstanding heares.

14 Fiersly at first those knights they did assaile,
    And drove them to recoile: but when againe
    They gave fresh charge, their forces gan to faile,
    Unhable their encounter to sustaine;
    For with such puissaunce and impetuous maine
    Those champions broke on them, that forst them fly,
    Like scattered sheepe, whenas the shepherds swaine
    A lyon and a tigre doth espye,
With greedy pace forth rushing from the forest nye.

15 A while they fled, but soone returnd againe
    With greater fury, then before was found;
    And evermore their cruell capitaine
    Sought with his raskall routs t'enclose them round,
    And overrun to tread them to the ground.
    But soone the knights with their bright-burning blades
    Broke their rude troupes, and orders did confound,
    Hewing and slashing at their idle shades;
For though they bodies seem, yet substaunce from them fades.

16 As when a swarme of gnats at eventide
  Out of the fennes of Allan do arise,
  Their murmuring small trompets sounden wide,
  Whiles in the aire their clustring army flies,
  That as a cloud doth seeme to dim the skies;
  Ne man nor beast may rest or take repast
  For their sharpe wounds, and noyous injuries,
  Till the fierce northerne wind with blustring blast
Doth blow them quite away, and in the ocean cast.

17 Thus when they had that troublous rout disperst,
  Unto the castle gate they come againe,
  And entraunce crav'd, which was denied erst.
  Now when report of that their perlous paine,
  And combrous conflict, which they did sustaine,
  Came to the ladies eare, which there did dwell,
  She forth issewed with a goodly traine
  Of squires and ladies equipaged well,
And entertained them right fairely, as befell.

18 Alma she called was, a virgin bright,
  That had not yet felt Cupides wanton rage;
  Yet was she woo'd of many a gentle knight,
  And many a lord of noble parentage,
  That sought with her to lincke in marriage:
  For shee was faire, as faire mote ever bee,
  And in the flowre now of her freshest age;
  Yet full of grace and goodly modestee,
That even heaven rejoyced her sweete face to see.

19 In robe of lilly white she was arayd,
  That from her shoulder to her heele downe raught;
  The traine whereof loose far behind her strayd,
  Braunched with gold and pearle, most richly wrought,
  And borne of two faire damsels which were taught
  That service well: her yellow golden heare
  Was trimly woven, and in tresses wrought,
  Ne other tire she on her head did weare,
But crowned with a garland of sweete rosiere.

I

20 Goodly she entertaind those noble knights,
And brought them up into her castle hall;
Where gentle court and gracious delight
Shee to them made, with mildnesse virginall,
Shewing herselfe both wise and liberall.
There when they rested had a season dew,
They her besought of favour speciall
Of that faire castle to affoord them vew:
She graunted, and them leading forth, the same did shew.

21 First she them led up to the castle wall,
That was so high as foe might not it clime,
And all so faire and fensible withall;
Not built of bricke, ne yet of stone and lime,
But of thing like to that Aegyptian slime,
Whereof king Nine whilome built Babell towre:
But O great pitty, that no lenger time
So goodly workmanship should not endure:
Soone it must turne to earth: no earthly thing is sure.

22 The frame thereof seemd partly circulare,
And part triangulare, O worke divine;
Those two the first and last proportions are;
The one imperfect, mortall, fæminine;
Th' other immortall, perfect, masculine;
And twixt them both a quadrate was the base,
Proportiond equally by seven and nine;
Nine was the circle set in heavens place:
All which compacted made a goodly Dyapase.

23 Therein two gates were placed seemly well:
The one before, by which all in did pas,
Did th' other far in workmanship excell;
For not of wood, nor of enduring bras,
But of more worthy substance fram'd it was:
Doubly disparted, it did locke and close,
That when it locked, none might thorough pas,
And when it opened, no man might it close;
Still open to their friends, and closed to their foes.

24 Of hewen stone the porch was fairely wrought,
 Stone more of valew, and more smooth and fine,
 Then jet or marble far from Ireland brought;
 Over the which was cast a wandring vine,
 Enchaced with a wanton yvie twine:
 And over it a faire portcullis hong,
 Which to the gate directly did incline
 With comely compasse, and compacture strong,
Neither unseemly short, nor yet exceeding long.

25 Within the barbican a porter sate,
 Day and night duely keeping watch and ward;
 Nor wight, nor word mote passe out of the gate,
 But in good order, and with dew regard;
 Utterers of secrets he from thence debard,
 Bablers of folly, and blazers of crime:
 His larum bell might lowd and wide be hard
 When cause requird, but never out of time;
Early and late it rong, at evening and at prime.

26 And round about the porch on every syde
 Twise sixteene warders sat, all armed bright
 In glistring steele, and strongly fortifide:
 Tall yeomen seemed they, and of great might,
 And were enraunged ready still for fight.
 By them as Alma passed with her guestes,
 They did obeysaunce, as beseemed right,
 And then againe returned to their restes:
The porter eke to her did lout with humble gestes.

27 Thence she them brought into a stately hall,
 Wherein were many tables faire dispred,
 And ready dight with drapets festivall,
 Against the viaundes should be ministred.
 At th' upper end there sate, yclad in red
 Downe to the ground, a comely personage,
 That in his hand a white rod menaged;
 He steward was hight Diet; rype of age,
And in demeanure sober, and in counsell sage.

28 And through the hall there walked to and fro
   A jolly yeoman, marshall of the same,
   Whose name was Appetite; he did bestow
   Both guestes and meate, whenever in they came,
   And knew them how to order without blame,
   As him the steward bad. They both attone
   Did dewty to their lady, as became;
   Who, passing by, forth led her guestes anone
Into the kitchin rowme, ne spard for nicenesse none.

29 It was a vaut ybuilt for great dispence,
   With many raunges reard along the wall,
   And one great chimney, whose long tonnell thence
   The smoke forth threw. And in the midst of all
   There placed was a caudron wide and tall
   Upon a mighty furnace, burning whot,
   More whot then Aetn', or flaming Mongiball:
   For day and night it brent, ne ceased not,
So long as any thing it in the caudron got.

30 But to delay the heat, least by mischaunce
   It might breake out, and set the whole on fyre,
   There added was by goodly ordinaunce
   An huge great paire of bellowes, which did styre
   Continually, and cooling breath inspyre.
   About the caudron many cookes accoyld
   With hookes and ladles, as need did require;
   The whiles the viaundes in the vessell boyld,
They did about their businesse sweat, and sorely toyld.

31 The maister cooke was cald Concoction,
   A carefull man, and full of comely guise:
   The kitchin clerke, that hight Digestion,
   Did order all th' achates in seemely wise,
   And set them forth, as well he could devise.
   The rest had severall offices assind;
   Some to remove the scum, as it did rise;
   Others to beare the same away did mind;
And others it to use according to his kind.

     *   *   *   *   *   *

33 Which goodly order, and great workmans skill
   Whenas those knights beheld, with rare delight
   And gazing wonder they their minds did fill;
   For never had they seene so straunge a sight.
   Thence backe againe faire Alma led them right,
   And soone into a goodly parlour brought,
   That was with royall arras richly dight,
   In which was nothing pourtrahed nor wrought;
Not wrought, nor pourtrahed, but easie to be thought.

34 And in the midst thereof upon the floure
   A lovely bevy of faire ladies sate,
   Courted of many a jolly paramoure,
   The which them did in modest wise amate,
   And each one sought his lady to aggrate:
   And eke emongst them little Cupid playd
   His wanton sportes, being returned late
   From his fierce warres, and having from him layd
His cruell bow, wherewith he thousands hath dismayd.

35 Diverse delights they found themselves to please;
   Some song in sweet consort, some laught for joy;
   Some plaid with strawes, some idly sat at ease,
   But other some could not abide to toy,
   All pleasaunce was to them griefe and annoy:
   This frownd, that faund, the third for shame did blush,
   Another seemed envious, or coy,
   Another in her teeth did gnaw a rush:
But at these straungers presence every one did hush.

36 Soone as the gracious Alma came in place,
   They all attonce out of their seates arose,
   And to her homage made with humble grace:
   Whom when the knights beheld, they gan dispose
   Themselves to court, and each a damzell chose:
   The prince by chaunce did on a lady light,
   That was right faire and fresh as morning rose,
   But somewhat sad, and solemne eke in sight,
As if some pensive thought constraind her gentle spright.

37 In a long purple pall, whose skirt with gold
    Was fretted all about, she was arayd;
    And in her hand a poplar braunch did hold.
    To whom the prince in courteous maner sayd;
    Gentle Madame, why beene ye thus dismaid,
    And your faire beautie doe with sadnes spill?
    Lives any, that you hath thus ill apayd?
    Or doen you love, or doen you lack your will?
  Whatever be the cause, it sure beseemes you ill.

38 Faire sir, (said she, halfe in disdaineful wise,)
    How is it, that this word in me ye blame,
    And in yourselfe doe not the same advise?
    Him ill beseemes anothers fault to name,
    That may unwares be blotted with the same:
    Pensive I yeeld I am, and sad in mind,
    Through great desire of glory and of fame;
    Ne ought I weene are ye therein behind,   [find.
  That have twelve months sought one, yet no where can her

39 The prince was inly moved at her speach,
    Well weeting trew, what she had rashly told;
    Yet with faire semblaunt sought to hide the breach,
    Which chaunge of colour did perforce unfold,
    Now seeming flaming whot, now stony cold:
    Tho turning soft aside, he did inquyre
    What wight she was, that poplar braunch did hold:
    It answered was, her name was Prays-desire,
  That by well doing sought to honour to aspire.

40 The whiles, the Faery knight did entertaine
    Another damsell of that gentle crew,
    That was right faire and modest of demaine,
    But that too oft she chaung'd her native hew:
    Straunge was her tyre, and all her garment blew,
    Close rownd about her tuckt with many a plight:
    Upon her fist the bird which shonneth vew,
    And keepes in coverts close from living wight,
  Did sit, as yet ashamd, how rude Pan did her dight.

41 So long as Guyon with her commoned,
   Unto the ground she cast her modest eye,
   And ever and anone with rosie red
   The bashfull bloud her snowy cheekes did dye,
   That her became, as polisht yvory
   Which cunning craftesman hand hath overlayd
   With faire vermilion or pure castory.
   Great wonder had the knight to see the mayd
So straungely passioned, and to her gently said:

42 Faire damzell, seemeth by your troubled cheare,
   That either me too bold ye weene, this wise
   You to molest, or other ill to feare
   That in the secret of your hart close lyes,
   From whence it doth, as cloud from sea, arise:
   If it be I, of pardon I you pray;
   But if ought else that I mote not devise,
   I will, if please you it discure, assay
To ease you of that ill, so wisely as I may.

43 She answerd nought, but more abasht for shame
   Held downe her head, the whiles her lovely face
   The flashing bloud with blushing did inflame,
   And the strong passion mard her modest grace,
   That Guyon mervayld at her uncouth cace;
   Till Alma him bespake, Why wonder yee,
   Faire sir, at that, which ye so much embrace?
   She is the fountaine of your modestee,
You shamefast are, but Shamefastnesse itselfe is shee.

44 Thereat the Elfe did blush in privitee,
   And turnd his face away; but she the same
   Dissembled faire, and faynd to oversee.
   Thus they awhile with court and goodly game
   Themselves did solace each one with his dame,
   Till that great ladie thence away them sought
   To vew her castles other wondrous frame.
   Up to a stately turret she them brought,
Ascending by ten steps of alablaster wrought.

45 That turrets frame most admirable was,
  Like highest heaven compassed around,
  And lifted high above this earthly masse,
  Which it survewd, as hils doen lower ground:
  But not on ground mote like to this be found:
  Not that, which antique Cadmus whylome built
  In Thebes, which Alexander did confound;
  Nor that proud towre of Troy, though richly guilt,
From which young Hectors bloud by cruell Greekes was spilt.

46 The roofe hereof was arched over head,
  And deckt' with flowres and herbars daintily;
  Two goodly beacons, set in watches stead,
  Therein gave light, and flam'd continually:
  For they of living fire most subtilly
  Were made, and set in silver sockets bright,
  Cover'd with lids deviz'd of substance sly,
  That readily they shut and open might.
O who can tell the prayses of that makers might?

47 Ne can I tell, ne can I stay to tell,
  This parts great workemanship and wondrous powre,
  That all this other worldes worke doth excell,
  And likest is unto that heavenly towre
  That God hath built for his owne blessed bowre.
  Therein were divers roomes, and divers stages;
  But three the chiefest and of greatest powre,
  In which there dwelt three honorable sages,
The wisest men, I weene, that lived in their ages.

48 Not he, whom Greece, the nourse of all good arts,
  By Phoebus doome the wisest thought alive,
  Might be compar'd to these by many parts:
  Nor that sage Pylian syre, which did survive
  Three ages, such as mortall men contrive,
  By whose advise old Priams cittie fell,
  With these in praise of pollicies mote strive.
  These three in these three roomes did sundry dwell,
And counselled faire Alma how to governe well.

49 The first of them could things to come foresee;
    The next could of thinges present best advize;
    The third things past could keepe in memoree:
    So that no time, nor reason could arize,
    But that the same could one of these comprize.
    Forthy the first did in the forepart sit,
    That nought mote hinder his quicke prejudize:
    He had a sharpe foresight, and working wit,
That never idle was, ne once would rest a whit.

50 His chamber was dispainted all within
    With sondry colours, in the which were writ
    Infinite shapes of thinges dispersed thin;
    Some such as in the world were never yit,
    Ne can devized be of mortall wit;
    Some daily seene, and knowen by their names,
    Such as in idle fantasies do flit;
    Infernall hags, centaurs, feendes, hippodames,
Apes, lyons, aegles, owles, fooles, lovers, children, dames.

51 And all the chamber filled was with flyes
    Which buzzed all about, and made such sound
    That they encombred all mens eares and eyes,
    Like many swarmes of bees assembled round,
    After their hives with honny do abound.
    All those were idle thoughts and fantasies,
    Devices, dreames, opinions unsound,
    Shewes, visions, sooth-sayes, and prophesies;
And all that fained is, as leasings, tales, and lies.

52 Emongst them all sate he which wonned there,
    That hight Phantastes by his nature trew;
    A man of yeares yet fresh, as mote appere,
    Of swarth complexion, and of crabbed hew,
    That him full of melancholy did shew;
    Bent hollow beetle browes, sharpe staring eyes
    That mad or foolish seemd: one by his vew
    Mote deeme him borne with ill disposed skyes,
When oblique Saturne sate in th' house of agonyes.

53 Whom Alma having shewed to her guestes,
    Thence brought them to the second roome, whose wals
    Were painted faire with memorable gestes
    Of famous wisards, and with picturals
    Of magistrates, of courts, of tribunals,
    Of commen wealthes, of states, of pollicy,
    Of lawes, of judgements, and of decretals;
    All artes, all science, all philosophy,
And all that in the world was aye thought wittily.

54 Of those that rowme was full; and them among
    There sate a man of ripe and perfect age,
    Who did them meditate all his life long,
    That through continuall practise and usage
    He now was growne right wise, and wondrous sage:
    Great pleasure had those stranger knights to see
    His goodly reason and grave personage,
    That his disciples both desir'd to bee:
But Alma thence them led to th' hindmost roome of three.

55 That chamber seemed ruinous and old,
    And therefore was removed far behind,
    Yet were the wals, that did the same uphold,
    Right firme and strong, though somewhat they declind;
    And therein sat an old oldman halfe blind,
    And all decrepit in his feeble corse,
    Yet lively vigour rested in his mind,
    And recompenst them with a better scorse:
Weake body well is chang'd for minds redoubled forse.

56 This man of infinite remembrance was,
    And things foregone through many ages held,
    Which he recorded still, as they did pas,
    Ne suffred them to perish through long eld,
    As all things els, the which this world doth weld;
    But laid them up in his immortall scrine,
    Where they for ever incorrupted dweld:
    The warres he well remembred of king Nine,
Of old Assaracus, and Inachus divine.

57 The yeares of Nestor nothing were to his,
  Ne yet Mathusalem, though longest liv'd;
  For he remembred both their infancies:
  Ne wonder then if that he were depriv'd
  Of native strength now that he them surviv'd.
  His chamber all was hangd about with rolles
  And old records from auncient times deriv'd,
  Some made in books, some in long parchment scrolles,
That were all worm-eaten and full of canker holes.

58 Amidst them all he in a chaire was set,
  Tossing and turning them withouten end;
  But for he was unhable them to fet,
  A little boy did on him still attend,
  To reach, whenever he for ought did send;
  And oft when thinges were lost, or laid amis,
  That boy them sought, and unto him did lend:
  Therefore he Anamnestes cleped is;
And that old man Eumnestes, by their propertis.

59 The knights there entring did him reverence dew,
  And wondred at his endlesse exercise.
  Then as they gan his librarie to vew,
  And antique registers for to avise,
  There chaunced to the princes hand to rize
  An auncient booke, hight *Briton Moniments*,
  That of this lands first conquest did devize,
  And old division into regiments,
Till it reduced was to one mans governments.

60 Sir Guyon chaunst eke on another booke,
  That hight *Antiquitie of Faerie* lond:
  In which when as he greedily did looke,
  Th' off-spring of Elves and Faries there he fond,
  As it delivered was from bond to hond:
  Whereat they burning both with fervent fire
  Their countries auncestry to understond,
  Crav'd leave of Alma and that aged sire
To read those bookes; who gladly graunted their desire.

CANTO X.

A chronicle of Briton kings,
From Brute to Uthers rayne;
And rolles of Elfin emperours,
Till time of Gloriane.

1 WHO now shall give unto me words and sound
   Equall unto this haughtie enterprise?
   Or who shal lend me wings, with which from ground
   My lowly verse may loftily arise,
   And lift it selfe unto the highest skies?
   More ample spirit, then hitherto was wount
   Here needes me, whiles the famous auncestries
   Of my most dreaded soveraigne I recount,
By which all earthly princes she doth farre surmount.

2 Ne under sunne, that shines so wide and faire,
   Whence all that lives does borrow life and light,
   Lives ought that to her linage may compaire;
   Which though from earth it be derived right,
   Yet doth it selfe stretch forth to heavens hight,
   And all the world with wonder overspred;
   A labor huge, exceeding far my might:
   How shall fraile pen, with feare disparaged,
Conceive such soveraine glory and great bountihed?

3 Argument worthy of Maeonian quill;
   Or rather worthy of great Phoebus rote,
   Whereon the ruines of great Ossa hill, .
   And triumphes of Phlegraean Jove, he wrote,
   That all the gods admird his loftie note.
   But if some relish of that heavenly lay
   His learned daughters would to me report
   To decke my song withall, I would assay
Thy name, O soveraine Queene, to blazon farre away.

4 Thy name, O soveraine Queene, thy realme and race,
From this renowmed prince derived arre,
Who mightily upheld that royall mace
Which now thou bear'st, to thee descended farre
From mightie kings and conquerours in warre,
Thy fathers and great grandfathers of old,
Whose noble deedes above the northerne starre
Immortall Fame for ever hath enrold;
As in that old mans booke they were in order told.

5 The land, which warlike Britons now possesse,
And therein have their mightie empire raysd,
In antique times was salvage wildernesse,
Unpeopled, unmannurd, unprovd, unpraysd;
Ne was it island then, ne was it paysd
Amid the ocean waves, ne was it sought
Of merchants farre for profits therein praysd;
But was all desolate, and of some thought
By sea to have bene from the Celticke mayn-land brought.

6 Ne did it then deserve a name to have,
Till that the venturous mariner that way
Learning his ship from those white rocks to save,
Which all along the southerne sea-coast lay
Threatning unheedie wrecke and rash decay,
For safeties sake that same his sea-marke made,
And nam'd it Albion. But later day,
Finding in it fit ports for fishers trade,
Gan more the same frequent, and further to invade.

7 But farre in land a salvage nation dwelt
Of hideous giants, and halfe beastly men,
That never tasted grace, nor goodnesse felt,
But wild like beasts lurking in loathsome den,
And flying fast as roebucke through the fen,
All naked without shame, or care of cold,
By hunting and by spoiling lived then;
Of stature huge, and eke of courage bold,
That sonnes of men amazd their sternesse to behold.

8 But whence they sprong, or how they were begot,
　Uneath is to assure ; uneath to wene
　That monstrous error which doth some assot,
　That Dioclesians fiftie daughters shene
　Into this land by chaunce have driven bene,
　Where companing with feends and filthy sprights
　They brought forth giants, and such dreadfull wights
As farre exceeded men in their immeasurd mights.

9 They held this land, and with their filthinesse
　Polluted this same gentle soyle long time ;
　That their owne mother loathd their beastlinesse,
　And gan abhorre her broods unkindly crime.
　All were they borne of her owne native slime;
　Until that Brutus anciently deriv'd
　From royall stocke of old Assaracs line,
　Driven by fatall error, here arriv'd,
And them of their unjust possession depriv'd.

10 But ere he had established his throne,
　And spred his empire to the utmost shore,
　He fought great battels with his salvage fone ;
　In which he them defeated evermore,
　And many giants left on groning flore:
　That well can witness yet unto this day
　The westerne Hogh, besprincled with the gore
　Of mighty Goëmot, whom in stout fray
Corineus conquered, and cruelly did slay.

11 And eke that ample pit, yet farre renownd
　For the large leape, which Debon did compell
　Coulin to make, being eight lugs of grownd,
　Into the which returning backe he fell:
　But those three monstrous stones doe most excell
　Which that huge sonne of hideous Albion,
　Whose father Hercules in Fraunce did quell,
　Great Godmer threw, in fierce contention,
At bold Canutus ; but of him was slaine anon.

12 In meed of these great conquests by them got,
 Corineus had that province utmost west
 To him assigned for his worthy lot,
 Which of his name and memorable gest
 He called Cornewaile, yet so called best;
 And Debons shayre was that is Devonshyre:
 But Canute had his portion from the rest,
 The which he cald Canutium, for his hyre;
Now Cantium, which Kent we commenly inquire.

13 Thus Brute this realme unto his rule subdewd,
 And raigned long in great felicitie,
 Lov'd of his friends, and of his foes eschewd:
 He left three sonnes, his famous progeny,
 Borne of faire Inogene of Italy;
 Mongst whom he parted his imperiall state,
 And Locrine left chiefe lord of Britany.
 At last ripe age bad him surrender late
His life, and long good fortune unto finall fate.

14 Locrine was left the soveraine lord of all;
 But Albanact had all the northerne part,
 Which of himselfe Albania he did call;
 And Camber did possesse the westerne quart,
 Which Severne now from Logris doth depart:
 And each his portion peaceably enjoyd,
 Ne was there outward breach, nor grudge in hart,
 That once their quiet government annoyd;
But each his paines to others profit still employd.

15 Untill a nation straung, with visage swart,
 And courage fierce, that all men did affray,
 Which through the world then swarmd in every part,
 And overflowd all countries far away,
 Like Noyes great flood, with their importune sway,
 This land invaded with like violence,
 And did themselves through all the north display:
 Untill that Locrine for his realmes defence,
Did head against them make, and strong munifence.

16 He them encountred, a confused rout,
   Foreby the river that whylome was hight
   The auncient Abus, where with courage stout
   He them defeated in victorious fight,
   And chaste so fiercely after fearefull flight,
   That forst their chiefetaine, for his safeties sake,
   (Their chiefetaine Humber named was aright,)
   Unto the mightie streame him to betake,
Where he an end of battell and of life did make.

17 The king returned proud of victorie,
   And insolent wox through unwonted ease,
   That shortly he forgot the jeopardie,
   Which in his land he lately did appease
   And fell to vaine voluptuous disease:
   He lov'd faire Ladie Estrild, lewdly lov'd,
   Whose wanton pleasures him too much did please,
   That quite his hart from Guendolene remov'd,
From Guendolene his wife, though alwaies faithful prov'd.

18 The noble daughter of Corinëus
   Would not endure to be so vile disdaind,
   But, gathering force, and courage valorous,
   Encountred him in battell well ordaind,
   In which him vanquisht she to fly constraind:
   But she so fast pursewd, that him she tooke
   And threw in bands, where he till death remaind;
   Als his faire leman flying through a brooke
She overhent, nought moved with her piteous looke.

19 But both her selfe, and eke her daughter deare
   Begotten by her kingly paramoure,
   The faire Sabrina almost dead with feare,
   She there attached, far from all succoure:
   The one she slew in that impatient stoure,
   But the sad virgin innocent of all,
   Adowne the rolling river she did poure,
   Which of her name now Severne men do call:
Such was the end that to disloyall love did fall.

20 Then for her sonne, which she to Locrin bore,
   Madan was young, unmeet the rule of sway,
   In her owne hand the crowne she kept in store,
   Till ryper ears he raught, and stronger stay:
   During which time her powre she did display
   Through all this realme, the glorie of her sex,
   And first taught men a woman to obay:
   But when her sonne to mans estate did wex,
She it surrendred, ne her selfe would lenger vex.

21 Tho Madan raignd, unworthie of his race;
   For with all shame that sacred throne he fild.
   Next Memprise, as unworthy of that place,
   In which being consorted with Manild,
   For thirst of single kingdom him he kild.
   But Ebranck salved both their infamies
   With noble deedes, and warreyd on Brunchild
   In Henault, where yet of his victories
Brave moniments remaine, which yet that land envies.

22 An happy man in his first dayes he was,
   And happie father of faire progeny:
   For all so many weekes as the yeare has,
   So many children he did multiply;
   Of which were twentie sonnes, which did apply
   Their minds to praise and chevalrous desire:
   Those germans did subdew all Germany,
   Of whom it hight; but in the end their sire
With foule repulse from Fraunce was forced to retire.

23 Which blot his sonne succeeding in his seat,
   The second Brute, the second both in name,
   And eke in semblance of his puissance great,
   Right well recur'd, and did away that blame
   With recompence of everlasting fame.
   He with his victour sword first opened
   The bowels of wide Fraunce, a forlorne dame,
   And taught her first how to be conquered;
Since which, with sundrie spoiles she hath been ransacked

K

24 Let Scaldis tell, and let tell Hania,
 And let the marsh of Estham bruges tell,
 What colour were their waters that same day,
 And all the moore twixt Elversham and Dell,
 With bloud of Henalois which therein fell.
 How oft that day did sad Brunchildis see
 The *greene shield* dyde in dolorous vermell?
 That not *scuith guiridh* it mote seeme to bee
But rather *y scuith gogh*, sign of sad crueltee.

25 His sonne king Leill by fathers labour long,
 Enjoyd an heritage of lasting peace,
 And built Cairleill, and built Cairleon strong.
 Next Huddibras his realme did not encrease,
 But taught the land from wearie warres to cease.
 Whose footsteps Bladud following, in arts
 Exceld at Athens all the learned preace,
 From whence he brought them to these salvage parts,
And with sweet science mollifide their stubborne harts.

26 Ensample of his wondrous faculty,
 Behold the boyling baths at Cairbadon,
 Which seeth with secret fire eternally,
 And in their entrails, full of quicke brimston,
 Nourish the flames, which they are warm'd upon,
 That to their people wealth they forth do well.
 And health to every forreine nation:
 Yet he at last, contending to excell
The reach of men, through flight into fond mischief fell.

27 Next him king Leyr in happie peace long raind,
 But had no issue male him to succeed,
 But three faire daughters, which were well uptraind
 In all that seemed fit for kingly seed;
 Mongst whom his realme he equally decreed
 To have divided. Tho when feeble age
 Nigh to his utmost date he saw proceed,
 He cald his daughters, and with speeches sage
Inquyrd, which of them most did love her parentage.

28 The eldest Gonorill gan to protest,
   That she much more than her owne life him lov'd;
   And Regan greater love to him profest
   Then all the world, when ever it were proov'd;
   But Cordeill said she loved him, as behoov'd:
   Whose simple answere, wanting colours faire
   To paint it forth, him to displeasance moov'd,
   That in his crowne he counted her no haire,
But twixt the other twaine his kingdom whole did shaire.

29 So wedded th' one to Maglan king of Scots,
   And th' other to the king of Cambria,
   And twixt them shayrd his realme by equall lots;
   But, without dowre, the wise Cordelia
   Was sent to Aganip of Celtica.
   Their aged syre, thus eased of his crowne,
   A private life led in Albania
   With Gonorill, long had in great renowne,
That nought him griev'd to beene from rule deposed downe.

30 But true it is that, when the oyle is spent,
   The light goes out, and weeke is throwne away;
   So when he had resignd his regiment,
   His daughter gan despise his drouping day,
   And wearie waxe of his continuall stay;
   Tho to his daughter Regan he repayrd,
   Who him at first well used every way;
   But when of his departure she despayrd,
Her bountie she abated, and his cheare empayrd.

31 The wretched man gan then avise too late,
   That love is not, where most it is profest;
   Too truely tryde in his extremest state;
   At last resolv'd likewise to prove the rest,
   He to Cordelia him selfe addrest,
   Who with entyre affection him receav'd,
   As for her syre and king her seemed best;
   And after all an army strong she leav'd,
To war on those, which him had of his realme bereav'd.

32 So to his crowne she him restor'd againe,
　　In which he dyde, made ripe for death by eld,
　　And after wild it should to her remaine :
　　Who peaceably the same long time did weld,
　　And all mens harts in dew obedience held;
　　Till that her sisters children, woxen strong
　　Through proud ambition, against her rebeld,
　　And overcommen kept in prison long,
Till wearie of that wretched life her selfe she hong.

33 Then gan the bloudy brethren both to raine:
　　But fierce Cundah gan shortly to envie
　　His brother Morgan, prickt with proud disdaine
　　To have a pere in part of soveraintie ;
　　And kindling coles of cruell enmitie,
　　Raisd warre, and him in battell overthrew:
　　Whence as he to those woodie hills did flie,
　　Which hight of him Glamorgan, there him slew:
Then did he raigne alone, when he none equall knew.

34 His sonne Rivall' his dead rowme did supply;
　　In whose sad time bloud did from heaven raine.
　　Next great Gurgustus, then faire Caecily,
　　In constant peace their kingdomes did containe,
　　. After whom Lago, and Kinmarke did raine,
　　And Gorbogud, till farre in yeares he grew:
　　Then his ambitious sonnes unto them twaine
　　Arraught the rule, and from their father drew;
Stout Ferrex and sterne Porrex him in prison threw.

35 But O, the greedy thirst of royall crowne,
　　That knowes no kinred, nor regardes no right,
　　Stird Porrex up to put his brother downe;
　　Who unto him assembling forreine might,
　　Made warre on him, and fell himselfe in fight:
　　Whose death t' avenge, his mother mercilesse,
　　Most mercilesse of women, Wyden hight,
　　Her other sonne last sleeping did oppresse,
And with most cruell hand him murdred pittilesse.

36 Here ended Brutus sacred progenie,
    Which had seven hundred years this sceptre borne
    With high renowme, and great felicity :
    The noble braunch from th' antique stocke was torne
    Through discord, and the royall throne forlorne.
    Thenceforth this realme was into factions rent,
    Whilest each of Brutus boasted to be borne,
    That in the end was left no moniment
Of Brutus, nor of Britons glory a...ncient.

37 Then up arose a man of matchlesse might,
    And wondrous wit to menage high affaires,
    Who stird with pitty of the stressed plight
    Of this sad realme, cut into sundry shaires
    By such as claymd themselves Brutes rightfull haires,
    Gathered the princes of the people loose
    To taken counsell of their common cares ;
    Who with his wisedom won, him streight did choose
Their king, and swore him fealty to win or loose.

38 Then made he head against his enimies,
    And Ymner slew of Logris miscreate ;
    Then Ruddoc and proud Stater, both allyes,
    This of Albanie newly nominate,
    And that of Cambry king confirmed late,
    He overthrew through his owne valiaunce ;
    Whose countries he redus'd to quiet state,
    And shortly brought to civill governaunce,
Now one, which earst were many, made through variaunce.

39 Then made he sacred lawes, which some men say
    Were unto him reveald in vision ;
    By which he freed the traveilers high way,
    The churches part, and ploughmans portion,
    Restraining stealth and strong extortion ;
    The gracious Numa of great Britanie :
    For till his dayes, the chiefe dominion
    By strength was wielded without pollicie :
Therefore he first wore crowne of gold for dignitie.

40 Donwallo dyde, (for what may live for ay ?)
    And left two sonnes, of pearelesse prowesse both,
    That sacked Rome too dearely did assay,
    The recompence of their perjured oth;
    And ransackt Greece wel tryde, when they were wroth;
    Besides subjected France and Germany,
    Which yet their praises speake, all be they loth,
    And inly tremble at the memory
Of Brennus and Bellinus, kings of Britany.

41 Next them did Gurgunt, great Belinus sonne,
    In rule succeede, and eke in fathers praise;
    He Easterland subdewd, and Denmarke wonne,
    And of them both did foy and tribute raise,
    The which was dew in his dead fathers dayes:
    He also gave to fugitives of Spayne,
    Whom he at sea found wandring from their wayes,
    A seate in Ireland safely to remayne,
Which they should hold of him as subject to Britayne.

42 After him raigned Guitheline his hayre,
    The justest man and trewest in his dayes,
    Who had to wife Dame Mertia the fayre,
    A woman worthy of immortall prayse,
    Which for this realme found many goodly layes,
    And wholesome statutes to her husband brought:
    Her many deemd to have beene of the Fayes,
    As was Aegerie that Numa tought:
Those yet of her be Mertian lawes both nam'd and thought.

43 Her sonne Sifillus after her did rayne,
    And then Kimarus, and then Danius;
    Next whom Morindus did the crowne sustaine;
    Who, had he not with wrath outrageous,
    And cruell rancour dim'd his valorous
    And mightie deeds, should matched have the best
    As well in that same field victorious
    Against the forreine Morands he exprest;
Yet lives his memorie, though carcas sleepe in rest.

44 Five sonnes he left begotten of one wife,
   All which successively by turnes did raine:
   First Gorboman, a man of vertuous life;
   Next Archigald, who for his proud disdaine
   Deposed was from princedome soveraine,
   And pitteous Elidure put in his sted;
   Who shortly it to him restord againe,
   Till by his death he it recovered;
But Peridure and Vigent him disthronized.

45 In wretched prison long he did remaine,
   Till they out raigned had their utmost date,
   And then therein reseized was againe,
   And ruled long with honorable state,
   Till he surrendred realme and life to fate.
   Then all the sonnes of these five brethren raynd
   By dew successe, and all their nephewes late;
   Even thrise eleven descents the crowne retaynd,
Till aged Hely by dew heritage it gaynd.

46 He had two sonnes, whose eldest called Lud
   Left of his life most famous memory,
   And endlesse moniments of his great good:
   The ruin'd wals he did reædifye
   Of Troynovant, gainst force of enimy,
   And built that gate, which of his name is hight,
   By which he lyes entombed solemnly.
   He left two sonnes, too young to rule aright,
Androgeus and Tenantius, pictures of his might.

47 Whilst they were young, Cassibalane their eme
   Was by the people chosen in their sted,
   Who on him tooke the royall diademe,
   And goodly well long time it governed;
   Till the prowd Romanes him disquieted,
   And warlike Caesar, tempted with the name
   Of this sweet island, never conquered,
   And envying the Britons blazed fame,
(O hideous hunger of dominion) hither came.

48 Yet twise they were repulsed backe againe,
   And twise renforst backe to their ships to fly;
   The whiles with blood they all the shore did staine,
   And the gray ocean into purple dy:
   Ne had they footing found at last perdie,
   Had not Androgeus, false to native soyle,
   And envious of uncles soveraintie,
   Betrayd his countrey unto forreine spoyle,
Nought els but treason from the first this land did foyle.

49 So by him Caesar got the victory,
   Through great bloudshed, and many a sad assay,
   In which himselfe was charged heavily
   Of hardy Nennius, whom he yet did slay,
   But lost his sword, yet to be seene this day.
   Thenceforth this land was tributarie made
   T' ambitious Rome, and did their rule obay,
   Till Arthur all that reckoning defrayd:
Yet oft the Briton kings against them strongly swayd.

50 Next him Tenantius raignd, then Kimbeline,
   What time th' eternall Lord in fleshly slime
   Enwombed was, from wretched Adams line
   To purge away the guilt of sinfull crime.
   O joyous memorie of happy time.
   That heavenly grace so plenteously displayd;
   (O too high ditty for my simple rime.)
   Soone after this the Romanes him warrayd;
For that their tribute he refusd to let be payd.

51 Good Claudius, that next was emperour,
   An army brought, and with him battell fought,
   In which the king was by a treachetour
   Disguised slaine, ere any thereof thought:
   Yet ceased not the bloudy fight for ought:
   For Arvirage his brothers place supplide
   Both in his armes and crowne, and by that draught
   Did drive the Romanes to the weaker side,
That they to peace agreed. So all was pacifide.

52 Was never king more highly magnifide,
   Nor dred of Romanes, then was Arvirage,
   For which the emperour to him allide
   His daughter Genuiss' in marriage:
   Yet shortly he renounst the vassallage
   Of Rome againe, who hither hastly sent
   Vespasian, that with great spoile and rage
   Forwasted all, till Genuissa gent
Persuaded him to ceasse, and her lord to relent.

53 He dyde; and him succeded Marius,
   Who joyd his dayes in great tranquillity.
   Then Coyll; and after him good Lucius,
   That first received Christianity,
   The sacred pledge of Christes Evangely,
   Yet true it is, that long before that day
   Hither came Joseph of Arimathy,
   Who brought with him the holy grayle, (they say,)
And preacht the truth; but since it greatly did decay.

54 This good king shortly without issew dide,
   Whereof great trouble in the kingdome grew,
   That did her selfe in sundry parts divide,
   And with her powre her owne selfe overthrew,
   Whilest Romanes daily did the weake subdew:
   Which seeing, stout Bunduca up arose,
   And taking armes the Britons to her drew;
   With whom she marched straight against her foes,
And them unwares besides the Severne did enclose.

55 There she with them a cruell battell tride,
   Not with so good successe, as she deserv'd;
   By reason that the captaines on her syde,
   Corrupted by Paulinus, from her swerv'd:
   Yet such, as were through former flight preserv'd,
   Gathering againe, her host she did renew,
   And with fresh courage on the victor serv'd:
   But being all defeated, save a few,
Rather then fly, or be captiv'd, her selfe she slew.

56 O famous moniment of womens prayse,
Matchable either to Semiramis,
Whom antique history so high doth raise,
Or to Hypsiphil', or to Thomiris:
Her host two hundred thousand numbred is,
Who whiles good fortune favoured her might,
Triumphed oft against her enemis;
And yet, though overcome in haplesse fight,
She triumphed on death, in enemies despight.

57 Her reliques Fulgent having gathered,
Fought with Severus, and him overthrew;
Yet in the chace was slaine of them, that fled:
So made them victours, whom he did subdew.
Then gan Carausius tirannize anew,
And gainst the Romanes bent their proper powre;
But him Allectus treacherously slew,
And tooke on him the robe of emperoure;
Nath'lesse the same enjoyed but short happy howre.

58 For Asclepiodate. him overcame,
And left inglorious on the vanquisht playne,
Without or robe or rag to hide his shame:
Then afterwards he in his stead did rayne;
But shortly was by Coyll in battell slaine:
Who after long debate, since Lucies time,
Was of the Britons first crownd soveraine:
Then gan this realme renew her passed prime:
He of his name Coylchester built of stone and lime.

59 Which when the Romanes heard, they hither sent
Constantius, a man of mickle might,
With whome king Coyll made an agreement,
And to him gave for wife his daughter bright,
Faire Helena, the fairest living wight,
Who in all godly thewes and goodly prayse
Did far excell, but was most famous hight
For skill in musicke of all in her dayes,
As well in curious instruments, as cunning layes.

60 Of whome he did great Constantine beget,
   Who afterward was emperour of Rome;
   To which whiles absent he his mind did set,
   Octavius here lept into his roome,
   And it usurped by unrighteous doome:
   But he his title justifide by might,
   Slaying Traherne, and having overcome
   The Romane legion in dreadfull fight:
So settled he his kingdome, and confirmd his right:

61 But wanting issew male, his daughter deare
   He gave in wedlocke to Maximian,
   And him with her made of his kingdome heyre,
   Who soone by meanes thereof the empire wan,
   Till murdred by the freends of Gratian.
   Then gan the Hunnes and Picts invade this land,
   During the raigne of Maximinian;
   Who dying left none heire them to withstand,
But that they overran all parts with easie hand.

62 The weary Britons, whose war-hable youth
   Was by Maximian lately led away,
   With wretched miseries and woefull ruth
   Were to those pagans made an open pray,
   And daily spectacle of sad decay:
   Whom Romane warres, which now foure hundred years
   And more had wasted, could no whit dismay;
   Till by consent of Commons and of Peares,
They crownd the second Constantine with joyous teares.

63 Who having oft in battell vanquished
   Those spoilefull Picts and swarming Easterlings,
   Long time in peace his realme established,
   Yet oft annoyd with sundry bordragings
   Of neighbour Scots, and forrein scatterlings,
   With which the world did in those dayes abound,
   Which to outbarre, with painefull pyonings
   From sea to sea he heapt a mightie mound,
Which from Alcluid to Panwelt did that border bound.

64 Three sonnes he dying left, all under age;
   By meanes whereof their uncle Vortigere
   Usurpt the crowne during their pupillage;
   Which th' infants tutors gathering to feare,
   Them closely into Armorick did beare:
   For dread of whom, and for those Picts annoyes,
   He sent to Germanie straunge aid to reare;
   From whence eftsoones arrived here three hoyes
Of Saxons, whom he for his safetie imployes.

65 Two brethren were their capitayns, which hight
   Hengist and Horsus, well approv'd in warre,
   And both of them men of renowmed might;
   Who making vantage of their civile jarre,
   And of those forreiners which came from farre,
   Grew great, and got large portions of land,
   That in the realme ere long they stronger arre
   Then they which sought at first their helping hand,
And Vortiger enforst the kingdome to aband.

66 But, by the helpe of Voytimere his sonne,
   He is againe unto his rule restord;
   And Hengist, seeming sad for that was donne,
   Received is to grace and new accord,
   Through his faire daughters face, and flattring word:
   Soone after which, three hundred lords he slew
   Of British bloud, all sitting at his bord;
   Whose dolefull moniments who list to rew,
Th' eternall marks of treason may at Stonheng vew.

67 By this the sonnes of Constantine, which fled,
   Ambrose and Uther, did ripe yeares attaine,
   And here arriving, strongly challenged
   The crowne which Vortiger did long detaine:
   Who flying from his guilt, by them was slaine;
   And Hengist eke soone brought to shamefull death.
   Thenceforth Aurelius peaceably did rayne,
   Till that through poyson stopped was his breath;
So now entombed lies at Stoneheng by the heath.

68 After him Uther, which Pendragon hight,
Succeeding—There abruptly it did end,
Without full point, or other cesure right;
As if the rest some wicked hand did rend,
Or th' author selfe could not at least attend
To finish it: that so untimely breach
The prince him selfe halfe seemed to offend;
Yet secret pleasure did offence empeach,
And wonder of antiquitie long stopt his speach.

69 At last, quite ravisht with delight, to heare
The royall ofspring of his native land,
Cryde out, Deare countrey, O how dearely deare
Ought thy remembraunce and perpetuall band
Be to thy foster childe, that from thy hand
Did commun breath and nouriture receave?
How brutish is it not to understand
How much to her we owe, that all us gave,
That gave unto us all whatever good we have.

70 But Guyon all this while his booke did read,
Ne yet has ended: for it was a great
And ample volume, that doth far excead
My leasure so long leaves here· to repeat:
It told how first Prometheus did create
A man, of many parts from beasts deriv'd,
And then stole fire from heaven to animate
His worke, for which he was by Jove depriv'd
Of life him selfe, and hart-strings of an aegle riv'd.

71 That man so made he called Elfe, to weet
Quick, the first authour of all Elfin kind;
Who wandring through the world with wearie feet,
Did in the gardins of Adonis find
A goodly creature, whom he deemd in mynd
To be no earthly wight, but either spright,
Or angell, th' authour of all woman kind;
Therefore a Fay he her according hight,
Of whom all Faeryes spring, and fetch their lignage right.

72 Of these a mightie people shortly grew,
  And puissant kings, which all the world warrayd,
  And to them selves all nations did subdew:
  The first and eldest, which that scepter swayd,
  Was Elfin; him all India obayd,
  And all that now America men call:
  Next him was noble Elfinan, who layd
  Cleopolis foundation first of all:
But Elfiline enclosd it with a golden wall.

73 His sonne was Elfinell, who overcame
  The wicked Gobbelines in bloudy field:
  But Elfant was of most renowmed fame,
  Who all of christall did Panthea build:
  Then Elfar, who two brethren gyantes kild,
  The one of which had two heads, th' other three:
  Then Elfinor, who was in magick skild;
  He built by art upon the glassy see
A bridge of bras, whose sound heavens thunder seem'd to be.

74 He left three sonnes, the which in order raynd,
  And all their ofspring, in their dew descents;
  Even seven hundred princes, which maintaynd
  With mightie deedes their sundry governments;
  That were too long their infinite contents
  Here to record, ne much materiall:
  Yet should they be most famous moniments,
  And brave ensample, both of martiall
And civil rule to kinges and states imperiall.

75 After all these Elficleos did rayne,
  The wise Elficleos in great majestie,
  Who mightily that scepter did sustayne,
  And with rich spoyles and famous victorie
  Did high advaunce the crowne of Faery:
  He left two sonnes, of which faire Elferon
  The eldest brother did untimely dy;
  Whose emptie place the mightie Oberon
Doubly supplide, in spousall, and dominion.

76 Great was his power and glorie over all,
   Which him before, that sacred seate did fill,
   That yet remaines his wide memoriall :
   He dying left the fairest Tanaquill,
   Him to succeede therein, by his last will :
   Fairer and nobler liveth none this howre,
   Ne like in grace, ne like in learned skill ;
   Therefore they Glorian call that glorious flowre :
Long mayst thou, Glorian, live in glory and great powre.

77 Beguild thus with delight of novelties,
   And naturall desire of countreys state,
   So long they red in those antiquities,
   That how the time was fled they quite forgate
   Till gentle Alma seeing it so late,
   Perforce their studies broke, and them besought
   To thinke how supper did them long awaite :
   So halfe unwilling from their bookes them brought,
And fayrely feasted, as so noble knights she ought.

CANTO XI.

The enimies of Temperaunce
Besiege her dwelling place;
Prince Arthure them repelles, and fowle
Maleger doth deface.

1 WHAT warre so cruel, or what siege so sore,
As that, which strong Affections do apply
Against the fort of Reason evermore,
To bring the sowle into captivity :
Their force is fiercer through infirmitie
Of the fraile flesh, relenting to their rage ;
And exercise most bitter tyranny
Upon the parts, brought into their bondage :
No wretchednesse is like to sinfull vellenage.

2 But in a body which doth freely yeeld
His partes to reasons rule obedient,
And letteth her that ought the scepter weeld,
All happy peace and goodly government
Is settled there in sure establishment.
There Alma like a virgin Queene most bright,
Doth florish in all beautie excellent ;
And to her guestes doth bounteous banket dight,
Attempred goodly well for health and for delight.

3 Early before the morne with cremosin ray
The windowes of bright heaven opened had,
Through which into the world the dawning day
Might looke, that maketh every creature glad,
Uprose Sir Guyon, in bright armour clad,
And to his purposd journey him prepar'd :
With him the palmer eke in habit sad
Him selfe addrest to that adventure hard :
So to the rivers side they both together far'd.

4 Where them awaited ready at the ford
   The ferriman, as Alma had behight,
   With his well-rigged boate : they goe abord,
   And he eftsoones gan launch his barke forthright.
   Ere long they rowed were quite out of sight,
   And fast the land behind them fled away.
   But let them pas, whiles wind and weather right
   Do serve their turnes : here I a while must stay,
To see a cruell fight doen by the Prince this day.

5 For all so soone, as Guyon thence was gon
   Upon his voyage with his trustie guide,
   That wicked band of villeins fresh begon
   That castle to assaile on every side,
   And lay strong siege about it far and wide.
   So huge and infinite their numbers were,
   That all the land they under them did hide ;
   So fowle and ugly, that exceeding feare
Their visages imprest, when they approched neare.

6 Them in twelve troupes their captein did dispart,
   And round about in fittest steades did place,
   Where each might best offend his proper (part,)
   And his contrary object most deface,
   As every one seem'd meetest in that cace.
   Seven of the same against the castle gate
   In strong entrenchments he did closely place,
   Which with incessaunt force and endlesse hate
They battred day and night, and entraunce did awate.

7 The other five, five sundry wayes he set
   Against the five great bulwarkes of that pile,
   And unto each a bulwarke did arret,
   T' assayle with open force or hidden guile,
   In hope thereof to win victorious spoile.
   They all that charge did fervently apply
   With greedie malice and importune toyle,
   And planted there their huge artillery,
With which they dayly made most dreadfull battery.

L

8 The first troupe was a monstrous rablement
  Of fowle misshapen wights, of which some were
  Headed like owles, with beckes uncomely bent,
  Others like dogs, others like gryphons dreare;
  And some had wings, and some had clawes to teare:
  And every one of them had lynces eyes,
  And every one did bow and arrowes beare:
  All those were lawless lustes, and corrupt envies,
And covetous aspectes, all cruel enimies.

9 Those same against the bulwarke of the Sight
  Did lay strong siege and battailous assault,
  Ne once did yield it respit day nor night;
  But soone as Titan gan his head exault,
  And soone againe as he his light with hault,
  Their wicked engins they against it bent;
  That is each thing, by which the eyes may fault.
  But two then all more huge and violent,
Beautie and money, they that bulwarke sorely rent.

10 The second bulwarke was the Hearing sence,
  Gainst which the second troupe dessignment makes;
  Deformed creatures, in straunge difference,
  Some having heads like harts, some like to snakes,
  Some like wild bores late rouzd out of the brakes:
  Slaunderous reproches, and fowle infamies,
  Leasinges, backbytinges, and vaine-glorious crakes,
  Bad counsels, prayses, and false flatteries.
All those against that fort did bend their batteries.

11 Likewise that same third fort, that is the Smell,
  Of that third troupe was cruelly assayd;
  Whose hideous shapes were like to feends of hell,
  Some like to houndes, some like to apes, dismayd;
  Some like to puttockes, all in plumes arayd;
  All shap't according their conditions:
  For, by those ugly formes, weren pourtrayd
  Foolish delights and fond abusions,
Which do that sence besiege with light illusions.

12 And that fourth band, which cruell battry bent
    Against the fourth bulwarke, that is the Tast,
    Was as the rest, a grysie rablement,
    Some mouth'd like greedy oystriges, some fast
    Like loathly toades, some fashioned in the wast
    Like swine; for so deformd is luxury,
    Surfeat, misdiet, and unthriftie wast,
    Vaine feasts, and idle superfluity:
All those this sences fort assayle incessantly.

13 But the fift troupe most horrible of hew
    And fierce of force, is dreadfull to report;
    For some like snailes, some did like spyders shew,
    And some like ugly urchins thicke and short:
    Cruelly they assayled that fift fort,
    Armed with dartes of sensuall delight,
    And feeling pleasures, with which day and night
Against that same fift bulwarke they continued fight.

14 Thus these twelve troupes with dreadfull puissaunce
    Against that castle restlesse siege did lay,
    And evermore their hideous ordinance
    Upon the bulwarkes cruelly did play,
    That now it gan to threaten neare decay:
    And evermore their wicked capitaine
    Provoked them the breaches to assay,
    Sometimes with threats, sometimes with hope of gaine,
Which by the ransack of that peece they should attaine.

15 On th' other side, th' assieged castles ward
    Their steadfast stonds did mightily maintaine,
    And many bold repulse, and many hard
    Atchievement wrought with perill and with payne,
    That goodly frame from ruine to sustaine:
    And those two brethren giantes did defend
    The walles so stoutly with their sturdie maine,
    That never entraunce any durst pretend,
But they to direfull death their groning ghosts did send.

L 2

16 The noble virgin, ladie of the place,
  Was much dismayed with that dreadfull sight;
  For never was she in so evill cace;
  Till that the Prince seeing her wofull plight,
  Gan her recomfort from so sad affright,
  Offring his service and his dearest life
  For her defence against that carle to fight,
  Which was their chiefe and th' author of that strife:
She him remercied as the patrone of her life.

17 Eftsoones himselfe in glitterand armes he dight,
  And his well proved weapons to him hent;
  So taking courteous conge he behight
  Those gates to be unbar'd, and forth he went.
  Fayre mote he thee, the prowest and most gent;
  That ever brandished bright steele on high:
  Whom soone as that unruly rablement
  With his gay squire issuing did espy,
They reard a most outrageous dreadfull yelling cry:

18 And therewithall attonce at him let fly
  Their fluttring arrowes, thicke as flakes of snow,
  And round about him flocke impetuously,
  Like a great water flood, that tombling low
  From the high mountaines, threates to overflow
  With suddein fury all the fertile plaine,
  And the sad husbandmans long hope doth throw
  Adowne the streame, and all his vowes make vaine:
Nor bounds nor banks his headlong ruine may sustaine.

19 Upon his shield their heaped hayle he bore,
  And with his sword disperst the raskall flockes,
  Which fled asonder, and him fell before,
  As withered leaves drop from their dried stockes,
  When the wroth western wind does reave their locks.
  And underneath him his courageous steed,
  The fierce Spumador, trode them down like docks.
  The fierce Spumador borne óf heavenly seed;
Such as Laomedon of Phœbus race did breed.

20 Which suddeine horrour and confused cry
   Whenas their capteine heard, in haste he yode
   The cause to weet, and fault to remedy:
   Upon a tygre swift and fierce he rode,
   That as the winde ran underneath his lode,
   Whiles his long legs nigh raught unto the ground;
   Full large he was of limbe, and shoulders brode,
   But of such subtile substance and unsound,   [bound:
That like a ghost he seem'd whose grave-clothes were un-

21 And in his hand a bended bow was seene,
   And many arrowes under his right side,
   All deadly daungerous, all cruell keene,
   Headed with flint, and feathers bloudie dide;
   Such as the Indians in their quivers hide:
   Those could he well direct and streight as line,
   And bid them strike the marke, which he had eyde;
   Ne was there salve, ne was there medicine,
That mote recure their woundes; so inly they did tine.

22 As pale and wan as ashes was his looke,
   His bodie leane and meagre as a rake,
   And skin all withered like a dryed rooke,
   Thereto as cold and drery as a snake,
   That seem'd to tremble evermore, and quake:
   All in a canvas thin he was bedight,
   And girded with a-belt of twisted brake:
   Upon his head he wore an helmet light,
Made of a dead mans skull, that seemd a ghastly sight.

23 Maleger was his name, and after him
   There follow'd fast at hand two wicked hags,
   With hoarie lockes all loose, and visage grim;
   Their feet unshod, their bodies wrapt in rags,
   And both as swift on foot as chased stags;
   And yet the one her other legge had lame,
   Which with a staffe all full of litle snags
   She did support, and Impotence her name:
But th' other was Impatience, arm'd with raging flame.

24 Soone as the carle from farre the Prince espyde
Glistring in armes, and warlike ornament,
His beast he felly prict on either syde,
And his mischievous bow full readie bent,
With which at him a cruell shaft he sent:
But he was warie, and it warded well
Upon his shield, that it no further went,
But to the ground the idle quarrell fell:
Then he another and another did expell.

25 Which to prevent, the Prince his mortall speare
Soone to him raught, and fierce at him did ride,
To be avenged of that shot whyleare:
But he was not so hardie to abide
That bitter stownd, but turning quicke aside
His light-foot beast, fled fast away for feare:
Whom to pursue, the Infant after hide
So fast as his good courser could him beare:
But labour lost it was to weene approch him neare.

26 For as the winged wind his tigre fled,
That vew of eye could scarse him overtake,
Ne scarse his feet on ground were seene to tred;
Through hils and dales he speedie way did make,
Ne hedge ne ditch his readie passage brake,
And in his flight the villein turn'd his face,
(As wonts the Tartar by the Caspian lake,
When as the Russian him in fight does chace,)
Unto his tygres taile, and shot at him apace.

27 Apace he shot, and yet he fled apace,
Still as the greedy knight nigh to him drew;
And oftentimes he would relent his pace,
That him his foe more fiercely should pursew:
Who when his uncouth manner he did vew,
He gan avize to follow him no more,
But keepe his standing, and his shaftes eschew,
Until he quite had spent his perlous store,
And then assayle him fresh, ere he could shift for more.

28 But that lame hag, still as abroad he strew
   His wicked arrowes, gathered them againe,
   And to him brought, fresh battell to renew;
   Which he espying, cast her to restraine
   From yielding succour to that cursed swaine,
   And her attaching thought her hands to tye;
   But soone as him dismounted on the plaine
   That other hag did farre away espy
Binding her sister, she to him ran hastily;

29 And catching hold of him, as downe he lent,
   Him backwarde overthrew, and downe him stayd
   With their rude hands and griesly graplement;
   Till that the villein, comming to their ayd,
   Upon him fell, and lode upon him layd:
   Full litle wanted, but he had him slaine,
   And of the battell balefull end had made,
   Had not his gentle squire beheld his paine,
And commen to his reskew, ere his bitter bane.

30 So greatest and most glorious thing on ground
   May often need the helpe of weaker hand;
   So feeble is mans state, and life unsound,
   That in assurance it may never stand,
   Till it dissolved be from earthly band.
   Proofe be thou, Prince, the prowest man alive,
   And noblest borne of all in Briton land;
   Yet thee fierce fortune did so nearely drive,
That had not grace thee blest, thou shouldest not survive.

31 The squire arriving, fiercely in his armes
   Snatcht first the one, and then the other jade,
   His chiefest lets and authors of his harmes,
   And them perforce withheld with threatned blade,
   Least that his lord they should behind invade;
   The whiles the Prince prickt with reprochfull shame,
   As one awakt out of long slombring shade,
   Reviving thought of glorie and of fame,
United all his powres to purge himselfe from blame.

32 Like as a fire, the which in hollow cave
　　Hath long bene underkept, and downe supprest,
　　With murmurous disdaine doth inly rave,
　　And grudge, in so streight prison to be prest,
　　At last breakes forth with furious unrest,
　　And strives to mount unto his native seat;
　　All that did earst it hinder and molest,
　　It now devoures with flames and scorching heat,
And carries into smoake with rage and horror great.

33 So mightily the Briton prince him rouzd
　　Out of his holde, and broke his caitive bands ;
　　And as a beare, whom angry curres have touzd,
　　Having off-shakt them and escapt their hands,
　　Becomes more fell, and all that him withstands
　　Treads down and overthrowes. Now had the carle
　　Alighted from his tigre, and his hands
　　Discharged of his bow and deadly quar'le,
To seize upon his foe flat lying on the marle.

34 Which now him turnd to disavantage deare ;
　　For neither can he fly, nor other harme,
　　But trust unto his strength and manhood meare,
　　Sith now he is farre from his monstrous swarme,
　　And of his weapons did himselfe disarme.
　　The knight yet wrothfull for his late disgrace,
　　Fiercely advaunst his valorous right arme,
　　And him so sore smote with his yron mace,
That groveling to the ground he fell, and fild his place.

35 Wel weened he that field was then his owne,
　　And all his labour brought to happie end;
　　When suddein up the villein overthrowne
　　Out of his swowne arose, fresh to contend,
　　And gan himselfe to second battell bend,
　　As hurt he had not bene. Thereby there lay
　　An huge great stone, which stood upon one end,
　　And had not bene removed many a day :
Some land-marke seem'd to be, or signe of sundry way :

36 The same he snatcht, and with exceeding sway
   Threw at his foe, who was right well aware
   To shunne the engine of his meant decay;
   It booted not to thinke that throw to beare,
   But ground he gave, and lightly leapt areare;
   Eft fierce returning, as a faulcon faire,
   That once hath failed of her souse full neare,
   Remounts againe into the open aire,
And unto better fortune doth herselfe prepaire:

37 So brave returning, with his brandisht blade,
   He to the carle himselfe againe addrest,
   And strooke at him so sternely, that he made
   An open passage through his riven brest,
   That halfe the steele behind his backe did rest;
   Which drawing backe, he looked evermore
   When the hart bloud should gush out of his chest,
   Or his dead corse should fall upon the flore;
But his dead corse upon the flore fell nathemore:

38 Ne drop of bloud appeared shed to bee,
   All were the wounde so wide and wonderous
   That through his carcasse one might plainely see.
   Halfe in amaze with horror hideous,
   And halfe in rage to be deluded thus,
   Againe through both the sides he strooke him quight,
   That made his spright to grone full piteous;
   Yet nathemore forth fled his groning spright,
But freshly as at first, prepard himselfe to fight.

39 Thereat he smitten was with great affright,
   And trembling terror did his hart apall;
   Ne wist he what to thinke of that same sight,
   Ne what to say, ne what to doe at all:
   He doubted least it were some magicall
   Illusion, that did beguile his sense,
   Or wandring ghost that wanted funerall,
   Or aerie spirit under false pretence,
Or hellish feend raysd up through divelish science.

40 His wonder farre exceeded reasons reach,
　　That he began to doubt his dazeled sight,
　　And oft of error did him selfe appeach:
　　Flesh without bloud, a person without spright,
　　Wounds without hurt, a body without might,
　　That could doe harme, yet could not harmed bee,
　　That could not die, yet seem'd a mortall wight,
　　That was most strong in most infirmitee;
Like did he never heare, like did he never see.

41 A while he stood in this astonishment,
　　Yet would he not for all his great dismay
　　Give over to effect his first intent,
　　And th' utmost meanes of victorie assay,
　　Or th' utmost issew of his owne decay.
　　His owne good sword Mordure, that never fayld
　　At need, till now, he lightly threw away,
　　And his bright shield that nought him now avayld;
And with his naked hands him forcibly assayld.

42 Twixt his two mightie armes him up he snatcht,
　　And crusht his carcasse so against his brest,
　　That the disdainfull soule he thence dispatcht,
　　And th' ydle breath all utterly exprest:
　　Tho when he felt him dead, a downe he kest
　　The lumpish corse unto the senselesse grownd;
　　Adowne he kest it with so puissant wrest,
　　That backe againe it did alofte rebownd,
And gave against his mother earth a gronefull sownd.

43 As when Joves harnesse-bearing bird from hie
　　Stoupes at a flying heron with proud disdaine,
　　The stone-dead quarrey falls so forciblie,
　　That it rebownds against the lowly plaine,
　　A second fall redoubling backe againe.
　　Then thought the Prince all peril sure was past,
　　And that he victor onely did remaine;
　　No sooner thought, then that the carle as fast
Gan heap huge strokes on him, as ere he down was cast.

44 Nigh his wits end then woxe th' amazed knight,
And thought his labor lost, and travell vaine,
Against this lifelesse shadow so to fight:
Yet life he saw, and felt his mightie maine,
That whiles he marveild still, did still him paine;
For thy he gan some other wayes advize,
How to take life from that dead-living swaine,
Whom still he marked freshly to arize
From th' earth, and from her wombe new spirits to reprize.

45 He then remembred well, that had bene sayd,
How th' Earth his mother was, and first him bore;
She eke so often, as his life decayd,
Did life with usury to him restore,
And raysd him up much stronger then before,
So soone as he unto her wombe did fall:
Therefore to ground he would him cast no more,
Ne him commit to grave terrestriall,
But beare him farre from hope of succour usuall.

46 Tho up he caught him twixt his puissant hands,
And having scruzd out of his carrion corse
The lothfull life, now loosd from sinfull bands,
Upon his shoulders carried him perforse
Above three furlongs, taking his full course,
Until he came unto a standing lake;
Him there into he threw without remorse,
Ne stird, till hope of life did him forsake:
So end of that carles dayes and his owne paines did make.

47 Which when those wicked hags from farre did spy,
Like two mad dogs they ran about the lands,
And th' one of them with dreadfull yelling cry,
Throwing away her broken chaines and bands,
And having quencht her burning fier brands,
Hedlong her selfe did cast into that lake;
But Impotence with her owne wilfull hands
One of Malegers cursed darts did take,
So riv'd her trembling hart, and wicked end did make.

48 Thus now alone he conquerour remaines:
  Tho comming to his squire, that kept his steed,
  Thought to have mounted, but his feeble vaines
  Him faild thereto, and served not his need,
  Through losse of bloud which from his wounds did bleed,
  That he began to faint, and life decay:
  But his good squire, him helping up with speed,
  With stedfast hand upon his horse did stay,
And led him to the castle by the beaten way.

49 Where many groomes and squiers readie were
  To take him from his steed full tenderly;
  And eke the fairest Alma met him there
  With balme, and wine, and costly spicery,
  To comfort him in his infirmity:
  Eftsoones she causd him up to be convayd,
  And of his armes despoyled easily;
  In sumptuous bed she made him to be layd,
And all the while his wounds were dressing, by him stayd.

CANTO XII.

Guyon by palmers governance,
Passing through perils great,
Doth overthrow the Bowre of Blisse,
And Acrasie defeat.

1 Now gins that goodly frame of Temperance
Fairely to rise, and her adorned hed
To pricke of highest praise forth to advance,
Formerly grounded, and fast setteled
On firme foundation of true bountihed;
And this brave knight, that for this vertue fights,
Now comes to point of that same perilous sted,
Where Pleasure dwelles in sensuall delights
Mongst thousand dangers and ten thousand magick mights.

2 Two dayes now in that sea he sayled has,
Ne ever land beheld, ne living wight,
Ne ought save perill, still as he did pas:
Tho when appeared the third morrow bright
Upon the waves to spred her trembling light.
An hideous roaring far away they heard,
That all their senses filled with affright;
And streight they saw the raging surges reard
Up to the skyes, that them of drowning made affeard.

3 Said then the boteman, Palmer stere aright,
And keepe an even course; for yonder way
We needes must passe (God doe us well acquight,)
That is the Gulfe of Greedinesse, they say,
That deepe engorgeth all this worldes pray;
Which having swallowd up excessively,
He soone in vomit up againe doth lay,
And belcheth forth his superfluity,
That all the seas for feare doe seeme away to fly.

4 On th' other side an hideous rocke is pight
  Of mighty magnes stone, whose craggie clift
  Depending from on high, dreadfull to sight,
  Over the waves his rugged armes doth lift,
  And threatneth downe to throw his ragged rift
  On whoso cometh nigh; yet nigh it drawes
  All passengers, that none from it can shift:
  For, whiles they fly that gulfes devouring jawes,
They on the rock are rent, and sunck in helplesse wawes.

5 Forward they passe, and strongly he them rowes,
  Untill they nigh unto that gulfe arrive,
  Where streame more violent and greedy growes:
  Then he with all his puissance doth stryve
  To strike his oares, and mightily doth drive
  The hollow vessell through the threatfull wave;
  Which, gaping wide to swallow them alive
  In th' huge abysse of his engulfing grave,
Doth rore at them in vaine, and with great terror rave.

6 They, passing by, that griesly mouth doe see
  Sucking the seas into his entralles deepe,
  That seemd more horrible than hell to bee,
  Or that darke dreadfull hole of Tartare steepe,
  Through which the damned ghosts doen often creep
  Backe to the world, bad livers to torment:
  But nought that falles into this direfull deepe,
  Ne that approcheth nigh the wide descent,
May backe returne, but is condemned to be drent.

7 On th' other side they saw that perilous rocke,
  Threatning it selfe on them to ruinate,
  On whose sharp clifts the ribs of vessels broke;
  And shivered ships, which had bene wrecked late,
  Yet stuck, with carcases exanimate
  Of such, as having all their substance spent
  In wanton joyes and lustes intemperate,
  Did afterwardes make shipwracke violent
Both of their life and fame for ever fowly blent.

8 For thy this hight the Rock of vile Reproch,
  A daungerous and detestable place,
  To which nor fish nor fowle did once approch,
  But yelling meawes, with seagulles, hoarse and bace,
  And cormoyrants, with birds of ravenous race,
  Which still sat waiting on that wastfull clift
  For spoile of wretches, whose unhappie cace,
  After lost credit and consumed thrift,
At last them driven hath to this despairefull drift.

9 The palmer seeing them in safetie past,
  Thus said; Behold th' ensamples in our sights
  Of lustfull luxurie and thriftlesse wast:
  What now is left of miserable wights,
  Which spent their looser daies in lewd delights,
  But shame and sad reproch, here to be red
  By these rent reliques speaking their ill plightes?
  Let all that live hereby be counselled
To shunne Rocke of Reproch, and it as death to dred.

10 So forth they rowed, and that ferryman
  With his stiffe oares did brush the sea so strong,
  That the hoare waters from his frigot ran,
  And the light bubbles daunced all along,
  Whiles the salt brine out of the billowes sprong.
  At last farre off they many islands spy
  On every side floting the floods emong:
  Then said the knight. Loe I the land descry,
Therefore old syre thy course do thereunto apply.

11 That may not be, said then the ferryman,
  Least we unweeting hap to be fordonne:
  For those same islands, seeming now and than,
  Are not firme land, nor any certein wonne,
  But straggling plots, which to and fro do ronne
  In the wide waters: therefore are they hight
  The Wandring Islands: therefore doe them shonne;
  For they have oft drawne many a wandring wight
Into most deadly daunger and distressed plight.

12 Yet well they seeme to him, that farre doth vew,
  Both faire and fruitfull, and the ground dispred
  With grassie greene of delectable hew,
  And the tall trees with leaves apparelled
  Are deckt with blossomes dyde in white and red,
  That mote the passengers thereto allure;
  But whosoever once hath fastened
  His foot thereon, may never it recure,
But wandreth ever more uncertein and unsure.

13 As th' isle of Delos whylome men report
  Amid th' Aegaean sea long time did stray,
  Ne made for shipping any certaine port,
  Till that Latona travelling that way,
  Flying from Junoes wrath and hard assay,
  Of her faire twins was there delivered,
  Which afterwards did rule the night and day:
  Thenceforth it firmely was established,
And for Apolloes temple highly herried.

14 They to him hearken, as beseemeth meete;
  And passe on forward: so their way does ly,
  That one of those same islands, which doe fleet
  In the wide sea, they needes must passen by,
  Which seemd so sweet and pleasant to the eye,
  That it would tempt a man to touchen there:
  Upon the banck they sitting did espy
  A daintie damsell dressing of her heare,
By whom a little skippet floting did appeare.

15 She them espying, loud to them gan call,
  Bidding them nigher draw unto the shore,
  For she had cause to busie them withall;
  And therewith loudly laught: but nathemore
  Would they once turne, but kept on as afore:
  Which when she saw, she left her lockes undight,
  And running to her boat withouten ore,
  From the departing land it launched light,
And after them did drive with all her power and might.

16 Whom overtaking, she in merry sort
　　Then gan to bord, and purpose diversly;
　　Now faining dalliance and wanton sport,
　　Now throwing forth lewd words immodestly;
　　Till that the palmer gan full bitterly
　　Her to rebuke, for being loose and light:
　　Which not abiding, but more scornfully
　　Scoffing at him that did her justly wite,
She turnd her bote about, and from them rowed quite.

17 That was the wanton Phaedria, which late
　　Did ferry him over the Idle Lake:
　　Whom nought regarding, they kept on their gate,
　　And all her vaine allurements did forsake;
　　When them the wary boateman thus bespake;
　　Here now behoveth us well to avyse,
　　And of our safety good heede to take;
　　For here before a perlous passage lyes,
Where many mermayds haunt, making false melodies.

18 But by the way there is a great quicksand,
　　And a whirlepoole of hidden jeopardy;
　　Therefore, Sir Palmer, keepe an even hand;
　　For twixt them both the narrow way doth ly.
　　Scarse had he said, when hard at hand they spy,
　　That quicksand nigh with water covered;
　　But by the checked wave they did descry
　　It plaine, and by the sea discoloured:
It called was the quicksand of Unthriftyhed.

19 They passing by, a goodly ship did see
　　Laden from far with precious merchandize,
　　And bravely furnished, as ship might bee,
　　Which through great disaventure, or mesprize,
　　Her selfe had runne into that hazardize;
　　Whose mariners and merchants with much toyle
　　Labour'd in vaine to have recur'd their prize,
　　And the rich wares to save from pitteous spoyle;
But neither toyle nor travell might her backe recoyle.

M

20 On th' other side they see that perilous poole,
   That called was the Whirlepoole of Decay;
   In which full many had with haplesse doole
   Beene suncke, of whom no memorie did stay:
   Whose circled waters rapt with whirling sway,
   Like to a restlesse wheele, still running round,
   Did covet, as they passed by that way,
   To draw the boate within the utmost bound
Of his wide labyrinth, and then to have them dround.

21 But th' heedful boateman strongly forth did stretch
   His brawnie armes, and all his body straine,
   That th' utmost sandy breach they shortly fetch,
   Whiles the dred daunger does behind remaine.
   Suddeine they see from midst of all the maine
   The surging waters like a mountaine rise,
   And the great sea puft up with proud disdaine,
   To swell above the measure of his guise,
As threatning to devoure all, that his powre despise.

22 The waves come rolling, and the billowes rore
   Outragiously, as they enraged were,
   Or wrathfull Neptune did them drive before
   His whirling charet for exceeding feare;
   For not one puffe of winde there did appeare;
   That all the three thereat woxe much afrayd,
   Unweeting what such horrour straunge did reare.
   Eftsoones they saw an hideous hoast arrayd
Of huge sea monsters such as living sence dismayd.

23 Most ugly shapes, and horrible aspects,
   Such as dame Nature selfe mote feare to see,
   Or shame, that ever should so fowle defects
   From her most cunning hand escaped bee:
   All dreadfull pourtraicts of deformitee:
   Spring-headed hydraes; and sea-shouldring whales;
   Great whirlpooles, which all fishes make to flee;
   Bright scolopendraes arm'd with silver scales;
Mighty monoceros with immeasured tayles;

24 The dreadfull fish, that hath deserv'd the name
Of Death, and like him lookes in dreadfull hew;
The griesly wasserman, that makes his game
The flying ships with swiftnesse to pursew;
The horrible sea-satyre, that doth shew
His fearefull face in time of greatest storme
Huge ziffius, whom mariners eschew
No lesse than rockes, (as travellers informe,)
And greedy rosmarines with visages deforme.

25 All these, and thousand thousands many more,
And more deformed monsters thousand fold,
With dreadfull noise and hollow rombling rore
Came rushing in the fomy waves enrold,
Which seem'd to fly for feare them to behold:
Ne wonder, if these did the knight appall;
For all that here on earth we dreadfull hold,
Be but as bugs to fearen babes withall,
Compared to the creatures in the seas entrall.

26 Feare nought, (then saide the palmer well aviz'd,)
For these same monsters are not these in deed,
But are into these fearefull shapes disguiz'd
By that same wicked witch, to worke us dreed,
And draw from on this journey to proceede.
Tho lifting up his vertuous staffe on hye,
He smote the sea, which calmed was with speed,
And all that dreadfull armie fast gan flye
Into great Tethys bosome, where they hidden lye.

27 Quit from that danger forth their course they kept;
And as they went they heard a ruefull cry
Of one, that wayld and pittifully wept,
That through the sea th' resounding plaints did fly:
At last they in an island did espy
A seemely maiden, sitting by the shore,
That with great sorrow and sad agony
Seemed some great misfortune to deplore,
And lowd to them for succour called evermore.

28 Which Guyon hearing, streight his palmer bad
   To stere the boate towards that dolefull mayd,
   That he might know and ease her sorrow sad:
   Who, him avizing better, to him sayd;
   Faire sir, be not displeased, if disobayd:
   For ill it were to hearken to her cry;
   For she is inly nothing ill apayd;
   But onely womanish fine forgery,
Your stubborne hart t'affect with fraile infirmity.

29 To which when she your courage hath inclind
   Through foolish pitty, then her guilefull bayt
   She will embosome deeper in your mind,
   And for your ruine at the last awayt.
   The knight was ruled, and the boateman strayt
   Held on his course with stayed stedfastnesse,
   Ne ever shruncke, ne ever sought to bayt
   His tyred armes for toylesome wearinesse,
But with his oares did sweepe the watry wildernesse.

30 And now they nigh approched to the sted
   Where as those mermayds dwelt: it was a still
   And calmy bay, on th' one side sheltered
   With the brode shadow of an hoarie hill;
   On th' other side an high rocke toured still,
   That twixt them both a pleasaunt port they made,
   And did like an halfe theatre fulfill:
   There those five sisters had continuall trade,
And usd to bath themselves in that deceiptfull shade.

31 They were faire ladies, till they fondly striv'd
   With th' Heliconian maides for maistery;
   Of whom they over-comen were depriv'd
   Of their proud beautie, and th' one moyity
   Transform'd to fish for their bold surquedry;
   But th' upper halfe their hew retained still,
   And their sweet skill in wonted melody;
   Which ever after they abusd to ill,
T' allure weake travellers, whom gotten they did kill.

32 So now to Guyon, as he passed by,
    Their pleasaunt tunes they sweetly thus' applide;
    'O thou faire sonne of gentle Faery,
    That art in mighty armes most magnifide
    Above all knights, that ever battell tride,
    O turne thy rudder hither-ward a while:
    Here may thy storme-bet vessell safely ride;
    This is the port of rest from troublous toyle,
The worlds sweet in, from paine and wearisome turmoyle.

33 With that the rolling sea resounding soft,
    In his big base them fitly answered;
    And on the rocke the waves breaking aloft
    A solemne meane unto them measured;
    The whiles sweet Zephyrus lowd whisteled
    His treble, a straunge kinde of harmony;
    Which Guyons senses softly tickeled,
    That he the boteman bad row easily,
And let him heare some part of their rare melody.

34 But him the palmer from that vanity
    With temperate advice discounselled,
    That they it past, and shortly gan descry
    The land, to which their course they leveled;
    When suddeinly a grosse fog over spred
    With his dull vapour all that desert has,
    And heavens chearefull face enveloped,
    That all things one, and one as nothing was,
And this great universe seemd one confused mas.

35 Thereat they greatly were dismayd, ne wist
    How to direct theyr way in darkenesse wide,
    But feard to wander in that wastfull mist,
    For tombling into mischiefe unespide:
    Worse is the daunger hidden, then descride.
    Suddeinly an innumérable flight
    Of harmefull fowles about them fluttering, cride,
    And with their wicked wings them ofte did smight,
And sore annoyed, groping in that griesly night.

36 Even all the nation of unfortunate
　 And fatall birds about them flocked were,
　 Such as by nature men abhorre and hate,
　 The ill-faste owle, deaths dreadfull messengere,
　 The hoars night-raven, trump of dolefull drere,
　 The lether-winged bat, dayes enimy,
　 The ruefull strich, still waiting on the bere,
　 The whistler shrill, that whoso heares doth dy,
The hellish harpies, prophets of sad destiny.

37 All those, and all that els does horrour breed,
　 About them flew, and fild their sayles with feare:
　 Yet stayd they not, but forward did proceed,
　 Whiles th' one did row, and th' other stifly steare;
　 Till that at last the weather gan to cleare,
　 And the faire land itselfe did plainly show.
　 Said then the palmer, Lo where does appeare
　 The sacred soile, where all our perils grow;
Therefore, Sir Knight, your ready armes about you throw.

38 He hearkned, and his armes about him tooke,
　 The whiles the nimble boat so well her sped,
　 That with her crooked keele the land she strooke,
　 Then forth the noble Guyon sallied,
　 And his sage palmer, that him governed;
　 But th' other by his boate behind did stay.
　 They marched fairly forth, of nought ydred,
　 Both firmely armd for every hard assay,
With constancy and care, gainst daunger and dismay.

39 Ere long they heard an hideous bellowing
　 Of many beasts, that roard outrageously,
　 As if that hungers point or Venus sting
　 Had them enraged with fell surquedry;
　 Yet nought they feard, but past on hardily,
　 Untill they came in vew of those wild beasts,
　 Who all attonce, gaping full greedily,
　 And rearing fercely their upstarting crests,
Ran towards to devour those unexpected guests.

40 But soone as they approcht with deadly threat,
 The palmer over them his staffe upheld,
 His mighty staffe, that could all charmes defeat:
 Eftsoones their stubborne courages were queld,
 And high advaunced crests downe meekely feld;
 Instead of fraying, they themselves did feare,
 And trembled, as them passing they beheld:
 Such wondrous powre did in that staffe appeare,
All monsters to 'subdew to him, that did it beare.

41 Of that same wood it fram'd was cunningly,
 Of which Caduceus whilome was made,
 Caduceus, the rod of Mercury,
 With which he wonts the Stygian realmes invade
 Through ghastly horrour and eternall shade;
 Th' infernall feends with it he can asswage,
 And Orcus tame, whom nothing can persuade,
 And rule the Furyes when they most doe rage;
Such vertue in his staffe had eke this palmer sage.

42 Thence passing forth, they shortly doe arrive
 Whereas the Bowre of Blisse was situate;
 A place pickt out by choice of best alive,
 That natures worke by art can imitate:
 In which whatever in this worldly state
 Is sweet, and pleasing unto living sense,
 Or that may dayntiest fantasie aggrate,
 Was poured forth with plentifull dispence,
And made there to abound with lavish affluence.

43 Goodly it was enclosed round about,
 As well their entred guestes to keepe within,
 As those unruly beasts to hold without;
 Yet was the fence thereof but weake and thin;
 Nought feard their force, that fortilage to win,
 But wisedomes powre, and temperaunces might,
 By which the mightiest things efforced bin:
 And eke the gate was wrought of substaunce light,
Rather for pleasure, then for battery or fight.

44 Yt framed was of precious yvory,
  That seemd a worke of admirable witt;
  And therein all the famous history
  Of Jason and Medaea was ywrit;
  Her mighty charmes, her furious loving fit;
  His goodly conquest of the golden fleece,
  His falsed faith, and love too lightly flit;
  The wondred Argo, which in venturous peece
First through the Euxine seas bore all the flowr of Greece.

45 Ye might have seen the frothy billowes fry
  Under the ship as thorough them she went,
  That seemd the waves were into yvory,
  Or yvory into the waves were sent;
  And other where the snowy substaunce sprent
  With vermell, like the boyes bloud therein shed,
  A piteous spectacle did represent;
  And otherwhiles with gold besprinkeled
Yt seemed th' enchaunted flame, which did Creusa wed.

46 All this and more might in that goodly gate
  Be red, that ever open stood to all,
  Which thether came: but in the porch there sate
  A comely personage of stature tall,
  And semblaunce pleasing, more then naturall,
  That travellers to him seemd to entize;
  His looser garment to the ground did fall,
  And flew about his heeles in wanton wize,
Not fit for speedy pace or manly exercize.

47 They in that place him Genius did call:
  Not that celestiall powre, to whom the care
  Of life, and generation of all
  That lives, perteines in charge particulare,
  Who wondrous things concerning our welfare,
  And straunge phantomes doth let us ofte foresee,
  And ofte of secret ill bids us beware:
  That is our Selfe, whom though we do not see,
Yet each doth in him selfe it well perceive to bee.

48 Therefore a god him sage antiquity
    Did wisely make, and good Agdistes call;
    But this same was to that quite contrary,
    The foe of life, that good envyes to all,
    That secretly doth us procure to fall
    Through guilefull semblaunts, which he makes us see.
    He of this gardin had the governall,
    And Pleasures porter was devizd to bee,
Holding a staffe in hand for more formalitee.

49 With diverse flowres he daintily was deckt,
    And strowed round about; and by his side
    A mighty mazer bowle of wine was set,
    As if it had to him bene sacrifide;
    Wherewith all new-come guests he gratifide:
    So did he eke Sir Guyon passing by;
    But he his idle curtesie defide,
    And overthrew his bowle disdainfully,
And broke his staffe, with which he charmed semblants sly.

50 Thus being entred, they behold around
    A large and spacious plaine, on every side
    Strowed with pleasauns; whose faire grassy ground
    Mantled with greene, and goodly beautifide
    With all the ornaments of Floraes pride,
    Wherewith her mother Art, as halfe in scorne,
    Of niggard Nature, like a pompous bride
    Did decke her, and too lavishly adorne,
When forth from virgin bowre she comes in th' early morne.

51 Thereto the hevens alwayes joviall
    Lookt on them lovely, still in stedfast state,
    Ne suffred storme nor frost on them to fall,
    Their tender buds or leaves to violate:
    Nor scorching heat, nor cold intemperate,
    T' afflict the creatures, which therein did dwell;
    But the milde aire with season moderate
    Gently attempred, and disposd so well,
That still it breathed forth sweet spirit and holesome smell:

52 More sweet and holesome, then the pleasaunt hill
  Of Rhodope, on which the nimphe, that bore
  A gyaunt babe, her selfe for griefe did kill;
  Or the Thessalian Tempe, where of yore
  Faire Daphne Phoebus hart with love did gore;
  Or Ida, where the gods lov'd to repaire,
  Whenever they their hevenly bowres forlore;
  Or sweet Parnasse the haunt of muses faire:
Or Eden selfe, if ought with Eden mote compaire.

53 Much wondred Guyon at the faire aspect
  Of that sweet place, yet suffred no delight
  To sincke into his sence nor mind affect;
  But passed forth, and lookt still forward right,
  Bridling his will and maistering his might:
  Till that he came unto another gate;
  No gate, but like one, being goodly dight
  With boughes and braunches, which did broad dilate
Their clasping armes in wanton wreathings intricate.

54 So fashioned a porch with rare device
  Archt over head with an embracing vine,
  Whose bounches hanging downe seemd to entice
  All passers by to taste their lushious wine,
  And did themselves into their hands incline,
  As freely offering to be gathered;
  Some deepe empurpled as the hyacint,
  Some as the rubine laughing sweetly red,
Some like faire emeraudes, not yet well ripened:

55 And them amongst some were of burnisht gold,
  So made by art to beautifie the rest,
  Which did themselves emongst the leaves enfold,
  As lurking from the vew of covetous guest,
  That the weake boughes with so rich load opprest
  Did bow adowne, as over-burdened.
  Under that porch a comely dame did rest
  Clad in faire weedes but fowle disordered,
And garments loose, that seemd unmeet for womanhed:

56 In her left hand a cup of gold she held,
   And with her right the riper fruit did reach,
   Whose sappy liquor, that with fulnesse sweld,
   Into her cup she scruzd with daintie breach
   On her fine fingers, without fowle empeach,
   That so faire wine-presse made the wine more sweet:
   Thereof she usd to give to drinke to each,
   Whom passing by she happened to meet:
It was her guise all straungers goodly so to greet.

57 So she to Guyon offred it to tast;
   Who taking it out of her tender hond,
   The cup to ground did violently cast,
   That all in peeces it was broken fond,
   And with the liquor stained all the lond:
   Whereat Excesse exceedingly was wroth,
   Yet no'te the same amend, ne yet withstond,
   But suffered him to passe, all were she loth;
Who nought regarding her displeasure forward goth.

58 There the most daintie paradise on ground
   Itselfe doth offer to his sober eye,
   In which all pleasures plenteously abownd,
   And none does others happinesse envye;
   The painted flowres, the trees upshooting hye,
   The dales for shade, the hilles for breathing space,
   The trembling groves, the christall running by;
   And that, which all faire workes doth most aggrace,
The art, which all that wrought, appeared in no place.

59 One would have thought, (so cunningly the rude
   And scorned partes were mingled with the fine,)
   That nature had for wantonesse ensude
   Art, and that art at nature did repine;
   So striving each th' other to undermine,
   Each did the others worke more beautifie;
   So diff'ring both in willes agreed in fine:
   So all agreed, through sweete diversitie,
This gardin to adorne with all varietie.

60 And in the midst of all a fountaine stood,
Of richest substance that on earth might bee,
So pure and shiny, that the silver flood
Through every channell running one might see;
Most goodly it with curious imageree
Was over-wrought, and shapes of naked boyes,
Of which some seemd with lively jollitee
To fly about, playing their wanton toyes,
Whylest others did themselves embay in liquid joyes.

61 And over all of purest gold was spred
A trayle of yvie in his native hew;
For the rich metall was so coloured,
That wight, who did not well avis'd it vew,
Would surely deeme it to bee yvie trew:
Low his lascivious armes adown did creepe,
That themselves dipping in the silver dew
Their fleecy flowres they fearfully did steepe,
Which drops of christall seemd for wantones to weepe.

62 Infinit streames continually did well
Out of this fountaine, sweet and faire to see,
The which into an ample laver fell,
And shortly grew to so great quantitie,
That like a little lake it seemd to bee;
Whose depth exceeded not three cubits hight,
That through the waves one might the bottom see,
All pav'd beneath with jaspar shining bright,
That seemd the fountaine in that sea did sayle upright.

* * * * *

69 On which when gazing him the palmer saw,
He much rebukt those wandring eyes of his,
And counseld well, him forward thence did draw.
Now are they come nigh to the Bowre of Blis,
Of her fond favorites' so nam'd amis;
When thus the palmer; Now sir, well avise;
For here the end of all our travell is:
Here wonnes Acrasia, whom we must surprise,
Els she will slip away, and all our drift despise.

70 Eftsoones they heard a most melodious sound,
  Of all that mote delight a daintie eare,
  Such as attonce might not on living ground,
  Save in this paradise, be heard elsewhere:
  Right hard it was for wight, which did it heare,
  To read what manner musicke that mote bee;
  For all that pleasing is to living eare
  Was there consorted in one harmonee;
Birdes, voices, instruments, windes, waters, all agree:

71 The joyous birdes, shrouded in chearefull shade,
  Their notes unto the voyce attempred sweet;
  Th' angelicall soft trembling voyces made
  To th' instruments divine respondence meet;
  The silver sounding instruments did meet
  With the base murmure of the waters fall;
  The waters fall with difference discreet,
  Now soft, now loud, unto the wind did call;
The gentle warbling wind low answered to all.

* * * * *

74 The whiles some one did chaunt this lovely lay;
  Ah see, whoso faire thing doest faine to see,
  In springing flowre the image of thy day;
  Ah see the virgin rose, how sweetly shee
  Doth first peepe foorth with bashfull modestee,
  That fairer seemes the lesse ye see her may;
  Lo see soone after, how more bold and free
  Her bared bosome she doth broad display;
Lo see soone after, how she fades, and falls away.

75 *So passeth, in the passing of a day,*
  Of mortall life the leafe, the bud, the flowre;
  Ne more doth flourish after first decay,
  That earst was sought to decke both bed and bowre
  Of many a ladie, and many a paramowre!
  Gather therefore the rose, whilest yet is prime,
  For soone comes age, that will her pride deflowre:
  Gather the rose of love, whilest yet is time,
Whilest loving thou mayst loved be with equall crime.

76 He ceast; and then gan all the quire of birdes
   Their diverse notes t'attune unto his lay,
   As in approvance of his pleasing words.
   The constant paire heard all that he did say,
   Yet swarved not, but kept their forward way
   Through many covert groves and thickets close,
   In which they creeping did at last display
   That wanton ladie, with her lover lose,
Whose sleepie head she in her lap did soft dispose.

*   *   *   *   *

79 The young man, sleeping by her, seemd to be
   Some goodly swayne of honorable place;
   That certes it great pittie was to see
   Him his nobility so foule deface:
   A sweet regard and amiable grace,
   Mixed with manly sternesse did appeare,
   Yet sleeping, in his well proportiond face;
   And on his tender lips the downy heare
Did now but freshly spring, and silken blossomes beare.

80 His warlike armes, the idle instruments
   Of sleeping praise, were hong upon a tree:
   And his brave shield, full of old moniments,
   Was fowly ras't, that none the signes might see;
   Ne for them, ne for honour cared hee,
   Ne ought that did to his advauncement tend;
   But in lewd loves, and wastfull luxuree,
   His dayes, his goods, his bodie he did spend:
O horrible enchantment, that him so did blend.

81 The noble elfe and carefull palmer drew
   So nigh them, minding nought but idle game,
   That suddein forth they on them rusht, and threw
   A subtile net, which only for that same
   The skilfull palmer formally did frame:
   So held them under fast; the whiles the rest
   Fled all away for feare of fowler shame.
   The faire enchauntresse, so unwares opprest,
Tryde all her arts, and all her sleights thence out to wrest;

82 And eke her lover strove; but all in vaine;
   For that same net so cunningly was wound,
   That neither guile nor force might it distraine.
   They tooke them both, and both them strongly bound
   In captive bandes, which there they readie found:
   But her in chaines of adamant he tyde;
   For nothing else might keepe her safe and sound:
   But Verdant (so he hight) he soone untyde,
And counsell sage in steed thereof to him applyde.

83 But all those pleasaunt bowres, and pallace brave,
   Guyon broke downe with rigour pittilesse:
   Ne ought their goodly workmanship might save
   Them from the tempest of his wrathfulnesse,
   But that their blisse he turn'd to balefulnesse,
   Their groves he feld, their gardins did deface,
   Their arbers spoyld, their cabinets suppresse,
   Their banket houses burne, their buildings race,
And of the fairest late, now made the fowlest place.

84 Then led they her away, and eke that knight
   They with them led, both sorrowfull and sad:
   The way they came, the same retourn'd they right,
   Till they arrived, where they lately had
   Charm'd those wild beasts, that rag'd with furie mad;
   Which, now awaking, fierce at them gan fly,
   As in their mistresse reskew, whom they lad;
   But them the palmer soone did pacify.   [did ly.
Then Guyon askt, what meant those beastes, which there

85 Said he, These seeming beasts are men in deed,
   Whom this enchauntresse hath transformed thus,
   Whylome her lovers, which her lusts did feed,
   Now turned into figures hideous,
   According to their mindes like monstruous.
   Sad end (quoth he) of life intemperate,
   And mournefull meed of joyes delicious:
   But palmer, if it mote thee so aggrate,
Let them returned be unto their former state.

86 Streightway he with his vertuous staffe them strooke,
    And streight of beasts they comely men became;
    Yet being men they did unmanly looke,
    And stared ghastly; some for inward shame,
    And some for wrath, to see their captive dame:
    But one above the rest in speciall,
    That had an hog beene late, hight Grille by name,
    Repined greatly, and did him miscall,
That had from hoggish forme him brought to naturall.

87 Said Guyon; See the mind of beastly man,
    That hath so soone forgot the excellence
    Of his creation, when he life began,
    That now he chooseth with vile difference
    To be a beast, and lacke intelligence.
    To whom the palmer thus; The donghill kind
    Delights in filth and foule incontinence:
    Let Grill be Grill, and have his hoggish mind:
But let us hence depart, whilest wether serves and wind.

NOTES.

INTRODUCTION.

1. The Introduction is addressed, courtier-fashion, to Queen Elizabeth. The Poet makes apology for his Faery-land. 'Truth is stranger than fiction:' who could have foreseen the discovery of Peru and Virginia? may there not be worlds in the moon and stars? And, after all, Faery-land is not so far off: the doubter, if he will search for it, may find it at home; for it is England, ruled by the fairest of Princesses. The Poet is fain thus to veil her glories under the misty shadows of Faery-land, lest men's eyes should be dazzled by them. He now prays the Queen to listen to the tale of Guyon, the Knight of Temperance.

2, 6. *tb' Indian Peru;*—' Indian,' because men had believed that America was India taken from the other side. See canto xi. st. 21, and note there. Peru, discovered by Vasco Nuñez de Balboa about A.D. 1513, was conquered by Pizarro in 1532.

8. *The Amazons buge river;*—the Amazon, in South America, the greatest river on the globe, runs a course of about 3000 (some say 4000) miles from source to sea, and in the rainy season is said to be thirty miles broad at its mouth. Yanez Pinçon first discovered the mouth of the river, A.D. 1500: but a Spaniard, Francesco d'Orillana, was the first who sailed down any part of it, in 1540. He reported that there was a community of female warriors on its banks; and the river was named after them. The scattered accounts of the Amazons were collected by Sir W. Raleigh, and are to be found in his History of the World, Life of Alexander the Great.

9. *fruitfullest Virginia;*—now one of the United States of America. When Sir W. Raleigh returned from his expedition in 1584 with a glowing report of the country discovered in North America, and laid the new lands at the feet of the ' Virgin Queen,' she was pleased to accept them, and to give them the name of Virginia. In 1589, after much outlay in unsuccessful attempts at colonisation, Sir Walter handed over his rights to a London Company, reserving to himself a royalty of one-fifth of all precious metals found there. The colony then prospered; and it is interesting to note that while the Dedication to the first edition of the Faery Queene (A.D. 1590) styles Elizabeth " Queene of England, Fraunce and Ireland," that of the

N

second edition (1596) adds the words "and of Virginia," shewing that the colony had risen to high credit in the interval.

8, 2. *from wisest ages;*—hidden from ages renowned for their wisdom : why then should our dull age think an undiscovered Faery-land impossible ?

9. *yet such to some appeare;*—such worlds (in the moon, stars, &c.) seem to some persons to exist.

4, 2. *in sondrie place;*—either, as the Prayer-book phrase 'in sundry places' = in many different spots ; or = in one distinct place separated off from all others. In the latter case the clause 'here sett in sondrie place' will come after 'find' : in the former case 'sett' will agree with 'signes.'

5. *no'te . . . trace;*—'knows not how to track out.' This Old English contraction is common in Spenser's writings.

9. *thy great auncestry;*—especially described in canto 10, where the two knights, Arthur and Guyon, find two books, 'Briton Moniments' and 'Antiquitee of Faery Lond,' and read in them 'their countreys auncestry.'

5, 1. The style of this high compliment is a kind of parody on' things divine : it is the veil on Moses' face transferred to the glory and majesty of the Queen.

4. *beames;*—notice the dissyllabic plural, a relic of the old Northern English dialects.

9. *great rule of Temp'raunce;*—thus Spenser states the subject of the Book. Guyon's part is to work out the triumph of moral virtue over the various temptations of vice.

CANTO I.

Archimago, having escaped out of Eden, sets himself to work fresh woe to the Red Cross Knight. He meets Sir Guyon attended by his Palmer, and with a false tale and the sight of the false grief of Duessa, pricks him to attack the Red Cross Knight. But Sir Guyon, seeing the cross on the other's shield, forbears to fight ; and they fall to friendly converse. Soon after they part in all good-will ; the Red Cross Knight disappears from the scene ; Archimago and Duessa flee discomfited. Sir Guyon presently finds the dying Amavia, by the side of her dead husband, with her little babe whose hands are bedabbled with her blood. . He bears her last words, the tale of excess in drink, and swears to avenge her on Acrasia (or Intemperance). Then he gives them decent burial, takes up the babe, and fares forth on his way.

1, 1. *That cunning architect,* &c. ;—sc. Archimago: see Bk. I. xii. 24-36. In Milton (Par. Lost, 4. 121) we have a like phrase, "Artificer of fraud :" both drawn from the Latin " sceleris infandi artifex."—Cic. Or. 48. Archimago and the Red Cross Knight are introduced in order to link together the First and Second Books, and to form a natural introduction to the new 'gest' or pageant of Sir Guyon.

7. *out of caytives bands;*—what is meant by 'he frees himself out of caytives hands'? Probably Spenser means 'out of the hands of those who

held him captive;' or 'out of the hands of the rascals,' his gaolers. ·It has been suggested that this is a misprint for 'caytive hands' = either 'hands of the base,' or = 'captivity' simply; or another misprint for 'caytive bands,' which would make the best sense: but then 'bands' occurs already as one of the rhymes of this stanza.

8. *his artes he moves;*—Proteus-like: cp. Virg. Aen. 1. 661, "novas artes . . . versat;" and 12. 397, "agitare . . . artes."

2, 2. *to worken;*—notice the old Southern infinitive. Spenser was not particular as to the dialect he used.

4. *onely* = special, as in the theological usage of the word: see Bk. I. vii. 50, 'mine onely foe.' 'Only' is first an adj., then an adv.

6. *his;*—i. e. the Red Cross Knight's.

3, 2. *food;*—peculiar spelling of *feud*. See Bk. I. viii. 9: in Bk. IV. i. 26, the word is spelt *feood*.

6. *fayre filed tong;*—he was a smooth-tongued rascal. See Glossary to Bk. I. *File.*

9. *For hardly, &c.;*—i. e. the man who has once been hit will not be likely to fall again into Archimago's hands.

4, 5. *ketch;*—note this spelling of the word 'catch.' answering to the now vulgar pronunciation.

5, 2. *to win occasion to his will;*—to get a good opportunity to work his will. Spenser personifies Occasion in canto iv, bringing her in as the mother and cause of Fury.

. 9. *no place appeared;*—i. e. he was armed cap-à-pie, and no unarmed spot could be seen from head to foot.

6, 8. *Sir Huon;*—Sir Huon of Bordeaux. He was King Oberon's favourite. In the romance named after him, Oberon, after many gifts and marks of good-will, makes him his successor in his kingdom of Faery-land. Todd adds that as such he obtained the kingly right of conferring knighthood. But in true days of chivalry, knighthood could be conferred not only by kings, but by any knight. Thus the dead Sir Launcelot knights the hero of one romance, the sword being placed in his skeleton hand: in history, Francis I requested the great Bayard to dub him a knight. So that no kingly powers were needed in the case of Sir Huon.

9. *King Oberon;*—King of Faery-land. In canto x. 75, Henry VIII of England is introduced under this name.

7, 2. *a comely Palmer;*—under the person of the Palmer Spenser wishes to indicate the prudence and sobriety which counsel aright in times of moral trial. The Palmer plays the part of a kind of Chorus; he brings sober reason to bear upon every question; his remarks throughout the Book are sententious and soothing. When he is hindered from following his master, the Knight falls into violent passions, and is wellnigh undone. He corresponds to the Mentor of Telemachus, a slow-paced "sage and sober sire," without imagination, aged and free from youthful temptations, clad in black. Spenser may have meant to shadow out also the Church, as the moral guide and teacher of noble spirits.

8, 3. *deceiptfull clew;*—the clew, or twisted hank of string, kept ready to be made into nets.

7. *seeke;*—2nd pers. sing. for seekest.

8, 9. *miser;*—an Italian and Latin usage. So Ariosto, Orl. Fur., "Chè 'l miser suole," &c.

9, 3. *Who;*—notice the Latinized construction. Modern writers would have broken the sentence, and begun again with ' He.'

8. *in place;*—favourite phrase with Spenser, either = ' here, in this place;' or (as we now say) ' in a position' to tell.

9. *thy sight ;*—Latinism = ' sight of thee.'

10, 4. *virgin cleene;*—so in Sir Bevis of Hampton, a romance which Spenser knew well, we have " But were she a maiden cleene."

11, 5. *looser;*—Spenser affects this Latin comparative = ' too loose'— dishevelled by her tormentor.

12, 3. *doen;*—here is a present tense plural which belongs rightly to the Midland dialects (see Morris and Skeat's Specimens, Introduction, p. xix); · another example of Spenser's seizing on antique forms from any part of England.

9. *The stricken deare;*—Shakespeare has the same epithet in Hamlet, act. 3. sc. 2:

> " Why, let the *stricken deer* go weep."

16, 6. *but doth the ill increase;*—an intricate construction, half interrogative, half direct. ' What boots it to lament ?—to do so, when the mischief is done, but increases the evil.'

9. *voluntarie;*—i. e. it was a feigned tale, and feigned grief throughout The ' gentle lady' was Duessa, the spirit of falsehood.

18, 9. *that quartred all the field;*—heraldic phrase. The red cross divided the whole ' field' of the shield into four equal quarters.

19, 7. *'armes be swore;*—swore the oaths usually taken when a knight first dons his armour.

8. *Th' adventure,* &c. ;—i. e. the succouring of Una.

20, 7. *blotted;*—ed. 1590, ' blotting.'

21, 4. *Duessa;*—in Book I she did her utmost to lead true men into false doctrine; here into immoral life.

22, 7. *Sith her,* &c. ;—cp. Book I. viii. 45.

23, 3. *To slug in slouth,* &c. ;—in Bunyan's Pilgrim's Progress, the Christian's course is first endangered by the Slough of Despond ; . Bunyan was drawing the spiritual, Spenser the moral state of man. This temptation to idle sensuality meets Guyon, the hero of morality, at the outset, just as Error met the Red Cross Knight at the beginning of his career. He was striving after truth and was tried by error; Guyon after moral perfectness and is tempted by idleness.

9. *as virtues like,* &c. ;—such good knights as Guyon and the Red Cross Knight ought to be friends by nature; but the Evil One sets them sometimes at variance.

25, 5. *but vaine;*—the phrase is a Latinism, ' at vanum ': ' vaine' being elliptical or adverbial.

8. *So . . . that;*—' ita . . . ut,' so angry *that,* &c.

26, 1. *to pricke;*—note this use of the infinitive.

3. *in the rest;*—this was a catch under the knight's right arm, into which the spear was lowered : not the place on the stirrup on which the lance is rested while the horseman is not riding a tilt. It is the " ferro *al*

petto del cavaliere, ove s'accomoda il calce della laucia per colpire." Cp.
Ariosto, Orl. Fur. 1. 61:
> "Sprona a un tempo, e la lancia in resta pone."

28, 3. Note the courtesy of 'well becommeth you, But me behoveth,'
&c.

7. *fayre image of that heavenly maid;*—i. e. the portrait of Queen
Elizabeth on Sir Guyon's shield. She is the Virgin of English sixteenth-
century courtier-chivalry. In the shows and tilts of her reign, her figure
was a favourite device. Camden, in his Remains, says that one of her
courtiers displayed on one such occasion a half zodiac on his shield, with
Virgo rising, and the motto "Jam redit et virgo:" a conceit in many ways
pleasing to the Queen.

29, 3. *each to other beare;*—note the pl. verb; 'each to other'='one
with another they.'

5. *mote I weet;*—answers nearly to our modern 'Might I know ..?'

30, 3. *A false*, &c.;—the construction is, '(It) once befell me to meet a
traitor.' Note the use of 'for': for Spenser's parallel use of 'from' see
note below, xii. 26.

31, 1. *earnest with game;*—so Chaucer, Prologue to the Milleres Tale,
78: "Men schulde nat make earnest of game."

8. *and that deare Crosse*, &c.;—in the same construction with 'you,'
a dative after 'happie chance.'

32, 5. *a saint with saints;*—the Red Cross Knight is also 'Saint George
of mery England.' Cp. Book I. x. 61.

33, 6. *whose pageant next ensues;*—pageants were favourite pastimes
at the Queen's court. Virtues and vices were therein personified. So in
st. 36. l. 3, we have
> 'To see *sad pageaunts* of mens miseries.'

The pageant that was about to follow was that of Sir Guyon, the subject of
the coming book. The Red Cross Knight now takes his farewell of the
audience, and puts his successor forward as the next actor.

7. *Well mote yee thee;*—'may you prosper.' See Glossary, *Thee.*

8. *thrise;*—edd. 1590, 1596, 'these'; but in 'Faults Escaped' at end
of ed. 1590, it is corrected to 'thrise.'

39, 4. *dolour;*—ed. 1596, 'labour.'

half dead, half quicke;—so in the Creeds "the quick and the
dead." See Glossary, *Quick.*

40, 4. *gore;*—ed. 1596, 'gold.'

41, 5. *yett being ded;*—in apposition to 'his'; 'his'='of him,'—'the
cheeks of him yet being dead.'

6. *seemd;*—'he seemed,' the personal pronoun being not rarely
omitted by Spenser.

44, 8. *your untimely date;*—the allotted, or given, end of her days,
coming before the kindly term of life; cp. Virg. Aen. 4; 697, of Dido,
"misera ante diem." These stanzas are modelled upon the description
of Dido's last moments. So the 'Therewith her dim eye-lids,' &c., is
imitated from Virgil's
> "Illa, graves oculos conata attollere, rursus Deficit,"

and 'Thrise he her reard,' &c., from "Ter se attollens," &c. (Aen. 4 690.)

45, 1. *eie-lids, On which the drery death did sit;*—so Homer, Il. 10. 91, speaks of sleep sitting on the eyes.

　2. *sad As lump of lead;*—so in viii. 30:
'With that his hand, more sad than lump of lead
Uplifting hye.'
See Glossary, *Sad.*

　47, 9. *now got, which;*—Latinism; 'the death, now got by me, which,' &c., i. e. the self-caused boon of death.

　50, 1. *ay the while;*—cp. the equivalent 'Woe worth (be to) the while,' &c. 'Ay' is our present 'Ah !'

　51, 2. *vile Acrasia;*—the Aristotelian ἀκρασία, that condition of man in which the due government of the appetites, or the combination of the elements of human nature, is neglected. She is the self-indulgent opposite of self-ruling Temperance. Spenser's Temperance is manly, not cloistered or retiring; the condition of the full-grown man, who has met his trials and fought them down, supported and guided by his monitor, 'the Palmer,' who may be either 'Conscience,' or 'God's Word,' or 'Reason,' or 'Sobriety.' Spenser here introduces the central figure of Evil, antagonist to Guyon, the central figure of Good. Her features are copied from the Homeric Circe.

　5. *a wandring island;*—one of the established properties of romance writers.

　52, 3. *with words and weedes,* &c.;—Hom. Od. 10. 234-236: probably also alluding to Rev. 14. 8; 17. 4.

　8. *palmers weed;*—the 'palmer's weed' was a very common disguise in romance ; so Sir Bevis says, "palmers weed thou shalt weare." The black robe and staff were an excuse for wandering anywhither, and therefore very suitable for a disguise. A distinction is drawn between palmer and pilgrim, to the effect that while the pilgrim was bound to some particular holy place or shrine, the palmer had a sort of general roving commission of a more permanent character. The *pilgrim* went from home to the shrine he had vowed to visit, and returned home again; the *palmer* had no home, and was a kind of permanent beggar. Chaucer in his Prologue 13 seems to favour a distinction:
"Thanne longen folk to gon on *pilgrimages*
And *palmeres* for to seeken straunge strondes."
Tyrwhitt, in his ed. of Chaucer, quotes Dante's Vita Nuova, "Chiamansi Palmieri, inquanto vanno oltra mare, laonde molte volte recano la palma." The *palmer* carried in his hand a staff of palm-tree wood, or a branch of it, whence his name. Consequently the name of Palmer belongs properly to those only who went as pilgrims to the Holy Land. And thus the author of the anonymous Passio S. Thomae Cant. (ed. Dr. Giles, p. 134) says, "Peregrinationis suae signum primi quidem *et soli* vel *a Christi sepulcbro* vel a sancto Iacobo revertentes, hi cochleas, *illi palmarum spatulas* referre consueverunt." The name, however, came to signify a homeless wanderer, under a religious guise and character. The journey to Jerusalem had a natural tendency to become discursive, whether undertaken by single pilgrims or crusading armies. Camden, Remains, Surnames, seems to recognise no difference: "As *palmer*, that is, *pilgrime,* for that they carried palme when they came from Jerusalem."

54, 1. Milton seems to have had this description in his mind when he drew the besotted revellers in his Comus, l. 524 sqq. The fall of Sir Mordant, and the miserable death of Amavia, are intended to express the consequences of intemperance in drink. (The English, thanks chiefly to their relations with the Dutch and Flemish, grew more drunken during the latter half of the sixteenth century than they had been before.)Camden, Britannia, speaking of the year 1581, says that up to that time there had been no habit of drunkenness in England, nor laws nor punishments for it. Spenser himself, View of the State of Ireland, says: "If it should be made a capital crime for the Flemmings to be taken in drunkenness, there should have been fewer Flemmings now;" shewing the character they had got for drinking. The chief drinks hitherto had been beer and mead, with sack for the upper classes; and even on these the English had a reputation for tippling: but the ardent spirits now brought in seem to have thrown the nation off its balance.

55, 6. *Bacchus with the Nymphe;*—i.e. as soon as the wine in her enchanted cup (Bacchus, god of wine) should be mixed with water (the Nymph of the stream). Heliod. Aethiop. Bk. 5. p. 234, has καθαρὰς τὰς νύμφας καὶ ἀκοινωνήτους τοῦ Διονύσου. Boyd, in his note on this passage, poetically suggests an allusion to the *dropsy!* which so often follows and punishes drunkenness.

56, 2. *off;*—ed. 1590, 'of.'

57, 1. This stanza and the 58th express, as at the outset, the general aim and 'moral' of the Book—the ruin of man through Passion, and his happiness if he can 'measure out a meane' through Temperance.

58, 8. *Reserve her cause,* &c.;—i.e. let us not judge her, but leave it to the last judgment of doomsday.

59, 1. *equall;*—ed. 1596, 'evill.'

5. *But both alike;*—'(to) both alike.'

7. The pagan notion of the want of funeral rites being a distress to the dead.

8. *For all,* &c.;—I count it altogether as great an evil to be badly (miserably) unburied, as to die miserably.

60, 3. *sad cypresse;*—see Book I. i. 8 (note). So Sidney, in his Arcadia, speaks of "cypress branches, wherewith in old times they were wont to dress graves."

8. *affection;*—here = sense of piety.

61, 1. *his;*—the neuter possessive pronoun 'it' was already in use, being a shortened form of the neuter 'hit'; but 'its' does not appear till close to the end of the sixteenth century.

2. *be cut a lock;*—so Iris is sent to cut a lock of Dido's hair. Aen. 4. 694, 704. Cp. also Euripides, Alcestis, 76. In these cases, however, the cutting off a lock of hair is supposed to release the dying spirit.

CANTO II.

Sir Guyon tries in vain to cleanse the babe's hands. He and the Palmer return with the infant to where they had left the horse, but find it stolen. They must fare afoot. Presently they come to a castle, where dwell three sisters, Medina, just moderation, and the two extremes, Elissa, too little, Perissa, too much. The strife between these two is pourtrayed, and the manner in which Medina moderates their wrath.

Heading, l. 2. *The face of Golden Meane;*—part for whole = the appearance, figure. The French *figure* is used for the *face* only, by an opposite idiom.

1, 6. *that;*—notice the three uses of 'that' in this passage; (1) the babe who; (2) in l. 8 = that which (now 'what'); (3) in l. 8 = so that.

2, 1. *borne under cruell starre;*—ἀστὴρ κακοποιός. It was believed that each man's fortunes throughout life depended upon the aspect of the heavens at the moment of birth. The whole life was influenced especially by the star that was rising at that moment, and by the stars which grouped themselves round that rising star, or were on or near the opposite extremity of the same diameter of the heavens. The benign stars were Venus, Jupiter, Luna, Virgo, Taurus; the malign, Saturn, Mars, Scorpio, Capricorn; the doubtful, Mercury, &c. See Smith's Dict. of Antiquities, art. Astrology.

2. *in dead parents,* &c.;—an allusion to the birth of the Phœnix, said to be sprung, according to one account, from his father's ashes.

8. *Such is the state of men;*—so Wolsey in Shakespeare's Henry VIII, act 3. sc. 2, exclaims,
"This is the state of men!"

3, 4. *His guiltie bandes;*—i. e. the babe's hands, which were guilty, either because they had dabbled in their mother's life-blood, or, possibly, because of the stain of their parents' crimes. The proposed reading 'guiltlesse' is without foundation.

4, 1. *He wist not;*—notice the two negatives; 'He did not know whether the offence was indelible, or whether,' &c. Compare the blood on Lady Macbeth's hands, Macbeth, act 5. sc. 1.

5. *hat'th;*—notice the harsh elision for metre and rhyme's sake.

7. *bath;*—change of construction from '*might* not be purged,' and 'imprinted *had.*'

5, 6. *secret vertues are infused,* &c.;—medicinal waters attracted much attention at the time. Spenser himself alludes to them in Bk. I. xi. 29, 30.

8. *Which, who,* &c.;—notice the involved construction. The meaning is, 'He who chooses them wisely, has often used them so as to produce (as proofs of their efficacy) surpassing wonders.'

6, 6. *later grace;*—some fountains are full of 'virtue' from their first source, others gain it by favour shewn later.

7, 2. *her nymph;*—the well or fountain is probably made fem. by Spenser, because fountains are always tenanted by nymphs; the A. S. *wyl* is masc., *wylle* fem.; the same word in Germ., *quelle*, is always fem.

7. *chace;*—does not rhyme with 'way,' &c. as it should do. But I know of no other reading.

8, 5. *deare besought;*—'deare' = earnestly. See Glossary. This is the tale of Arethusa, taken from Ovid, Metam. 5. 618, &c.

9, 1. Contrast with this the legend of St. Winifred's Well, which is the Christian form of the same thought.

8. *Ne lets her waves;*—in i. 40 we read, 'And the cleane waves with purple gore did ray;' which seems to contradict this passage. But to 'ray' may mean to 'streak' with blood, the blood not mixing with the water.

10, 7. *as a sacred symbole;*—Upton says that this passage images forth the rebellion of the O'Neals, and quotes Spenser's View of the State of Ireland: "As they under Oneale cry *Lanndarg-abo*, that is, the bloody hand, which is Oneales badge."

11, 2. *to the Palmer gave to beare;*—this does not agree with the statement in the Letter to Sir W. Raleigh. Spenser there says: 'The second day there came in a Palmer *bearing an Infant with bloody hands*;" that is, before the beginning of Sir Guyon's adventure.

9. *here fits not to tell;*—not here, but in iii. 4, so weaving skilfully the tale together.

12, 1. *all . . . algates;*—although . . . yet.

8. *fame;*—ed. 1590, 'frame,' wrongly.

13, 1. *three sisters;*—this is an allegory of the Aristotelian doctrine of the Mean. "Virtue, a mean between the extremes of excess and defect." The three sisters are named and described in stanzas 35–38. Spenser seems also to work in the Platonic theory of morals. For the 'too little' sister also shews a tendency towards *anger*, and the 'too much' one towards intemperate living. (See the next note.) It is worthy of remark that whereas Spenser set out with declaring that he would display 'the twelve private morall vertues, as Aristotle hath devised; the which is the purpose of these first twelve bookes,' we soon find that he wanders very far from the Aristotelian series. The first Book pourtrays Holiness, the second Temperance. But the first is really the triumph of Faith and Truth, and is far more intellectual and spiritual than moral; while the second covers almost the whole ground of the Aristotelian moral virtues.

2. *one syre by mothers three;*—connected, yet very different. An allusion to the theory laid out by Plato, Rep. Bk. 4. p. 439, and Bk. 9. p. 580. The three mothers will be λογιστική, ἐπιθυμητική, and θυμητική, the reasonable, the appetitive, the passionate or high-spirited elements of our nature: the 'one syre' is probably the human reason (λόγος).

4. *in equall fee;*—with equal right of holding or tenure. 'To hold in fee' is a feudal term, meaning to hold upon the tenure of a *feud* (*fee-od, fee-good,* that is, property held in fee). See Glossary, *Fee.*

6. *in partes;*—a Latinism, 'in partes,' i. e. on different sides or parties.

14, 5, *sober;*—an adverb in this place (= soberly), 'sober sad' balancing 'comely courteous.'

15, 6. *Above the reason,* &c.;—'ultra rationem'—beyond the proportion one would have expected from so young a person.

17, 2. *Sir Huddibras;*—i. e. rashness, the Greek θυμὸς, or θρασύτης its development. There is also in him the element of morose joylessness, which makes one think that Spenser intended to shadow forth the Puritans, who were already a strong party. It will be remembered that Samuel Butler gives this name to the hero of his burlesque on Puritanism.

18, 1. *Sans-loy;*—unbridled excess; the lawless side of unbelief, the 'unruly' and 'boldest boy' who outraged purity and truth alike.

19. These stanzas express the general opposition of extremes; answering to Aristotle's dictum that the extremes are opposed to one another and to the mean. We are now engaged with the general principles of morals, not with any of its special applications.

9. *themselves;*—if this pronoun refers to 'Both knightes and ladies,' it will mean, 'they prepared themselves, the knights to battle, the ladies to encourage their champions:' but 'themselves' probably refers only to the knights.

20, 5. *the scorned life to quell;*—each extreme strove to destroy its opposite, which it scorned.

7. *all that in did dwell;*—an elliptical expression: 'in' = therein, or = in that house.

21, 5. *sunbroad shield;*—so in Milton, Par. Lost, 6. 305 :

> "Two *broad suns* their shields
> Blazed opposite."

7. *their strife to understond;*—to interfere in, to run in underneath, and stop it. Or, possibly, only 'to learn what they were fighting about.'

22, 5. *As when* = like as when. The illustration is here preceded by that which it illustrates: 'The two turn upon Sir Guyon, like a bear and tiger which espying a traveller leave their strife and attack him.'

6. *on lybicke ocean;*—i. e. on the deserts of Africa, which are spread out in hillocks, like an ocean. Not on the *syrtes*, as some would have it. Upton quotes as an illustration the Greek phrase πελάγιόν τι χεῦμα, used of the desert. Spenser had in mind Virg. Georg. 2. 105,

> " Quem si scire velit, *Libyci* velit *aequoris* idem
> Discere quam multae Zephyro turbentur arenae."

23, 2. *boldly;*—ed. 1596, 'bloudy.'

3. *byte him nere;*—Warton says = 'to pierce him to the quick.'

24, 2. *Whom;*—the ship made personal, as seems always natural. A very fine stanza. Spenser is always fine in his naval similes. See note on xii. 19.

25, 7. *forcing to invade;*—using force so as to invade his foes and drive them back.

9. *So ... so* = As ... so.

26, 1. Sidney's Arcadia has a like fight between three knights at once.

4. *All for ... to gaine;*—analogous to the Greek use of the infinitive as a substantive neuter, εἰς τὸ κτᾶσθαι. Spenser also uses '*from* to ...' See note on 'from to,' xii. 26.

7. *He maketh, &c.;*—so Terence, Eunuch.,

> "In amore haec omnia insunt vitia, iniuriae,
> Bellum, pax rursum."

Cp. also Hor. Sat. 2. 3, 267.

27, 9. *to her ... to beare;*—'to heare to' used as we still use 'to hearken, listen to.' Cp. also the archaic 'to obey to.'

29, 2. *fell Erinnys;*—the Erinnyes were the Furies of Greek and Latin mythology. They were originally only personifications of the curses pronounced on a guilty criminal. These spirits of cursing sojourn in Erebus, until some curse duly pronounced on an offender calls them up to earth. They then pursue the guilty wretch with unrelenting steps, and bring down the curse upon his head. Their later name was 'the Eumenides' ('the well-disposed ones'); so called by the trembling flattery of the Greeks.

30, 2. *faire it to accord;*—to bring it to fair agreement.

32, 9. *Which to observe;*—Latin construction = 'and they assured (promised) to observe,' &c.

33, 5. *grace to reconcile;*—Latinism, 'gratiam conciliare,' to regain each other's favour.

34, 3. *fained cheare,* &c.;—they pretended to be of good cheer; the passions being not subdued, but held under for a time.

4. *could not colour;*—they could not so far disguise their feelings. The Latin rhetoricians used the term 'color' in the sense of speciously covering over a thing by argument.

7. *as doth an hidden moth The inner garment fret;*—cp. Ps. 39. 12, " Like as it were a *moth fretting a garment.*"

8. *not th' utter touch;*—*touch* is a verb; for *utter,* see Glossary.

35, 1. *Elissa;*—the personification of Moral Deficiency, the Aristotelian ἔλλειψις. Spenser probably derives the name from ἐλάσσων, 'too little.' It is curious that it should have also been so like one of the names of the Virgin Queen, the great but parsimonious Eliza.

did deeme Such entertainment base, &c.;—the churlishness of the Puritanic feeling which found fault with moderate feasting, &c. The Puritans revenged themselves on Spenser by forbidding the faithful to look into the Faery Queene.

36, 1. *Perissa;*—personification of Excess; from περισσή, 'too much.'

37, 1. *Fast;*—edd. 1590, 1596, 'first': but corrected in 'Faults Escaped,' 1590, to 'fast.'

2. *a mincing mineon;*—'an affected favourite.'

4. *a franker franion;*—'too free a companion.' Cp. Heywood's Edward IV (A.D. 1600):
"He's a *frank franion,* a merry companion."
See Glossary, *Franion.*

6. *malecontent;*—a term often used at that time of the Puritans. Todd quotes Barnabie Rich's 'Faults and nothing his Faults' in confirmation.

38, 1. *Medina;*—personifying the golden mean, halfway between the morose Puritanism of Elissa and the loose behaviour of Perissa.

5, 7. *forward paire, . . . froward paire;*—Excess is forward, or too bold, Defect froward, or wayward and dissatisfied. Upton says that the two knights, Sansloy and Huddibras, are the forward pair, the two ladies the froward pair. But this is an obvious mistake. The pairs are the two sets of knights and dames—Elissa with Huddibras, Perissa with Sansloy.

9. *her selfe in heed;*—kept due watch over her own conduct.

39, 3. *when lust,* &c.;—a well-known Homeric line translated;
ἀλλ' ὅποταν ποσίος καὶ ἐδητύος ἐξ ἔρον ἕντο.

39, 4. *She Guyon,* &c.;—this calling on the guest to relate his adventures is modelled on Dido and Aeneas, Virg. Aen. 1. 757–760, and 2. 1–5.

40, 1. Notice here how the poet never lets slip an occasion of praising Queen Elizabeth.

41, 1. *The richesse ... are heaped up;*—'richesse' is here, as often, a noun plural : there never seems to have been any distinct rule laid down, and grammarians err if they speak of 'riches' as a noun singular solely. The word is used in the English Bible of 1611 chiefly in the plural.

42, 1. *To her I homage,* &c.;—the feudal style, as befitting loyalty to chief and respect for lady, was much affected by the Elizabethan courtiers.

2. *In number,* &c.;—Spenser, as one who did not hold any sure position at court, would naturally take this opportunity of paying a graceful compliment to the gentlemen who surrounded the Queen. The allusion may refer specially to the Knights of the Garter, as seems probable from the phrase in line 4, ' Order of Maydenhead.'

6. *An yearely solemne feast;*—this alludes first to the plot of the whole work, which begins, according to the Letter of Sir Walter Raleigh, with this high festival, lasting twelve days, at which twelve knights come in, and undertake the twelve labours, which were intended to form the subject of the twelve Books.

' The day which first doth lead the yeare around' will mean, not the 1st of January, but March 25 ; spring-time, not mid-winter, according to the reckoning of that time. Edward III, before he established the order of the Garter, endeavoured to create an annual festival of the Knights of the Round Table, who were to be gathered out of all nations to his court. It is probably to this that Spenser here primarily alludes, rather than to the Order of the Garter, which Edward III established in its stead, when he found that, through the jealousy and antagonism of Philip of Valois, his first and grander plan could not be carried out.

In this line, the last word ' make,' the reading of all the old editions, is clearly a slip for ' hold.'

44, 2. This line is quoted by Warton as an instance of Spenser's weak elongations caused by exigency of the metre. He regards it as a lengthy paraphrase for the words ' three months have passed.' There are, however, those who will regard the image of the placid moon looking down upon the shadows of this nether world as something better than mere verbiage to fill up lines.

6. *Acrasia;*—the personification of ungoverned, unbridled life. See note on i. 51.

8. *and this,* &c.;—' and (so also is) this their son witness.'

45, 5. *Ill by ensaumple;*—this is the principle on which the Spartans shewed drunken Helots to their sons, that by seeing the example of evil they might learn to hate and avoid it.

46, 1. *now in ocean deepe,* &c.;—Orion and the Serpent are neighbouring constellations on the sidereal globe. Orion sets towards morning, and the poet means to say that the night was far spent. It is an astrological, rather than a classical allusion. One of the classical legends describe him as pursued and killed by a scorpion.

8. *the chaunged skyes;*—i. e. the variation in the position of the stars.

CANTO III.

Braggadocchio, having stolen Guyon's steed and spear, subdues Trompart, a weak but wily knave. Archimago, meeting them, incites the false knight to avenge him on the Red Cross Knight and Guyon, and promises to bring him Prince Arthur's sword. Braggadocchio is mortally affrighted by Belphoebe, the hunter-goddess.

Heading, l. 2. The metre is at fault here: it should have been printed
' getting Guy-
ons horse is made the scorne.'

1, 2. *Disperst the shadowes of the mistie night;*—cp. Virg. Aen. 4. 7,
"*Humentemque* Aurora polo dimoverat *umbram.*"
Also for ' purple beams,' see Virg. Aen. 6. 640,
"Largior hic campos aether et *lumine* vestit
Purpureo."
9. *many-folded;*—so the Virgilian *septemplex.* See note on v. 6.

2, 8. *Ruddymane;*—rouge-main, red-hand.

3, 3. *Patience perforce;*—a proverbial phrase quoted in Romeo and Juliet, act I. sc. 5 : " Patience perforce, with wilful choler meeting." Upton says that the whole proverb was " Patience perforce (or, *upon* force) is a medicine for a mad dog;" but it seems more probable that the shorter phrase was the real proverb. The meaning of the proverb is, ' What can't be cured must be endured.'

helplesse what may it boot;—a Latin arrangement of words = ' what may it profit a helpless man.'

4, 1. *a losell;*—sc. Braggadocchio, as the name signifies, a big bragging fool. He personifies Cowardice, and is the comic element in the Book.
4. *his kestrell kind;*—his low-bred hawk-nature. The kestrel was a hawk looked on with contempt by falconers, as being vain and cowardly.

5. *he;*—ed. 1596 repeats ' vaine' for ' he.'
9. *to court* = ' at court.' So in America 'to home' (cp. Germ. *zu haus*) is still used as we now use ' *at* home.'

6, 2. *One sitting;*—sc. Trompart, weak and deceitful, a flatterer and knave. The pair serve as a foil to the noble figures of Guyon and the Palmer, the sham knight and lying squire, to the true soldier and his grave adviser; and also lighten the tone of a Book otherwise filled with dark characters. More especially they form a contrast to the angry passions of the brothers Cymocles and Pyrocles.

7, 1. *the scarecrow;*—so called for his false bravery, terrible in appearance to the foolish and bird-witted, but really of no strength at all.
6. *dead dog;*—cp. 2 Sam. 9. 8; 16. 9; also 1 Sam. 24. 14.

8, 1. *dead-doing;*—Hom. Il. 18. 317, χεῖρας ἐπ' ἀνδροφόνους.
6. *kisse my stirrup;*—one of the established forms of homage was to hold the stirrup of one's lord.

8, 7. *as an offall;*—this word is not now used with the indefinite article, which here points out the true origin of the word. See Glossary, *Offall.*

9. *to hold of him in fee;*—term used properly of land, but here only of service "Feodum, or *fee*, is that [sc. land] which is held of some superior on condition of rendering him service, in which superior the ultimate property of the land resides." Blackstone, Comm. II. 7. 1. By the sixteenth century the term was quite degraded, and from the first sense of a recompense for service rendered, leading on to a return sense of service to be paid for the use of the land, it came to mean simply any recompense or gift; thence it reached the modern usage of 'fee' or payment of certain charges at law, &c. In the text it is used solely of *personal* service of a liegeman to his liege lord; 'to hold of him' meaning simply 'to be his subject, as a feudal inferior to his lord.'

9, 2. *this liegeman;*—Trompart. These are the two sides of low and cowardly depravity, the loud boasting bully and the supple foxy cheat; the stupid bully is the apparent master, but the sharp servant soon has the real command, his 'wylie-witted' nature taking advantage of the other's folly. One cannot help suspecting that Spenser had before his mind's eye some master and man at court.

11, 3. *in armour fayre;*—a slight confusion here : for Braggadocchio steals only the horse and spear from Sir Guyon. He may however be imagined to have worn some body armour of his own. On the other hand, in st. 15 of this canto he is advised to arm himself in surest steel that may be found.

5. *Eftsoones supposed;*—Archimago is a singular mixture of the ignorant and the magician : a character, in this respect, drawn very true to nature, the deceiver being made at the same time the most credulous of men. Spenser may have also meant to shew up the crafty shifts to which the Jesuit priests and emissaries in England were apt to resort.

12, 7. *now hath vowd;*—a common incident in Romance writing. In Ariosto, Orl. Fur. 23. 78, Mandricardo says,—
"Ho sacramento di non cinger spada
  Fin ch' io non tolgo Durindana al Conte."

14, 3. *gaged;*—left as gages, or hostages, in his power.

16, 6. *Is not enough*, &c. ;—notice the construction here : 'foure quarters of a man' is taken as = 'a man,' and followed by a sing. verb. The ' foure quarters of a man ' is only a piece of bombast in Braggadocchio's mouth.

17, 7. *seven knightes*, &c. ;—the character of the fire-eater and braggart was not an uncommon one in Spenser's time. Cp. Shakespeare's Falstaff, and Sir P. Sidney's Dametas in the Arcadia.

18, 6. *by my device;*—a knightly oath; 'by the device upon my shield' = by my knightly honour—the shield being supposed to represent the knight, and the device to express his character or qualities.

9. *that monster;*—that marvel.

20, 5. *their haire on end does reare;*—ed. 1590, 'does unto them affeare;' and in the 'Faults Escaped' at the end of that ed. the word ' unto' is corrected to ' greatly.'

21, 3. *crept into a bush;*—Dametas, in the Arcadia, does just the same, when the wild beasts are let loose.

7. *A goodly ladie*, &c. ;—Belphoebe, i. e. Queen Elizabeth, who much affected a likeness to the chaste Diana. With this picture may be compared that of Chastity in Milton's Comus, 420 sqq. The incident is very skilfully introduced here, by way of contrasting the pure Virgin Queen with the loose, idle Phaedria of canto vi.

22, 5. With this description of Belphoebe, the picture of Alcina (Ariosto, Orl. Fur. 7. 10) may well be compared. 'In her cheekes,' &c., answers to

> " Spargeasi per la guancia delicata
> Misto color di rose e di ligustri."

The picture of her hair in stanza 30 to

> " Bionda chioma lunga, ed annodata,
> Oro non è che più risplenda e lustri."

'Without blame' is the Homeric ἀμύμων, used sometimes of fair women (as of Nausicaa, Od. 7. 303). The 'ambrosial odours' may be drawn from Virgil, Aen. 1. 403, where, however, the phrase refers to the hair.

23, 8. *For, with dredd majestie*, &c. ;—so in Milton's Comus, l. 444, Diana

> " Set at nought
> The frivolous bolt of Cupid."

This stanza is probably intended as an answer to the attacks on the Queen's character and conduct which were very rife at this time.

24, 7. *Sweet wordes, like dropping honny ;*—so Solomon's Song, 4. 11.
8. *twixt the perles and rubins ;*—cp. Spenser's Sonnet, 81 :
" The gate, with perles and rubyes richly dight."
Both from Ariosto, Orl. Fur. 12. 94 :

> " Che dai coralli e dalle preziose
> Perle uscir fanno i dolci accenti mozzi."

25, 1. *Upon her eyelids*, &c. ;—so in Sonnet 40 :

> " When on each eyelid sweetly doe appeare
> An hundred Graces as in shade to sit."

And these again from Alcina, Ariosto, Orl. Fur. 7. 12 ; or from Tasso, Aminta, act 2. sc. 1, where Cupid sits

> " Sotto al ombra de le palpebre."

26, 4. *a silken Camus ;*—a thin transparent robe; twice used in Spenser of a silken dress. The word is a form of the word *chemise ;* see Glossary.
9. An unfinished line. There is another such in viii. 55, 'But to be ever bound—,' where, however, there is a reason for an abrupt break. Here it can only be accounted for by Spenser's unwillingness to use that ' padding' which the critics have so often accused him of. He would have had no difficulty in finishing the line, and finding a rhyme to 'about.' Indeed, some of his critics have had the goodness to finish it for him.

27, 1. Here the statues and coins bearing the figure of Diana have been exactly followed. Compare with this the account in Sidney's Arcadia of the dress of Pyrocles, when disguised as an Amazon.

28, 1. *faire marble pillours ;*—cp. Solomon's Song, 5. 15.
6. *she herself would grace ;*—would do herself honour, by moving in queenly sort, when " vera incessu patuit Dea."

30, 1. *golden wyre ;*—" Her haire as gold-wyre was seene."—Bevis of Hampton. Cp. Virg. Aen. 1. 318 :

> " dederatque comam diffundere ventis,
> Nuda genu."

31, 1. *Such as Diana,* &c.;—direct from Virg. Aen. 1. 498:
" Qualis in Eurotae ripis aut per iuga Cynthi
  Exercet Diana choros."

5. *that famous queene Of Amazons;*—Penthesileia. She came to the help of the Trojans, and was killed by Achilles, who bitterly mourned over the dying queen, by reason of her sex, her youth and beauty, and her bravery. But Spenser follows Dares Phrygius, c. 36 (whose history, translated by Lydgate, he probably knew), who makes her to be slain by Pyrrhus, Achilles' son.

32, 5. *both feare and hope;*—a delicate compliment to the awful benignity of the Queen's countenance.

7. *Hayle, groome;*—so Venus (Virg. Aen. 1.321) addresses the Trojans: " Heus, inquit, iuvenes."
The next stanza shews that Spenser had Virgil in his mind.

33, 2. *O goddesse,* &c.;—Virg. Aen. 1. 327, 328

34, 6. *to marke the beast;*—not the modern sporting term ' to mark a bird down,' but to strike it.

35, 4. *many bold emprize;*—Ariosto's phrase, Orl. Fur. 1. 1, " l'audaci imprese."

6. *she staid ;*—sc. her hand.

36. An admirable simile, and well sustained throughout.

38, 8. *above the moone ;*—the same inflated style well kept up; together with the low views of life and duty peeping through.

40–41. Admirable stanzas, "if we consider it the sense of the Princess, and as a short character of so active and glorious a reign."—Hughes. These stanzas may be well contrasted with the theory of life put out by Phaedria (canto vi.) especially in her song ' Behold O man,' &c. (st. 15-17). It is the praise of work opposed to that of idleness.

40, 6. *his mind Behaves with cares;*—occupies his mind with business and study.

42, 2. This is perhaps a picture of the vain and craven world endeavouring to sully the Queen's fair fame.

43, 9. *leave so proud disdayne ;*—leave behind her such a sense of her contempt for us.

45–46. The braggart admirably combines boasting with fear in these stanzas.

45, 4. *on foote ;*—i. e. ' one foot,' not = afoot,

46, 7. *to tread in dew degree ;*—to move along with equal paces, as befits a knight's charger.—The noble horse was wearied and fretted by the ignoble and unpractised rider. Braggadocchio now disappears from this Book. He reappears, Bk. III. viii ; and is finally detected and put to utter shame, Book V. iii.

CANTO IV.

Sir Guyon meets Furor dragging a handsome youth by his hair, and followed by Occasion, his mother. The Knight overcomes and binds both mother and son, and delivers Phedon, the luckless squire, who tells his sad history. Meanwhile comes a Varlet, running hastily; he reviles Sir Guyon, and bids him give place to his master Pyrocles, who is not far behind.

Argument, 3. *Phedon ;*--ed. 1590, Phaon.

1, 1. *I know not what,* &c.;--a Latin construction. This is a description of the Platonic εὐφυὴς, the well-bred, well-thewed, and, it must be confessed, the affected gentleman. It was the fashion of the society in which Spenser moved to be keenly sensitive as to the honour and duties of the estate of gentleman. The newer aristocracy of the reign prided themselves on their breeding and conduct, and despised the 'rascal rout' without stint. The feeling that can be traced here runs through Sir W. Raleigh's writings and acts, in a foppish strain : it also gives the colour to Sir P. Sidney's affected Arcadia throughout.

2. *by native influence ;*--by the star which rose at their birth.

7. *skill to ride ;*--the art of horsemanship throughout this period belongs specially to the gentleman. It was one of the characteristics of the true knight, that he could gracefully 'menage' his steed, it being an essential and prime element of chivalry. In our day, however, this 'mark of a gentleman,' the good seat, must be shared with circus riders and grooms.

2, 5. *who suffred not,* &c.;--the Palmer appears again as the Knight's constant monitor.

3, 2. *He saw,* &c.;--so Apoll.Rhodius, Argon 4. 1480, ἢ ἴδεν ἢ ἐδόκησεν ἐπαχλύουσαν ἰδέσθαι.

5. *a mad man ;*--Furor, or ungoverned anger : not Aristotle's Rashness, but excess of angry passion.

7. *a handsome stripling ;*--Phedon, a youth who has given himself up to ungovernable anger.

4, 1. *a wicked Hag ;*--Occasion. The idea which Spenser wishes to enforce by this description of Occasion, is that involved in the phrases 'an occasion of falling,' 'an occasion of wrath,' &c. It is not the same with the 'Occasio' (the nick of time, ξυροῦ ἀκμή) of the moralists, who was personified as a deity by the late Greeks and Latins, and was rather a good than an evil personage. In Greek Occasion was masculine, ὁ καιρὸς (sometimes εὐκαιρία, indicating that the *favourable* moment was what was meant by it). We have in Ausonius, Epigr. 12, an account of this deity and her companion Poenitentia (the penitence which follows after an opportunity *missed,* not after occasion seized). Phaedrus also describes this deity as male :

> "Cursu ille volucri pendens in novacula,
> Calvus, comosa fronte, nudo corpore.

O

Quem si occuparis, teneas; elapsum semel
Nec ipse possit Jupiter reprendere:
Occasionem rerum significat brevem."

Spenser describes her as lame of one leg (not necessarily lame of the *left*, or unlucky, leg, as some annotators hold, but, like Thersites in Homer, Il. 2. 2 ¹ 7, χωλὸs δ' ἔτερον πόδα, lame of one leg, but still swift as the wind). Her hair hangs down before her face, that no one may know her, till she is past; at the back of her head she is bald, that when once she is past, no one may be able to grasp her from behind;—for opportunity once missed never returns. This is expressed by the old proverb, "Fronte capillata, post est occasio calva," given in Dionysius Cato's Distichs, No. 17.

5, 1. *ber toung did walke;*—we now talk of the 'wag' of the ceaseless tongue.

6. *ber one leg;*—her staff was a leg to her, serving instead of the lame leg.

7. Picture of ungovernable fury; reason blinded by passion.

9, 4. *still cald upon;*—the Hag kept on inciting Furor to kill Guyon.

10, 2. *Not so, O Guyon, &c.*;—the prudent Palmer keeps his temper: i. e. the reasonable part of the tempted man cools the passionate.

11, 9. *The bankes are overflowen, &c.*;—this is rather a difficult simile. Spenser means to say that Fury is like a dam which blocks back the stream of moderation and reason and so causes an overflow; till it is removed the stream will not return to its orderly course.

14. The mastery of the strong man over the temptations of passion is finely given. It may be contrasted with the description of Pyrocles (canto vi. st. 41-50), or of Phedon (in this canto, st. 29-33), who give way to fury.

15, 1. *chaines;*—so Horace,
"Hunc frenis, hunc tu compesce catenis,"
speaking of Anger.

17, 1. This tale is taken straight from the story of Ginevra, Ariosto, Orl. Fur. 5, except that it is much shorter, and ends with this great and ungovernable outburst of passion, instead of with chill death by drowning.

6-9. In ed. 1590 the readings of these lines were—
"So one weake wretch, of many weakest *wretch*,
Unweeting, and unware of such mishap,
She brought to mischief through *ber guilful trech*,
Where this same wicked villein did me *wandring ketch*."
In ed. 1596 it was altered, evidently by Spenser himself, in order to keep it closer to Occasion.

20, 1. *Philĕmon;*—so Spenser reads Acrātes and Philotĭme in equal defiance of the proper quantities of the words.

21, 2. *to my spouse;*—the older use of this preposition. We still say 'took to wife.'

9. *that my falser friend;*—'that' is here a demonstr. pron.

22, 8. *the faith which she to me did bynd;*—did plight; note the same metaphor of obligation in Lat. "fidem *ligare.*"

24, 2. *bad boulted all the floure;*—'had distinguished the truth from the falsehood;' taken from the language and usage of millers, who use the word 'to bolt' of the separation of the bran from the flour. Cp. Chaucer, Nonnes Priors Tale, 415:

> "But yit I can not *bult it to the bren,*'

and Milton, Comus, 760:

> "I hate when Vice can *bolt* her arguments."

See Glossary.

25, 9. *That it should not,* &c.;—i.e. lest your beauty should outshine that of your mistress.

26, 1. *she;*—Fortune.

28, 4. *I not discerned;*—an Italian order of words, 'Io non vedeva.'

9. *wound of gealous worme;*—the sting of jealousy.

29, 1. *I bome returning . . . . . I slew her;*—the nom. pronoun is perhaps here repeated to give emphasis.

5. *That after soon;*—'id quod mox . . .'

7. *Demaunded;*—'I was asked for.'

32, 1. *Feare gave her wings;*—Virg. Aen. 8. 224:

> "Pedibus timor addidit alas,"

34, 2. *to affections;*—Latin use of the term = passions, violent emotions of the mind or the sensitive part of man.

5. *Whiles they are weake;*—a rendering of the old 'principiis obsta.'

8. *Gainst fort of reason;*—they besiege the reasonable part of man; a metaphor worked out into a complete allegory in canto ix.

9. *wrath,* &c.;—the Palmer, acting as Chorus, here sums up the matter neatly, and points the due moral.

35. Notice the interwoven construction of this stanza. It is a good specimen of the euphuistic style.

36. 5. *Least worse,* &c.;—"Sin no more lest a worse thing come unto thee."—John 5. 14.

7. *Phedon;*—ed. 1590, Phaon.

37, 2. *A varlet;*—Atin, sc. Strife: thus continuing the personification of the Vices and their attendants. Atin is a name drawn either from the Greek ἄτη, "the goddess of mischief, author of all blind, rash actions and their results." (Liddell and Scott.) As Mr. Gladstone says, Homeric Studies, vol. ii. p. 159, "Vigorous and nimble, she ranges over the whole earth for mischief;"—or more probably from the adj. ἄτος, as in Il. 5. 388, Ἄρης ἄτος πολέμοιο, an adj. which bears the sense of *insatiate,* and is used solely of fighting; for Atin is always drawn as eagerly exciting strife.

39, 1. *in presence came;*—Latin form, 'in praesentiam.'

8. *to purpose;*—either 'in reply to his conversation' (see Gloss. *Purpose*), or = *à propos,* to the point.

9. *not to grow of nought,* &c.;—' ex nihilo fit nil.'

41, 2. *Pyrocles;*—Spenser takes the name, but not the character, from Sidney's Arcadia. The two brethren of Anger are the anger of fire, and the anger as of the sea-waves, πυροκλέης, compounded of πῦρ, fire; and Cymocles, κυμοκλέης, of κῦμα, a billow. The student may compare the description of Pyrocles with Shakespeare's Hotspur, in King Henry IV, Part I.

Ed. 1590, 1596, 'Pyrrhocles;' but it is corrected in the 'Faults Escaped,' ed. 1590.

6. *Acrates;*—is intemperate love of pleasure (ἀκρατής), and

Despight is malicious resentment: personages not found in the classical mythologies. But Spenser always holds himself free to treat allegorical personages as he likes. His meaning being that the various forms of anger spring from the combination of ungoverned desires with malicious and resentful qualities, he expresses it by calling Pyrocles and Cymocles sons of Acrates and Despight.

41, 7. *Phlegeton;*—'the burning one.' Virgil (Aen. 6. 265) makes him both a god and an infernal river.

Jarre;—or quarrel; the ἔρις of Homer (Il. 11. 3, 73) a goddess who rouses men to war, and is the sister of Ares. She is also the " Discordia demens" of Virgil, Aen. 6. 280. She is described by Hesiod, Theog. 225, as daughter of Night.

8. *Herebus and Night;*—these are a classical pair. Erebus and Night (according to Hesiod, Theog. 125) were brother and sister, children of Chaos, and parents of Aether, Day, and Strife (Eris).

This line is one foot too long: possibly the words 'is sonne' ought to be omitted.

9. *Sonne of Aeternitie;*—this is not proper mythological genealogy. Herebus (see above) was son of Chaos. Eternity was not personified by the ancients.

42, 6. *matter make for him;*—give him material for his wrath to work on.

43, 9. *in his jeopardie;*—' his' here = of or from him, a Latin usage.

44, 6. *woe never wants,* &c. ;—' Misfortune is never lacking, when every occasion for it is seized on and employed.' This is also the key to the character given to Occasion by Spenser ;—' rash Occasion ' catches at every possible cause of quarrel.

45, 3. Compare with this scornful speech that of Juno to Venus, Virg. Aen. 4. 93, &c.

5. *thus to fight;*—so ed. 1596 ; ed. 1590 'that did fight.'

9. *abolish so reprochful blot;*—so Tacitus, Hist. 3. 24, has "abolere labem ignominiae."

CANTO V.

Pyrocles sets furiously on Guyon, but is quelled. He humbly begs leave to release Occasion and Furor; who, when set free, attack him and work him great woe. Atin, his varlet, flees, seeking Cymocles, whom he finds sleeping secure in Acrasia's island.

Argument.—The reading of ed. 1590 is here followed. In the ed. 1596 it is altered to

> 'Pyrocles does with Guyon fight,
>   And Furors *chayne unbinds,*
>   *Of whom sore hurt, for his revenge*
>   *Attin Cymocles finds.'*

1. 4. *perturbation;*—Upton notices that Spenser works out the four forms of perturbation given by Cicero (De Fin. 3. 11):

(1) Aegritudo, or sorrowful annoyance and distress, in the history of the bloody-handed babe.

(2) Formido, or fearfulness, in Braggadocchio.

(3) Libido, in the bower of Acrasia. ᒐᴜᵴᵗ

(4) Voluptas, or pleasure, in the idle ' jollity ' of Phaedria.

4, 5. *On his horse neck;*—notice this form of the gen.: ' horse ' = ' horses' or ' horse's,' as we now write it. Our ' horseback' is another instance of this use.

7. *So him, &c.*;—note the construction of this passage. The comma after ' low' ought to be omitted, as ' him dismounted low ' is the object after the verb 'did compel.'

5, 3. *Disleall knight;*—it was clean against the laws of chivalry to strike a horse. Spenser makes Guyon do it by accident, and his antagonist pretends to think it was done purposely. Sidney, in the Arcadia, has a corresponding passage: " Amphialus ... gave a mighty blow ... upon the shoulder of the Forsaken Knight, from whence sliding, it fell upon the neck of his horse, so as horse and man fell to the ground ... But the courteous Amphialus excused himself for having, against his will, killed his horse."

6, 3. *sevenfolded shield;*—the σάκος έπταβόειον of Ajax in Homer, Il. 7. 220, &c. So too Virgil, Aen. 12. 925, describes the shield of Turnus, " clypei extremos *septemplicis* orbes." Sidney, Arcadia, Bk. I, has " sevendouble shield," a less happy adjective.

7, 8. *inly bate;*—to *bite*, of a sword or sharp weapon, common in the Teutonic languages. Notice the strong form of the pret., like *ate*, pret. of ' to eat'; and *wan* of ' to win,' in vi. 41.

8, 7. *burtle round, &c.*;—to skirmish round one's antagonist, pressing him first from one side, then from the other: a part of the fencer's art. Ed. 1596 reads ' hurle,' but it is only a misprint.

9, 3. *Ne plate, ne male;*—see Bk. I. vi. 43, and Glossary.

10, 1. *Like as a lyon, &c.* ; — this is an early example of ' the lion and the unicorn fighting.' According to mediæval belief and early books on natural history, there was a constant feud between them. The unicorn is described by Cardan (who died 1576) as a rare animal, of the stature of a horse, weazel-coloured, with a stag's head, out of whose forehead sprang a single tapering central horn, some three cubits long. He has a short neck, sandy mane, slight and somewhat shaggy legs, and cloven hoofs. This is the creature as he is traditionally depicted as a supporter of the English royal coat of arms. Some held that he perished at the Deluge; others that he was still to be found in Arabia Deserta. It is recorded that in the year 1588 (only two years before the publishing of the Faery Queene) a poor woman found an unicorn's horn on the Suffolk coast. This was however, in all probability, the horn of a narwhal. The unicorn was brought into the English shield by James I. The supporters of the Scottish coat of arms were two unicorns; one of these the King imported with him, displacing Queen Elizabeth's red dragon. I do not know whether the hostility between England and Scotland is represented under the feud of " the lion and the unicorn fighting for the crown." (See Ann. and Mag. of Nat. Hist., Nov.1862.)

imperiall;—king of beasts.

2. *proud rebellious unicorn;*—so it is in Job 39. 9, 10, " Will the unicorn be willing to serve thee, or abide by thy crib ?" &c.

10, 7. *His precious borne,* &c.;—the unicorn's horn was supposed to have marvellous medicinal qualities.

11, 7. *to the saint;*—i. e. to the image of Queen Elizabeth, depicted on his shield.

12, 5. *on his brest,* &c.; — commentators confuse this action with the Biblical putting the 'foot upon the neck of an enemy.' They are quite different processes. The victor's foot was placed on the breast of a vanquished foe, when he bid him yield or die; but the foot upon the neck was symbolical of captivity. The defeated person prostrated himself upon his face, and the victor then set his foot on the back of his neck. For this 'foot on breast,' cp. Hom. 6. 65; Virg. Aen. 10. 495; Tasso, Gier. Lib. 9. 79.

8. *Ne deeme,* &c.;—two very difficult lines. Possibly ' deeme' should be considered equivalent to ' count ' or ' make ': it will then be = ' and do not make an unjust use of thy strength, under the doom (judgment) of fortune.' But this is very unsatisfactory. The meaning is more probably this, ' and do not think it is thy strength that has thus laid me low in dust through the unjust judgment of fortune.' The parenthesis ' maugre her spight' is most probably explained (and so Upton and Jortin take it) by considering ' maugre' as = ' a curse upon.' The ordinary meaning of the word = ' in spite of' makes no sense.

13, 4. *th' equall dye of warre;*—the ξυνὸς Ἄρης of the ancients. Some commentators propose to spoil the allusion by reading ' th' unequall,' for which there is neither authority nor reason.

15, 6. *to be lesser then himselfe;*—this is a classical construction, ἥττων εἶναι ἑαυτοῦ, ' minor seipso,' i. e. to fall below one's own proper moral level in consequence of defeat, and to be ' demoralised' or to be too much elated by victory, and to lose self-control.

9. *Vaine others overthrowes;*—' vaine ' is an adv. here, ' overthrowes' a verb, ' [He] overthrows others [in] vain, who,' &c. The influence of the Italian may be perhaps traced in Spenser's frequent omission of the personal pron.

16, 8. *Of curtesie;*—we now say ' *in* courtesy': ' of' was constantly so used; ' of thy great mercy' = out of, sign of a partitive genitive.

19, 3. *to her use;*—' to her usual way of life and habit.'

7. *garre;*—ed. 1596, ' do.'

20, 3. *his redeemer;*—this use of the word seems to shew that it had not in Spenser's time become specially theological and sacred.

21, 7. *vaine occasions;*—' with foolish causes as they arose.' Church, offended at the repetition of the word in this stanza, suggests ' encheasons' as an amendment, but without authority. Spenser is here ending the part played by Occasion, or opportunity of wrath, and naturally uses the term, though at the risk of being chargeable with tautology, as if he had said, ' Occasion seeks to influence Guyon with vain occasions.'

22, 7. *Stygian lake, ay burning bright;*—the Styx was a river, not a lake: nor did it ' burn bright,' but, on the contrary, was cold and dark; the loathsome river. Still Spenser has the authority of Virgil, Aen. 6. 134: " bis Stygios innare lacus.'

23. The picture of the angry man giving way to and overwhelmed by fury.

26, 2. *warlike prayse;*—Latin use of the word, answering to Virgil's 'laus.' Aen. 1. 465, 'sunt hic etiam sua praemia laudi.'

8. *And hong*, &c.;—cp. with this Hawes' Hist. de Graunde Amour (quoted by Todd):

> " Besides this gyaunt, upon everie tree
> I did se hang many a goodly shilde
> Of noble knightes."

Any insult to the shield was looked on as specially trying to the knightly temper. See Sansfoy's Complaint, Book I. iv. 41:

> " Even stout Sansfoy (O, who can then refrayn?)
> Where shield he beares renversed, the more to heap disdayn."

27, 2. *Acrasia;*—the personification of intemperance, Guyon's real opposite and opponent. Her description is partly drawn from Circe, partly, or chiefly, from the enchantress Alcina in Ariosto. Ariosto also drew from Circe, Hom. Od. 10. 210. The student should also compare Armida's garden and bower of bliss in Tasso, Gier. Lib. c. 16, and the revelry in Milton's Comus. Circe's lovers are all turned into swine, and have no choice or variety; Alcina's victims are made into plants, trees, rivers, as well as beasts; Spenser's Acrasia commutes hers into shapes of various animals, following each the bent of their character. Milton retains the human form, but gives an animal's head to each reveller; as does also Spenser, in describing the troops of evil spirits attacking Alma's castle in canto xi.

29, 8. *myld Zephyrus*, &c.;—Tasso, Gier. Lib. c. 16.

30, 2. *A gentle streame*, &c.;—Niccolo degli Agostini, in his continuation of Orlando Inam., 4. 9, has a passage like this. Cp. also Chaucer's description of the House of Morpheus, Boke of the Duchesse, 160. Also Faery Queene, Bk. I. i. 41.

31, 2. *the stately tree*, &c.;—Spenser means the poplar, which was dedicated to Alcides, i. e. Heracles. The legend runs thus:—Leuce, daughter of. Ocean, was loved by Pluto, god of the realms below. After her death a tree sprang up in Elysium, or on the shores of Acheron, called by her name, with leaves of two colours, dark above, white on the under side; (the Greek name for the poplar is λευκή), Leuce, which means ' white,' whence the Latin ' populus *alba*'). When Heracles returned from his visit to the infernal regions, he came up crowned with a wreath of this tree, signifying by its two-coloured leaves his conquest in the realms of light and darkness. For this cause whoever sacrificed to him wore a poplar-wreath. Cp. Virg. Eclogue 7. 61: " Populus Alcidae gratissima."

The poplar was not specially dedicated to Jove: his proper tree was the oak. In this Spenser is somewhat inaccurate, as was not uncommonly the case with his mythological allusions.

4. *whenas hee Gaynd in Nemea;*—here again Spenser is vague and incorrect. His 1st ed. 1590 read ' Netmus' in the text, ' Nemus' in the ' Faults Escaped.' There are no such places: and Spenser obviously meant throughout ' Nemea,' and was trusting to his memory. Even in ed. 1596 he accents the word wrongly, ' Neméa,' and to remedy this later editors altered the line to ' In Némea gayned goodly victorie,' without authority. In Bk. I. vii. 17 (where he is also speaking of ' great Alcides') he introduces

a place 'Stremona,' which has no existence. He is also incorrect in his statement. Heracles is not said in the legends to have had the poplar dedicated to him after the Nemean victory, nor was the poplar used as the victor's crown. In fact there is no connection between them. Heracles is related to have killed the lion there; and the Nemean games, first instituted by the 'Seven against Thebes,' were revived from that time, and celebrated in honour of Zeus.

36, 2. *Up, up,* &c.;—cp. Tasso, Gier. Lib. 16. 32 :
"Su, su : te il campo e te Goffredo invita
Te la fortuna e la vittoria aspetta."

6. *on senselesse ground;*—a Greek construction = senseless on ground. So also, vii. 34, Spenser has, 'to lack his greedie pray,' = 'the prey he was greedy after.' See also line 9, 'thy help, that here' = the help of thee, who, &c. This is the figure called *enallage* in grammar. So Soph. Antig. 793, νείκος ἀνδρῶν ξύναιμον, 'the kindred strife of heroes,' meaning 'the strife of kindred heroes.'

37, 3. *But he ;*—sc. Atin, who would not waste time in telling Cymocles more of his brother's mishap.

38, 9. *And Atin aie bim pricks,* &c.;—the part of the attendant upon wrath. He is to Cymocles what the Palmer is to Guyon. He is his monitor, but for evil, and is drawn true to life as such. The self-indulgent mind, passing into anger, is constantly stung with this sense of shame at slothfulness, and of wrong done to be avenged. He does not stop to enquire whether the wrong done is really a wrong or not, but rushes on into fury. He goads on his courser, and Atin follows fast behind, ceaselessly urging him on to greater wrath and haste.

CANTO VI.

Cymocles is waylaid by idle Pbaedria, wbo carries bim to ber floating island, where be is lulled to sleep in slotb. Atin can no longer prick bim on, for Pbaedria refused to take bim over in ber boat. Guyon also comes to the Idle Lake, and is also carried to the island, the Palmer likewise being left behind. He is attacked by Cymocles, wbo bas awaked out of bis sleep, and they figbt. Pbaedria separates them, and gladly carries Guyon to the other sbore. There be finds Atin, wbo reviles bim ; and afterwards sees the sad plight of Pyrocles, who is at last cured of bis burns by Arcbimago.

1, 1. *A barder lesson,* &c.;—this is the opposite to Aristotle's dictum, Eth. Nic. 3. 9, 2, χαλεπώτερον τὰ λυπηρὰ ὑπομίνειν ἢ τῶν ἡδονῶν ἀπέχεσθαι. Moralists can balance both, and divide either way. Hitherto Guyon has had to face only painful passions, the θυμικὸν, in his struggles against Furor, Occasion, and Pyrocles. He will now have to resist the seductions of pleasure—idleness, wealth, and immoral desire.

8. *ber ;*—ed. 1596 reads 'their,' an obvious carelessness.

3, 1. *a lady*, &c. ;—Phaedria, representing unmeasured mirth and wanton idleness ; the 'insolens laetitia' of Horace, Odes, 2. 3, 3. The name is derived from the Greek φαιδρός, bright, glittering. The character answers nearly to that βωμολοχία, unseasonable merriment, which Aristotle has described in his Ethics, 4. 8 : " They who exceed in fondness for what makes laughter seem to be βωμολόχοι and low, for they strive to put everything in a ridiculous light; and aim rather at raising a laugh, than at speaking what is seemly, nor do they spare the feelings of their butt;" which answers closely to the description of Phaedria in stanza 6.

4. *that nigh her breth was gone ;*—ed. 1590 reads, ' as merry as Pope Jone ;' but Spenser probably thought the allusion too low, and altered it in 1596.

5, 1. *Eftsoones her shallow ship*, &c. ;—this enchanted boat comes from Ariosto, Orl. Fur. 30. 11 :

> " Per l'acqua il legno va con quella fretta
> Che va per l'aria irondine che varca."

Or perhaps from Tasso, Gier. Lib. 15. 3, 6 :

> " Vider picciola nave, e in poppa quella
> Che guidar gli dovea, fatal donzella," &c.

6. *cut away;*—so in 1590, 1596. But it should be ' cut a way '— ' viam secare.' Cp. I. xi. 18, ' He cutting way,' &c.

8, 3. *of his way;*—of the path he ought to have followed, the object he had set before him.

7. *one sweete drop ;*—Lucr. 4. 1052 :

> " Dulcedinis in cor
> *Stillavit gutta.*"

10, 7. *Ne swelling Neptune, ne loud thundring Jove ;*—i. e. neither tempest nor thunder-storm.

11, 3. *an island waste and voyd ;*—this floating island is natural to romance. The first island of the kind is Delos, which wandered about the Ægean till Zeus chained it to the bottom of the sea, that it might be a safe birth-place for Apollo and Artemis. But it was also a natural phenomenon, not altogether uncommon on lakes whose shores are swampy and covered with vegetation. So Pliny (Epist. 8. 20) describes, as an eye-witness, floating islands on Lake Vadimo, large enough to carry cattle without sinking. They were made of reeds, grass, &c.

waste and voyd ;—not desolate in respect of vegetation, &c., but not inhabited by men.

12, 2. *like a little nest ;* Upton quotes Cicero de Or. 1. 44 : " ut Ithacam illam in asperrimis saxulis, *tanquam nidulum*, affixam sapientissimus vir immortalitati anteponeret."

13. Notice the harmonious chain, giving in itself the sense of music. Cp. c. 12. st. 70.

15. The ' love lay' sung to Cymocles is fashioned upon that which the enchanted voice sang to Rinaldo, Tasso, Gier. Lib. 14. 62. See also the boy's song in the poem called ' Britain's Ida,' printed in Spenser's works, but believed not to be his.

4. *nothing envious nature ;*—a Latin construction : ' nihil invida Natura.'

15, 8. These allusions, taken from St. Matthew, 6. 26–29, have been found fault with, as bringing things sacred into such a connection. But Spenser was desirous of shewing how luxury can distort truths to an immoral purpose.

16, 1. *The lilly, ladie of the flowring field;*—so Queen Katherine (Henry VIII. act 3, sc. 1) says, "Like the lily that once was mistress of the field."

2. *The Flowre-deluce ;*—the Fleur-de-lys or iris.　　.

17, 6. *What bootes it,* &c.;—the same argument is used by Comus to the lady in his speech beginning "O foolishness of men!" l. 706.

7. *in the maine ;*—the commentators observe that this must be understood of river or lake, not of the sea, whose waters are salt!

18, 7. *griesly ;*—so ed. 1596; ed. 1590 reads 'griesy,' as if a sluggish oily water: the 'Idle wave.' But the reading of 1596 is probably the best.

19, 8. *for price or prayers ;*—'aut prece aut pretio.'

20, 3. *obaying to ;*—a common construction at that time. Occurs thrice in Scripture: "his servants ye are *to* whom ye obey." It answers to the Latin usage, 'obedire, servire, alicui.'

9. *timely tides ;*—the tides in their due seasons.

sourse ;—except that 'course' is already appropriated in l. 6, it would have been natural to consider this a misprint. But Spenser perhaps wrote 'source,' to convey the impression that there was neither tide nor stream.

22, 9. *Mee litle needeth ;*—for this construction of the verb 'to need,' see note to Bk. I. x. 38.

23, 3. *Ne wind and weather,* &c.;—a proverbial expression.

8. *Better safe port then be in seas distrest ;*—' a safe port (is) better than (to) be . . .'

24, 6. *The fields did laugh ;*—'Prata rident.' Cp. also Psalm 65. 13.

26, 6. *fairly tempring ;*—i.e. 'keeping due bounds of temperance,' or keeping desire within fair bounds.

9. *time the tide renewd ;*—brought back the right season, or moment. There was no tide, in our sense of the word, in the Idle Lake ; so that the word must be used as meaning 'the right moment.' A. S. *tid.* Is there any allusion to the proverb 'Time and tide wait for no man'?

27, 1. *Cymochles bowre was spent ;*—i.e. the time of his drugged sleep was over.

5. *to steme ;*—to let evaporate his molten heart; let it pass off in steam of idleness.

9. *their ;*—edd. 1590, 1596. But it seems clear that 'there' is the right reading.

28, 7. *Loe, loe* = look, look, used as if it were an imperative. So Sir P. Sidney, in his Arcadia, Bk. ii., has, "Then lo, if Cupid be a god." 'Lo' is, however, only another form of the old interjection 'la': 'the modern *lo*,' says Mr. Earle (Philology of the English Tongue, p. 163), 'represents both the Saxon interjections *la* and *loc ;*' *loc* being our '*Look!*'

29, 2. *importune ;*—ed. 1596 reads, 'importance'—a mere blunder.　　.

3. *to field ;*—to battle-field, i.e. to fight. Notice the affected use of technical terms in this stanza—'haberjeons,' 'dismayld,' 'spelles,' 'entayld,' 'giambeux'—worthy of the Rime of Sir Topas, where Chaucer, making fun of interlarded speech, says, "His jambeux were of quirboily," i.e. his boots were of prepared leather (*cuir bouilli*). Fencers and the like have always affected French terms for their art.

31, 6. *as Titan shone;*—shone like the sun.

32, 5. *Ah well away;*—probably a corruption of the old cry, 'wala wa.'

7. *Wo worth the man;*—simply = 'woe be to the man,' or possibly 'woeful be the man.' 'Worth' is here the A. S. *weorð*, imper. of *weorðan*, to be. See Glossary. These two exclamations, as well as 'Harrow,' which usually goes with 'well away,' have perished out of common speech.

34, 3. *the which doe men in bale to sterve;*—'to do to sterve' = 'to do to die,' i. e. to cause their death. See Gloss. *Sterve*.

5. *Such cruell game, &c.;*—if you fight in your fashion, I cannot fight in mine.

35, 7. *Mars is Cupidoes frend;*—the story is told by Homer, Od. 8. 266.

36, 5. *Such powre have pleasing wordes;*—an allusion to Prov. 15. 1, 'A soft answer turneth away wrath.'

40, 2. *But sober Guyon, &c.;*—the mastery of passion in another form. Guyon resists the irritating assaults of angry railing and abuse.

41, 4. *wan.;*—old strong pret. of 'to win.' We still use another form of it, 'won.' It is here = had won; so in v. 7 can = could.

43, 7. *lent this;*—ed. 1590 reads 'lent but.this his.'

9. *What is thee betyde?*—'What has befallen thee?' 'thee' is a dat.: = 'what is come to thee?' See Gloss. *Betide*.

44, 9. *borne under unhappie starre;*—see notes on ii. 2, and ix. 52.

45, 5. *last death;*—as opposed to the 'dying daily, daily yet revive.'

46, 6. *The waves thereof, &c.;*—a sort of Lacus Asphaltites, or Dead Sea. Cp. Dante's 'la morta gora,' Inferno, c. 8. 31. But Tasso's description, Gier. Lib. 10. 62, comes nearer to Spenser's:—

"Questo è lo stagno in cui nulla di greve
Si getta mai, che giunga insino al basso;
Ma, in guisa pur d'abete o d'orno, leve
L'uom vi sornuota, e 'l duro ferro e 'l sasso."

47, 9. *a goodly arming sword;*—Archimago had somehow purloined *Morddure*, Prince Arthur's enchanted sword, for the use of Braggadocchio: it comes however to other uses. Enchanted weapons, especially swords, are common in romance.

48, 5. *weake hands;*—notice the ellipse of 'are the.'

8. *be needed more;*—in this place the verb 'to need' follows the more usual and modern construction = to require. See Book I. x. 38.

50, 9. *In flaming Phlegethon;*—the burning river of Hades. Spenser probably connects it with the description of the souls carried round in torment, described in the Mythus at the end of Plato's Phaedo; to which dialogue an allusion is also made in vii. 52. Cp. also Book I. v. 33,
'The fiery flood of Phlegeton,
Where as the damned ghostes in torments fry.'

51, 5. *fire too;*—ed. 1590 omits 'too'; and the line is eked out by writing 'fier,' as a dissyllable.

CANTO VII.

Guyon finds Mammon sunning his treasure, and is led by him through many temptations of avarice and ambition: be resists with a stedfast soul; and, after three days underground, returns to daylight, and swoons away.

Argument 2. *Sunning his threasure hore;*—Milton probably had this phrase in his mind when he wrote, Comus 398, "th' unsunned heaps of miser's treasure."

1. *As pilot,* &c.;—in Spenser's day the mariner seems to have sailed chiefly by the stars, applying to his chart ('card') and compass when fog or cloud blotted away the heavens. The fact was that neither chart nor compass were fully understood, or very safe guides; so that sailors found it more prudent to trust chiefly to 'a stedfast starre.' The earlier works on navigation mostly came (as one would expect) from Spain; but towards the end of the sixteenth century, as English and Dutch adventure grew, Englishmen also and Dutchmen turned their attention to the subject. The only 'card' in existence was that known as the 'plane chart,' which was full of inaccuracies, and a most unsafe guide, till Gerard Mercator published an universal map in 1569. This map, however, was not understood, and was believed to be still more dangerous than the old plane chart. Nor was it till 1592, two years after the publication of the Faery Queene, that its value began to be recognised. After that date the principles of navigation improved rapidly, chiefly through the writings of an Englishman, Edward Wright. It is curious to notice how the interest in seafaring shewn by Spaniards and Portuguese languished towards the end of the century, and how the Dutch and English took their place as the chief advancers of navigation.

8. *to them,* &c.;—directs by them.

9. *Winged vessel;*—so Pindar, Ol. 9. 36, ναὸς ὑποπτέρου, and Virg. Aen. 3. 520, 'velorum pandimus *alas*.' Any one who has ever seen a lateen-rigged vessel, sees at once that the metaphor is just.

2, 4. *himself with comfort feedes,* &c.;—not altogether our conception of the true magnanimous hero, to meditate on, and comfort himself with, his own 'vertues and praiseworthie deedes.' But it is quite after the pattern of Aristotle's magnanimous man, whose character to a certain extent enters into that of Sir Guyon. The humility which runs through the morality of Bunyan's Pilgrim's Progress, and forms one of the most beautiful elements in it, is wanting from this part of the Faery Queene.

3, 4. *An uncouth,* &c.;—Mammon, whose description may be drawn from the Aristophanic Plutus, God of Wealth. See Aristoph. Plut. 78. 84. 123. He is called filthy, αὐχμῶν, in miserable plight, μιαρώτατος, ἀθλίως διακείμενος, blind, timorous, δειλότατος. But probably Spenser had Piers Ploughman's Covetyse before his eyes. Passus Quintus de Visione.

> "Thenne com Covetyse,
> I couþe him not discreve
> So hungri and so holewe
> Sire Hervi him loked.

> He was bitel brouwed,
> Wiþ twei blered eiȝen
> And lyk a leþerne pors
> Lukede his chekes."

Chaucer, Rom. of the Rose, l. 202, draws Coveityse,—

> "Ful croked were hir hondis two;"

and Avarice (l. 211),—

> "Ful sade and caytif was she eek
> And also greene as ony leek.
> So yvel hewed was hir colour,
> .   .   .   .
> And thereto she was lene and megre."

Milton also (Par. Lost, 1. 678) has Mammon among his chiefs of Hell, though he conceives him as a very different personage.

9. *fire-spitting;*—T. Warton makes a comical eighteenth-century note on this word, to relieve Spenser from the odium of using the word 'spitting' in its vulgar sense. "*Spett* seems anciently," says he, "to have more simply signified *disperse*, without the low idea which we at present affix to it." Warton could never have seen a smith's forge in full blow, or he might have noticed that 'fire-spitting,' with the 'low idea we at present affix to it,' is the exact word to express the jets of fire, and the sparks spirting out from the heap of coals.

4, 4. *Well yet appeared;*—ed. 1596 reads 'it,' and puts a comma after 'appeared,' so as to seem to make a parenthetical sentence of these three words. The reading is however in all probability another instance of the carelessness of that edition.

5, 4. *Mulciber's devouring element;*—the 'elementum ignis,' whose presiding deity was Mulciber or Vulcan, or Hephaestos. He is called Mulciber, 'the soother,' either as a good omen, to avert or restrain the ravaging force of fire, or because of the power of heat and fire in ripening or in melting.

7, 3. *beapes;*—so ed. 1596: ed. 1590 reads 'hils.'

8, 1. *God of the world,* &c.;—bearing out the antithesis between "God and Mammon" indicated in St. Matthew 6. 24.

9, 1. *Wherefore if me,* &c.;—an allusion to the Temptation on the Mount. Cp. Berni's Orl. Inam. 1. 25. 19, where Orlando is made to refuse the temptations of wealth.

12—13. The student should notice the condensed description of the evils and crimes of wealth in these stanzas, especially in st. 13. The day-dreams of golden shores, so rife at the time, the adventure and rapine, the cruel treatment of innocent natives, and the deterioration of character in Spain and England, arising from the greed of wealth, give point and special meaning to these stanzas. It must be remembered that Spenser lived among the brilliant adventurers of the time.

3. *First got,* &c.;—so Juv. Sat. 14. 303, 304,

> "Tantis parta malis cura maiore metuque
> Servantur. Misera est magni custodia census."

14, 3. *in Caspian sea; . . . on Adrian gulf;*—the Caspian and the Adriatic Sea were famous among the ancients for their storms. Horace's "Dux inquieti turbidus Hadriae" (Od. 3. 3, 5) will occur to every one. Milton,

Par. Lost, 2. 714-716, describes Satan and Death as like two clouds on the Caspian.

14, 6. *sayd;*—the verb has for its direct subject 'Mammon,' not, as Mr. Todd says, an ellipse of 'he.'

15. 2, 3. *captiv'd . . . allowaunce;*—note the accenting of these words, *captiv'd, allowaúnce.*

4. *untroubled;*—Nature left to herself, not stimulated by 'conventional necessities.'

8. *bis;*—notice this singular pron. after 'streames.' The conception is that this is true of each stream.

braunching armes;—either = the tributary rivers, or = the divisions of a river near its mouth, carrying on the forced analogy between the human frame and a river's course from its 'head' downwards. Geography appeals wherever it can to the human figure—that microcosm—for its technical terms: *bead, foot* (of a mountain), *arm* of the sea, *mouth* of river, &c.

16, 6. *like cornfed steed;*—cp. Jer. 5. 8, and Hom. Il. 6. 506.

9. *the measure of her meane;*—the proper limit of her moderation between two extremes. Spenser holds closely to the Aristotelian Moderation.

17, 2. *bis great grandmother;*—Terra mater, the mighty grandmother, or first mother of all. Cp. Milton, Par. Lost, 1. 686,

> " with impious hands
> Rifled the bowels of their mother earth
> For treasures better ·hid."

6. *the matter;*—'materies,' or subject-matter. One of the chief characteristics of the golden age is its entire freedom from gold and its attendant evils. This is an interesting discussion of the two sides of the question as to the happiness of uncivilized man, long before the days of Rousseau's 'savage.'

18, 1. *let be;*—so the Germans say 'lass sein,' 'leave alone.'

4. *Thou that,* &c.;—Mammon's political economy of 'work and pay,' contrasted with the chivalrous notions of 'work and duty.'

19, 2. *I know it well be got;*—this form of the conditional sentence is peculiar; the use of the subj. gives much force and character to the sentence, which is perhaps heightened by the order of words 'well be got' for ' be well, fairly, got.'

4. *unrighteous lot;*—'iniqua sorte,' by unfair trickery or by violence and deceit.

21, 4. *Plutoes griesly rayne;*—' the infernal regions.' This usage of the word 'reign' (regnum) is followed by Gray, Elegy in a Churchyard,—

> " Molests her ancient solitary *reign.*"

5. *Payne;*—not suffering, but Poena, the avenging, punishing deity. This passage is modelled upon the fine lines in Virg. Aen. 6. 273. We have here Strife, answering to Virgil's ' discordia demens'; Feare, to Virgil's Metus; and Celeno to his Harpies. Virgil has nothing so fine as Spenser's Horror; and in point of terse description, this passage is unrivalled. Jealousy gnawing his lips, Fear flying to and fro in vain search of a safe refuge, Horror beating his iron wings, are splendid conceptions.

23, 6. *sad Celeno;*—the Harpy mentioned in Virg. Aen. 3. 245, which passage Spenser had in mind,

"Una in praecelsa consedit rupe Celaeno,
   Infelix vates, rumpitque hanc pectore vocem."
The Harpies are placed by Dante in his Inferno, c. 13. 1. 10. They had
faces and breasts of women, but wings and crooked birds' talons; they are
described as foul, ill-omened monsters.

24, 6. *gaped wide;*—was ever open; so Virg. Aen. 6. 127; Milton, Par.
Lost, 2. 884.

7. *be them parted ought;*—the door of the House of Riches adjoins
Hell-gate without any division between, and Sleep has his house on the other
side. The forms of Care, and Force, and Fraud are round the door of Riches,
just as Payne, Strife, &c., were before that of Pluto's realm. Hell is drawn
as a sort of unholy mean between the cares and toils of wealth on the one
side, and sloth and idleness upon the other.

25, 7. *next to death,* &c.;—cp. Hom. Il. 14. 231, ἔνθ' Ὕπνῳ ξύμβλητο
κασιγνήτῳ θανάτοιο, Virg. Aen. 6. 278, "Consanguineus Leti Sopor."

26, 7. *An ugly feend;*—the allegorical form of the penalty which awaits
the man who gives way to covetousness. This is expressed in various ways
in old legends, as, for example, in that of the shooting figure in the tale of
Pope Sylvester and the Enchanted Chamber, quoted by T. Warton in his
notes on this canto.

27, 3. *likt him best;*—notice this neuter usage, very common in sixteenth-
century English. 'To like,' as an impers., is now obsolete; a real loss to
the language.

28, 7. *Arachne;*—the spider; alluding to the cobwebs so common in
vaults.

29, 6. *a faint shadow of uncertain light;*—a fine conception, drawn from
Tasso, Gier. Lib. 13. 2,

          "Luce incerta e scolorita e mesta;"
or 14. 37,

          "Debile e incerta luce ivi si scerne,
             Qual, tra' boschi, di Cintia ancor non piena."
Cp. also Virg. Aen. 6. 268.

31, 3. *to them opened of his own accord;*—Acts 12. 20; Milton, Par.
Lost, 5. 254.

33, 8. These reflections on the superiority of the knight to wealth (also
of the 'gentleman' to the merchant and trader) are quite in the highest style
of the time. It must not be forgotten that these were the days in which,
through their mines &c., the Spaniards were essentially the 'purse-proud'
race, and duly hated by the English. Possibly, too, a little scorn for the
burghers of Holland, who had but lately shewn so little sense of Lord Leicester's splendour and blood, may have been working in Spenser's mind. Upton
quotes the saying of Cyrus to Croesus. See Plut. Apophthegmata.

34, 6. *More light,* &c.;—so Ariosto, Orl. Fur. 2. 50,—

          "Come casca dal ciel falcon maniero
             Che levar veggia l'anitra o 'l colombo."

35, 4. These forges are possibly taken from the Cyclopean furnaces in
Virg. Aen. 8. 418.

36, 1. *great bellows;*—Hom. Il. 18. 468; Virg. Aen. 8. 449.

37, 8. *he would retire ;*—Spenser often uses the imperf. ' would do ' for the pluperf. ' would have done.'

39, 3. *I need, . . . needeth me ;*—note the two uses of the verb ' to need,' and see note on Bk. I. x. 38.

41, 1. *Disdayne ;*—it is not clear what this personified quality does here, unless Spenser means to indicate the pride which accompanied the acquisition of wealth. Disdain is far better introduced in Bk. VI. vii.

6. *the Titans race ;*—the Titans were mythological giants, sons and daughters of Uranus and Gaia (Heaven and Earth) who usurped their father's dominion, and were afterwards quelled and banished to Tartarus by Zeus.

44, 2. *A route, &c. ;*—this is from the Apocalypse, 17. 3.

46, 2. *a great gold chaine ;*—this is from the σειρὴ χρυσείη, the golden chain let down from heaven to earth, at which the gods were to pull in order to see whether they were strong enough to drag Zeus out of heaven. Hom. Il. 8. 19. Applied however in a different sense, as the chain by which men strive to rise, the chain of ambition.

47, 1. *Some thought ;*—Spenser's reminiscences of court life, at least of the courtiers round the queen, were not altogether pleasing, as we see from his lines in ' Mother Hubberds Tale,' 877 sqq., where he describes the shifts and tricks of Renard (Reynold), and the way in which poor honest suitors are cozened and left to wait :—

> ' So pitifull a thing is suters state,
> Most miserable man, whom wicked fate
> Hath brought to court, to sue for had ywist,
> That few have found, and manie one hath mist.
> Full little knowest thou that hast not tride
> What hell it is, in suing long to bide :
> To loose good days, that might be better spent,' &c.

The whole passage is worth study, but too long for quotation.

49. *Philotime ;*—Φιλοτιμή, love of honour. Spenser here again takes no heed to the quantity of the penult., making it Philotime. Ambition

6. *From whence the gods ;*—this envy of the gods, which thrust Ambition out of heaven, is not found in classical mythologies.

50, 9. *causelesse ;*—here an adv. = ' without good cause.'

51, 4. *a gardin ;*—the garden of Proserpine, decked with flowers of Spenser's own just fancy. The grove of Persephone is mentioned in the Odyssey, 10. 509, as being on the outer borders of the earth, at the entrance to the lower world. Claudian, Rapt. Proserp. 2, 285, describes this garden as beautiful, Elysian.

8. *direfull deadly blacke ;*—see Dante, Inf. c. 13.

52, 1. *cypresse ;*—dedicated to death and funeral. See note on Book I 1. 8.

2. *trees of bitter gall ;*—Gerard's Herbal, iii. ch. 37, enumerates many gall-trees, i. e. trees that (like the oak, &c.) bear galls, astringent, bitter.

beben sad ;—the ebony-tree. This is the Ethiopian variety, which was black. Its juice was thought to be poisonous.

black bellebore ;—described in Gerard's Herbal, ii. ch. 377 ; a herb used for the curing of madness by the ancients. It had white and black varieties.

4. *Cold coloquintida;*—the colocynth, κολόκυνθις, or bitter gourd. Gerard's Herbal, ii. 343. The epithet ' cold' has puzzled commentators, as the plant grows in a hot climate. They have, however, discovered a German gourd, which seems to satisfy them. 'Cold' probably refers simply to the coldness of the fruit itself. A pumpkin always feels cold to the touch.

tetra mad;—this seems to be ' tetrum solanum' or deadly nightshade : ' mad' because supposed to cause madness.

5. *Mortall samnitis;*—no such plant can be found, says Upton, in any old Herbal. Nor have I found any such in the old books I have looked through. Upton suggests with probability that Spenser, who was not very accurate on such points, confused *samnite* with *sabine*, and meant the 'arbor sabina,' or savine, which is said in the Great Herball to be "a herbe in maner of a tre, and is comynly had in religious cloysters, and hath leves like ewe," a dark gloomy plant, with sundry deadly qualities.

cicuta bad;—hemlock, the poison with which Athens 'made to dy wise Socrates,' after his trial for 'corrupting youth, and dishonouring the gods.' During the night in which he drank the poison, he conversed on the immortality of the soul with his friends, as is set forth at length in Plato's Phaedo. But Spenser falls into error when he tells of his pouring out his 'last philosophy to the fair Critias.' Critias was one of the thirty tyrants, and so far from being at that time a disciple of Socrates, had been instrumental in setting public opinion against the philosopher, had been amongst the most violent of the Thirty, and had perished in battle full five years before the death of Socrates. The truth is that Spenser has mixed up Socrates with Theramenes, who perished in B.C. 404 in the same way. He owed his death entirely to Critias (who is said to have been formerly his friend), and when he drank off his hemlock-cup, he dashed the last drops on the ground, as though he were playing the game of cottabus,* saying, "I drink this to the health of lovely Critias." See Xen. Hell. II. 3. § 56. But neither do the last minutes of Socrates nor those of Theramenes correspond in reality with Spenser's lines.

54, 1. *golden apples;*—the garden of the Hesperides, the westernmost nymphs, could not have been far (in the mythological geography) from the district in which Homer places Proserpine's gardens ; see above, note on st. 51. Spenser makes the golden apple-tree of the Hesperides an off-shoot from this of Proserpine.

Hercules . . . Got from great Atlas daughters;—the eleventh of the labours of Heracles. Mythology shifted the golden apples from place to place : Heracles found them on mount Atlas; they were also placed near Cyrene, or in the islands off the western coast of Africa ; they were also put in the northern land of the Hyperboreans, guarded by the maidens, who, according to one account, were the daughters (as Spenser has it) of Atlas and Hesperis.

8. *And those, with which th' Euboean young man wan Swift Atalanta;*—Atalante, daughter of Jasus of Arcadia, was swiftest of mortals; she, desiring

---

* The Athenian gallants used to throw out the last drops of their beakers of wine, and drew auguries in love from the plash with which they fell.

to be ever virgin, made it the sole condition of marriage that her suitor should run a race with her; if he was beaten, he must die; if he outstripped her, he should have her to wife. Meilanion, one of her suitors (who is no-where else described as ' th' Euboean young man '), had received from Aphro-dite three golden apples; as he ran, and she began to distance him, he threw the apples one by one in front of her. She could not resist the temptation, but stayed thrice to pick them up; meanwhile Meilanion outran her, and won the race and a wife. The tale is told at length in Ovid, Metam. 10. 560 sqq., where the names are different. The fortunate suitor is there Hip-pomenes. Bacon is very fond of this tale, and alludes frequently to it : Advancement of Learning, I. II; Nov. Org. I. 70; Interpretation of Nature, cap. I; Filum Lab. § 5. He works it out as an allegory in the Wisdom of the Ancients, 25.

55, 2. *Acontius ;*—this is the tale of Acontius and Cydippe, told by Ari-staenetus, I. 10, and by Ovid, Heroides, 20, 21. Acontius gathered a κυδώ-νιον μῆλον (a citron or orange) in the garden of Venus, and having written on the rind the words νὴ τὴν Ἄρτεμιν Ἀκοντίῳ γαμοῦμαι, 'By Artemis, I will marry Acontius,'* threw it in her way. She took it in her hand, read out the inscription, and threw it from her. But Artemis heard the vow, and brought about the marriage.

4. *that famous golden apple ;*—the apple of discord. The story runs that Eris (strife or discord), (not ' false Ate,'—Spenser is again incorrect), being excluded from the nuptials of Peleus and Thetis, appeared, unasked, and threw in the midst a golden apple inscribed τῇ καλλίστῃ, 'To the fairest.' Forthwith Here, Aphrodite, and Athena began to strive for the palm of beauty : and to quiet them, and get them out of the way of the nuptials, Zeus ordered Hermes to take them to the shepherd Paris on mount Ida. Hence Spenser calls them ' the Idaean ladies.' Imperious Here, to win his vote, promised him sovereignty and wealth; Athena, glory and renown of war; fairest Aphrodite (Venus) offered him Helen as his wife. He adjudged the prize to Aphrodite, got Helen, whence sprang the Trojan war, 'which many noble Greekes and Trojans made to bleed.'

56, 8. *river of Cocytus ;*—Spenser somewhat enlarges upon this river. The old writers do not describe the souls as wallowing and wailing in it, as a penalty. Cp. Milton, Par. Lost, 2. 579.

57, 8. *One cursed creature ;*—Tantalus, whose punishment has become a proverb with us, as is seen by our verb ' to *tantalize.*' According to one account, he cut up his son Pelops, boiled him, and set him before the gods as a banquet (probably a traditional account of human sacrifice). Zeus, enraged at this, condemned him to stand up to his neck in a lake, whose waters he could never drink, with goodly fruit-branches just beyond his reach, for ever. Spenser puts it too strongly when he writes, ' Of whom high Jove *wont* whylome feasted bee.' One account makes him a guest at the table of Zeus; where his high honour (as has occurred at other tables of the great) turned his head—ἀλλὰ γὰρ καταπέψαι μέγαν ὄλβον οὐκ ἐδυνάσθη,

---

* An ambiguous oath—it might mean, ' By the hunter-goddess, I will only marry my dart,' i. e. I will continue unmarried.

Pind. Ol. 1. 87—and he prated of the secrets of the other world: whereupon Zeus punished him. His punishment is finely described by Homer, Od. 11. 581.

8. *sterved with hunger;*—note the limitation, shewing the passage of the word from its sense in Chaucer's time to the modern use. See Glossary, *Sterve.*

61, 2. *another wretch;*—Pontius Pilate. One legend has condemned him to dwell for ever on Mont Pilate, near Lucerne, in Switzerland, in a gloomy lake called the "Infernal Lake," whence "a form is often seen to emerge from the gloomy waters, and to go through the action of one washing his hands."

62, 8, 9. *The whiles . . . the whiles;*—shews the original use of 'whilst,' 'whiles,' 'while;' i. e. 'at one time,' 'at another time.'

64. 9. *did beguile the guyler of his prey;*—'cheated the tempter of his prey.'

[handwritten marginalia]

CANTO VIII.

The Palmer finds Guyon, lying in a swoon, and guarded by an Angel. While he tries to restore him, Pyrocles and Cymocles come up, guided by Archimago. Shamelessly they begin to spoil the helpless Knight; but Prince Arthur comes, and, after a stiff combat, slays them both. Guyon awakes, and does homage to the Prince; but Archimago and Atin flee away dismayed.

1, 2. This is perhaps the best-known and most beautiful passage in the Faery Queene. Mr. Keble quotes the second stanza in his ed. of Hooker's Works, E. P. 1. 4. 1, on the passage, "Desire to resemble him in goodness maketh them unweariable and even unsatiable in their longing to do by all means all manner good unto all the creatures of God, but especially unto the children of men."

1, 9. *to serve to wicked men;*—Latinism, 'servire alicui.'

2, 5. *to ayd us militant;*—'militant' here probably is an epithet of the angels, who 'for us fight.'

3, 7. *He heard a voyce;*—that of the ministering spirit watching over Sir Guyon.

5, 4. *above his equall peares;*—beyond the beauty of his equals in rank and age.

6. *Like Phoebus face, &c.;*—so Tasso's account of the angel Gabriel, Gier. Lib. 1. 13:

> "Tra giovane e fanciullo età confine
> Prese; ed ornò di raggi il biondo crine.
>   Ali bianche vestì, ch'han d'or le cime,
> Infaticabilmente agili e preste:
> Fende i venti e le nubi" . . . .

See also Milton, Par. Lost, 5. 276–285.

6, 1. *Like as Cupido on Idaean hill;*—The Idaeus Mons was a range in Phrygia, of very considerable extent. The only connection between it and Cupid is the tale of Paris, and the award of the apple of discord to Aphrodite.

6. *his goodly sisters, Graces three;*—fault is here again found with Spenser for inventing mythological genealogies at will. But it is evident that if the Graces were not Cupid's sisters, they ought to have been so: and, besides, while, according to the Odyssey, Hephaestos was the husband of Aphrodite, according to the Iliad he was the husband of Charis (or of Aglaia, one of the Charites). So that the relation was regarded as close, though the critics are right in saying that the Graces were not, classically speaking, the sisters of Cupid. Their names were Euphrosyne, Aglaia, Thalia, and they were counted to be the daughters of Zeus.

8, 6. *Against his foe and mine;*—violence and excess are foes to the Angels as well as to men; the Angel fulfils this promise by sending Prince Arthur at the last moment to succour the Palmer and save the Knight from spoliation. Thus the tale moves equably on.

9, 2. *his slow eyes;*—the Palmer is always drawn as a slow-moving prudence.

5. *his charge behight;*—'behight' is a part. agreeing with 'his charge.'

10, 9. *them combatted;*—the verb 'to combat' with an objective case is now usually confined to arguments, &c.—'to combat a proposition, a conclusion, a statement;' not a person. We prefer 'to combat *with* a person.'

12, 2. *foule bespake;*—spake foully to him: this form of the adv. 'foul,' for 'foully,' is much less common now than it was in Spenser's day. We retain it in 'right' as well as 'rightly,' 'bright' and 'brightly'; but there is a tendency (wrongly) to think it a vulgarism.

6, 7. *it selfe . . . his;*—note the absence still of the mongrel genitive 'its.' 'Its' or 'it's' seems first to have appeared in print in 1598, in Florio's 'A Worlde of Wordes,'—"for *its* owne sake." Shakespeare shews well the state of transition; he uses 'it' (= our present 'its') thirteen times, and 'it's' ten times. See article on *It* in Wright's Bible Word Book.

7. *crest with knightly stile;*—put upon his cowardly helmet's crest the stile or cognisance of a knight.

13, 7. *sleeping fame;*—i.e. fame of one that sleeps: a Greek construction. See above, note on v. 36, on the words 'on senselesse ground.'

14, 7. *The worth of all men,* &c.;—this is a travesty on Solon's famous dictum about 'seeing the end' before you decide as to a man's happiness.

16, 2. *For knighthoods love;*—for the love you have to your condition as knights. It was clean contrary to the laws of chivalry to despoil the body of a dead knight, though you might take his shield as sign of victory.

17, 5. *An armed knight;*—Prince Arthur, who appears in each Book to shew his perfect knighthood by succouring the good and crushing the evil. His entry here is very skilfully managed. He comes in for a very critical adventure, and one worthy of his dignity, while he still leaves to Sir Guyon the real completion of the task round which the book centres, the taming of Acrasia. Similarly, in Bk. I., he delivers St. George from prison, and slays the giant Pride; but he leaves the Red Cross Knight to fight the dragon, and in his turn to fulfil the main purpose of the book, the triumph of truth.

7. *coverd shield;*—the shield which, uncovered, could dazzle and confound all foes by its own virtue. See Bk. I. vii. 33. The 'heben spear' is also mentioned in st. 37.

19, 3. *that afford;*—to give him that sword; i.e. Morddure, Prince Arthur's enchanted sword, whose other name, in the legends, is Excalibur or Caliburn. See Tennyson's Morte d'Arthur. Enchanted swords are common in romance. Even in classical times we have the Styx-dipped sword of Turnus, and that of Hannibal (Sil. Ital. 1. 429-432), which old Temisus had made in an enchanted fire. Such were 'Crocea Mors,' Caesar's fabled sword, and Belisarda, Ruggiero's weapon (Berni, Orl. Innam. 2. 17. 13). Orlando's is called Durenda (Ariosto, Orl. Fur. 41. 83). Chaucer tells us of the sword sent to Cambuscan. Cervantes hits the same point when he makes Don Quixote tell Sancho that he must get himself such a weapon. Such swords would wound even enchanters, and would refuse to harm their own master.

20, 2. *Merlin;*—in the history of Prince Arthur Merlin watches over the Prince, and, by means of his enchantments, arms him with miraculous weapons.

5. *The metall,* &c.;—this recipe for the forging of an enchanted sword is chiefly classical. *Medaewart* is not the mongrel *medica* (sainfoin), and *wart,* but *mede wart, meadow*-plant. This mixing of the metal with Medaewart is the first step; the second is that it was wrought in Aetna's flames, i.e. at Vulcan's forge, under the roots of Aetna, at which Aeneas' arms are forged at his mother's request. The last step is the dipping seven times in Styx, even as the sword of Turnus was dipped (Virg. Aen. 12. 91).

21, 6. *Morddure;*—'the hard-biter.' Fr. *mordre, dur.*

24, 3. *fatall date;*—see note on Bk. I. ix. 45.

3, 4. *Or . . . Or;*—now more usually 'whether . . . or,' or omitting whether, 'did he, or did he not.'

25, 5. *whose honourable sight;*—either 'whose honourable appearance,' or a classical construction = 'the sight of whom, an honourable man,' as opposed to the two caitiffs.

26, 5. *oddes,* &c.;—when in one's favour, of course.

27, 7. *Not to debate;*—some such ellipsis as '[I do] not [come, or intend] to fight.' I do not intend to make a fighting ground of a challenge of your right to do this. We will waive that point, and not consider what your 'just wrongs' are.

28, 4. *from to wreake;*—the infin. with prep. 'from,' corresponding to the phrase '*for* to do.' See note on xii. 26.

29, 3. *nephewes sonne;*—i.e. great-grandson. A rendering of the phrase in the second commandment, "visiting the iniquity of the fathers upon the children, unto the third and fourth generation of them that hate me." Exod. 20. 5.

30, 2. These villain phrases of Pyrocles contrast strongly with and heighten the effect of Prince Arthur's gentle breeding.

4. *Termagaunt;*—this oath occurs again in Bk. VI. vii. 47, 'Oftentimes by Termagant and Mahound swore.' In the thirty-third stanza we find Cymocles swearing by Mahoune. It is said that the Christians in the Middle Ages thought (among endless misconceptions) that Termagaunt was a Saracenic deity. The origin of the term is unknown. 'Ter magnus,' a

Latin Trismegistus, is suggested, but is mere conjecture. Others propose the A. S. *tyr*, used as a prefix, denoting 'very,' 'exceedingly,' and *mœgan, main* strength, and so make it = the very powerful one. The name *Trivigant* seems the most probable origin of the word. It is possible that the latter part of the word, *-magaunt*, may conceal the name of *Mabound*, or Mahomet; if so, it is simply the invocation of the Prophet. The word has now come to mean only a scolding woman. *Curmudgeon* is probably the same word; the male grumbler, answering to the female shrew. The subject is discussed at greater length in the Glossary, *Termagaunt.*

31, 7. *The law of armes;*—another of the many examples of the language of chivalry in the sixteenth century.

35, 3. *his ground to traverse wide;*—i. e. to shift his ground repeatedly, so as to escape their onslaughts, which he was not sufficiently armed to resist.

9. *Them;*—i. e. the 'double battry,' here taken as though it were a plural, and = 'two battering rams.'

her bulwarke;—note how many substantives still have genders—so 'tower' here is feminine, influenced by Lat. *turris* or Fr. *tour*, both of which are feminine.

37, 9. *Loe where the dreadfull Death,* &c.;—possibly suggested, as some have thought, by the pictures in the Dances of Death, in which the figure of Death sometimes is drawn standing behind his victim.

39, 9. *him forst his foot revoke;*—Latin phrase, 'revocare pedem.'

40, 4. *so wisely as he ought;*—'he' is the right hand. Ed. 1590 reads 'so well as he it ought,' but Spenser seems to have thought the phrase awkward.

41, 5. *twise so many fold;*—simply = twice so many (as to Pyrocles).

42, 1. *As salvage bull;*—this illustration is drawn from the national bull-baitings. The opening of it is like the opening of a passage in Ariosto, Orl. Fur. 11. 42, " Come toro selvatico, ch'al corno," &c.

44, 8. *bit no more;*—ed. 1590 reads ' bit not thore,' where ' thore' must be = thorow, *through.*

46, 9. *lenger day;*—we say ' a day longer.'

47, 9. *Tho when this breathlesse woxe, that,* &c.; —' this' is Pyrocles, ' that,' Prince Arthur.

48, 8. *prince Arthur;*—edd. 1590, 1596 read 'Sir Guyon,' which is an obvious oversight. A cotemporary marginal MS. note in ed. 1590 corrects to ' Prince Arthur,' and all the later editions have accepted the correction.

49, 3. *the dint deceiv'd;*—i. e. the blow deceived him, by failing to make the cut it ought to have made.

51, 1. *great mind;*—magnanimity—the special quality of heroes, and, above all, of Spenser's Arthur the ' magnificent.'

5. *thy dismall day;*—thy day of evil fate. So Shakespeare, Macbeth, 3. 5, couples *dismal* with fatal :

> " This night I 'll spend
> Unto a *dismall* and a fatal end."

See Gloss. *Dismall.*

53, 2. *her senceless foe;*—' her senseless-making foe,' the swoon.

54, 6. *to discourse the whole debate;*—' to tell him the whole battle.'

55, 4. *patrone of bis life;*—the Latin 'vitae patronus.'

56, 1. *the Infant;*—Prince Arthur is again so called in Bk. VI. viii. 25. "In our early poetry applied to the son of a king."—Richardson. But he gives no instance of this except from Spenser. It is most probable that Spenser adopted the term from the 'Infant of Spain'—a title which must have been familiar in his day.

what need;—note the ellipsis here.

6. *I have done my dew in place;*—'have done what was my duty in this place,' or, 'as I found it to my hand.' The English conception of Duty as the ruling principle of a man's acts. (So end the violent passions. They have made a long struggle for mastery, but are now finally brought under. Τὸ λυπηρὸν is conquered ; Temperance has still to achieve the harder victory—over τὸ ἡδὺ, the seductions of pleasure.

CANTO IX.

Prince Arthur and Sir Guyon go on their way till nightfall, when they espy the House of Temperance, abode of Alma, sore bested by many villains, who also fall on the Knights, but are scattered. Alma opens her gates to them, and shews them all the marvels of the place.

Argument 1, 4. *flight;*—ed. 1596 reads 'fight.'

This Canto contains a special allegory within the main one. It shadows out, with many quaint fancies, the soul (*Alma, anima*) dwelling in the body (the House of Temperance). Body and soul are assaulted by many foes, who strive to occupy the senses, and so to get footing within, and to lead captive the soul. (The subject became a favourite one with religious writers, and others. Fletcher's Purple Island is an allegorical poem on man; Bunyan's Mansoul is a spiritualised, or perhaps rather a Puritanised, form of the struggle here pourtrayed.) The enemies here drawn are moral (according to Spenser's general conception of this Book): in Bunyan they are spiritual. The soul displays her dwelling-place to her visitors. The frame of it, described in stanzas 21-32, gives us the 'dwelling of clay' (st. 21), the mystical harmonies of body and soul (st. 22), the mouth (st. 23), the lips (st. 24), the tongue (st. 25), the teeth (st. 26), then eating and appetite (st. 27, 28), then the stomach, lungs, digestion, &c. (st. 29-32). After that come various moral qualities, seated in the breast (st. 33-43), especially Prays-desire, or love of approbation (st. 36-39), and Modesty (st. 40-43). Then the mental qualities. The head, their seat, is first described, with the hair and eyes (st. 45, 46). Lastly are pourtrayed the three dwellers in the brain, Imagination (st. 49-52), Judgment (st. 53), and Memory (st. 54-58). 1. The subject is formally introduced in the first stanza.

1, 9. *in this place;*—i.e. in Book II, and especially in Canto viii, we have 'both one and other' in the dignity and chivalric purity of Arthur and Guyon, and in the ungoverned baseness of Pyrocles and Cymocles.

2, 9. *the substance dead ;*—i. e. it is only a picture of the living lady.

3–5. The praises of Queen Elizabeth ; they run through the usual scale, but none the less express the genuine feeling of the time. Men were willing to make of her a kind of Protestant Madonna, and to dedicate themselves to her service ; that service being also felt to be the service of truth and liberty.

6, 6. *mongst knights of Maydenhed ;*—the Order of the Garter may here be signified ; but Spenser probably only meant that all who entered the Queen's service became champions of her purity.

9. *Artbegall ;*—the hero of Book V, 'the legend of Artegall or of Justice.' Under his person is probably intended Arthur, Lord Grey of Wilton, Lord Deputy of Ireland, Spenser's honoured patron.

Sophy ;—would doubtless have been the hero of one of the later unwritten books. We may conjecture from the name that the book would have treated of the struggle between Wisdom (σοφία) and Folly.

7, 1. *Certes,* &c. ;—there are two movements throughout the Faery Queene : (1) that of the several knights, the servants of the Queen, fulfilling each his own task of resisting some force of malignant evil ; and (2) that of Prince Arthur, who is gradually and very skilfully displayed before us, as the Briton Prince in search for Gloriana, whom he had seen in a vision only. This latter movement forms the under-current, but was doubtless designed to become more and more clear as the action of the poem proceeded.

5. *Now hath the sunne with his lamp-burning light*
    Walkt round about the world ;—

Ed. 1590 reads
        ' Seven times the sunne with his lamp-burning light
        Hath walkte about the world ;'
shewing that Spenser at first meant to describe Prince Arthur as having already spent seven years in his quest of the Faery Queene ; but that on second thoughts he considered that too long a space, and altered it to. *one* year.

8, 1. *Fortune, the foe,* &c. ;—cp. Seneca, Herc. Fur. 523 : " O Fortuna, viris invida fortibus."—Upton. There is probably an allusion to the popular old ballad of " Fortune, my foe," of which the first verse has been preserved by Malone, beginning
        " Fortune, my foe, why dost thou frown on me,
        And will my fortune never better be ? "

9, 1. *weete ;*—edd. 1590, 1596 read ' wote,' but the cotemporary marginal corrector of ed. 1590 writes ' weete,' which is required by the rhyme.

13, 2. *A thousand villeins ;*—these are the evil desires, vices, temptations, which beset man's moral nature. There is also a bye allusion to the outbreaks of the ' villenage,' jacquerie, &c., who with rude assault, and weapons of the field, attacked the feudal castles ; possibly also a slight allusion to the wild Irish, of whom Spenser was presently to have such sad experiences. As, in Spenser's mind, the castle and its lord represented knowledge, virtue, civilisation, the part of the gentleman ; so the rude clown and serfs represented ignorance, brutality, the ungentle character. We must not forget that Spenser despised the ' raskall rout,' and had no sympathy for any but the gentleman-class.

7. *staves in fier warmed ;*—cp. Stat. Theb. 4. 64:
> " pars robora flammis
> Indurata diu."

15, 3. *their cruell capitaine;*—Maleger, afterwards described in c. xi.
20–22. He is the incarnation of evil and malignant passions, lord of all
temptations.

5. *overrun to tread them, &c.* ;—a Latin use, " superatos ad terram
dejicere."

6. *bright-burning blade ;*—the metaphor is the same as that of the
substantive ' brand,' because a sword flashes like a blazing torch.

16, 1. *a swarm of gnats ;*—cp. Hom. Il. 2. 469 :
> ἠΰτε μυιάων ἀδινάων ἔθνεα πολλά,
> αἵ τε κατὰ σταθμὸν ποιμνήϊον ἠλάσκουσι
> ὥρῃ ἐν εἰαρινῇ . . .

and 'their *clustring* army' from Il. 2. 89 :
> βοτρυδὸν δὲ πέτονται.

2. *the fennes of Allan ;*—an Irish experience of the poet. The " Bog
of Allen" is the general name for a set of turbaries, spread over a wide surface, across the centre of the country, from Wicklow Head to Galway, and
from Howth Head to Sligo, all on the east bank of the Shannon.

17, 9. *as befell ;*—' as was proper and seemly,' answering to the German
phrase, " Wie befohlen ist."

19, 5. *two faire damsels ;*—the commentators suggest Plato's ἐπιθυμητικὴ
and θυμητικὴ, under proper governance. But this is doubtful.

21, 5. *of thing like, &c.* ;—the ' clay' of which man is made. Gen. 2. 7,
" The Lord God formed man of the dust of the ground."

that Aegyptian slime ;—here Spenser wrote Aegyptian for Assyrian.
Herodotus speaks of the bitumen or ' slime' found in the Cissian territory,
and of that used for the walls of Babylon (Hdt. 1. 179).

6. *Whereof King Nine, &c.* ;—Ninus, the eponymic and mythical
founder of Nineveh, is nowhere spoken of as being the builder of ' Babell
towre,' unless he be regarded as the same with Nimrod, the Scriptural founder
of Babylon.

22, 1. *The frame thereof, &c.* ;—this quasi-Platonic passage has much
exercised the ingenuity of expounders. Sir Kenelm Digby made it the subject of a long letter addressed—it is a curious illustration of the age—to a
sea-captain, " To Sir E. Esterling (or Stradling), aboard his ship."
He holds that the circle is man's soul ; the triangle, his body ; the quadrate,
the four principal ' humours' of man's body, viz. choler, blood, phlegm,
melancholy ; the seven, the seven planets ; the nine, the nine orders of
angels, which have to do with man's soul.

There are those who less eruditely imagine the circle to be man's head ;
the triangle, to be formed by his legs and the ground ; the square, " 'twixt
them both," to be the trunk of the body, of a rough oblong form. But this
gives no explanation of the three last lines of the stanza.

The true explanation seems to be that (1) the circle is (as Sir Kenelm
says) the soul, the most perfect figure, and, according to Pythagorean
language, of the masculine gender ; (2) the triangle, also, is the body, the
least perfect figure, as including least amount of space, and so fulfilling worst

the special function of a figure; and also feminine by reason of its feeble-
ness and inferiority. (3) But the quadrate, betwixt them both, is the
ancient τετράκτυs or fountain of perpetual nature: a sacred quaternion, embracing all the members, elements, powers, and energies of man, as Hierocles
says, ἁπλῶς τὰ ὄντα πάντα ἡ τέτρας ἀνεδήσατο. (Hierocl. p. 169. Cp. also
Cic. de Nat. Deor. 2, 33.) In the proportion by 'seven and nine' (4) 'seven'
relates to the seven planets, whose influences on man's life and nature are
mysteriously great: see the treatment of the subject in the first book of the
Astronomica of Manilius. The subject is also handled in the same way in
Cicero's Somnium Scipionis (from the sixth book of his De Republica. Ma-
crob. 1. 6.) It forms a usual part of the speculations of the Neo-Platonists
as to the relations between mind and matter. (5) 'Nine,' 'the circle set
in heaven's place,' is obviously the ninth orb of the heavenly sphere, en-
folding all things, the "Summus ipse Deus." And (6) the whole 'compacted
made a goodly Dyapase,' i. e. the διὰ πασῶν, the harmony of all the members and elements together was goodly. In other words, Man, the microcosm,
like the great world, and acted on by that great world, is, according to this
philosophy, that "noblest work of God," as we have it in Dryden's Ode on
St. Cecilia's Day:
             "The Diapason closing full in man."
Cp. also Pliny, Nat. Hist. 2. 22, where, speaking of the Pythagorean system,
he sums it up thus: "Ita septem tonos effici, quam *diapason* harmoniam
vocant, hoc est universitatem concentus."

   23, 2. *The one;*—sc. the mouth. With this fanciful description of the
parts of man's body cp. Eccles. 12. 4. Upton also quotes Plato, Timaeus,
1. 4, and Cic. de Nat. Deor. 2. 54, &c.
   24, 1. *the porch;*—the lips.
      3. *Marble far from Ireland brought;*—Todd says, "Near Kilcolman
(the poet's seat) there was, it seems, a red and grey marble quarry: see
Smith's Hist. of Cork, 1. 343."
      4. *a wandring vine;*—probably the beard and moustache.
      6. *a fayre portcullis;*—the nose.
   25, 1. *a porter;*—the tongue, kept in due restraint.
   26, 2. *Twise sixteen warders;*—the teeth on the upper and lower jaw.
   27, 8. *hight Diet;*—the proper requirement of man's diet, &c., and the
connection of health with moral life, were much pondered in Spenser's time.
We see this in Bacon, who, a few years later, busied himself much with
speculations and experiments on different kinds of food, &c.
   28, 2. *a jolly yeoman;*—appetite, vigorous and healthy, like a yeoman
fresh from his fields.
   29, 1. *It was a vaut,* &c.;—the kitchens of the time were often large
vaulted rooms, built for a great consumption of provender.
      3. *one great chimney;*—as may still be seen in the Glastonbury
kitchen.
      5. *a caudron;*—the digestive process. The Hindus hold that one of
the functions of fire is digestion. One Hindu writer bids the reader press his
hand on his ears, and he will then hear the inward roaring of this fire!
      7. *flaming Mongiball;*—Upton quotes L'Adone del Marino, "Fumar
Etna si vede e *Mongibello,*" adding that 'or' here is not a disjunctive particle,

but that Etna and Montgibel are two names for the same mountain. Mont-gibel is the Arabic name for Etna; *jebel* being Arabic for a mountain.

30, 4. *a huge great paire of bellowes ;*—the lungs.

33, 6. *a goodly parlour ;*—the heart, abode of the affections and moral qualities.

34, 2. *A lovely bevy of faire ladies;*—the feelings, tastes, &c., of the heart—music, laughter and joy, flattery, envy, &c.

35, 8. *another in her teeth did gnaw a rush;*—a curious picture of man-ners, intended to express anger or moroseness. In a letter to Thomas à Becket (Giles, Patres Eccl. Angl. vol. 39, p. 260) we find a curious de-scription of the passion of Henry II. "Rex itaque solito furore succensus pileum de capite projecit, . . . stratum sericum quod erat supra lectum manu propria removit, et, quasi in sterquilinio sedens, coepit *straminis masticare festucas"*—began to gnaw the rushes of the floor.

36, 5. *themselves to court;*—to act in courteous style, according to the proper and polite ways of knights at court.

8. *sad and solemne ;*—Prays-desire, or love of the approbation of the good, is dressed in purple and gold, imperially, and is staid and solemn, as one who has noble aims and high desires.

37, 3. *a poplar branch ;*—Spenser is still thinking of the tree sacred to Hercules, and therefore symbolical of high adventure. Possibly he also thought that victors in the games were crowned with it.

38, 9. *sought one;*—i. e. the Faery Queene, in whose presence he desired to be honoured. See also stanza 7 of this canto.

40, 1. *The whiles,* &c.;—Sir Guyon's characteristic is moderation and modesty. The strong and true knight is also bashful and shy.

7. *the bird,* &c.;—the owl; symbolical here of a retiring disposition. It does not appear from mythology how Pan maltreated her. There is a story that Pan had a daughter named Iynx, who was afterwards changed by Juno into a bird. But I know of no tale of Pan and the owl.

41, 7. *castory;*—edd. 1590, 1596 read 'lastery'; but it is corrected to 'castory' in 'Faults Escaped' at end of ed. 1590.

44, 7. *other wondrous frame;*—the head.

8. *a stately turret ;*—so Cicero, Tusc. Quaest. 1. 10, says, "in capite, *sicut in arce,* posuit."

9. *ten steps of alablaster;*—the neck; though why 'ten steps' does not appear.

45, 6. *antique Cadmus whylome built ;*—the acropolis of Thebes, called Cadmeia, named after Cadmus the Phoenician (or Egyptian).

7. *which Alexander did confound ;*—in the year 335 B.C. Alexander marched upon Thebes, which had a second time revolted since Philip's death, took the city by assault, and then razed it to the ground, with the exception of the house of Pindar.

8. *though richly guilt ;*—these words have been pointed out as an in-stance of an unnecessary filling up of a line. But they are quite defensible when we recollect that Oriental cities sometimes had coloured walls, and even gilded ones. So Herodotus, 1. 98, describes the seven walls of Ecbatana as all having coloured battlements; the sixth silvered, the seventh gilt.

9. *From which young Hectors bloud,* &c. ;—referring probably to the

fate of young Astyanax, Hector's son, whom the Greeks hurled headlong
from the battlements of Ilium (Ov. Met. 13. 415).

46, 1. *The roofe;*—the upper part of the skull.

    2. *deckt with flowres and berbars;*—hair and eyebrows.

    3. *set in watches stead;*—'in the place of watchmen:' so Cic. de Nat.
Deor. 2. 56, has "Oculi, *tanquam speculatores.*"

47, 4. *likest is,* &c.;—allusion to Gen. 1. 27.

    8. *three honorable sages;*—these are:

        (1) Imagination, looking on to the future; youthful, poetical.

        (2) Judgment, deciding calmly on the present; manly, philo-
sophical.

        (3) Memory, looking back to the past; aged, historical.

48, 1. *Not he, whom,* &c.;—Socrates, whom the Delphic Oracle declared
to be the wisest man alive (Plat. Apol. pp. 21, 25). This, he says, was because he knew how ignorant he was.

    4. *that sage Pylian syre;*—Pylian Nestor, τριγέρων; he had ruled
over three generations of men, and was appealed to throughout the siege of
Troy as an oracle. His opinion was equal to that of the gods. His medi-
ation reconciled Agamemnon and Achilles, and his advice helped greatly
towards the fall of Ilium.

    49, 7. *quicke prejudize;*—the Imagination does not really *judge,* it pre-
judges; moving too fast for the Reason.

50, 3. *Infinite shapes,* &c.;—the creations of the imagination.

51, 1. *flyes Which buzzed;*—the idle thoughts and fantasies of imagination.

    8. *visions;*—note that this word is a trisyllable, just as in the line
before it *opinions* is a four-syllabled word; the Latin or French pronunciation
still prevailing. So also in the next stanza we have *melancholy,* which
shews the same influence.

    52, 2. *Phantastes;*—φαντάστης, from φαντασία, the 'fantastic' or imagi-
native faculty. Note the *melancholy* side of the quality: what we call the
'sadness of youth.'

    8. *with ill disposed skyes;*—with the stars arranged unluckily: so =
'borne under evill starre.'

    9. *When oblique Saturn sate in th' house of agonyes;*—'oblique Sa-
turne' was of all planets the most malign; Propertius, El. 4. 1. 86:

        "Est grave Saturni sidus in omne caput."

He was considered *cold* and blighting; Virg. Geor. 1. 336:

        "Frigida Saturni . . . . . stella;"

and Lucan 1. 651:

        "summo si frigida caelo
    Stella nocens nigros Saturni accenderet ignes."

So Chaucer, Knightes Tale, l. 1585, has "pale Saturnes the colde." Saturn
goes on to say,

        "Myn is the drenchyng in the see so wan;
        Myn is the prisoun in the derke cote;
        Myn is the stranglyng and hangyng by the throte;
        The murmur, and the cherles rebellyng;
        The groynyng, and the pryvé enpoysonyng,

I do vengance and pleyn correctioun,
Whyles I dwelle in the signe of the lyoun.
Myn is the ruen of the hihe halles,
The fallyng of the toures and the walles
Upon the mynour or the carpenter.
I slowh Sampsoun in schakyng the piler.
And myne ben the maladies colde,
The derke tresoun, and the castes olde;
Myn lokyng is the fadir of pestilens."

(Knightes Tale, 1598–1611.)

the house of agonyes;—in astrology 'house' is the τέμενος οὐρανοῦ, the district of the heavens in which a planet rises. 'Agonyes' refers to the belief (alluded to in the Knightes Tale, 1592, 1593) that under Saturn strife and contention (ἀγῶνες) largely prevail. So the almanack called "the Compost of Ptholomeus" tells us that "the children of the sayd Saturne shall be great jangeleres and chyders . . . they will never forgyve tyll they be revenged of theyr quarell;" and agayn, "When he doth reygne, there is moche debate." (Quoted by Dr. Morris, on Chaucer's Knightes Tale, l. 1593.)

53, 2. *second roome;*—the seat of the Judgment (or Reason); all civil, political, or philosophical learning.

7. *decretals;*—Spenser probably only means 'decrees;' he would hardly allude to the Papal decretals; unless he means by 'lawes,' 'judgements,' 'decretals' to signify all law civil or canon.

54, 9. *bindmost roome;*—seat of memory.

56, 8. *The warres . . . of King Nine;*—these wars exist only in imagination.

9. *old Assaracus;*—mythical king of Troy, son of Tros, father of Capys, great-grandfather of Aeneas.

Inachus divine;—a river god, and also king of Argos. He is called son of Oceanus and Tethys, and gives his name to the river Inachus.

58, 3. *But for* = 'but for that,' 'but inasmuch as.'

8. *Anamnestes;*—the Reminder, ἀναμνήστης, from ἀνάμνησις, the faculty by which the lost links of memory are recovered. Ingenious critics suggest that Memory ought to need no helper, and propose to read Anagnostes, or the 'Reader'; alleging that ancient libraries used to have a 'Lector' or ἀναγνώστης appointed as an official in them. But Spenser knew well that aged Memory always does need a 'reminder,' to bring out hidden stores of knowledge.

9. *Eumnestes;*—of good memory, εὐμνήστης, of 'infinite remembrance.'

59, 6. *Briton Moniments;*—the "Monumenta Britannica," or a fabulous chronicle of the earliest times. Spenser made large use of Holinshed's Chronicle, as well as of Hardyng's.

9. *one mans governments;*—this does not relate, as might seem at first sight, to the so-called Heptarchy, and its end; but to the legendary reduction of all the petty kingdoms of Britain under the rule of King Arthur.

60, 2. *Antiquitie of Faerie lond;*—an imaginary chronicle, whose aim is to glorify the parentage and character of Queen Elizabeth.

4. *Th' off-spring;*—i. e. the origin, not the descendants. So confirming the view taken in note on Bk. I. vii. 30.

CANTO X.

Prince Arthur reads 'Briton's Moniments,' from the beginning to the days of Uther: and Sir Guyon the 'Antiquitie of Faerie Lond,' down to the days of Gloriana.

1, 1. *Who now,* &c.;—straight from Ariosto, Orl. Fur. 3. 1:

"Chi mi darà la voce e le parole
Convenienti a si nobil soggetto?
Chi l'ale al verso presterà, che vole
Tanto, ch' arrivi all' alto mio concetto?
Molto maggior di quel furor che suole
Ben or convien che mi riscaldi il petto
Chè questa parte al mio signor si debbe,
Che canta gli Avi, onde l'origin ebbe."

This Canto, by far the dullest of all, has for its real aim the praises of Elizabeth. It is, however, interesting as shewing the attention given at that time in literary circles to archæological questions; an attention altogether uncritical, but giving evidence of the newly-aroused national life and feeling. Men were moved to study the origines of their race. Holinshed's Chronicle had not long been published (first ed. is dated 1587): Camden's Britannia was also new (first ed. 1586), and Stowe had appeared in 1574.

3, 1. *Maeonian quill;*—the pen of Homer, who was called Maeonian, or Maeonides, from the ancient name of Lydia, to which country he was supposed by some to belong.

2. *great Phoebus rote;*—Apollo's lyre; the god of music and poetry. He was supposed to be the inspirer of poets. So Odysseus (Od. 8. 488) tells Demodocus the bard, that either the Muse has taught him, or Apollo.

3. *the ruines of great Ossa hill,* &c.;—the assault of the giants upon heaven, and their defeat by Zeus, Virg. Georg. 1. 281:

" Ter sunt conati imponere Pelio Ossam
Scilicet, atque Ossae frondosum involvere Olympum:
Ter pater exstructos disiecit fulmine montes."

4 *Phlegraean Jove;*—rightly so styled in this place, as the conflict between him and the giants was said to have taken place at Phlegra (Pallene).

he wrote;—a bold usage = 'he described' or sung.

7. *His learned daughters;*—the Muses. They are attributed to many parents: (1) Uranus and Gaia (Heaven and Earth); (2) Aether and Gaia (Air and Earth); (3) Zeus and Mnemosyne (Memory); (4) Zeus and Plusia; (5) Zeus and Moneta; (6) Zeus and Athene; (7) Pierus and a Nymph; (8) Apollo.

4, 2. *This renowmed prince;*—that is, Prince Arthur.

5, 5. *Ne was it island then;*—a curious forecast of a geological truth. Sammes (Britannia, c. 4) says, "That this Island hath been joyned to the opposite continent, by a narrow isthmus between Dover and Bullen, or thereabouts, hath been the opinion of many : As of Antonius Volsius, Dom. Marius Niger, Servius Honoratus, our countryman John Twine, and the French poet Du Bartas." And Camden, Brit. (publ. 1586) writes, " Inter Cantium enim et Caletum, Galliae ita in altum se evehit, et adeo in arctum mare agitur, ut perfossas ibi terras antea exclusa admisisse maria opinentur nonnulli." The same was thought to have been the case with Sicily, as Virgil notes, "Hesperium Siculo latus abscidit." .

9. *the Celticke mayn-land;*—properly so called, ' Gallia Celtica.'

6, 3. *those white rocks;*—there are cretaceous cliffs, (1) on the coast of Yorkshire (Flamborough Head); (2) on the Norfolk coast (Hunstanton Cliff to Cromer); (3) at the North Foreland in Kent; (4) at the South Foreland, from Deal to Hythe (to which district Spenser probably alludes more particularly); (5) in Sussex (Beachy Head to Brighton); (6) in the Isle of Wight (at St. Helen's on the east and at the west to the Needles); (7) along a portion of the Dorset coast (ending at Weymouth); and (8) on the Devonshire shore (about Sidmouth).

6. *safeties sake;*—ed. 1590, ' safety' (as a trisyllable).

7. *nam'd it Albion;*—the chroniclers hold that this name comes from the giant Albion (cp. st. 11). Or from *alb*, white, or from *alp*, a pasture, or from *Albine*, daughter of the mythical Dioclesian.

7, 2. *hideous giants;*—so Geoffry of Monmouth has it, c. 9 : " Erat tunc nomen insulae Albion, quae nemine exceptis paucis gigantibus inhabitabatur."

7. *lived then;*—ed. 1590 reads ' liveden,' an old pret. inflexion which Spenser seems to have thought too archaic.

8, 3. *That monstrous error, &c.;*—all this is direct from Hardyng's Chronicle, c. 1 and 5. He gives the tale (describing the daughters of ' Dioclesian, King of Greece,' as *thirty*, not *fifty*); and adds also that he considers it to be false and without foundation. In the legend these ' thirty daughters' are described as performing the feat of Danaides, with whom they are evidently confounded. Holinshed (Hist. of Engl. 1. 3) explains how the name of ' Dioclesian' got into the legend. He rebukes the ignorance of the chroniclers in supposing ' Danaus' was a short way of writing ' Dioclesianus.'

9, 3. *their owne mother;*—i. e. Albion. Spenser hints that, like the classical Gigantes, these British giants were earth-born (γηγενεῖς).

6. *Brutus;*—this legendary Brutus is always described as descended from Aeneas. His coming to Albion is described by Hardyng, c. 11. Robert of Gloucester fixes the date of his arrival at 1132 B.C. Holinshed puts it at 1116, Stow at 1108. He is said to have landed at Totnes in Devon, with his comrade Corineus.

7. *old Assaracs line;*—cp. Virg. Georg. 3. 35, "Assaraci proles." See note on ix. 56, 9.

10, 3. *He fought great battels;*—Hardyng says :

" The giauntes als he sleugh doune beelive

Through all the lande in battaile mannely:
And lefte no moo but Gogmagog onely."

7. *Th: westerne Hogb;*—Camden calls it " the Haw" in his Britannia
(Devonshire). It is now " the Hoe," near Plymouth.

8. *migbty Goëmot;*— otherwise called Goemagot, or Gogmagog.
Geoffry of Monmouth (c. 9) says, " ille (Goemagot) per abrupta saxa cadens
in multa frustra dilaceratus est, et fluctus sanguine maculavit." Cp. also
Hardyng, c. 12, for this conquest of Corineus. Holinshed says Gogmagog
was thrown over the cliffs near Dover. (Hist. of Eng. 2. 4.)

11, 6. *bideous Albion;*—a legendary giant, whose history is given in
Holinshed, 1. 3.

7. *Hercules in Fraunce did quell;*—a curious mixture of classical with
mediæval legend. Robert of Gloucester says that Hercules was in France
with Brutus. Holinshed tells us that Hercules fought a terrific battle with
Albion on the Rhone, and eventually defeated him by showers of stones,
which still lie there, in the district called the Crau. .(Hist. of Eng. 1. 3.)

9. *Canutus;*—another of the legendary companions of Brutus, epo·
nynious of Cantium or Kent.

12, 5. *He called Cornewaille;*—so stated in Geoffry of Monmouth, c. 9.

6. *tbat is Devonsbyre;*—I have not succeeded in finding the legends of
Godmer, Debon, and Canutus.

13, 5. *faire Inogene of Italy;*—Robert of Gloucester (who spells the name
' Innogen'), describes her as the wife of Brute, daughter of Pandras, king of
Greece, not Italy.

7. *Locrine . . . cbiefe lord of Britany;*—Hardyng, c. 15 and 17:
" On Locryne it should ever be homage."
' Britany' here means Britain.

14, 2, 3. *Albanact . . . Albania;*—Hardyng, c. 15:
" Fro Humber north unto the Northwest sea
Of all Britaine, which he called *Albanye*
For *Albanacte* the kyng therof to be."

5. *Logris;*—all to the east of Severn, and "from the south sea unto
the river of Humber." (Holinshed, Hist. of Eng. 2. 5.)

6. *eacb bis portion peaceably enjoyd;*—so Hardyng, c. 17:
" And reyned so bylyfe in one assente," &c.

15, 1. *Untill,* &c.;—this incursion of Huns or Scythians is described in
full in Hardyng, c. 18.

9. *munifience;*—ed. 1596 has ' munificence.'

16, 3. *Abus;*—the Humber. Abus is probably a form of the British *aber*,
a river mouth.

17, 6, 8. *faire . . . Estrild . . . Guendolene;*—see Hardyng, c. 18. Estrild
is described as a ' young damsel of excellent beauty,' daughter of a certain
king of Scythia, taken captive in the battle on the Humber.—Holinshed,
Hist. of Engl. 2. 5.

18, 4. *battell well ordaind;*—Latin phrase, " praelio bene ordinato."
(Upton.)

19, 3. *Sabrina;*—daughter of Estrild, drowned in the Severn; narrated by
Hardyng, c. 18.

5. *in tbat impatient stoure;*—ed. 1590 reads ' upon the present stoure.'

20, 1. *Then for her son* . . . ;—'for' here = 'seeing that,' 'forasmuch as.'

2. *Madan;*—Hardyng, c. 20, who says she governed for him fifteen years.

  rule of sway;—ed. 1590 reads 'rule to sway.' The 'rule of sway' = 'active government.' The 'rule to sway' would = 'to sway (hold) the sceptre.'

21, 3. *Memprise;*—Hardyng, c. 20; Holinshed, Hist. of Engl. 2. 5. Manild, his brother, is called 'Manlius' by Holinshed, 'Maulyne' by Hardyng.

  6. *Ebranck;*—the legendary founder of Eber-wik (or Caer-Ebrank), Everwyk (Eber's town), i. e. York. See Hardyng, c. 21. He had twenty wives, twenty sons and thirty daughters; so that 'as many weekes,' &c., is not quite right, unless we take the fifty lunar weeks in the solar year. According to Hardyng, he "warred in Gaule," which would do, perhaps, for Henault, Hainault. His sons, according to this same authority, conquered Germany. There is no trace of his warring on Brunchild.

22, 7. *germans . . . Germany;*—the derivation is as correct as the rest of the history.

23, 2. *The second Brute;*—this was Brutus Greneschilde. See Hardyng, c. 22. It is this prince who is said by Holinshed to have gone over into 'Henaud,' and to have warred with 'king Brinchild,' who gave him a sore repulse. (Hist. of Engl. 2. 5.) Milton, Hist. of Britain, Bk. I, says that Jacobus Bergomas and Lassabeus, in their account of Hainault, give these fables.

  6. *first opened The bowels of wide Fraunce;*—he is said to have passed into Armorica, and to have given to that district a name derived from his own, i. e. Brittany.

24. The quaint proper names heaped together in this stanza remind us of Milton's delight in such displays; e. g. Par. Lost, 4. 268–283.

  1. *Scaldis;*—the river Scheldt.

  Hania;—the country of Hainault in Belgium. Milton says it is a river. The Henalois below are the men of Hainault.

  2. *Estbam bruges ;*—Bruges, in Belgium.

  8. *scuith guiridh;*—Welsh for a 'green shield;' *y scuith gogh,* 'the red shield.' It had been green, but was dyed red in the blood of the men of Hainault.

25, 1. *Leill ;*—see Hardyng, c. 23 : founder of Caerleill (Carlisle) and Caerleon (Chester, otherwise called *Leon*-cester, Leicester, 'Legionum castra'). *Caer,* British for 'city.'

  4. *Huddibras;*—called 'Ludhurdibras' by Holinshed, 'Rudhudebras' by Hardyng, c. 24.

  6. *Bladud following,* &c. ;—famed for his learning, as Hardyng says, c. 25 :

  "When at Athenes he had studied clere,
  He brought with hym iiii philosophiers wise
  Schole to holde in Brytayne and exercyse.
   Stamforde he made that Stamforde hight this daye
   In whiche he made an universitee," &c.

26, 2. *the boyling baths at Cairbadon ;*—Spenser follows Geoffry of Mon-

Q

mouth, c. 14, "Ædificavit urbem *Kaer-badum,* quae nunc *Badus* nuncupatur."
See Hardyng :
　　　　" Cair Bladud, so that nowe is Bath, I rede."
Holinshed (Descr. of Engl. 2. 23) gives a long account of the Bath waters,
under the name of *Caer-bledud.*

　　26, 9. *through flight,* &c. ;—" And to shew his cunning in other points,
upon a presumptuous pleasure which he had therein, he tooke upon him *to
flie in the aire,* but he fell upon the temple of Apollo, which stood in the
citie of Troynovant, and there was torne in peeces." Holinshed, 2. 5. And
Hardyng :
　　　　" And afterward a Featherham he dight
　　　　　To flye with wynges as he could best descerne,
　　　　　He flyed on high to the temple Apolyne,
　　　　　And ther brake his necke, for all his great doctrine."

　　27, 1. *king Leyr ;*—this legend, so familiar to us through Shakespeare, is
best given by Robert of Gloucester; also by Holinshed (Hist. Engl. 2. 5),
and by Hardyng more briefly, c. 26.

　　29, 1. *Maglan ;*—' Duke of Albania,' or ' Albanie' (N. England), according
to Holinshed and Hardyng.

　　2. *the king of Cambria ;* — ' Henninus' in Holinshed; ' Evin ' in
Hardyng.

　　5. *Aganip of Celtica ;*—Holinshed says : " one of the princes of Gallia
(which now is called France), whose name was Aganippus, hearing of the
beautie, womanhood, and good condition of the said Cordeilla, desired to
have hir in mariage," &c. " This Aganippus was one of the twelve kings
that ruled Gallia in those daies."

　　32, 3. *after wild,* &c. ;—i. e. left the kingdom by will to Cordelia.

　　9. *her selfe she hong ;*—Hardyng, c. 28, says :
　　　　" For sorow then, she sleugh hir selfe for tene."
We may notice that the legend, as treated by Shakespeare, differs very much ·
from that of the chroniclers, who restore Lear to his throne and honours, nor
do they say he was blind.

　　33, 2. *Cundah ;*—' Condage' in Hardyng, 30; ' Cunedag' in Holinshed,
2. 6.

　　8. *hight of him Glamorgan ;* — Holinshed says (Hist. Engl. 2. 8) :
" that countrie tooke name of him, being there slaine, and so is called to
this daie *Glan Margan,* which is to meane in our English tong, Margans
land."

　　34, 2. *bloud did from heaven raine ;*—Hardyng, 30 :
　　　　" And rayned bloodde thesame, iii dayes also,
　　　　　Greate people dyed, the land to mykell woo."
So too Holinshed, 2. 7.

　　3. *great Gurgustus ;*—why ' great'? Hardyng, 30, says of him that
he reigned
　　　　" In mykill ioye and worldly selynesse,
　　　　　Kepyng his landes from enemyes as a manne,
　　　　　But drunken he was eche daye expresse,
　　　　　Unaccordynge to a prince of worthynesse."

　　4. *In constant peace ;*—not so Hardyng, 30 :—

" In whose tyme eche man did other oppresse
The lawe and peace was exiled so indede
That ciuill warres and slaughter of men expresse,
And murderers foule throgh all his lande, dayly,
Without redres or any remedy."

8. *Arraught the rule;*—not according to Holinshed and Hardyng.

35, 3. *Stird Porrex up, &c.;*—there is a very pardonable confusion in this history; the chroniclers being uncertain whether Ferrex killed Porrex, or Porrex Ferrex. Spenser follows Geoffry of Monmouth, c. 16. But Holinshed and Hardyng make Ferrex the slayer. Geoffry also gives us their mother's name, ' Wyden.'

9. *him murdred, &c.;*—so Hardyng, c. 30:
" Ther mother that Indon hight,
To Ferrex came, with her maydens all in ire
Slepyng in bed slew hym upon the night,
And smote hym all on peces sett on fyre,
With suche rancor that she could not ceas,
Which, for passyng yre, was mercyles."
So Spenser calls her " his mother *mercilesse.*"

36, 6. *into factions rent;*—so Hardyng, c. 31.

37, 1. *Then up arose;*—finely introduced. We do not learn the name of this matchless hero till st. 40, '*Donwallo* dyed.' He is called in Holinshed " Mulmucius Dunwallo" (Hist. Engl. 3. 1), and by Hardyng (c. 31) 'Moluncius.'

Sammes, Brit. p. 172, gives his laws, seven in number, dealing, as Spenser gives them (st. 39), with temples of the gods, highways, and plough-lands, and restraint of robbery.

39, 6. *The gracious Numa;*—the legendary lawgiver and second King of Rome, to whom Donwallo may well be likened.

9. *first wore crowne of gold;*—so Holinshed says : " He ordained him . . . a crowne of gold ; and because he was the first that bare a crowne here in Britaine, he is named the first King of Britaine." And Hardyng :
" The first he was, as chroniclers expresse,
That in this isle of Brytein had *croune of golde,*
For all afore copre and gilt was to beholde."

40, 2. *two sonnes ;*—Belinus and Brennus.

3. *That sacked Rome ;*—Holinshed (Hist. Engl. 3. 2, 3) tells us that after many adventures, Brennus, who had married the daughter of the " Duke of Allobrog," came into Britain to overthrow his brother. But being reconciled by their mother, they both set forth against Gallia and Rome. They reached Clusium, besieged it, made treaty with the Romans, broke it— " their perjured oth"—and took and sacked Rome. The date assigned is B. C. 365. (Hardyng, c. 32.)

41, 1. *Gurgunt ;*—Holinshed, Hist. Engl. 3. 5.

3. *Easterland subdewd, and Denmarke wonne ;*—i. e. the Danes and dwellers in North-eastern Europe. Holinshed and Hardyng only record his triumphs over the Danes.

6. *fugitives of Spayne ;*— Holinshed (Hist. Engl. 3. 5) says : " he encountred with a navie of 30 ships, besides the Iles of Orkenies. These ships

were fraught with men and women, and had for their capteine one Bartholin, who, being brought into the presence of King Gurguint, declared that he with his people were banished out of Spaine, and were named Balenses, or Baselenses, and had sailed long on the sea, to the end to find some prince that would assigne them a place to inhabit, to whom they would become *subjects, and hold of him* as of their sovereigne governor." Spenser, l. 9, reproduces this phrase almost literally :

"Which they *should hold of him as subject* to Britayne."

See also Robert of Gloucester, who is eloquent on the praises of Ireland. This is a manifesto, to shew the right of England over Ireland in the days of Queen Elizabeth, and to justify her severe measures, in which Spenser had necessarily taken some part.

42, 1. *Guitheline, &c.* ;—so Hardyng, c. 35, whom Spenser here follows almost literally :

> "Guytelyn his sonne gave reigne *as heyre*
> Of all Brytayn, aboute unto the sea,
> *Who wedded was to Marcyan full fayre*
> That was so wyse in her femynites,
> That lawes made of her syngularytes,
> That called were *the lawes Marcyane*
> In Britayne tongue, of her owne witte alone."

"These lawes," says Holinshed, "Alfred . . . translated also out of the British tong into the English Saxon speech, and then they were called after that translation, Marchen a lagh, that is to meane, the lawes of Marcia." (They were really *Border*-laws).

43, 8. *the forreine Morands* ;—Holinshed, Hist. Engl. 3. 6 : " In his daies, a certaine king of the people called Moriani . . . landed in Northumberland . . ." " These people I take to be either those that inhabited about Terrouane and Calice, called Morini, or some other people of the Galles or Germaines."

44, 6. *pitteous Elidure* ;—so called because he had pity on, and abdicated in favour of, his deposed brother Arthegal, or Archigald. (Hardyng, c. 37.) Holinshed (Hist. Engl. 3. 7) says : " For this great good-will and brotherly love by him shewed thus towards his brother, he was surnamed The Godly and Vertuous." And Hardyng, c. 38 :

> "He was so full of all *pytee*
> That in all thynge mercy he dyd preserve."

9. *Vigent* ;—' Vigenius,' Holinshed ; ' Iugen,' Hardyng.

45, 1. *In wretched prison, &c.* ;—Hardyng, c. 38 :

> "And prisoner hym full sore and wrongfullye
> All in the towre of Troynovante for thy."

3. *then therein reseized was againe* ;—Hardyng, c. 39 :

> "Eledour was kyng all newe made againe,
> Thrise crowned."

6. *Then all the sonnes* ;—Spenser closely follows Holinshed, who merely mentions these thirty-three kings, saying that 182 years must be apportioned among them, and adding that there is no certainty among authors on the subject. But Hardyng goes through them diligently by name.

9. *aged Hely* ;—eponymous of the ' Isle of *Ely.* '

46, 1. *Lud ;*—Holinshed, Hist. Engl. 3. 9; Hardyng, c. 40, 41.

    4. *The ruin'd wals ;*—Hardyng says :

> "With walles faire, and towres fresh about
> His citie great of Troynovaunt, full fayre,
> Full well he made, and batelled throughout ;
> And palays fayre, for [royalles to appeare]
> Amendyng other defectyfe and unfayre,
> From London stone to his palays royall
> That now *Ludgate* is knowen over all."

He says he built hard by Ludgate his palace and a temple, and then

> "He died so, and in his temple fayre
> Entombed was."

    5. *Troynovant ;*—that is, London, the city of the *Trinobantes;* there is of course no ground for the old derivation from ' Troia nova,' new Troy, the city founded by Brutus, and named after the home of his fathers.

    8. *too young to rule aright ;*—so Hardyng :

> "Which were to young to rule the heritage."

47, 5. *Till the proud Romanes,* &c.;—55 B.C. Hardyng, c. 42, says:

> "In which tyme so came Caesar Iulius
> Into the lande of Fraunce that nowe so hight ;
> [And on a daye walkyng up and downe full right]
> On the sea syde, wher he this lande did see,
> Desyryng sore [of it] the soverayntee,
> His nauye greate, with many soudyoures
> To sayle anone into this Britayn made,
> In Thamis aroue, wher he had ful sharpe shores (stowres ?)
> . . . wher, after battayle, smythen and forfought
> Iulius fled, and there preuayled nought."

Caesar's true reason was not a mere ' hideous hunger of dominion,' but a clear opinion that unless the Druid power in Britain, its stronghold, were quelled, he could never hold Gaul securely.

48, 1. *Yet twise,* &c. ;—Hardyng gives it thus, c. 43 :

> "came to Brytayn again
> Into Thamis, where Cassibelayn tho
> Great pyle of tree and yron sette hym again,
> His shippes to peryshe, and so he did certain
> Through which greate parte of his nauy was drowned
> And [some other] in batayl wer confounded.
> Then fled he eft with shippes that he had
> Into the lande of Fraunce," &c.

Caesar, Comment. Bk. 4. 5, only makes *two* descents, in 55 and 54 B.C., and neither of these into the Thames at all. He landed both times somewhere near the South Foreland. Nor was he ever repulsed by the Britons, though his successes were of but small value. For it is very clear, after all, that he got very little hold on Britain. After his second incursion he withdrew on receiving the nominal submission of Cassibelan, some slaves, and a quantity of pearls. But Britain remained as she was, and the tribute was never paid.

48, 6. *Androgeus ;*—Hardyng (whom Spenser follows here) describes this
in c. 44.

49, 4. *Nennius, whom he yet did slay, But lost his sword ;*—Hardyng,
c. 41 :

> "But Neminus, brother of Cassybalayne,
> Full manly fought on Iulius tymes tweyne.
> With strokes sore ayther on other bette,
> But [at the laste this prynce syr] Iulius
> *Crosea mors* his swerde in shelde sette
> Of the manly worthy sir Neminus;
> (Which of manly force and myght vigorous)
> The swearde he brought away out of the felde,
> As Iulius it [set faste] in his shelde.
> Through which stroke sir Neminus then died.
> . . . . *Crosea mors* his swearde layde by his syde
> Which he [brought from] Iulius that tyde."

So also the story is told by Geoffry of Monmouth. This tale is doubtless
connected with that sword which Caesar is said to have lost in the Gallic
War.

8. *Till Arthur,* &c. ;—Spenser means that Britain continued subject to
Rome till Arthur delivered her. As to this subjection, even Holinshed, Hist.
Engl. 3. 16, says, " Cesar might seem rather to have shewed Britaine to the
Romans than to have delivered possession of the same."

50, 2. *What time ;*—so Holinshed and Hardyng.

9. *For that their tribute,* &c. ;—this is told, not of Kimbeline, but of
his son and successor Guyder.

51, 1. *Good Claudius ;*—Emperor, A.D. 41, was of Sabine origin, born at
Lyons. He spoke but a barbarous Latin, and preferred Greek; he was
proud of his Gallic birthplace, and hated Rome. A fragment of his speech
in the Senate, advocating the claims of the Gaelic chiefs to a seat in that
assembly, is still preserved in the museum at Lyons. This friendliness for
the Gael is doubtless the origin of the title ' good,' which scarcely bears its
proper moral significance in this case. This is probably the answer to Mr.
Church's question: " But why does he call him *good*?" Claudius came
into Britain A.D. 43.

3. *In which the king,* &c. ;—so Hardyng, c. 45 :

> " One Hamon rode faste into the route
> Havyng on him the Britains sygne of warre
> Who, in the prees, slewe the Kyng Guyder."

6. *Arvirage ;*—Hardyng, c. 46 :

> " His brothers armis upon hymself he cast ;
> And Kyng was then of all Great Britain."

52, 4. *His daughter Genuiss' ;*—so says Geoffry of Monmouth, Holinshed
(Hist. Engl.), Hardyng, c. 46.

All these details are wanting in the Roman histories, and are in fact inci-
dents of romance. As we have now reached a time of historic names, it
becomes needful to separate what is mythical from what is historical.

5. *Yet shortly*, &c.;—So Hardyng:
    "After agayne, the Kyng truage denyed,
    And none wolde paye; wherefore Vespasian
    Hyther was sent."

6. *who bither*, &c.;—'who'=Rome in the person of her Emperor Claudius. Vespasian came into Britain, 43 A.D., as 'legatus legionis;' the same year in which Claudius himself was there.

53, 3. *good Lucius, That first received Christianity;*—" The early Welsh notices, and the Silurian Catalogues of Saints state that Lleurwg, called also Lleufer Maur, 'the great light'=*Lucius* (*lux*), applied to Rome for spiritual instruction, and that in consequence four teachers, Dyfan, Ffagan, Medwy, and Elfan were sent to him by Pope Eleutherius." (Smith's Dict. of Biogr., Lucius.) Bede gives in substance the same account, giving the date A.D. 156. The tale is possible; but King Lucius is a very shadowy personage of no historical certainty.

So in Geoffry of Monmouth, 2. 1. This King Lucius is said by Hardyng to have received two " holye menne, Faggan and Dunyen," from Pope Eleutherius. Another account describes him as going a pilgrimage and suffering martyrdom at Chur (Coire) in the Grisons, where the cathedral is dedicated to him.·

5. *The sacred pledge;*—sc. Baptism.

6. *Yet true it is;*—the very dubious legend of Joseph of Arimathea who, according to Hardyng, c. 47, and Holinshed (Hist. Engl. 4. 5), came into England, and made many converts. The tale runs that Joseph, carrying the Holy Grayle with him, set forth in a boat, which guided itself through the Pillars of Hercules, across the main sea, into the Bristol Channel. She went steadily on, till she grounded in a marshy spot, since called Glastonbury. There Joseph landed, and in sign of possession, planted his staff, which took root, and became the famous Glastonbury thorn.

8. *the holy grayle;*—either (1) the dish off which our Lord ate the Passover; or (2) the 'sanguis realis,' or actual blood of our Saviour. But see Gloss. *Grayle*. The quest of the Sangreal forms a large element in the Mort d'Arthur.

54, 6. *Bunduca;*—better known as Boadicea. Her story is handed down to us by Tacitus, 14. 31–37. She was aroused in A.D. 62 by the infinite wrongs the Romans had done her family; and raising the Iceni and Trinobantes, she stormed and took the Roman position of Camalodunum. Afterwards she defeated Petilius Cerealis. The Britons next seized London, even then a great emporium, and also Verulamium. In these places the Britons are said to have taken and slain ruthlessly nearly 70,000 Romans or their allies. Boadicea was afterwards utterly defeated by Suetonius Paulinus. Robert of Gloucester, Geoffry of Monmouth, Hardyng, give no account of her; but Holinshed gives her history, and describes her at length, Hist. Engl. 4. 10, 11:

"Hir mightie tall personage, comelie shape, severe countenance, and sharpe voice, with hir long and yellow tresses of haire reaching downe to hir thighes, hir brave and gorgeous apparelle also caused the people to have hir in great reverence. She wore a chaine of gold, great and verie massie, and was clad in a lose kirtle of sundrie colours, and aloft thereupon she had a

thicke Irish mantell; hereto in hir hand she bare a speare, to shew hirselfe
the more dreadfull."

54, 9. *besides the Severne;*—we do not know where the battle was fought;
but it could not have been in West England. Boadicea was an eastern
queen; her successes were at Camalodunum (Colchester), London, and Verulamium (St. Alban's), all in the East of England. Her followers were Iceni
and Trinobantes, eastern tribes.

Spenser's account differs from that given by Holinshed. He says that
after her defeat by Suetonius, "those that escaped would have fought a new
battell, but in the meane time Voadicea deceased of a naturall infirmitie, as
Dion Cassius writeth, but other say that she poisoned hir selfe, and so died,
because she would not come into the hands of hir bloodthirsty enimies."

55, 2. *Not with so good success,* &c.;—in this great battle the Romans
had but 10,000 men, while Boadicea commanded (it is said) 230,000. The
Romans took up a strong position, and utterly defeated the barbarians with
immense slaughter: 80,000 are said to have perished. It is obvious that the
figures cannot be trusted.

56, 2. *Semiramis;*—the mythical founder of Nineveh, wife of Ninus.
Her beauty and bravery placed her among memorable women.

4. *Hypsiphil';*—was, in the legends, Queen of Lemnos. Her one feat
(Apollod. 3. 6. 4) was that of saving her father when the Lemnian women
slew all the men on the island. It is hard to see why she has been selected
by Spenser among the heroic parallels to Boadicea.

Thomiris;—Tomyris is described by Herodotus (1. 205) as a heroic
queen of the Massagetae, who resisted and defeated Cyrus.

57, 1. *Fulgent;*—Hardyng, c. 52:
> "the northern Brittons,
> With Fulgen stode, was Kyng of Scotlande bore."

2. *Fought with Severus;*—Julius Séverus is described by Dion Cassius
(69. 13) as a legate of Hadrian, and for a time governor of Britain. He
built the wall (*Murus Britannicus*) between the Tyne and the Solway. The
chroniclers confound the Picts' Wall with this. Hardyng (c. 53) says:
> "From Tynmouth to *Alclud* his fayre citee,"

Alcluid being on the Clyde (Dumbarton) where the Picts' Wall, running
from the Frith of Forth, ended.

5. *Then gan Carausius;*—M. Aurelius Valerius Carausius, a native
of the district of the Menapi, a poor pilot, being set by Maximian over the
cruisers who watched the pirates swarming in and out of the mouths of
the Rhine and Scheldt, fled with his fleet to Britain, gained over the legions
there stationed, and assumed the title of Augustus. He was eventually
recognised as colleague by Diocletian and Maximian. Spenser refers to his
resistance to Maximian when he writes that he
> 'Gainst the Romanes bent their proper powre,'

though he is not very exact in saying so. He was murdered by Allectus, his
chief officer (as Spenser says, l. 7) in the year A.D. 293.

8. *And tooke on him,* &c.;—Allectus did assume the purple, and wore
it for three years—that was his 'short happy howre.' In 296 Constantius
sent against him Asclepiodotus with army and fleet, and subdued him.

58, 2. *on the vanquisht plaine ;*—either = 'vanquished on the plaine,' or = 'on the plain of his defeat.'

4. *Then afterwards ;*—it does not appear that this was the case. There is no proof that Asclepiodotus was ever Emperor. Hardyng calls him "Duke of Cornwayle" (c. 56). In c. 57 he says he "was crowned Kyng agayne."

5. *Coyll ;*—Hardyng (c. 58) gives us this prince:

> " For whiche duke Coyle agayne him rose ful hote,
> The duke Caire Colun (that hight) Coylus,
> Whiche cytee [now] this daye Colchester hight,
> Then crowned was."

9. *Coylchester ;*—Colchester is so called either from its older name Camulodunum, Camalo-chester, or more probably from the Latin Colonia, Coln-chester. It was the first of the Roman colonies in Britain, and is mentioned by the name of *Caer* Colun, in Nennius. By the time of Boadicea there were three important Roman cities in Britain, Camulodunum, London, and Verulamium. So that 'Coylchester' existed long before Spenser's King Coyll the Second.

59, 2. *Constantius ;*—Constantius Chlorus established his authority in Britain A.D. 296, at the time of the overthrow of Allectus, but did not come into the island till rather later. He died at Eboracum (Everwyk, York) in 306, while on an expedition against the Picts.

4. *his daughter bright, Faire Helena, the fairest living wight ;*—Spenser attributes to her some of the qualities of the original Helena, the bane of Troy. Her origin seems to have been humble; nor is there any foundation for the legend adopted by Spenser from Hardyng, c. 59, 60, and Holinshed, Hist. Engl. 4. 28 : "His first wife Helen, the daughter (as some affirme) of Coell late king of the Britains."

She was repudiated by Constantius when he was raised to the dignity of Caesar, because he wanted, for state reasons, to marry Theodora, stepchild of Maximian.

60, 1. *great Constantine ;*—surnamed Magnus, son of Constantius and Helena, born A.D. 272. He was emperor from A.D. 306 to 337.

4. *Octavius ;*—not a historic personage, nor is *Traherne.* The legend is given by Holinshed, Hist. Engl. 4. 29, and by Hardyng, c. 63, who calls Octavius "Duke of Westesax."

61, 1. *wanting issew male ;*—Constantine, on the contrary, had four sons: Crispus; Constantinus II, 'the younger;' Constantius II; and Constans. None of his daughters married Maximian : one of them was named Helena Flavia Maximiana, whence the error may have sprung.

2. *to Maximian ;*—there were two Maximians emperors : (1) Maximianus I, surnamed Herculius, whose stepdaughter Constantius Chlorus married. He formed a close alliance with Constantine, and gave him his daughter Fausta ; but afterwards, intriguing against him in the south of France, he was ordered to choose the manner of his death, and strangled himself, A.D. 310. (2) Maximianus II, who is also called Galerius. He was never on friendly relations with Constantine.

5. *Gratian ;*—was not born till A.D. 359. Nor is there any founda-

tion in history for this murder 'by the freends of Gratian:' Maximian strangled himself forty-nine years before Gratian was born.

61, 6. *Then gan*, &c.;—the chroniclers are fond of these Huns. Geoffry
of Monmouth, I. II, tells us of their entry into Britain under Humber their
chief. The Scots and Picts were probably natives of Ireland.

7. *Maximinian*;—it is not quite clear who this is; but Spenser probably meant Maximus, who, in the time of Gratian, was in Britain, A.D. 368,
and remained there as general for several years. Fuller, Ch. Hist. I. cent. iv.
§ 22, says he " for a time valiantly resisted the Scots and Picts, which cruelly
invaded and infested the south of Britain."

62, 8. *by consent of Commons and of Peares*;—a curious anachronism.

9. *the second Constantine*;—Spenser must here mean Constantine the
'tyrant,' who was raised to the purple by the British legions (scarcely by
'Commons and Peares') A.D. 407. See Holinshed, Hist. Engl. 5. I; Hardyng, c. 65:
> "The Scottes and Peightes he venged and overcam."

Robert of Gloucester says:
> "þe Brytones nome þo Costantyn, and glade þoru all þyng   ·
>   In þe toun of Cicestre crouned hym to here kyng."

63, 2. *Picts, and swarming Easterlings*;—the Picts and Northmen. For
Easterling see Gloss.

9. *from Alcluid to Panwelt*;—this is the 'Picts' wall' from the Forth
to the Clyde. This wall is said to have been built by Carausius, A.D. 285.
There is not the slightest reason for thinking that Constantine had any hand
in it. 'Panwelt' or Panvahel on the Firth of Forth is Falkirk; Alcluid,
often mentioned by old chroniclers, is at or near Dumbarton, on the Clyde.
This great wall can still be traced over a large part of its course. The
chroniclers seem to confuse this wall with that from the Tyne to the Solway;
which was the Murus Britannicus, called sometimes Severus', sometimes
Hadrian's wall.

64, I. *Three sonnes*;—Constantius, who was dull of wit, and therefore
made a monk; Aurelius Ambrose; and Uther (afterwards) Pendragon.
Hardyng, c. 65.

2. *Vortigere*;—Vortigern is a British king who is said by the chroniclers to have been the first to call in the Saxons, through fear of the Picts.

5. *Them closely into Armorick did beare*;—Holinshed, Hist. Engl.
5. I: "With all speed got them to the sea, and fled into little Britaine," i.e.
Brittany or Armorica.

8. *three boyes Of Saxons*;—so Hardyng, c. 67:
> "In shyppes thre arryued so there in Kent."

Gildas, c. 23, says: "Tribus ut lingua ejus exprimitur *Cyulis*, ut nostra,
longis navibus," i.e. "three *keels*."

65, 2. *Hengist and Horsus*;—Saxon chiefs, according to the early historians. It is noticeable that their names both signify 'horse' (cp. mod.
Danish and Germ. *Hengst*, and Engl. *Horse*, Germ. *Ross*.) Historians are
divided as to the fact of their existence. Hengist is said to have established ·
himself in Kent A.D. 454. Holinshed, Hist. Engl. 5. 2, 3; Hardyng, c. 67.

9. *enforst*;—ed. 1590 reads 'have forst.'

66, I. *Vortimere his sonne*;—a brave British prince who steadily and successfully stemmed the Saxon incursions. This semi-legendary period is found at large in Nennius, c. 45–52; also in Holinshed, Hist. Engl. 5. 3; Hardyng, c. 67; Bede's Gesta Anglorum; Gildas; and William of Malmesbuɒy.

5. *Through his faire daughters face,* &c.;—Rowan, or Rowena, for love of whom Vortiger abandoned his own wife; so restoring Hengist to favour. The chroniclers tell us she saluted Vortiger with the word 'Wassal,' to which he made reply (through the interpreter) 'Drink hail;' whence came those words into English speech as salutations.

6. *Soone after which ;*—"They invited the British to a parley and banquet on Salisbury plain; where, suddenly drawing out their *seaxas,* concealed under their long coats, they made their innocent guests with their blood pay the shots of their entertainment. Here Aurelius Ambrosius is reported to have erected that monument of Stonehenge to their memory."— Fuller, Ch. Hist. I. cent. v. § 25. This close commentary on this stanza is, of course, of no historical value. The Druid circles of Stonehenge were standing centuries before the period of this doubtful banquet and massacre. See also Holinshed, Hist. Engl. 5. 5 and 8; Hardyng, c. 68 and 70.

67, 1. *the sonnes of Constantine . . . . Ambrose and Uther ;*—Ambrose, or Aurelius Ambrosius, a semi-mythical character, "is said to be extracted of the Roman race" (Fuller, Ch. Hist. I. cent. v. § 28), and is described as attacking Vortigern in Wales at his castle of Generen, where he set fire to his castle, and burnt him with it. He is also reported to have been a great champion of the British race.

68, 1. *Uther ;*—the great *Pendragon* (a title borne by British chiefs as defenders of their race), is said to have kept up the strife against the Saxons, and to have been the father of Arthur. Cp. F. Q. Bk. I. vii. 31. Hardyng, c. 71:

> " His brother Uter at Caergwent was crouned
> In trone royall then fully was admit:
> Twoo dragons made of gold royall that stound,
> (That one) offred of his devout wit,
> In the mynster there, as he [had] promit:
> That other before hym euer in battaile bare
> Of gold in goulis, wher so he gan to fare.
> And for he bare the dragon so in warre
> The people all hym called then Pendragon
> For his surname, in landes nere and farre,
> Whiche is to say in Britayn region
> In theyr langage, *the head of the dragon.*"

2. *There abruptly ;*—the plan which Spenser is working out does not allow him to go on any farther. Otherwise Prince Arthur would learn his own parentage and dignities long before his time; for Uther is Arthur's father. So he rends the MS. at this point abruptly.

69, 2. *royall ofspring ;*—the pedigree or descent of kings. This use of 'ofspring' proves that 'ofspring auncient,' Bk. I. vi. 30, means 'ancient descent' or origin.

70, 1. *Guyon . . . his booke did read ;*—this was the 'Antiquitee of Faerie lond;' the imaginative and poetical account of the parentage and descent of Queen Elizabeth.

70, 5. *Prometheus ;*—the myth relates how Prometheus (forethought) and Epimetheus (afterthought) were sons of the Titan Iapetus; and how (according to one account) Prometheus saved mankind from ruin at the hands of Zeus, and bestowed on them many useful gifts, fire, the practical arts, &c.; (according to another account) how he first fashioned man out of earth and water, and afterwards stole fire from heaven to animate his work.   The first story is to be found in Aeschylus' Prometheus, the latter (which Spenser follows) in Ovid, Met. i. 81.

8. *for which,* &c. ;—so in Aeschylus, Prom. 1015.   But Spenser deviates from the established tale in saying that Jove deprived him of life ; the essence of his punishment was the constant renewal of his ' hart-strings,' i. e. his liver, and the continuance of his life.

71, 1. *Elfe, to weet Quick ;*—this name of the first man is purely imaginary, nor does Elfe mean ' quick,' i. e. living.   See Gloss. *Elf.*

4. *in the gardins of Adonis ;*—Adonis being wounded, Aphrodite sprinkled nectar on his blood, and flowers immediately sprang up.   This is one side of it.   The other legend makes Adonis the Sun-god, and his garden the garden of the Sun.   In this garden the first man might well walk and meet with the ' goodly creature,' mother of all Fairies, and eventually of Queen Elizabeth.

72, 6. *all that now America men call ;*—which Spenser still attaches on to India, as we have before noticed.

8. *Cleopolis ;*—Spenser's name for London.   See Bk. I. vii. 46, and x. 58.

73, 4. *Panthea ;*—supposed by some to be Windsor.   See Bk. I. x. 58.

75, 1. *Elfcleos ;*—coming after the seven hundred princes who reigned in order, was Henry VII of England, who reigned from A. D. 1485 to 1509.

2. *Elfcleos ;*—in line 1 this word is four-syllabled ; here only three-syllabled.

6. *He left two sonnes ;*—scarcely correct, as he outlived the elder.

Elferon The eldest brother ;—Prince Arthur, firstborn son of Henry VII, born A.D. 1486, married to Katharine of Aragon in 1501, ' untimely died' in 1502.

8. *the mightie Oberon ;*—Prince Henry, afterwards Henry VIII, born A.D. 1491.   Spenser is right in saying he supplied Prince Arthur's place in ' spousall,' for he married Katharine of Aragon, his brother's widow, in 1509.   But it can hardly be said that he supplied his place ' in dominion,' as Arthur never came to the throne.

76, 4. *the fairest Tanaquill ;*—Queen Elizabeth, to whom Spenser gives this name, that of a British Princess.   Cp. Bk. I. Introd. ii.

5. *Him to succeede therein ;*—Spenser says nothing about Edward VI and Mary, artistically (and courtier-like) conceiving that the force of the passage would be broken if anything were interposed between the great Harry and his lordly daughter.

by his last will ;—the will of King Henry VIII, dated 30 Dec. 1546, bequeaths the Crown of England to Prince Edward and his heirs: in default of such heirs, then to any other offspring of himself and " Queen Katherine that now is, or of any other our lawfull wife that we shall hereafter marie." [Indicating that this part of the will was drawn up at a much earlier date than the signature.]   In default of such male heirs, then the Crown was to go to Mary and her heirs: "and if it fortune that our said daughter do die without issue . . . we will that . . . the said imperyall crowne·. . . *shall wholely remaine and come to our said daughter Elizabeth*," upon certain stringent conditions as to the marriages of Mary and Elizabeth.   The will goes on to leave the Crown conditionally, after Elizabeth, to the 'Lady Frances' and the 'Lady Eleanor,' the two daughters of Mary his sister, widow of Louis XII, and afterwards wife of Charles Brandon, Duke of Suffolk.   He passes over her sister Margaret, who in 1501 had married James IV, King of Scotland, and had afterwards been Regent during the minority of James V, 1513-1516; and consequently passes over Mary Queen of Scots, who had been reigning in Scotland since the sixth day of her life in 1542 (King James her father died 14 Dec. 1542; she had been born on the 8th).

CANTO XI.

Sir Guyon and the Palmer set forth by sea to reach Acrasia's Island.   Meanwhile the foul spirits assault the castle of Alma, under their captain, Maleger.   Prince Arthur sallies forth upon them, and after infinite pains, drowns Maleger, and puts the whole rout to flight.

1. This stanza sets forth the aim of the Canto—which is, to describe the Soul attacked by the temptations of the five Senses.   This idea is worked out in Bunyan's allegory of Mansoul.   There the powers of evil beleaguer man, who is rescued by the divine aid of "the Captain of our Salvation."   While, however, Bunyan's aim was religious edification, Spenser's was the expression of moral conflict.   He as carefully excludes the religious side from this allegory as he had introduced and enforced it in that of the Red Cross Knight.

2. A beautiful picture of the soul ruling over a pure and well-ordered body. This is a reminiscence of Spenser's Platonic studies.

3, 2. *The windowes of bright heaven;*—so Gen. 7. 11.

4, 7. *let them pas;*—they are resumed in Canto xii.

6, 1. *in twelve troupes;*—i. e. *seven* deadly sins; and *five* vices which attack the five senses.

3. *offend his proper part,* &c.;—i. e. do most damage to that part of man (that sense, &c.) to which he was most akin, or to which he was most properly opposed.

7, 1. *The other five,* &c.;—against the "five senses."
    1. Against the sight, the lust of the eyes.
    2. Against the hearing, the spirit of falsehood.
    3. Against the smell, the delights of odours, &c.
    4. Against the taste, greediness and gluttony.
    5. Against the touch, all manner of carnal delights.

8, 1. *The first troupe;*—such, Upton remarks, is Alcina's crew, Ariosto, Orl. Fur. 6. 61.   So also Comus:—"Rout of monsters, headed like sundry sorts of wild beasts."

9, 9. *they that bulwarke sorely rent;*—ed. 1590 reads, 'they against that bulwarke lent.'

10, 2. *dessignment ;*—ed. 1590, 'assignment.'

11, 4. *Some like to boundes, some like to apes, dismayd;*—the old conception of vice taking form of different animals. Mediæval symbolism used animals on both sides—as signs of virtue or of vice; the lion, the dog (he however was both good and bad), the leopard, the eagle, &c. were symbolical of noble qualities; the fox, the ape, the swine, &c. of evil passions. This symbolism culminates in the old satire of Reynard the Fox.

For '*dismayd,*' see Glossary.

14, 3. *ordinance ;*—the commentators here hold learned controversy as to whether Spenser is justified in firing off guns in a faery tale, or whether 'ordinance' may not signify 'battering engines.'

15, 6. *those two brethren giantes ;*—Prince Arthur and Timias his squire—unless indeed it is a slip, and Spenser was thinking of Sir Guyon as still in the castle.

16, 9. *the patrone of her life ;*—Latinism, her *patronus,* defender.

17, 5. *Fayre mote be thee ;*—'well might he prosper.' See Gloss. *Thee.*

18, 2. *thicke as flakes of snow;*—so Hom. Il. 12. 156, 278; Virg. Aen. 12. 610.

4. Fine simile of the mountain torrent. Cp. Hom. Il. 4. 452; Virg. Aen. 2. 305; Ariosto, Orl. Fur. 39. 14; Tasso, Gier. Lib. 19. 46.

8. *vowes make vaine ;*—so Pliny has "preces irritae.' With this passage cp. Ovid, Met. 1. 272:

"Sternuntur segetes, et deplorata coloni
     Vota iacent, longique perit labor irritus anni."

9. *headlong ruine ;*—Latinism, 'praeceps ruina.' So 'caeli ruina,' of the downfall of a thunderstorm.

19, 7. *The fierce Spumador ;*—Prince Arthur's steed. The horses of great knights, down to Rosinante, have always had high-sounding names. 'Spumador,' the foaming, bit-champing steed.

9. *Such as Laomedon of Phoebus race did breed ;*—the 'horses of Laomedon,' mentioned by Homer (Il. 5. 265 sqq.), had been originally given by Zeus to Laomedon's grandfather Tros, in return for his son Ganymede. From Tros they descended to Ilus, from Ilus to Laomedon, Priam's father. So that Laomedon cannot be said to have bred them, though Homer tells us that Anchises did succeed in secretly obtaining some half-divine foals from them for his son Aeneas. Nor are they said to be related to the horses of Phoebus, the Sun.

20, 2. *their capteine ;*—Maleger. Very finely conceived is this incarnation of Passions; worn out with evil desires, as the name implies (*malus, aeger*), terrible to others, and miserable in himself, dried up with the heat of immoral life, followed by two hags, Impotence, the curse of powerlessness, the consequence of that life, and feverish Impatience. His terrible tenacity of life, and activity in mischief, his recovery of strength by every contact with earth, his final defeat and death, drowned in a 'standing lake,' are all remarkably spirited.

21, 5. *Such as the Indians, &c. ;*—this refers doubtless to the North

American Indians, whose bows and arrows may have been brought over among the curiosities collected by Raleigh in Virginia.

23, 8, 9. *Impotence . . . Impatience;*—Passion followed by weakness, a weakness that leads on to new excesses; and by Impatience of all control 'armed with raging flame.'

25, 1, 2, *speare Soone to him raught;*—either took it from the hand of his squire, or drew it close in to himself, and laid it in the rest.

9. *to weene approch;*—we 'think of approaching,' and rarely use the infin. without its sign 'to'; except in the case of auxiliary verbs, 'I must go,' 'I shall live,' and a few others, as 'to let be,' 'to hear tell,' 'I saw him come,' 'I bid them wait.'

26, 7. *As wonts the Tartar,* &c.;—the Tartar is here the lineal descendant of the Parthian, whose method of flying and fighting was proverbial. The reference to the Russian is less curious than it might seem; for in the reign of Ivan the Terrible, the Cossacks and Tartars ravaged the banks of the Wolga and the shores of the Caspian Sea, and in A. D. 1577 the Czar sent troops against them, whose work in clearing those districts may well have been reported to the English by the merchants. They had been the chief sufferers, and would doubtless have communications with England.

27, 5. *Who;*—ed. 1590, 'but.'

28, 29. The struggle of the virtuous man with weakness and impatience.

29, 5. *lode upon him layd;*—a proverbial expression: cp. the common English phrase, 'to come down *heavily*' on a person.

30, 4. *That in assurance;*—perhaps an anti-Calvinistic reflection. Man can have no absolute assurance till the end. Even a Prince Arthur may be nearly overcome.

9. *grace thee blest;*—had not God's favour defended him. So in Bk. I. ix. 28, 'God from him me blesse.'

survive;—edd. 1590, 1596 'revive,' but corrected in the 'Faults Escaped' of 1590.

32, 6. *strives to mount,* &c.;—the notion of the older physicists that the element of Fire was confined here below, and was ever striving to rise to its natural sphere, the outermost of the four concentric circles.

33, 2. *Out of his bolde;*—must here mean 'out of the bonds in which he was holden.'

3. *And as a beare;*—an allusion to the then popular sport of bear-baiting. 'As' must here be taken as = 'like,' and thus the object to 'becomes more fell, &c.' will be Prince Arthur. Or 'as' = 'is as,' and then 'becomes, &c.' will be referred to the bear. The parallel of the simile, in that case, is not drawn out at all, but left to the reader's imagination.

34, 2. *nor other barme;*—'nor do harm to any other person' (or 'to the other,' Arthur).

9. *fild his place;*—'lay along covering his allotted amount of ground,' his " six-feet of land."

35, 9. *signe of sundry waye;*—a stone set to indicate that two roads separated from that point. Cp. Virg. Aen. 12. 896:

> " Saxum circumspicit ingens,
> Saxum antiquum, ingens, campo quod forte iacebat,
> Limes agro positus, litem ut discerneret arvis "

36, 6. *as a faulcon*, &c.;—simile drawn from the craft of falconry. Spenser delights to take his illustrations from the amusements of the gentlemen of his age.

39, 7. *wandring ghost that wanted funerall;*—a classical allusion mixed up with the thoroughly romantic characteristics of this conflict. The Greeks and Latins believed that if a man's body lay unburied, his spirit wandered about, refused admission to Charon's boat, and unable to appear before the Judges below.

40, 4. *a person without spright;*—'a body without a spirit,' like a mask without a face behind it; Lat. *persona*, a mask.

43, 1. *Joves harnesse-bearing bird;*—the eagle bears Jove's 'harness,' his thunder-bolts, in his claws. Cp. Virg. Aen. 1. 394.

4. *That it rebounds ;*—a bird falling dead would scarcely rebound in fact, however heavy its fall, as all its elasticity would be lost.

44, 7. *dead-living swaine;*—alive while dead, having no 'spirit,' yet having 'soul,' motion, passion, breath.

9. *and from her wombe,* &c.;—like the fabled Antaeus whom Heracles slew. See Lucan. Phars. 4. 615 sqq.

46, 1. *Tho up he caught him ;*—Cp. Tasso, Gier. Lib. 19. 17:

> "Nè con più forza da l'adusta arena
> Sospese Alcide il gran gigante, e strinse." (Upton.)

5. *taking his full course;*—probably equivalent to 'reckoning the whole distance traversed.'

48, 6. *That he began to faint,* &c.;—the deadly faintness which ensues after a terrible wrestling with temptations. The human soul comes out victorious, but with suffering. We are reminded of Him, to whom after the great victory over the tempter, angels came and ministered.

CANTO XII.

Sir Guyon comes at last to the Bower of Bliss, in which Acrasia dwells. Here he lands, and enters her gardens, passing, by the help of his monitor the Palmer, through another subtle series of temptations. At last he finds the enchantress lying asleep: he seizes and binds her fast. Then he breaks down the Bower, and releases, through the virtue of the Palmer's staff, all her wretched victims, save only Grille the hog, who chooses to continue in that estate.

1, 1. *Now gins that goodly frame of Temperance,* &c.;—the poet feels that he draws towards the end of his long task, and he rises to the occasion. This last Canto is full of passages of very great beauty, and is perhaps the most striking part of all the Faery Queene.' The influence of Spenser's imagination and rich colouring is seen as clearly in Keats as in any later poet, though there are others who (like Fletcher, in his Purple Island) have copied him more closely.

that;—edd. 1590, 1596 'this,' but corrected in 'Faults Escaped,' 1590.

8. *Pleasure;*—that is, Acrasia. Spenser, putting this trial last and counting it as worst, accepts the old Greek saying, that 'It is harder to fight against pleasure than against pain.'

2, 6. *An hideous roaring,* &c. ;—so Hom. Od. 12. 202 :

καπνὸν καὶ μεγὰ κῦμα ἴδον, καὶ δοῦπον ἄκουσα·
τῶν δ' ἄρα δεισάντων ἐκ χειρῶν ἔπτατ' ἐρετμά·
βόμβησαν δ' ἄρα πάντα κατὰ ῥόον.

8, 4. *the Gulfe of Greedinesse;*—this is the Charybdis of the ancients, ever regarded as a type of greediness. Hom. Od. 12. 235 ; Virg. Aen. 3. 420.

9. *doe seeme away to fly;*—Ps. 114. 3, "The sea saw that, and fled."

4, 1. *an hideous rocke,* &c.;—so the rock of Scylla is described by the ancients ; but instead of the horrible sea-monster dwelling in it, Spenser has given it magnetic qualities.

2. *mighty magnes stone;*—the magnet is named from Magnesia, whence it was supposed to come. Lucr. 6. 909 :

"Quem Magneta vocant patrio de nomine Graiei,
Magnetum quia sit patriis in finibus ortus."

9. *wawes;*—'waves'; not 'woes,' as has been suggested.

6, 1. *doe;*—ed. 1590, 1596 'did,' corrected to 'doe' in 'Faults Escaped,' 1590.

8, 1. As on the one side is Charybdis or greediness, past which snare the Knight rows unscathed, so on the other side is Scylla, 'the Rock of vile Reproch,' the place of broken credit and repute, arising from extravagance. The Knight is made to run the gauntlet of every kind of excess in pleasure : first gluttony, then vain show, next the wandering islands, i. e. listless idleness, and so on up to Acrasia's Bower.

11, 3. *seeming now and than;*—appearing at intervals upon the sea.

13, 1. *th' isle of Delos,* &c.;—Delos, says the legend, was at first a floating island; but Zeus anchored it to the sea-bottom with an adamantine chain, that it might be a safe resting-place for Latona, who was flying from the wrath of Here (Juno). There she brought forth twin children, Apollo and Artemis. The island was afterwards consecrated to Apollo, to whom it was held to belong absolutely. Thucydides, 3. 104, gives an account of the purification of Delos at the time of the Peloponnesian war. See Ovid, Met. 6. 186 ; Virg. Aen. 3. 73.

15, 8. *the departing land;*—departing, either because her boat left it, or because, being a wandering island, it drifted away from her.

16, 2. *to bord, and purpose diversly;*—to address them, and try all manner of talk.

18, 7. *the checked wave;*—any one will understand this who has watched the tide running upon sands.

19, 1. *a goodly ship did see,* &c. ;—the shipwreck of some noble gentleman, well equipped, but cast away through unthrift and careless living. The time was that of a newly-awakened interest in seafaring : gentlemen fitted out gallant ships, and sailed them themselves. One feels the power of the sea, and, probably, the influence of Raleigh, in these descriptive passages.

Raleigh, the poet's most intimate friend, was just at this time especially keen on such adventure.

21, 3. *tb' utmost sandy breacb ;*—the very end of the sandbank, on which the sea was breaking.

23, 6. *Spring-beaded bydraes ; and sea-sbouldring wbales ;*—i. e. Hydras with many heads springing from their necks, and whales which from their bigness shoulder away the waves from them. The hydra is an amphibious monster, a huge water-snake, seven-headed ; whenever one head was cut off, two new ones instantly sprang up in its place. Hence the epithet 'spring-headed.'

7 *wbirlpooles ;*—Gesner, vol. iii. p. 256 (1558), says, " *Wbirlpoole* ab Anglis dictus cetus balaena est. Videtur a vorticibus, quos turbinis instar in aqua excitat, nomen habere." In Job 41. 1, *leviatban* is rendered in the margin, 'a whale or *wbirlpool.*' This whale was also called *tburlepoole.*

8. *scolopendraes ;*—a marine insect, a palm long, said by Avicenna to have forty-four legs, like a centipede. Its bite was poisonous, and it had a sting in its tail. This is probably not the monster meant by Spenser.

9. *monoceros ;*—the narwhal, a whale scarcely known when Spenser wrote. Or he may mean the sword-fish, which has only one 'horn,' and is a sufficiently formidable sea-monster. See Gesner, Hist. Animalium, vol. iii. p. 645 (1558): " Monoceros est monstrum marinum, habens in fronte cornu maximum, quo naves obvias penetrare potest ac destruere, et hominum multitudinem perdere." He also, p. 247, gives a picture of the monoceros of Olaus Wormius, but deems it fabulous.

Notice the halting of this line. 'Mighty monóceros with unmeasúred tayles.'

24, 1. *The dreadfull fisb ;*—Gesner (p. 249) says that *Mors* is another name for the 'Rosemary.' On p. 498 he describes a big brute, half sea-calf, half hippopotamus, as the *Moriz.*

3. *The griesly wasserman ;*—Gesner (pp. 519-522) gives some varieties of these maritime demons, with their portraits. There seems to have been a water-monk, and a water-bishop; both under the heading " Homo marinus."

5. *sea-satyre ;*—Gesner (p. 1197) gives us this monster as " Pan, vel Satyrus marinus," with his picture, and calls it a " daemon marinus."

7. *ziffius ;*—Gesner (p. 249) classes ziffius under the whales. His account of him is that " if you saw his face, you would say it was utterly monstrous ; if the abyss of his mouth, you would flee as from the picture of death ; if his eyes, you would shudder; if his whole body, you would declare there was nothing like it in the world." Gesner's picture bears out his description.

9. *greedy rosmarines ;*—Gesner (p. 249) pourtrays the *Rosmarus* among the whales. He says of him that he is as big as an elephant ; that he climbs up the shore and eats grass ; and when he wants to sleep, hangs himself by his teeth to a rock. He then slumbers so soundly that fishermen can throw ropes and nets round him and capture him.

26, 5. *draw from on tbis journey to proceede ;*—notice this construction, 'from to proceed.' The substantival use of the infin. is common to many languages. So Schiller's famous " *Sterben* ist nichts; doch *leben* und nich *seben*—Dass ist das Unglück." (Wilhelm Tell.) Once grant this substantival infin., and the use of the preposition with it, whether 'for to' or 'from to,' becomes perfectly natural, though our language rather shrinks from the use of abstract forms, and has gradually dropped these phrases. The 'for' early became quite pleonastic; as in the English Bible of 1611, Matt. xxvii. 6, " It is not lawful *for to* put them into the treasury," where the force of the preposition is quite lost. 'For to' is still retained in vulgar speech.

6. *vertuous staffe ;*—his miraculous staff, having 'virtue' in it. Tasso's Ubaldo has a similar wand: Gier. Lib. 14. 73; 15. 49. It is the proper accompaniment of all workers of wonders or magicians, from Moses' rod downwards.

9. *great Tethys bosome ;*—Tethys, daughter of Uranus and Gaea, was Ocean's wife, and sea-gods and sea-monsters were her offspring.

30, 2. *it was a still,* &c. ;—This is Virgil's bay, Aen. 1. 159 sqq.

7. *did like an balfe theatre fulfill ;*—completed a semicircle (not an *amphitheatre,* as Upton says), which looked down on the quiet bay and sands.

31, 1. *They were faire ladies,* &c. ;—Spenser has, as usual, altered the classical legend to his own. mind. The Sirens were mythical ladies, who had the power of enchanting passers-by to their ruin. They are not mermaids in classical times; late poets grant them wings, but make no other deviation from human form. They were not five in number, but two or three.

2. *With th' Heliconian maides ;*—the Muses, who had their especial seat upon the eastern side of Mount Helicon, where was a grove sacred to them, and the well-known fountain of Aganippe. Pindar calls the Muses (Isthm. 7 (8). 126) Ἑλικώνιαι παρθένοι. This musical contest between Sirens and Muses answers to no classical legend; but it is well conceived. The student will do well to contrast this passage of Spenser with the account of the Sirens in the Odyssey (12. 166–200). Spenser's bay has a modern beauty about it, which Homer's Siren Island misses; his description of the Sirens is more grotesque than Homer's, as we should expect in a 'Gothic' poem. The two songs are very different in tone and character: Spenser's suggests sweet rest and quiet after storm; Homer's tempts Ulysses by a promise of an epic upon the labours of Troy. The harmony of nature, also a more modern conception, comes out very clearly in Spenser, st. 33. We feel his exquisite sense of harmonious sounds, for which this canto is remarkable throughout. The victory of Sir Guyon over this temptation is far nobler than that of Ulysses, who, bound doubly and trebly to the mast, with gesture and voice beseeches his sailors (whose ears are stopped with wax, so that they cannot hear) to loose him, that he may go to them. Finally, Spenser's passage avoids the grim accessories of the shore strewed with dead men's bones and garbage. (Od. 12. 45, 46.) It would have jarred on the sense of calm sweetness' and beauty ; it would have lessened the force of the temptation, had Guyon espied these evidences of the Sirens' deadly power. On the whole, Homer is more forcible, Spenser more beautiful.

32, 8. *the port of rest;*—so Tasso, Gier. Lib. 15. 63.

34, 5. *a grosse fog ;*—notice the sharp clear touches with which the poe: paints the coming on of a fog.

36, 4. *The ill-faste owl ;*—see Bk. I. v. 30, and note there.

36, 5. *The boars night-raven;*—always regarded as a weird, uncanny bird. See Milton, Allegro:

> "Where brooding darkness spreads her jealous wings,
> *And the night-raven sings.*"

6. *The . . . bat, dayes enimy ;*—naturally introduced in the dark fog.

7. *The ruefull strich, still waiting on the bere ;*—the screech-owl. Also called the *lich*-owl, or bird of death. So Ovid, Met. 10. 452 :

> " Ter omen
> Funereus bubo letali carmine fecit."

So also Drayton's Owl (quoted by Nares), has:

> "The shrieking *litch-owl*, that doth never cry
> But boding death, and quick herself inters
> In darksome graves, and hollow sepulchres."

9. *The bellish harpies ;*—see above, vii. 23.

37, 8. *The sacred soile ;*—Latinism, *sacer*, accursed. So i. 51 :

> ' Shonne
> The cursed land, where many wend amis.'

38, 3. *crooked keele ;*—i. e. at the bow of the boat.

41, 2. *Caduceus ;*—Mercury's rod; it was an olive-branch, or wand, around which two snakes were twined. He used it to quell all discord and disturbance. It is said that Apollo invented it, and exchanged it for a lyre.

4. *With which he wonts the Stygian realmes invade ;*—So Virgil, Aen. 4. 242 :

> " Tum virgam capit: hac animas ille evocat Orco
> Pallentes, alias sub Tartara tristia mittit."

And Horace, Od. 1. 10, 18 :

> " Virgaque levem coerces
> Aurea turbam."

42, 2. *the Bowre of Blisse ;*—upon this description Spenser has expended all the riches of his imagination. His Faery-land is intended to heighten the contrast between the good and the evil land—that of Queen Elizabeth, the Faery Queene, and that of vice and luxury. It also heightens the continual triumph of virtue over the most seductive forms of temptation. Compare Tasso's Bower of Armida, Gier. Lib. 15 and 16.

43, 5. *Nought feard their force, that fortilage to win, But, &c. ;*—this seems to signify that ' their force' (i. e. the power of the wild beasts without) in no respect frightened them (' feared' is so used by Spenser = to affear, or terrify), lest they should get in; but Wisdom and Temperance did frighten them. The fence was ' weake and thin ;' but the guests feared not the beasts without ; what they really feared was Wisdom and Temperance, against whom the mightiest fence would have been powerless.

44, 4. *Jason and Medaea ;*—Love and Magic ; and then ' falsed faith' when Jason deserted Medea for Creüsa, Creon's daughter. The latter part of the tale is worked out by Euripides, Medea ; also by Ovid, Met. 7.

8. *The wondred Argo ;*—the famous ship of the Argonauts.

45, 6. *like the boyes bloud ;*—the blood of Medea's children murdered by her in her terrible revenge.

9. *th' enchaunted flame, &c. ;*—Medea sent Glauce (or Creüsa) a magical medicated robe, which destroyed her by fire when she put it on.

47, 1. *him Genius did call;*—there were two sorts of genius (according to Servius ad Aen. 6. 743), good and bad. Spenser here follows that division. See the passage from Natalis Comes, 4. 3, quoted by T. Warton.

2. *Not that celestial powre;*—this 'Genius' of the Romans was an emanation from the gods. To him the marriage-bed was sacred ('lectus *genialis*'), as Spenser hints in this place; he was the spirit of renovation and plenty; he inspired good thoughts, warned men of evil, escorted them to another world. They were called Daemons by the Greeks.

8. *That is our Selfe;*—Spenser inclines to the opinion of those who make the Socratic Daemon only a Conscience, or Moral Sense. The ancients never confound these 'guardian angels' with the men whose interests they watched over.

48, 2. *good Agdistes;*—Agdistis is a mythical being, connected with Phrygian rites of worship, and with the symbolical worship of the powers of nature. Hesychius and Strabo make Agdistis the same as Cybele. The ancients did not connect this being with the Genius. This connection comes from Natalis Comes, 4. 3 (quoted by T. Warton).

50, 5. *Floraes pride:*—the wedding of Nature and Art in gardening.

51, 1. *bevens alwayes joviall;*—'joviall' is 'sub Jove,' clear, serene. Cp. Tasso, Gier. Lib. 15. 9.

52, 1. *the pleasaunt hill Of Rhodope;*—a desolate, high mountain on the frontiers of Thrace and Macedonia: far from being a 'pleasant hill.' There was on it a great sanctuary of the Thracian Dionysus. Spenser's notion of it comes from Ovid, Met. 10. 86 sqq.

2. *on which the nimphe, &c.;*—this story is told in Plutarch, De Fluv. p. 23; and is alluded to by Ovid, Met. 6. 87. (Upton.)

4. *Thessalian Tempe;*—here too the scenery is wild and grand, not soft and garden-like, as Spenser conceives. Tempe is a long, deep defile, difficult of access, five miles long, with steep, frowning cliffs.

6. *Ida;*—the famous hill of Phrygia.

8. *Parnasse;*—the hill sacred to Apollo and the Muses.

9. *Eden selfe;*—Spenser is blamed for mixing sacred conceptions with classical; as also in Bk. I. x. 54.

57. Compare with this stanza Milton's account of the brothers breaking Comus' cup, Comus 651.

58, 9. *The art, &c.;*—'ars celare artem.' So Tasso, Gier. Lib. 16. 9, whence this description is largely drawn:

"L'arte, che tutto fa, nulla si scopre."

59. This stanza comes straight from Tasso, Gier. Lib. 16. 10; and the fountain from the same, 15. 55, &c.

70, 6. *what manner musicke;*—the Old English usage of 'manner,' common in Chaucer. So Spenser also uses 'mister,' 'what mister wight,' Bk. I. ix. 23.

71. Notice the extraordinary art with which this sequence is carried on. The intricacy of it is intended to give a sense of infinitely complicated, and so harmonious and gentle, sounds; while out of it all arises the sweet human voice of one who sings. Cp. Tasso, Gier. Lib. 16. 12.

74. For this love lay, cp. Ariosto, 1. 58; but especially Tasso, Gier. Lib. 16. 14, on which it is modelled.

J. C. Walker quotes a stanza from G. Niccolo degli Agostini, 4. 7, whence Spenser seems to have drawn this image of the rose almost literally.

3. *the image of thy day;*—the likeness of thy day of life. This is the old strain of "Gather your rosebuds," &c., the Epicurean "Carpe diem."

75, 6. *Gather therefore,* &c.;—so Ariosto, Orl. Fur. 1. 58:

"Corrò la fresca e mattutina rosa
Che tardando stagion perder potria."

79, 7. *Yet sleeping ;*—absolute nom. = 'he yet sleeping.'

80, 2. *sleeping praise ;*—Latinism, praise being used as Virgil uses "laus" = virtus.

81, 4. *A subtile net ;*—this is drawn from Vulcan's cunning net, with which he captures Mars and Venus, in the Iliad. Cp. also Ariosto, Orl. Fur. 15. 56.

85, 1. *These seeming beasts ;*—again the menagerie of Circe.

5. *like monstruous ;*—in shape they have become monstrous, like their disordered minds.

86, 7. *Grille ;*—the hoggish mind alone refuses to be restored to human shape. The incident is found in Plutarch's Dialogue, περὶ τοῦ τὰ ἄλογα λόγῳ χρῆσθαι. An allusion also to 2 Pet. 2. 22, perhaps. The force and vigour of these last touches are very remarkable. The poet does not end with abstract moralities or reflections. The work is done; one touch of the grotesque relieves the sense of sadness caused by the breaking-down of the earthly Paradise. Grille shews, more plainly than a dozen ethical stanzas would have done, the degradation and loss of human qualities, of self-respect, of aims above sense, which are the natural outcome of the life of sensual delights, however beautiful and refined. The victorious Knight has done his work without a word: and, with the sententious Palmer, spurns from him the degraded brute, and departs.

GLOSSARY.

List of Books cited, with explanation of references.

Dictionaries, Glossaries.

Baretti : Italian Dictionary. 1839.
Bartsch : Chrestomathie de l'ancien Français. 1880 (Glossaire).
Brachet : French Dict., translated by Kitchin. 1878.
Burguy : Glossaire de la langue d'Oïl. 1856.
Catholicon Anglicum : ed. Herrtage, E. E. T. S. 1882.
Chaucer : ed. Morris. 1880 (Glossary).
Chaucer 1 : ed. Morris, Prologue, &c. ⎫
Chaucer 2 : ed. Skeat, Prioresses Tale, &c. ⎬ Glossaries.
Chaucer 3 : ed. Skeat, Man of Lawe, &c. ⎭
Coleridge : Glossarial Index. 1852.
Cotgrave : French and English Dict. 1611.
Davies : Supplementary English Glossary. 1881.
Diez : Etymologisches Wörterbuch. 1878.
Ducange : Lexicon Manuale ; Maigne D'Arnis. 1866.
Fick : Wörterbuch der Indogerman. Sprachen. 1874.
Florio : Italian and English Dict. 1659.
Gloss. 1 : Glossary to Faery Queene, Book i. Clarendon Press, 1881.
Grein : Glossary to Anglo-Saxon Poetry. 1861.
Halliwell : Dict. of Archaic and Provincial Words. 1874.
Hilpert : German-English Dict. 1857.
Heliand : ed. Heyne (Glossary).
Icel. Dict. : Icelandic Dict. by Cleasby and Vigfusson. 1874.
Jamieson : Scottish Dict. 1867.
Leo : Angelsächsisches Glossar. 1877.
M.S. 1 : Specimens of Early English, ed. R. Morris. 1882.
M.S. 2 :   „   „   „   „   ed. Morris and Skeat. 1873.
Nares : Glossary. 1876.
O'Reilly : Irish-English Dict. 1864.
Palsgrave : L'Esclaircissement de la langue Française. 1530.
P. Plowman, C. P. : ed. Skeat, Clarendon Press. 1869.
Prompt. Parv. : Promptorium Parvulorum, ed. Way. 1865.
Richardson : English Dict. 1867.
Roquefort : Glossaire de la langue Romane. 1808.
Schmid : Gesetze der Angelsachsen. 1858 (Glossar.).
Schmidt : Shakspere Lexicon. 1874.
Skeat : Etymological Dict. of Eng. Lang. 1882.
Stratmann : Dict. of the Old Eng. Lang. 1873.
Sweet : Anglo-Saxon Reader. 1879 (Glossary).
Trench : Select Glossary. 1879.

Webster-Mahn : English Dict. 1875.
Weigand : Deutsches Wörterbuch. 1878.

Grammars, Philological Works.

Curtius : Grundzüge der Griechischen Etymologie. 1873.
Earle : Philology of the English Tongue. 1879.
Morris : Historical Outlines of English Accidence. 1876.
M. Müller : Lectures on the Science of Language. 1871.
M. Müller, Chips : Chips from a German Workshop. 1875.
P. Plowman : notes to, by Skeat : E. E. T. S. 1877.
Rhŷs : Lectures on Welsh Philology. 1879.
Sweet : A. S. Reader (with grammar). 1879.

Texts.

Ancren Riwle : ed. Morton. Camden Soc. 1853.
A. S. Chron. : Two Saxon Chronicles, ed. Earle. 1865.
Chanson de Roland : ed. Gautier. 1881.
More's Utopia : translated by Robynson, ed. Lumby. 1879.
Spenser : Complete Works, ed. Morris. 1879.
Wiclif, N. T. : New Test., ed. Skeat. 1879.
Wiclif, O. T. : Old Test. 1881.

Abbreviations (Languages).

A. S. = Anglo-Saxon.
Du. = Dutch.
Fr. = French.
O. Fr. = Old French.
Ger. = German.
Go. = Gothic.
Gr. = Greek.
Heb. = Hebrew.
It. = Italian.
Lat. = Latin.
L. Lat. = Late Latin.

M. E. Middle English.
M. H. G. = Middle High German.
O. H. G. = Old High German.
O. N. = Old Norse (Icelandic).
O. S. = Old Saxon.
Scot. = Lowland Scotch.
Sk. = Sanscrit.
Sp. = Spanish.
Sw. = Swedish.
W. = Welsh.

Other Abbreviations.

adj. = adjective.
adv. = adverb.
cp. = compare.
exx. = examples.
pl. = plural.

pp. = past participle.
pret. = preterite.
sb. = substantive.
s. v. = sub verbo (under the word).
vb. = verb.

Initials.

A. V. = Authorised Version.
C. T. = Canterbury Tales.

F. Q. = Faery Queene.
P. L. = Paradise Lost.

N.B. The semicolon stop ';' before forms is equivalent to the symbol —
in Skeat's Etymological Dict., and is to be read 'directly derived from,' or
'borrowed from.' The abbreviation 'cp.' is equivalent to Skeat's symbol +,
and is used to introduce cognate forms, having no part in the direct history
of the word.

A.

Abace, i. 26, to lower; O. Fr. *abaisser* (Bartsch); L. Lat. *abassare* (Ducange); *ad + bassare*; from *bassus*, low, prop. stout, short (Diez, p. 45); see **Bace.**

Aband, x. 65, to abandon; contracted from *abandon*; see Halliwell; O. Fr. *abandoner*, to give up into the power of another (Bartsch), from *à bandon*, at the free will, discretion of any one; O. Fr. *bandon* (L. Lat. *bandonem**) is from L. Lat. *bandum* or *bannum*, an order, decree, from O. H. G. *ban*, a proclamation. For this meaning of *bandon*, 'free disposal, unfettered authority,' cp. Chanson de Roland, 2703, 'All Spain will be to-day *en lur bandun*,' i. e. in their power, en leurs mains.

Abate, ii. 19, to beat down; O. Fr. *abatre* (Bartsch); L. Lat. *abbattere*; see Brachet (s. v. *abattre*).

Abord, vi. 4. For *on board*; see Skeat (s. v. *A-* prefix).

Abash, vii. 42, to frighten, amaze; M. E. *abaischen*, cp. Wiclif, Mk. 5. 42, 'Thei weren *abaischid* with a greet stonying,'=obstupuerunt stupore magno (Vulgate); O. Fr. *esbahiss-*, stem of pres. part. of *esbahir* (Fr. *ébahir*), to astonish; *es* (=Lat. *ex*, out, often, intensive) + *bahir*, to be amazed, to cry *bah!* For the final *-sh*, Fr. *-iss*, see Skeat (s. v. *abash*).

Abusion, deceit, fraud; M. E. *abusioun* (Chaucer); see also Halliwell; O. Fr. *abusion* (Bartsch) from *abuser*, to use amiss; from Lat. *abusus*, pp. of *abuti*, to misuse; *ab + uti*.

Abyde, i. 20; **Aby,** viii. 33; used with 'dearely,' to suffer for a thing; so Shakespeare 'lest thou *abide* it dear,' Mids. Nt. Dream,

iii. 2. 175, where the first quarto has '*aby*,' the latter being the correct form; M. E. *abyen*, to buy off (Chaucer); A. S. *ábycgan*; *á-* (intensive) + *bycgan*, to buy; see Skeat (s. v. *abide*, 2).

Accloye, vii. 15, to stop up, encumber, choke (with weeds); see Halliwell, Palsgrave; O. Fr. *cloyer* in *encloyer*, to stop up (Cotgrave), a form of O. Fr. *cloër* (mod. *clouer*) to nail, fasten up; from O. Fr. *clo* (mod. *clou*), a nail; Lat. *clavum*, acc. of *clavus*, a nail; see Skeat (s. v. *cloy*).

Accorage, ii. 38, to encourage; Fr. *accourager* (Cotgrave); see **Corage.**

Accord, ii. 30, to bring to terms, reconcile a matter; Fr. *accorder* (Cotgrave); L. Lat. *ac-cordare*, to bring to terms (Ducange); from *ad + cord-*, stem of *cor*, the heart.

Accord, iv. 21; ix. 2; x. 66, agreement; a subst. formed from the above.

According, x. 71, accordingly; so Shakespeare, see Schmidt.

Accourting, ii. 16, entertaining courteously; see **court.**

Accoyl, ix. 30, to gather together; O. Fr. *acoillir* (mod. *accueillir*); L. Lat. *accollegere*); *ad + colligere.*

Achates, ix. 31, provisions, lit. purchases; M. E. *achates* (Chaucer); Fr. *achat, achet*, a thing purchased (Cotgrave); from O. Fr. *achater, acater, achapter* (Bartsch); L. Lat. *accaptare*; Lat. *ad + captare*; see Brachet (s. v. *acheter*). Another form of *achates* is M. E. *acates*, victuals, delicacies, whence *acatour* (*catour*), a buyer of provisions, whence our *cater*, to buy provisions; see Skeat.

Acquight, xii. 3, to deliver; Fr. *acquiter* (Cotgrave); L. Lat. '*ac-*

quietare, quietum et securum red-
dere, absolvere—vox forensis' (Ducange) ; from L. Lat. *quietus,* out
of debt. Gloss. I, Acquite.

Address, iii. 1, to prepare, clothe,
arm ; O. Fr. *adresser, adrecier*
(Bartsch) ; L. Lat. *addretiare* (Ducange), a verb formed from L.
Lat. *drictus,* Lat. *directus,* straight.

Admire, Introd. 4, to be surprised ;
Fr. *admirer* ; Lat. *admirari* ; see
Trench.

Advaunce, iv. 46 ; xi. 34, to bring
forward, to raise, iv. 36, to show,
boast ; so Shakespeare, see Schmidt
(s. v. *advance*) ; *advance* is a mis-
taken form, in the 16th cent., for
M. E. *avancen* (Stratmann) ; Fr.
avancer, from *avant,* before ;
avant = Lat. *ab + ante* ; see Brachet.

Advise, avise, avize, vii. 38 ; ix.
38 ; x. 31 ; xii. 17, to consider
(a reflexive, vi. 46) ; i. 31 ; ix. 59,
to look at ; vi. 27, to advise, ad-
monish ; O. Fr. *aviser,* to be of
opinion, from *avis,* an opinion,
a word due to the phrase *il m'est
a vis,* my opinion is that . . . ; *vis*
= Lat. *visum,* that which has
seemed good to one.

Advizement, v. 13, consideration ;
ix. 9, advice ; see Halliwell.

Affeare, iii. 20 (ed. 1590), 45 ;
xii. 2 ; to frighten ; M. E. *afered*
(Chaucer) ; A. S. *áféran* (Grein),
from *fér,* a sudden peril, fear ;
orig. used of the peril of travelling ; related to A. S. *(ge)faran,*
to go, travel ; cp. Ger. *Gefahr,*
danger.

Affoord, vi. 19, to yield, to consent ; see Shakespeare (Schmidt,
s. v. *afford*) ; M. E. *aforthen,*
to provide ; A. S. *geforðian,* to
further, provide ; see Skeat.

Affrap, i. 26, to strike sharply ; It.
affrappáre (Baretti), from *frap-
páre* ; Fr. *frapper* ; O. N. *hrapa,*

to rush, to bluster (Icel. Dict.) ;
see Diez, p. 588.

Affright, iv. 30, terror, fright ; not
to be confused with *affret,* furious
onset (F. Q. III. ix. 16), a word
probably connected with It. *frétta,*
haste.

Affront, v. 20, to face ; O. Fr.
afronter (Burguy) ; L. Lat. *affron-
tare* (Ducange), from Lat. *ad +
front-,* stem of *frons,* the forehead.

Affyaunce, iv. 21, betrothal ; O.Fr.
afiance, a promising, from *afier,*
to promise faithfully (Bartsch) ;
L. Lat. *affidare* (Ducange), from
Lat. *fidem,* faith.

Afore, iv. 4 ; xii. 15, before (of
place and time) ; A. S. *onforan.*

Against, ix. 27, in provision for
the time when ; so Shakespeare
(Schmidt).

Aggrace, xii. 58, to lend a charm
to ; It. *aggraziáre* (Baretti). Gloss.
I, Agraste. viii. 56, goodwill,
favour.

Aggrate, ix. 34 ; xii. 42, 85, to
please ; It. *aggratare* (Florio) ;
L. Lat. *aggratare* ; hence O. Fr.
agreër. See Agree.

Aghast, viii. 4, struck with horror ;
M. E. *agaste* (Chaucer 2) pret. of
agasten, to terrify. Gloss. I.

Agonyes (House of), ix. 52, the
districts of the heavens in which
the planet Saturn rises ; see note.

Agree, iv. 3, to settle, quiet, appease ; O. Fr. *agreër,* to please
(Bartsch) ; L. Lat. *aggratare,*
from Lat. *gratum,* pleasing. See
Aggrate.

Agrise, vi. 46, to disfigure horribly.
This usage of the word seems
peculiar to Spenser. A. S. *á-grys-
an,* to fear greatly, to be horri-
fied (Leo) ; cp. Ger. *er-grausen,*
to fear, to horrify.

Aguise, i. 21, 31 ; vi. 7, to dress
out, adorn ; from guize.

Alablaster, ix. 44, alabaster; so Shakespeare (Schmidt); M. E. see Catholicon Anglicum; O. Fr. *alabastre* (mod. *albâtre*); Lat. *alabaster*; Gr. ἀλάβαστρον, ἀλάβαστος.

Alarmes, vi. 34, summons to arms, notice of hostile attack; see Shakespeare (Schmidt); O. Fr. *alarme* (Bartsch); It. *all' arme*, to arms! The word *alarum* is merely a Northern Eng. form of *alarm*; see Skeat; see **Larum-bell.**

Albe, vi. 4; viii. 28, although. Gloss. I.

Algates, i. 2; ii. 12, wholly, altogether; v. 20, 37, at all events, by all means; Jamieson. M. E. *algatis*, omnimodo (Catholicon Anglicum). Lit. by all ways; *gate* means a way; O. N. *gata*, a path, road; cp. Ger. *gasse*, a street. See **Gate.**

All, i. 46, altogether; so in various dialects (Halliwell).

Allegaunce, v. 13, allegiance, the duty of a subject to his *liege* lord, from Fr. *ligence*, liegemanship (Cotgrave), from O. Fr. *lige*, *liege*: see **Liege.**

Als, i. 7, 40, also. Gloss. I.

Amate, i. 6, ii. 5, to daunt, stupefy; Fr. *amatir*, *emmatir*, 'to amate, quaile' (Cotgrave), from O. Fr. *mat*, beaten, subdued, weak (Bartsch). *Mat* was orig. a chess term, like our *mate* in *checkmate*, which represents the Pers. *shâh mât*, 'the king is dead.' *Mât* is of Semitic origin, being from the Arab. *mâta*, he died.

Amate, ix. 34, to keep company with, from *mate* = M. E. *make*; A. S. *maca* (*ge-maca*), a mate, an equal; see Skeat (s. v. *mate*).

Ambrosiall (odours), iii. 22, 'Ambrosia deorum unguentum est,' cp. Virgil Aen. i. 403; Gr. ἀμβροσία, the food, ointment, &c., of the immortal gods; from ἀμβρόσιος immortal.

Amenage, iv. 11, to manage, control; a form of the verb **menage.**

Amenaunce, viii. 17; ix. 5, behaviour, see Halliwell; Fr. *amener*, to conduct, from *mener*, to manage, conduct, lead (Cotgrave); Lat. *minare*, to drive cattle (Andrews).

Amove, i. 12; vi. 37, to move; see Halliwell. Gloss. I.

Annoy, ii. 43; ix. 35: x. 64, annoyance, vexation; vii. 15; x. 14, to vex, trouble; *annoy* represents the Lat. *in odio*, in hatred. Gloss. I.

Anone, i. 13; ix. 28, anon, forthwith; A. S. *on án*, in *one* (moment), see Grein, p. 31, where it may be seen that the general meaning of *on án* is 'once for all.'

Antickes, iii. 27; vii. 4, odd, fanciful figures (wrought). *Anticke* orig. an adj., a doublet of *antique* (Lat. *antiquus*, *anticus*). Cotgrave gives s. v. *Antique*, 'taillé à antiques, cut with *anticks*, or with *antick*-works.' See Skeat.

Apayd (Ill), ix. 37; xii. 28, ill treated, lit. ill-satisfied; cp. Chaucer 2, 'evel *apayed*'; O. Fr. *apaier*, to satisfy (Bartsch); Lat. *ad + pacare*, to satisfy. See Wiclif N. T. (Glossary).

Appall, ii. 32; xi. 39, to weaken. See Skeat for examples of the word with this, the usual M. E. meaning. Etymology uncertain; prob. connected with *pall*, to wane, decay; see Schmidt.

Appeach, viii. 44; xi. 40, to censure, accuse; see Halliwell, Schmidt; *appeach*, a corrupted form of *impeach*; M. E. *apechen* for *empechen*; O. Fr. *empescher*, to hinder, stop, embarrass (Bartsch); cp. Skeat (s. v. *impeach*). See **Empeach.**

Approvaunce, xii. 76, approval;

from Fr. *approuver*; Lat. *appro-bare.*

Approv'd, iii. 15, proved, tried; so Fr. *approuvé* (Cotgrave).

Arber, v. 29; vii. 53; **arbour,** vi. 2, a bower made of branches of tiees; M. E. *herber* (*erber*), a garden of herbs, an orchard, a bower; O. Fr. *herbier* (*erbier*); Lat. *herbarium*, a collection of herbs; the word *arbour* has nothing in the world to do with *harbour.*

Arboret, vi. 12, a shrub; but generally the word means a place where trees are planted; cp. Ducange, '*Arborea*, locus arboribus consitus, Fr. *arboie, arboret*.' *Arboreta* and *arboretum* are also found in L. Lat. in this sense. *Arbustum* is the Class. Lat. form. Milton uses the word *arboret* in the sense of shrub, P. L. ix. 437. Cp. Richardson.

Aread (areed), i. 7; iii. 14; v. 16, to interpret, explain, tell; A. S. *á-rǽdan*, to explain (Leo, p. 446); cp. Ger. *er-rathen*. See **Read.**

Areare, xi. 36, back; M. E. *arere*; O. Fr. *arier, ariere*; Lat. *ad + retro*, backward. See Brachet (s. v. *arrière*), and Skeat (s. v. *arrears*).

Argo, xii. 44, Jason's ship; Gr. Ἀργώ, 'the swift,' from ἀργός, swift; so Liddell and Scott.

Arras, ix. 33, tapestry hangings of rooms, woven with figures; often in Shakespeare, see Schmidt. So named from Arras in Artois, France, where it was first made. See Halliwell.

Arraught, x. 34, seized by violence; see Halliwell (s.v. *araught* and *arraught*); pret. of M. E. *arechen*, to attain, reach (Richardson, Halliwell); A. S. *á-rǽcan* (Sweet). See Gloss. 1. **Raught.**

Arret, viii. 8; xi. 7, to entrust,

allot; M. E. *aretten*, to ascribe, impute (Chaucer 1), cp. Wiclif, N.T., Glossary; L. Lat. *arretare, arrectare*, to decree, decide, also to accuse (Ducange); Lat. *ad + reputare*, to count, reckon. According to Cowell's Interpreter a person is *arretted* 'that is charged with a crime.' 'Rider translates the word by *ad rectum vocatus.*' Halliwell (s. v. *arette*).

Artillery, xi. 7, machines of war, including cross-bows, etc. in early times; O. Fr. *artillerie* (Bartsch); L. Lat. *artillaria*, from *artillare** to make machines, a vb. inferred from the sb. *artillator*, a maker of machines (Ducange). From *arti-*, crude form of *ars*, art; see Skeat.

Askaunce, vii. 7, obliquely, with a sidelong glance. See Schmidt under *askance, askaunt* (*ascaunt*). Etymology doubtful.

Aspéctes, xi. 8; xii. 23, appearances; so Milton, Comus, 694, 'What grim aspécts are these, These ugly-headed monsters?'; Lat. *aspectus.*

Assay, iv. 40, proved value, cp. F. Q. I. ii. 13; vii. 34, an attempt; i. 35; iii. 12; viii. 7, 36; x. 49; xii. 13, 38. hostile attempt, attack; O. Fr. *essai*, a trial; Lat. *exagium*, a trial of exact weight; Gr. ἐξάγιον, a weighing. See Gloss. 1. Hence to *assay*, viii. 22, to attempt (with acc.); iv. 8; vi. 7; ix. 42; x. 3, to try, endeavour (with infin.); ii. 24; iv. 6; vi. 23; x. 40, to assail; O. Fr. *assaier* (Bartsch) = *assaier*, from *essai.*

Assieged, xi. 15, besieged; the verb *assege* is used in Holinshed, Hist. Eng. p. 44 (Halliwell); see **Siege.**

Assind, viii. 11, assigned; Fr. *as-signer*; Lat. *assignare.*

Assott, x. 6, to befool; Fr. *assoter*,

to besot (Cotgrave), from O. Fr. *sot*, a fool (Bartsch); L. Lat. *sottus* 'stolidus, bardus,—simplex, hinc Carolus *Sottus*, qui vulgo *Simplex*' (Ducange). Derivation unknown. For two suggested etymologies see Diez, p. 347 (s. v. *zote*).

Assoyle, v. 19, to loose; for exx. see Nares, Richardson (s. v. *assoil*); O. Fr. *asoldre*; Lat. *absoluere*; see Brachet (s. v. *absoudre*).

Atchiev'ment, i. 8, exploit; Fr. *achevement*, an atchievement (Cotgrave), from *achever*, to perform thoroughly, lit. to bring to a head, from O. Fr. *a chef* = Lat. *ad caput*. *Hatchment*, the escutcheon of a deceased person publicly displayed, is a corruption of *atch'ment*, the shortened form of *atchievement*. See Richardson (s. v. *hatchment*).

At one, i. 29, reconciled; M. E. *at oon*, *at on*; 'heo were al *at on*,' i. e. they were all agreed, Rob. of Glouc. p. 113; from this phrase arose the words *atone*, *atonement*; see Skeat's masterly article s. v.; **attone**, i. 42, together; **attonce**, iv. 18, together, at once; M. E. *attones*; *ones* = A. S. *ánes* (semel) the gen. case of *án*. For the adverbial genitive see Earle, pp. 431, 480.

Attach, x. 19; xi. 28, to seize, to take and hold fast; M. E. *attache*, Catholicon Anglicum; L. Lat. *attachiare*, 'apud leguleios Anglos, prehendere, reum vincire' (Ducange); O. Fr. *atachier*, to fasten (Bartsch), whence the two Fr. forms *attacher* and *attaquer*, see Brachet. Gloss. 1.

Attend, x. 68, to wait; Fr. *attendre*.

Atweene, vi. 32, between; prob. from A. S. *on tweónum*, in two parts, where *tweónum* is dat. pl.

of *tweón*, double (Chaucer 3, s. v. *atwinne*).

Aumayld, iii. 27, enameled, furnished with a glass-like coating; '*ammell*, esmailler' (Palsgrave); '*amell*, or enamell' (Cotgrave, s. v. *Email*); Fr. *esmail* (mod. *émail*), cp. It. *smalto*; L. Lat. *smaltum* (Ducange); see Diez p. 296, Skeat (s. v. *enamel*). For *aum-* = *am-* cp. Eng. *avaunt* = Fr. *avant*, *daunger* (Chaucer) = O. Fr. *dangier*, *pawn* (a pledge = Fr. *pan*).

Avale, ix. 10, to dismount; O. Fr. *avaler*, to descend, often in Chanson de Roland; from *aval*, down, Lat. *ad vallem*. Gloss. 1.

Avauntage, v. 9, advantage; Fr. *avantage*; the *d* in the modern form is an impertinent intrusion; for the *au* = *a* see **aumayld**.

Avaunting, iii. 6, advancing; distinct from the word in More's Utopia, 'they rejoyse and *avaunt* (boast) themselves, if they vanquishe their enemies by craft,' p. 133; where '*avaunt* is only *vaunt* (Fr. *vanter*, L. Lat. *vanitare*) with the *a* prefixed.'

Avize : see **Advise**.

Ay, i. 60, ever; O. N. *ei*, *ey*, ever; cp. A. S. *á*, aye, ever; Go. *aiw*; see Skeat (s. v. *aye*).

Ayery, viii. 5, airy, passing through the air; cp. Shakespeare, K. John, iii. 2. 2, 'some *airy* devil.'

Aygulet, iii. 26, aglet, tag of a lace, see Halliwell, p. 31; Fr. *aiguillette*, a point (Cotgrave), dimin. of *aiguille*, a needle; L. Lat. *acucula*, dimin. of *acus*; see Brachet.

Ayme (By), vi. 10, direct, straight; M. E. *aimen*, to estimate; O. Fr. *aesmer*; L. Lat. *adaestimare*; see Skeat (s. v. *aim*).

B.

Bace, ii. 41, low in place; this world is *base* as contrasted with heaven, see Schmidt for Shake-spearian exx. ; xii. 8, deep-voiced, *bass*; see **Abace.**

Badge, i. 27, mark, cognizance; M. E. *bage* or *badge* = banidium (Prompt. Parv.) ; L. Lat. *bagea, bagia*, 'signum, insigne quoddam' (Ducange). Derivation unknown.

Bait, i. 4, enticement to bite ; the vb. to *bait* is O. N. *beita,* to make to bite. Gloss. 1.

Bale, ii. 45 ; iv. 29, mischief, trou-ble ; vi. 34 ; vii. 23, grief, sorrow ; A.S. *bealu*, disaster, harm (Grein); hence **balefull,** ii. 2 ; **baleful-nesse** xii. 83.

Bane, xi. 29, ruin, destruction ; M. E. *bane* (Chaucer 1); O. N. *bani*, violent death, cognate with *ben*, a mortal wound ; cp. Go. *banja*, a wound, A. S. *bana*, a murderer, Gr. φόνος, murder, see Curtius, p. 300.

Banket, xi. 2, a rich entertain-ment, feast ; so Palsgrave, pp. 454, 804 ; Fr. '*banquet*, a banket' (Cotgrave), dimin. of *banc*, a bench ; M. H. G. *banc.*

Barbes, ii. 11, trappings for a horse, horse-armour protecting forehead, neck, chest, and back; *barbe*, a corruption of *barde* (Nares) ; Fr. *barde*, hence *bardé*, armed, of a horse (Bartsch) ; L. Lat. *barda* (Ducange); see Diez, p. 42.

Barbican, ix. 25, 'a casemate, or a hole in a town-wall to shoot out at,' so Cotgrave, s. v. *Barba-cane*, who goes on to say 'some hold it also to be a Sentrie, Scout-house, and thereupon our Chaucer useth the word *Barbican* for a watch-tower, which in the Saxon tongue was called a *Borough-ken-ning*'; L. Lat. *barbacana*, pro-pugnaculum exterius, quo portae muniuntur (Ducange). Etymo-logy unknown.

Bash, iv. 37, to be ashamed; for

exx. see Nares ; short for *abash*; M. E. *abaischen* ; see **Abash.** In this passage however the meaning of the word has been probably in-fluenced by the words *base, abase*, see **Abace,** and so to *bash* has here the connotation of to lower, to look down.

Bastard, iii. 42, low-born ; O. Fr. *bastard*, i. e. *fils de bast*, lit. 'the son of a pack-saddle,' not of the marriage-bed; see Diez, p. 45. Gloss. 1.

Bate, v. 7, bit ; see Halliwell ; A.S. *bát*, pret. sing. of *bítan*, to bite (Sweet, lxx).

Battailous (aray), vii. 37 ; viii. 22, ready for battle, combative ; see Nares; cp. Milton P. L. vi. 81, 'in *battaillous* aspect,' and Pattison's Milton, p. 14, 'the *battailous* canticles of his prose pamphlets.'

Bauldricke, iii. 29, belt ; see Nares (s. v. *Baldrick*). Gloss. 1.

Bayt, xii. 29, to give rest to, to cause to *abate* ; short for **abate.**

Becke, xi. 8, beak, bill; Fr. *bec.*

Bedight (Ill), i. 14, disfigured ; see also **dight.**

Beduked, vi. 42, dipped ; from to *duck*; cp. Du. *duiken*, to stoop, dive, Ger. *tauchen.*

Beene, i. 1, 52, to be (infin.) ; M. E. *been* ; A.S. *beón*, to be ; for root cp. Lat. *fu-i* ; Gr. φύ-ειν, see Curtius, p. 305 ; ii. 3, pl. 3 pers., so A. S. *beón*, they be, pres. subj.; cp. Shakespeare, Peric. ii. Prol. 28, 'where, when men *been*, there's seldom ease' (Gower loq.).

Beetle (browes), ix. 52, beetling or prominent ; cp. M. E. *bytel-browed* (P. Plowman, p. 117); see Skeat (s. v. *beetle* 3).

Befell, ix. 17, was fitting, an un-usual meaning of the vb. to *befall*, A. S. *be-feallan*, to happen.

Behave, iii. 40, to manage, govern

(trans.) ; A. S. *be-hæbban*, lit. to surround, then, to restrain, detain, cp. Lu. 4. 42, 'hi *behafdon* hine,' they detained him ; *behæbban* a compound of A. S. *habban*, to have, hold ; see Skeat.

Behest, iii. 32, see Gloss. 1. **Beheast**.

Behight, (pret.) iv. 43 ; ix. 17, ordered ; (pp.) iii. 1, promised ; viii. 9, entrusted ; M. E. *biháten*, to promise (Stratmann) ; A. S. *behátan*, to promise, A. S. Chron. an. 1012 ; a compound of *hátan*, to call, command.

Belamoure, vi. 16, a lover ; see Nares ; Fr. *Bel amour*.

Belamy, vii. 52, a dear friend, fair friend ; M. E., see Chaucer 3 ; cp. Halliwell ; Fr. *Bel ami*.

Belgards, iii. 25, pretty looks, amorous glances ; see Richardson ; Fr. *bel égard* ; from O. Fr. *esgarder*, to look (Bartsch).

, **Bend**, iii. 27 ; vii. 30 ; a band ; Fr. *bende, bande*, a band, a stripe (Cotgrave) ; a term used in Heraldry.

Bend, iv. 31 ; vii. 1 ; viii. 32 ; xi. 9, 12, 35, to direct (oneself, one's course, sword, spear, engines, etc.) for many Shakespearian exx. see Schmidt ; so Milton, P. L. ii. 729, 'to *bend* that mortal dart.'

Bene (ye), i. 33 ; ii. 5 ; viii. 13, ye be, are ; see **Beene**.

Bere, xii. 36, bier, a frame on which a corpse is borne ; M. E. *beere* ; A. S. *bǽr* ; from *beran*, to bear.

Bereave, vii. 19, to take away ; A. S. *bereáfian*, A. S. Chron. an. 975 ; see **Reave**.

Besits, vii. 10, it befits, becomes ; Gloss. 1. **Sits**.

Bespeak, i. 8 (and often) ; to address, speak to ; Gloss. 1.

Bestad, i. 52, situated, circumstanced ; Gloss. 1. **Bestedd**.

Bestow, ix. 28, to place, lodge, stow ; so often in Shakespeare, see Schmidt ; M. E. *bistowen* (Stratmann), from *stowen*, to put in a place, from A. S. *stów*, a place (often occurring in place-names), see Sweet.

Beteeme, viii. 19, to deliver, give ; for exx. see Richardson, Nares, Schmidt, also note on Hamlet i. 2. 141, Clar. Press. ed. To *beteem* means to 'think fit,' hence to permit, allow, give ; from *teem*, to think fit (for exx. see Halliwell) ; cp. Du. *betamen*, to beseem. *Beteem* does not appear in English before the 16th century. See New English Dictionary.

Bever, i. 29 ; v. 6, the part of the helmet which, when let down, covered the face ; Fr. *bavière*, a beaver, a bib (Cotgrave). Gloss. 1.

Bevy, ix. 34, a company (of ladies) ; so generally, see Richardson ; cp. It. *beva*, a bevy (Florio) ; a flock of pheasants called a 'bevy,' see Florio (s. v. *cováta*). Probably from O. Fr. *bevee*, a drinking, the orig. sense of *bevy* being a company for drinking.

Bittur, vii. 50, bittern, a bird of the heron tribe ; M. E. *bitoure*, *bytoure* (Chaucer) ; Fr. '*butor*, a bittor' (Cotgrave) ; L. Lat. *butorius*, cp. *butire*, to cry like a bittern (Ducange). For the suffixed *n* in the modern form *bittern*, cp. *marten*, for *marterne = marter*, Fr. *martre* ; also *wyvern = M. E. wivere*, O. F. *wivre* (mod. *givre*), a viper.

Blame, viii. 16, to injure ; O. Fr. *blasmer*. Gloss. 1.

Blazers, ix. 25, proclaimers. Gloss. 1. **Blaze**.

Blend, vii. 10 ; xii. 80, to blind ; A. S. *blendan*, to make blind (Leo) ; **blent**, iv. 7, blinded.

Blent, iv. 26; v. 5; xii. 7, defiled, stained, obscured, lit. mixed, confused; pp. of vb. to *blend*; A. S. *blandan*, to mix (Sweet).

Blive, iii. 18; **bylive,** viii. 18, forthwith, quickly; M. E. *bi live*, quickly; A. S. *bi life*, with life, see Stratmann (s. v. *lif*). See Nares, Coleridge. The word occurs in Burns' Cotter's Saturday Night, in the sense of 'presently': '*Belyve* the elder bairns came drappin in.' Gloss. I. **Bilive.**

Bord, ii. 5; iv. 24; ix. 2, to address, accost; 'I'll *board* (accost) him presently,' Hamlet ii. 2. 171, so frequently in Shakespeare, see Schmidt; a metaphorical expression from boarding a ship, see Nares (s. v. *boord*); cp. Fr. '*aborder*, to approach, accoast' (Cotgrave).

Bord, xii. 16, to jest; for exx. see Nares (s. v. *bourd*); Fr. '*bourder*, to bourd or jeast with' (Cotgrave), from *bourde*, a jest. See Skeat (s. v. *bourd*).

Bordraging, x. 63, border ravaging, border raid; cp. 'nightly *bordrags*,' Colin Clout, 266.

Boult, iv. 24, to sift meal; to *boulte* = Fr. *bulter* (Palsgrave); mod. Fr. *bluter*; O. Fr. *buleter* for *bureter*, to sift through cloth (Burguy); L. Lat. *buratare* (Ducange); from O. Fr. *bure*, coarse woollen cloth; L. Lat. *burra*, coarse red cloth, from Lat. *burrus*, reddish; Gr. πυρρός, from πῦρ, fire.

Bountihed, x. 2; xii. 1, generosity; the suffix answers to A. S. *hád*, faculty, quality, which is used also as a suffix, as in *cildhád*, childhood; cp. in mod. Eng. *Godhead*; see Earle, p. 308, M. Müller, Chips, 4. 91. *Bounty* = Fr. *bonté*; O. Fr. *bonteit* (Bartsch); Lat. acc. *bonitatem*.

Bourne, vi. 10, boundary; often in Shakespeare, see Schmidt; Fr. *borne*, also *bonne* (Cotgrave), also spelt *bodne* (Burguy); L. Lat. *bodina* (Ducange). Derivation unknown.

Bownd, iv. 43, ready to go; formed with excrescent *d* from M. E. *boun*, ready (Chaucer); O. N. *búinn*, prepared, pp. of *búa*, to make ready, see Icel. Dict.

Bowre, iv. 24; xii. 83, a chamber; M. E. *bour* (Chaucer 1); A. S. *búr*, a lady's apartment, as opposed to the 'hall' where all assemble, A. S. Chron. an. 755; from *búan*, to dwell; see Icel. Dict. (s. v. *búa*, to dwell). Gloss. I.

Brake, xi. 10, 22, tangle of a wood, fern; M. E. *brake* (Prompt. Parv.); A. S. *bracce*, fern (Cockayne's Leechdoms, gloss.). The original sense of the word seems to have been rough or 'broken' ground (cp. Ger. *brach*), as well as the overgrowth spreading on it; see Skeat. Cp. Halliwell (s. v. *breach, fallow*).

Bravely, xii. 19, splendidly. Gloss. I. **Brave.**

Bray, i. 38, to make a loud noise; M. E. *brayen* (Prompt. Parv.); O. F. *braire*, 'to *bray* as a deere doth, or other beest' (Palsgrave), used of any loud sound, even of the 'fast, thick warble' of the nightingale, see Diez, p. 532; L. Lat. *bragire* (Ducange). Gloss. I.

Breaches, vii. 28, stalactites.

Breaded, ii. 15, braided, entwined; M. E. '*breiden, braiden*, necto, torqueo' (Prompt. Parv.); A. S. (ge)*bregdan, brédan*, to weave, lit. to turn about quickly, to brandish (Sweet); see Icel. Dict. (s. v. *bregða*).

Brent, vi. 49, burnt; M. E. *brent*, pp. of *brennen* (Chaucer 1) for *bernen,* Ancren Riwle, p. 306; A. S. *byrnan* (Grein); cp. Ger. *brennen.*

Brimston, x. 26, sulphur; M. E. *brenstoon,* so Wiclif, Deut. 29. 23, lit. burn-stone; cp. O. N. *brennisteinn*; see above.

Brond, viii. 22, 37, a sword; M. E. *brond,* ensis, Will. of Palerne, 1244, so in A. S., see Grein; ii. 29; iii. 18, a brand, a burning piece of wood. Cognate with **brent**; see Skeat (s. v. *brand*). The sword-blade was called a *brand* or *brond* from its brightness, so in O. Fr. *brant,* see Bartsch, and Chanson de Roland, 1067.

Brood, vii. 8, a brooding place.

Brutenesse, viii. 12, brutality; Fr. *brut* (Cotgrave); Lat. *brutus,* stupid. The suffix *-nesse* is the oblique form of A. S. *-nes* or *-nis* (Sweet lxxxv). Of this suffix *-nis* the original formative is *-is* = Go. *-assus,* the *n* being due to a frequency of contact, as in Go. *gudjin-assus,* the priestly office; so in English *a newt* now stands for *an ewt,* and *a nickname = an eke-name.* See Earle, p. 302, for interesting remarks on this suffix; also Weigand (s. v. *-nis*).

Buff, ii. 23; v. 6, a blow; Fr. *buffe,* a buffet (Cotgrave).

Bug, iii. 20; xii. 25, a terrifying object; often in Shakespeare, see Schmidt; *bug* = Fr. ' gobelin' (Cotgrave); cp. Coverdale's version, Ps. 91. 5, ' thou shalt not nede to be afrayed for eny *bugges* by night ' (timore nocturno, Vulg.); see Skeat.

Bulwarke, viii. 35; xi. 7, a rampart, propugnaculum; occurs in the Bible and in Shakespeare; M. E. *bulwerke,* Lydgate, see Richardson; O. Fr. *bollewerque* (Roquefort); M. H. G. *bolewerc.* The Fr. *boulevard* is a corrupt

form of *bolewerc.* See Diez, p. 530, Weigand, p. 244.

Burganet, viii. 45, a close-fitting helmet; *burgonet,* Shakespeare (Schmidt); Fr. ' *bourguignotte,* a burganet, hufkin, or Spanish murrion' (Cotgrave); prop. the casque of a ' *Bourguignon,* a Burgonian,' i.e. Burgundian (Cotgrave); see Nares. A burgonet is figured in Clark's Introd. to Heraldry (see Glossary).

Busie, xii. 15, to occupy, engage attention; A. S. *(ge)bysgian* (Sweet), from *bysig,* active.

Buskin, iii. 27, a legging; for *bruskin*; O. Du. *brozeken,* dimin. of *broos*; O. Du. *brozeken* is related to Fr. *brodequin* (Cotgrave); cp. It. *borzacchino*; Sp. *borcegui*; Port. *borzeguins*; see Diez, p. 61. Etymology unknown.

Bynempt, i. 60, named (of a solemn vow); a rare word revived by Spenser; also used by Thomson in imitation of Spenser, see Castle of Indolence, c. ii. 32, ' a fiery-footed boy, *Benempt* Dispatch'; A. S. *be-nemnan,* asserere, stipulari (Grein); cp. Beowulf, 1098, ' Fin Hengeste áðum *be-nemde,*' Fin to Hengest with oaths declared.

C.

Cabinet, xii. 83, an arbour in a garden, so Cotgrave (s. v. *cabinet*).

Caduceus, xii. 41, ' the rod of Mercury'; Lat. *cādúceus*; Doric καρύκιον (Attic καρύκειον), ' the herald's wand'; the Lat. form is prob. an instance of popular etymology, being influenced by *cadere,* *caducus,* and the idea of ' falling'; see Curtius, p. 430.

Calmy, xii. 30, sheltered (of a bay); see Richardson; from Fr. *calme,* still, quiet (Cotgrave); allied to Prov. *chaume,* the time

when the flocks rest; Fr. *chommer*
(mod. *chômer*) to rest from work ;
from L. Lat. *cauma*, the heat of
the sun (whence, time for rest);
see Mayor's Bede (glossary) ; Gr.
καῦμα, heat ; see Diez, p. 78.

Camus, iii. 26, a thin robe (of
silk) ; see Halliwell (s. v. *camis*) ;
L. Lat. *camisia.* Diez, p. 80,
quotes Jerome, ' solent militantes
habere lineas quas *camisias* vocant,' see Lewis and Short, Lat.
Dict. s. v. Hence Fr. *chemise*
(Burguy). Etymology unknown.

Can, i. 31 ; xii. 15, an auxiliary
verb with pret. meaning, did; in
A. S. *can* is in form a pret., in
sense a present, meaning ' know '
(Morris, p. 183). Gloss. 1.

Cancred, i. 1, corrupt ; from Lat.
cancer, an ' eating ' tumour, lit.
a crab.

Card, vii. 1, a chart, a marine map;
Shakespeare, Macbeth i. 3. 17,
' the shipman's *card* '; Fr. *carte*,
a card (Cotgrave) ; L. Lat. *carta* ;
Lat. *charta* ; Gr. χάρτη, a leaf of
paper ; see M. Müller, i. 107.

Carde, vi. 16, to comb wool ; Fr.
carder (Cotgrave), from *carde*, a
thistle; L. Lat. *cardus* ; Lat.
carduus, from Lat. *cârere*, to
scratch wool ; see Fick, iv. 59.

Carle, vii. 43; xi. 37, a churl; Shakespeare, Cymb. v. 2. 4 ; O. N. *karl*,
prop. a man, see Icel. Dict., Fick
vii. 43. Hence the famous name
Charlemagne (Chanson de Roland), i.e. Karl the Great. Gloss. 1.

Cast, i. 48, 52; iv. 30; xi. 28, to
plan, resolve; 'I *caste*, I deter-
myne, or purpose a thyng, Je
determine' (Palsgrave) ; O. N.
kasta, to cast, to throw. Gloss. 1.

Castory, ix. 41, a colour, red or
pink ; Lat. (medical) *castoreum*, a
substance taken from the ' castor '
or beaver ; see Larousse, Encyclop.
s. v. *Castoréum*, ' L'analyse chim-

ique a trouvé dans cette substance
un principe colorant rougeâtre.'

Caytive, i. 1 ; iii. 7 ; iv. 16 ; viii. 12,
37, vile, base, also wretch; *caitiff*,
often in Shakespeare, see Schmidt;
M. E. *caityf* (Chaucer 3); O. Fr.
caitif, captive, wretched (Chanson
de Roland) ; L. Lat. *captivus*, vilis.
(Ducange); Lat. *captivus*, captive.
Gloss. 1.

Centaur, ix. 50, a creature half man
and half horse ; Lat. *centaurus* ;
Gr. κένταυρος.

Cesure, x. 68, a breaking off ; Lat.
cæsura.

Chaffar, v. 3, to chaffer, exchange ;
M. E. *chaffare*, vb. (Chaucer),
from *chaffare*, 'a bargaining';
chapfare, Ayenbite of Inwyt, meaning lit. ' a price business,' from A.S.
ceáp, price + *faru*, business. *Ceáp*
is not a word of Teutonic origin,
being closely connected with O.H.G.
choufo, which is the Lat. *caupo*, a
huckster—a word borrowed by the
Germans in commerce; see Skeat.
Gloss. 1. **Keepe.**

Chalenge, i. 12, to track, follow ;
an extension of one of the old
meanings of *challenge*, ' to accuse';
M. E. ' *chalange*, calumniari' (Catholicon Anglicum); O. Fr. *chalon-
gier, calengier*, to claim (Bartsch) ;
from *chalonge, calenge*, an accusation ; Lat. *calumnia*, a false
accusation ; see Skeat.

Champion, ii. 18, he who fights
for a person; O. Fr. *champion*
(Bartsch), *campiuns*, Chanson de
Roland ; L. Lat. *campionem*, from
campus, a duel,' combat ; Lat.
campus, a field. Gloss. 1.

Charm, v. 27 ; xii. 49, to affect by
magic power ; from Fr. *charme* =
Lat. *carmen*, a verse, a formula of
incantation.

Chaufe, Chauffe, iii. 46; iv. 32,
to chafe ; O. Fr. *chaufer*, to make
warm (Bartsch); Prov. *calfar* ;

It. *calefare*; Lat. *calefacere*; see Brachet. Gloss. 1.

Cheare, ii. 34; vi. 10, cheerfulness; x. 30, food, entertainment; see *cheer* in Shakespeare (Schmidt); O. Fr. *chiere, chere, cier,* the face, then, the look, the look of welcome (Bartsch); L. Lat. *cara,* a face; see Diez, p. 87.

Chevisaunce, ix. 8, achievement; gen. an agreement, bargain, purchase, for exx. see Richardson (s.v. *cheve*); Fr. ' *chevissance,* an agreement or composition made between a creditor and debtor' (Cotgrave), from *chevir,* to finish (Bartsch) = O. Fr. venir a *chief* (*caput*), to come to a head; see Diez, p. 545. There is a M. E. *cheviss* (= O. Fr. *chevir*), meaning 'to achieve one's purpose'; see M. S. ii. p. 212. Cp. **atchiev'**-ment.

Childe, viii. 7, a youth trained to arms, a young knight (a not unusual meaning of the word in old romances); see Nares; M. E. *Child* (*Thopas*), see Skeat's note, Chaucer 2, p. 159; *child* = Lat. 'comes' in Trevisa's Higden, Rolls Ser. No. 41, vii. 123; A. S. *cild,* the child of a noble house, also, used as a title, A. S. Chron., an. 1074. Cp. the use of *enfant* (= infans) in the Chanson de Roland. See **Infant.**

Choler, ii. 23, anger; often in Shakespeare, see Schmidt; Fr. ' *cholere* (now *colère*), choler, anger, also the humour termed choler' (Ćotgrave); Lat. *cholera,* the jaundice, also the bile; Gr. χολέρα, the cholera, from χολή, bile; cp. χόλος, bile, wrath.

Cicuta, vii. 52, hemlock; a Latin word.

Cleeped, iii. 8; ix. 58, called; Shakespeare, 'Love's Labour's Lost,' v. 1. 24, 'he *clepeth* a calf

cauf'; M. E. *clepen* (Chaucer 1); A. S. *cleopian, clipian* (Sweet).

Clew, i. 8, a ball of thread; in Shakespeare, All's Well, i. 3. 188; M. E. *clewe* (Stratmann); A. S. *cliwe, cleowen,* globus (Grein); see Skeat.

Clifte, vii. 23, 28, a cliff; see Halliwell; M.E. *clif,* so A.S., see Grein; the orig. sense prob. 'a climbing place'; cp. O. N. *klif* with *klifa,* to climb; see Skeat.

Coast (on even), iii. 17, on equal terms; cp. ' *coste à coste,* equally' (Cotgrave).

Coloquintida, vii. 52, colocynth, a kind of gourd growing wild; Shakespeare, Othello, i. 3. 355, 'as bitter as coloquintida'; Gr. κολοκυνθίδα, acc. of κολοκυνθίς, also κολοκύντη, so named from its colossal size; see Skeat.

Combrous, ix. 17, troublesome; see Nares, *comberous,* to *comber.* Gloss. 1.

Commoned, ix. 41, communed.

Commons, x. 62, the common people (opposed to the nobility); so in Shakespeare, see Schmidt; Fr. ' *commune,* the common people' (Cotgrave); L. Lat. *commune,* incolarum urbis aut oppidi universitas (Ducange).

Compacture, ix. 24, a joining together; Lat. *compactura.*

Comportaunce, i. 29, behaviour; cp. Fr. ' *comportement,* comportment, behaviour' (Cotgrave), from *se comporter,* to carry oneself, behave.

Comprize, ix. 49, to draw a conclusion; from O.Fr. *compris,* pp. of *comprendre;* Lat. *comprehendere.*

Conduct, ii. 25, handling (of a sword); cp. Pope, Rape of the Lock, iv. 124, 'the nice *conduct* of a clouded cane.'

Congé, i. 34; iii. 2; xi. 17, leave, farewell; Fr. ' *congé,* leave, per-

mission, dismission (Cotgrave);
O. Fr. *eumgiet* (Bartsch); L. Lat.
eomiatus, permission, authoriza-
tion; Lat. *commeatus*, leave of
absence, from *commeare*, to go,
travel; see Brachet.

Consort, vii. 22, company, fellow-
ship; Shakespeare, Two Gent. of
Verona, iv. 1. 64, 'will thou be
of our *consort*?'; v. 31; ix. 35,
harmonious music; Shakespeare,
ibid. iii. 2. 84, 'visit by night your
lady's chamber-window with some
sweet *consort*.'

Consorted, xii. 70, combined, as-
sociated.

Contrive, ix. 48, to wear out,
spend; for exx. see Nares, Richardson; cp. 'totum hunc *contrivi*
diem,' Ter. Hec. 5. 3. 17; *contrivi*,
pret. of *conterere*, to wear out.
Not the same word as mod. E.
contrive.

Cordwayne, iii. 27, Spanish leather
from *Cordova*; also spelt *cordevan*,
cordovan, see Nares, Richardson;
M. E. '*cordewayn*, aluta' (Catho-
licon Anglicum); Fr. *cordouan*;
L. Lat. *cordoanus* (Ducange), from
Cordoa, a spelling of Cordova
(Lat. *Corduba*); see Diez, p. 108.

Corse, v. 23; ix. 55, body; O. Fr.
cors (Bartsch). Gloss. 1.

Cott, vi. 9, a little boat; Ir. '*cot*, a
small boat' (O'Reilly).

Couch, v. 3, to lay (the spear in the
rest). Gloss. 1.

Countenaunce, ii. 16, to show
forth by look.

Countervayle, vi. 29, to counter-
balance; so in Shakespeare, Rom.
and Jul. ii. 6. 4; Peric. ii. 3. 56;
O. Fr. *contrevaloir*; It. *contrav-
valére*; Lat. *contra* + *valere*.

Courd, viii. 9, cherished, brooded
over; M. E. *couren*, to cower.
A Scandinavian word, cp. Swed.
kura, to settle to rest as birds do;
see Skeat (s.v. *cower*).

Court, ii. 35, courteous attention.
Gloss. 1.

Couth, vii. 58, could; M. E. *couthe*,
coude, pret. of *cunnen*, posse, scire
(Stratmann, p. 107); A. S. *cúðe*,
pret. of *cunnan* (Sweet); see Earle,
p. 162.

Covetise, vii. 12, 15, covetousness.
Gloss. 1.

Coward (adj.), viii. 12; O. Fr.
couard, *coard*, lit. an animal that
drops his tail, or that shows his
tail, turns tail; O. Fr. *coe* (Lat.
cauda) a tail + the suffix -*ard*, of
Teutonic origin, for which suffix
see M. Müller, Chips, iv. 91; see
Skeat.

Crack, i. 12, to impair, weaken; a
favourite word of Shakespeare's,
see Schmidt; A. S. *cearcian* (Leo).

Crake, xi. 10, a bragging; so Shakespeare uses to *crack*, to bluster,
cracker, a blusterer, swaggerer, see
Schmidt.

Cremosin, xi. 3, crimson; It. *cre-
misíno*, crimson-coloured, from *cré-
misi*, crimson; Arab. *qermez*, adj.
qermazi; from Sk. *krimi-ja*, i. e.
produced by an insect. The colour
is so called because produced by
the cochineal insect (L. Lat. *grana*).
Gloss. 1. **Graine.**

Crest, viii. 12, the top of the helmet
whence the plume falls; Fr.'*creste*,
a crest, comb' (Cotgrave); Lat.
crista, a comb on a bird's head.
In heraldry the 'crest' is the cognizance worn above the helmet to
distinguish such as had superior
military command.

Culver, vii. 34, a dove; M. E.
culver = Lat. *columba*, Mk. 1. 10
(Wiclif); A. S. *culfre*, prob. a corruption of the Lat. *columba*.

D

Dalliaunce, ii. 35; vi. 8, 21, trifling,
idle talk; a Miltonic word; prop.
lingering, loitering, cp. Shakespeare,

1 Hen. VI, v. 2. 5; M. E. *dalien*, supposed to be a form of *dwelien*, to be foolish, connected with M. E. *dwellen*, to linger; see Skeat. For Fr. suffix -*ance*, see Earle, p. 330, Brachet, p. cix.

Damnifyde, vi. 43, injured. Gloss. 1. *Damnify*.

Damozell, and **Damzell,** i. 19, maiden. Gloss. 1.

Dan, ii. 7, a title prefixed to the god Faunus; in Chaucer commonly given to monks, but also prefixed to the names of persons of all sorts (Chaucer 1); O. Fr. *dans* (Bartsch), cp. Chanson de Roland, 1367, *danz* Oliviers, mon seigneur Olivier; Lat. *dominus*. Used in a kind of jocular way by Shakespeare, e. g. '*Dan* Cupid,' L. L. L. iii. 182.

Dapled, i. 18, spotted (of an animal); M. E. *dappel*, a spot, *dappel-gray* (Chaucer 2); O. N. *depill*, a spot, orig. a little pool; see Skeat.

Darraine, ii. 26, to prepare, get ready (battle). Gloss. 1.

Date, i. 44, assigned term of life. Gloss. 1.

Dayes-man, viii. 28, an umpire or arbitrator; occurs Job 9. 33; for other exx. see Nares, Richardson. In the judicial language of the middle ages, words for 'day' were specially applied to the day appointed for hearing a cause, or for the meeting of an assembly. So L. Lat. *dies* (Ducange); for Teutonic equivalents see Wedgwood (s.v. *day*). Hence the use of *day* in the sense of 'judgment,' as in the compound *dayesman*. Cp. 1 Cor. 4. 3, ἡμέρα (*dies*, Vulgate) = judgment, see Stanley's note; and for the same idiom in Hebrew cp. Is. 2. 12.

Dayntest, xii. 42, nicest, most fastidious. Gloss. 1. **Daint**.

Deare, ii. 39, earnestly; v. 38, sorely; xi. 34, true, inmost; for

these senses of 'dear' cp. Shakespeare (Schmidt); A. S. *deóre*, carus, pretiosus, nobilis (Sweet); cp. O. H. G. *tiuri*; Ger. *theuer*.

Dearnly, i. 35, mournfully; also spelt *dernly*, see Nares, Richardson; M. E. *derne, dernliche*, obscurus, obscure (Stratmann); A. S. *dirne*, secret, hidden (Sweet); cp. Ger. *Tárn*-kappe, the mantle of concealment in the Nibelungenlied (Weigand).

Debate, i. 6, to contend, combat; Shakespeare, Lucr. 1421; Fr. '*debatre*, to debate, contend' (Cotgrave).

Debonaire, vi. 28, gentle; so Shakespeare, Troil. 1. 3. 235; M. E., see Chaucer 1; O. Fr. *debonaire*, gracious (Bartsch); cp. Chanson de Roland, 2252, 'E! gentilz hum, chevaliers *de bon aire*,' translated by Gautier, 'Ah! gentilhomme, chevalier *de noble lignée*.' See Diez, p. 6.

Decay, viii. 51, xi. 36, death, destruction; so Shakespeare often (Schmidt); from the verb *decay*; O. Fr. *decaer*; *caer, cader* (Bartsch) = Lat. *cadere*, to fall; see Skeat.

Décretals, ix. 53, prob. decrees; L. Lat. *decretalia* not *decretales* (Romanorum Pontificum), see Ducange.

Deface, xi. 6, to destroy; **defaste,** iv. 14, destroyed; so in Shakespeare (Schmidt); Fr. '*desfacer*, as *effacer*, to efface, deface, wipe away, to abolish' (Cotgrave), from *face*; Lat. *facies*.

Deforme, xii. 24, misshaped, illfavoured; cp. Milton, P. L. ii. 706; xi. 494; Lat. *deformis*.

Delay, vi. 40; ix. 30, to temper; for exx. see Richardson, Trench; Fr. *delayer*, to soften, dilute (Cotgrave); Prov. *deslegar*; It. *dileguare*; Lat. *dis + liquare*; see Diez p. 119. A different word from *delay*, to put off; O. Fr. *delayer*, *delaier* (Bartsch); Lat. *dilatare*; see Ducange.

Delve, viii. 4, a hole, cave; M. E. Wiclif, 2 Chron. 34. 11, *delves =* ' lapicidinæ' (Vulgate); from *delven*, to dig (Stratmann); A. S. *delfan* (Sweet).

Demayne, viii. 23; ix. 40, treatment, demeanour; M. E. *demeane*, behaviour (Chaucer), from *demeynen*, to control; O. Fr. *demener*, to guide (Bartsch); see Skeat (s.v. *demean*).

Dempt, vii. 55, deemed, judged; A. S. *déman*, from *dóm*, a decision (Sweet).

Demure, i. 6, modest; cp. Trench; so used without any insinuation of unreality by Shakespeare; O. Fr. *de murs*, of manners; Lat. *mores*; so Skeat.

Depainted, v. 11, depicted; M. E. *depeynted* (Chaucer 1).

Depart, x. 14, to part, divide; ' I *departe*. Je desmesle' (Palsgrave), M.E., see Chaucer 1 Wiclif, N.T.; Fr. *departir* (Cotgrave).

Der-doing, vii. 10, dare-doing.

Derring doe, iv. 42, deeds of daring; so Nares; M.E., Chaucer, Troilus, ' In *dorryng don* that longeth to a knyght,' see Academy, No. 469.

Desarts, ii. 29, a phonetic spelling for *deserts* ; cp. the family name *Clark* from *clerk* : see Skeat, Notes and Queries, 6th S. iii. 4.

Descrive, iii. 25, to describe; ' I *descryve*, je blasonne, je descrips' (Palsgrave); see Nares; M.E. *descriven* ; O. Fr. *descrivre*; Lat. *describere*; see Skeat.

Despight, i. 14 and freq., malice, contemptuous hate ; O. Fr. *despit*. Gloss. 1. Hence **despiteously,** vi. 29.

Dessignment, xi. 10, an attempt (to attack); Shakespeare, Oth. ii. 1. 22, ' their *designment* halts.'

Devise, ix. 42, guess, imagine; ix. 59, to treat of; see Shakespeare (Schmidt); Fr. *deviser* (Cotgrave), from L. Lat. *divisa*, a division, mark, device. **deviz'd,** i. 31, painted as a *device*.

Diademe, vii. 13, a fillet on the head worn by rulers ; Gr. διάδημα, what is bound round.

Diapase, ix. 22, harmony, a whole octave ; for *diapason*; Gr. διαπασῶν, the concord of the first and last notes of an octave; see Skeat.

Dight, to arrange, dress (very freq.); A. S. *dihtan*. Gloss. 1.

Dilate, xii. 53, to spread abroad; Fr. *dilater* (Cotgrave) ; Lat. *dilatare*.

Discreet, xii. 71, distinct, measured ; Lat. *discretus*, pp. of *discernere*, to separate.

Discure, ix. 42, to discover, disclose ; for *discover*, see Nares, Halliwell.

Disease, ii. 12, 24, to deprive of ease. Gloss. 1.

Dishable, v. 21, to disparage; ' to *disable*, to disgrace by bad report or censure ' (Nares); for *hable =* *able*, cp. More's Utopia, passim ; O. Fr. *habile* ; Lat. *habilis* ; see Skeat (s. v. *able*).

Disleall, v. 5, disloyal; M. E. *lel* ; Norm. Fr. *leal* ; O. Fr. *leial* ; Lat. *legalis*; see Skeat (s. v. *loyal*).

Dismall, vii. 26 ; viii. 51, ill-boding, fatal ; so in Shakespeare often (Schmidt) ; a difficult word, in old books the usual phrase is ' *dismal* days ' (Trench), which may refer to tithing-time ; O. Fr. *dismal*; Lat. *decimalis*, from *decima*, a tithe ; see Skeat.

Dismay, viii. 7 ; ix. 34, to deprive of power ; this is the etymological meaning of the word ; see Gloss. 1.

Dismayd, xi. 11, deformed ; *dis* + *made*.

Dismayle, vi. 29, to injure the *mail* ; see **Male.**

Disparaged, x. 2, rendered inferior in ability; M. E. *desparagen*, to lower in rank or estimation (Stratmann); Fr.*desparager*(Cotgrave), from *parage*, rank; L. Lat. *paragium*, *paraticum* (Ducange), from Lat. *par*, equal.

Dispence, ix. 29, expenditure; Fr. *despense* (Cotgrave). Gloss. 1.

Display, v. 30, to unfold, spread out; O. Fr. *despleier*; from Lat. *plicare*, to fold; see Skeat.

Disports, vi. 26, acts of playfulness. Gloss. 1.

Dispred, v. 29, to spread abroad; for exx. see Richardson.

Disthronize, x. 44, to dethrone; 'Desthroner, to *disthronize*, or unthrone' (Cotgrave).

Distraine, xii. 82, to pull asunder, break (of a net); Fr. *destraindre* (Cotgrave); Lat. *distringere*.

Ditt, vi. 13; **ditty**, x. 50, a theme for song. Gloss. 1.

Diverse, ii. 3, distracting; Lat. *diversus*.

Do, i. 25, 'to *do* him rew,' to make him repent. Gloss. 1.

Doole, xii. 20, grief; see Richardson (s. v. *dole*); M. E. *dole* in Chaucer; also *doel*, see Stratmann; O. Fr. *doel*, *duel* (mod. *deuil*), verbal subst. of *doloir* (Lat. *dolere*, to grieve.

Doome, ix. 48, judgment, decision, M. E. *dom*; A. S. *dóm*, lit. a thing set, decided on, from *dó-n*, to set, do; from *dóm* comes the vb. to *deem*, A. S. *déman*, to give a *doom*; for change of *ó* into *é*, see Skeat, Preface xiii.

Drapets, ix. 27, cloths; dimin. of Fr. *drap*; L. Lat. *drappus*. Origin uncertain, see Diez, p. 123.

Draught, x. 51 (rhymes with *ought*, *fought*, see Earle, p. 152), a stratagem; cp. Halliwell, '*draught* (2), a spider's web. Metaph. a snare to entrap any one.'

Drent, vi. 49, drowned; pp. of to drench; M. E. *drenchen*, pp. *dreint*; A. S. *drencan*, causal of *drincan*; see Stratmann, Skeat. For vowel-change, cp. M. E. *sengen*, A. S. (*be*) *sengan*, to singe, causal of *singan*, to sing; and see **Feld**.

Drere, xii. 36; **dreriment**, i. 15; iv. 31, grief. Gloss. 1.

Drift, xii. 8, a driving.

Drive, i. 55, to hasten; cp. Germ. *treiben*.

Driven, vii. 5, beaten, of gold; so Germ. *treiben*.

Drouth, vii. 58, drought, thirst; see Halliwell, Schmidt; M. E. *drouhthe*, P. Plowman, A. text: A. S. *drugaðe*, from *drugian*, to dry; see Skeat. For suffix *-að* (*oð*), denoting action, see Sweet, lxxxv.

E.

Easterland, x. 41, the eastern land; here prob. east Germany.

Easterlings, x. 63, people of the east; in this passage prob. the inhabitants of Norway and Denmark, see citation from Holinshed in Richardson. Later the word *Easterlings* or *Esterlings* was a name for the Hanse merchants, see Skeat (s. v. *sterling*), and Davies (s. v. *Easterling*). For an account of the suffix -*ling*, see Earle, p. 300, and Weigand (s. v. -*ling*).

Eath, iii. 40; iv. 11, easy; M. E. *eað* (Stratmann); A. S. *eáðe* (Grein); cp. O. S. *óði* (Heliand).

Eden, xii. 52, the first residence of man; a Hebrew word, Gen. ii. 15, but perhaps of Accadian origin, and standing for the Accadian *edin*, plain or valley, a word borrowed by the Semitic Babylonians and Assyrians under the form *edinu*; so Sayce in Academy, No. 496.

Eft, iii. 21; iv. 18; xi. 36, afterwards, again, forthwith; A.S. *æft, eft,* again.

Eftsoones, i. 8 (and freq.), soon after, forthwith. Gloss. 1.

Eke, ii. 34, also; M. E. *ec,* see M.S. 1; A. S. *eác,* from the verb *écan,* to increase; cp. Germ. *auch,* Dan. *og* (and); see Skeat.

Eld, ix. 56, old age; M. E. *elde;* A. S. *eldo, yldo,* see Stratmann, Leo. Gloss. 1.

Elfe, x. 71, ' *Elfe,* to weet Quick,' i. e. living, the name of the man 'authour of all Elfin kind' who was created by Prometheus; M. E. *elf, alfe,* see Stratmann, p. 21; A. S. *elf, ælf* (Leo). Origin doubtful, but see Curtius, p. 293. Gloss. 1.

Embatteiled, v. 2, armed for battle; a favourite word with Milton, cp. P. L. vi. 16, '*embattel'd* squadrons bright'; for Shakespeare's use of *embattle* see Schmidt.

Embaye, i. 40; viii. 55, to bathe; see Nares. Gloss. 1. Is this form due to a confusion of the letter *þ* with the letter *y*?

Embayle, iii. 27, 'to enclose, or pack up as in a *bale*' (Nares); Fr. ' *emballer,* to packe up' (Cotgrave). The word *bale,* a package, is the same as *ball,* a spherical body; see Skeat.

Embosome, iv. 25, to foster, to receive within the *bosom;* for exx. see Richardson.

Emboyle, iv. 9; v. 18, to boil (with anger).

Embrace, i. 26, to brace, fasten, or bind; Fr. ' *embrasser* son escu, to put his shield upon his arme, to buckle his shield unto his arme' (Cotgrave).

Embracement, iv. 26, embrace; for exx. see Richardson; often in Shakespeare, see Schmidt.

Embrave, i. 60, to decorate; for exx. see Richardson. Gloss. 1. Brave.

Embrew, i. 40, to moisten, drench; Fr. ' *s'embruer,* to imbrue himselfe with' (Cotgrave). Gloss. 1. Imbrew.

Eme, x. 47, uncle; still used in N. of England, see Jamieson; M. E. *ém, eam* (Stratmann); A. S. *eám* (Sweet); cp. Du. *oom;* Germ. *ôheim* (Weigand).

Emeraude, xii. 54, emerald; M. E. *emeraude;* Fr. ' *esmeraude,* an emerauld' (Cotgrave); Lat. *smaragdus;* Gr. σμάραγδος; see Skeat.

Emmove, i. 50, to move; Fr. ' *esmouvoir,* to stirre up' (Cotgrave).

Emongst, ix. 52, amongst; the form *emonge* occurs in Gower, see Richardson; for various other forms see Stratmann (s. v. *mang*); the *t* is merely excrescent (as often after *s*), cp. *whilst, amidst; amonges* is an adverbial form in *-es,* orig. a gen. sing., for which adverbial inflexion see Earle, p. 480, Sweet, lxxxix; *among* stands for A. S. *onmang = on mange* or *on gemange,* in a crowd; see Skeat.

Empayre, x. 30, to diminish; M. E. *enpeiren* (Stratmann, p. 149); O. Fr. *empeirier, enpirer* (Bartsch), cp. Cotgrave, '*empirer,* to *impaire,* make worse'; L. Lat. *impeiorare* (Ducange), from Lat. *peior,* worse.

Empeach, vii. 15, to hinder; for exx. in this sense see citations from Holland in Skeat (s. v. *impeach*); M. E. in Chaucer (Richardson); Fr. ' *empescher,* to hinder, impeach' (Cotgrave); O. Fr. *empescher* (Bartsch); see **appeach.**

Empight, iv. 16, pret., fixed, settled (of a dart). Gloss. 1. Pight.

Emprise, vii. 39, an undertaking;

Fr. *emprise* (Cotgrave, Bartsch). Gloss. I.

Enchace, ix. 24, to adorn, embellish; Fr. '*enchasser* en or, to enchace or set in gold' (Cotgrave). Gloss. I.

Enchaunter, i. 5, a magician, lit. one who repeats a *chant*, a charmer; from the vb. *enchant*; M. E. *enchaunten* (Chaucer); O. Fr. *enchanter* (Bartsch); Lat. *incantare*, to repeat a chant; see Skeat.

Encheason, i. 30, reason, cause, occasion; M. E. *enchesoun* (Chaucer), see also Stratmann, p. 149; O. Fr. *enchaison*, an occasion (Roquefort); from *encheoir* (Burguy), *chaoir, cader*, to fall (Bartsch); Lat. *cadere*.

Engin, iv. 27, wiles, deceit; Fr. '*engin*, understanding, policie, reach of wit, also, suttletie, fraud, craft' (Cotgrave); O. Fr. *engien*, wiliness (Bartsch); Lat. *ingenium*, used of 'natural abilities, cleverness.'

Englut, ii. 23, to devour; Shakespeare (Schmidt); Fr. '*engloutir*, to inglut, ingulfe' (Cotgrave); Lat. *glutire*, to swallow.

Engore, viii. 42, to pierce; from the vb. to *gore*, to pierce, which is formed from M. E. *gare, gore*, a spear; A. S. *gár* (Sweet); = O. H. G. *gér, kér*; cp. the Gaulish *gaesum* in Virgil, A. viii. 662.

Engrave, i. 60, to inter, bury; for exx. see Trench. Gloss. I.

Enhaunse, vi. 31; vii. 44, to raise, lift up; prop. to further, advance a thing; M. E. *enhansen* (Stratmann). Gloss. I.

Enlarge, v. 19, to set at large. Gloss. I.

Enlumine, ix. 4, to illumine; Fr. '*enluminer*, to illuminate, inlighten' (Cotgrave); Lat. *lumen*, light.

Ensue, iii. 2, to follow after; often in Shakespeare, see Schmidt; O. Fr. *ensuir*. Gloss. I.

Entayle, iii. 27; vi. 29, to carve, cut into; **entayle**, vii. 4, ornamental work cut on gold (cp. It. *intáglio*); M. E. *entailen*, to cut or carve in an ornamental way; O. Fr. *entaillier* (Bartsch), from *taillier*, to cut; L. Lat. *taleare*, to cut (Ducange), from Lat. *talea*, a cutting from a plant; see Diez, p. 313, Brachet (s. v. *tailler*).

Enterpris, i. 19, to undertake; for its use as a verb, cp. Skeat (s. v.); O. Fr. *entreprise, entreprinse* (Bartsch); from *entrepris*, pp. of *entreprendre*, to undertake; L. Lat. *interprendere* (Ducange).

Enterprize, ii. 14, to receive (as a host his guests); this sense apparently peculiar to Spenser, see Richardson.

Entertaine, ix. 6, to receive; so freq. in Shakespeare, see Schmidt; O. Fr. *entretenir*, to receive (Bartsch); L. Lat. *intertenere*, to support, maintain (Ducange).

Entertainment, ii. 35, hospitality; see above.

Entrall, xii. 25, the inward part, depth (bowels); a spelling of the word *entrails*; Fr. '*entrailles*, the intrals, intestines' (Cotgrave); L. Lat. *intralia*, also (and more correctly) *intranea*, in the Lex Salica, see Ducange; Lat. *interanea*, intestines. For the change from *n* to *l* cp. *Palermo* from Lat. *Panormus*, see Brachet, xcvii.

Entrayle, iii. 27, to twist, entwine, interlace; prob. from Fr. *treiller*, to lattice (Cotgrave), from *treille*, an arbour of intertwining trees; Lat. *tricla, trichila*, a bower, arbour; see Brachet (s. v. *treille*), Skeat (s. v. *trellis*).

Entyre, v. 8; viii. 15, wholly; Fr. '*entier*, intire, whole' (Cotgrave); Lat. *integrum*.

Envy, ii. 19, to feel jealousy at;
Fr. '*envier,* to envie' (Cotgrave);
from Fr. *envie* = Lat. *invidia.*

Enwombed, i. 50, pregnant; x. 50,
enclosed in the womb; cp. Shakespeare, All's Well, i. 3. 150.

Equipaged, ix. 17, arrayed, equipped; the vb. from the sb. *equipage*
in Spenser's Sheph. Kal. Oct. 114;
Fr. '*equipage,* equipage, furniture,
good armour' (Cotgrave); from
équiper, esquiper; O. N. *skipa,* to
arrange. Gloss. 1.

Erne, iii. 46, to yearn, to long for;
see Halliwell; *erne* apparently =
M. E. *3ernen*; A. S. *gyrnan,* to
be desirous, from *georn,* desirous
(Sweet); see Skeat (s. v. *yearn*).

Errant, i. 19, 51, 'the *errant*
damozell,' '*errant* knighte'; from
O. Fr. *errer, edrar,* to travel
(Bartsch); L. Lat. *iterare,* iter-
facere (Ducange), from Lat. *iter*;
see Burguy. Gloss. 1.

Error, x. 9, wandering; Lat. *error.*

Erst, ix. 17, previously; also **earst.**
Gloss. 1.

Evangely, x. 53, Gospel; Fr. *evan-
gile* (Cotgrave); L. Lat. *evan-
gelium*; Gr. εὐαγγέλιον, N. T.

Exanimate, xii. 7, lifeless; the
word occurs in Thomson's Spring,
1052; Lat. *exanimatus.*

Exprest, xi. 42, pressed, squeezed
out; *press* is Fr. *presser*; Lat. *pressare,* frequentative formed from
pressus, pp. of *premere.*

Expyre, viii. 24, 'to *expire* a date,'
to fulfil, come to the end of, a
term; the vb. used transitively as
the Lat. *exspirare,* to breathe out.

Extent, vii. 61, stretched out; pp.
of the vb. *extend.*

F.

Faerie, Faery, (1) Introd. 1, 4,
'land of *Faery,*' ix. 4, 'Queene of

Faerie,' enchantment; the subst.
used adjectivally by collocation
(Earle, p. 400), ix. 9, '*Faerie*
court'; i. 6; ii. 40; ix. 60,
'*Faerie* land'; Introd. 5; i. 17;
vi. 36; vii. 42, '*Faerie* knight';
(2) used for *fay* (a use pecu-
liarly English), vii. 38, '*Faeries*
sonne'; ix. 60, 'Elves and *Faeries*';
cp. x. 71. M. E. *faerie, fairye,*
enchantment, fairy land (Stratmann, Chaucer 2); O. Fr. *faerie,*
enchantment, from *fae* (Fr. *fée*),
see **fay.** Cp. Skeat (s. v. *fairy*).

Fail, v. 11, to deceive; Fr. '*faillir,*
to faile, to deceive' (Cotgrave);
Lat. *fallere.*

Fain, Fayn, ii. 34; vii. 61, to
feign, pretend; M. E. *feynen,*
feinen (Stratmann); O. Fr. *feindre,*
faindre (Bartsch); Lat. *fingere.*

Faine, vi. 1, gladly; A. S. *fægen,*
glad (Sweet). Gloss. 1. **Fayne.**

Faine, xii. 74, to desire; M. E.
faine, to be glad (M. S. 2); see
above.

Faitour, faytour, i. 30; iv. 30,
'false *faitour,*' cheat, deceiver;
O. Fr. '*faitour,* créateur' (Bartsch).
Gloss. 1.

Falsed, i. 1; xii. 44, falsified; so
Chaucer; *false* from Lat. *falsus,*
pp. of *fallere,* to deceive. Gloss. 1.

Fantasy, xii. 42, fancy; M. E.
fantasie (Chaucer 2); Fr. *fantasie*
(Cotgrave); L. Lat. *fantasia,*
phantasia; Gr. φαντασία in Acts
xxv. 23, 'pomp.' Hence **fantasticke,** vi. 7, fanciful.

Fare, i. 2, 4, to travel, speed; M. E.
faren (Chaucer 2); A. S. *faran*
(Leo), usually (*ge*)*faran* (Sweet);
cp. Goth. *faran,* to go, Germ.
fahren, cognate with Lat. *-per-* in
experior; see Skeat.

Faste, xi. 12, faced; cp. xii. 36,
ill-faste.

Fatall, xii. 36, of ill omen; so in
Shakespeare often, see Schmidt;

Lat. *fatalis,* from *fatum,* what is spoken, fate.

Fault, xi. 9, to err; see Richardson, citation from Cheke.

Favourlesse, ix. 7, not showing favour.

Fay, ii. 43; x. 42, 71, a supernatural being in the mythology of romance; the word does not occur in Shakespeare; Milton, Od. Nat. 235, sings how ' the yellow-skirted *Fayes.* Fly after the night-steeds, leaving their moon-loved maze'; O. Fr. *fee,* a witch, enchantress (Bartsch); L. Lat. *fata,* a goddess of destiny; cp. It. *fata,* Port. *fada,* Sp. *hada,* a fay, a witch; from Lat. *fatum,* what is spoken, fate; hence **faerie**; see Brachet (s.v. *fée*).

Fealty, x. 37, true service, fidelity; O. Fr. *fealte, feelteit*; Lat. *fidelitatem*; for loss of *d* see Brachet, Introd. sect. 120.

Fear, xii. 25, to affright, to terrify; so in Shakespeare often, see Schmidt.

Fee, vii. 56, reward, recompense (fruit of a tree); ii. 13; iii. 8, ' in *fee,*' as a reward, payment; M. E. *fee, fe, feo, feoh,* property, hence a grant of land, payment; A. S. *feó, feoh,* cattle, property, money; see Leo, A. S. Chron. an. 865; cp. O. N. *fé,* Goth. *faihu,* cognate with Lat. *pecus*; see Skeat. Gloss. 1.

Feend, vii. 26; ix. 50, a fiend, an unfriendly supernatural being; M. E. *feend* (Chaucer 2); A. S. *feónd,* a foe, a fiend (Sweet), properly pres. pt. of *feón,* to hate; cp. O. N. *fjándi,* Ger. *feind*; see Skeat.

Feld, vi. 32; xii. 40, let fall; pret. of to *fell,* A. S. *fellan,* formed as a causal by vowel-change from *fallan* (*feallan*), to fall; cp. **drent.**

Fell, viii. 31, fierce, cruel; M. E.

fel (Chaucer 2); A. S. *fel,* as in comp. *wæl-fel,* slaughter-fierce (Leo); cp. O. Fr. *fel,* in oblique case *felon* (Bartsch), see Chanson de Roland.

Felon, viii. 30, a wretch, criminal; O. Fr. *felon* (see above); cp. L. Lat. *fello* (Ducange).

Fensible, ix. 21, fit for defence; for exx. see Richardson; *fence* is merely an abbreviation for *defence*; see Skeat.

Ferry, vi. 19, a ferry-boat; to ferry, A. S. *ferian, ferigan,* to carry, is causal of *faran,* to fare.

Fetch, xii. 21, ' they *fetch* the sandy breach,' they reach, arrive at; the orig. notion of to *fetch* seems to be ' to go to find'; M. E. *fecchen* Stratmann); A. S. *feccan* in John iv. 7; see Skeat, p. 790.

Fett, ix. 58, to fetch; M. E. *fette* (Stratmann, p. 167); A. S. *fetian,* see Sweet.

Field, i. 18, (in heraldry) the surface of the shield, containing the charges; so in Shakespeare figuratively, Lucrece 58, and cp. Pericles, i. 1. 37, ' yon *field* of stars.' The Fr. equivalent is *champ,* L. Lat. *campus* (Ducange).

Field, vi. 29, battle in the 'champ clos'; cp. stanza 28, ' thyselfe prepaire to *batteile.*' So L. Lat. *campus* = duellum, single combat (Ducange).

Fine, xii. 59, ' in *fine,*' in the end; Fr. *enfin.*

Firme, vii. 1, to fix firmly; Lat. *firmare.*

Fits, ii. 11, it is fitting; M. E. *fitten,* to arrange; O. N. *fitja,* to knit together, see Skeat.

Fitt, iv. 14; vi. 21; vii. 66, an attack (of fury, of merriment, of weakness); M. E. *fit* (Stratmann); A. S. *fit,* a struggle (Leo).

Flamed, vi. 8, inflamed.

Fleet, vii. 14, to move swiftly;

M. E. *fleten, fleoten,* to float, swim ; A. S. *fleótan.*

Flit, iv. 38 ; vi. 20, 38 ; xii. 44, flee, swift.

Flitting, viii. 2, fleeting, moving.

Flore, xi. 37, ground ; A. S. *flór* (Sweet) ; cp. Ir. *lár* (Fick, iv. 498).

Flowre-deluce, vi. 16, the white lily ; *flower-de-luce* in Shakespeare, see Schmidt ; M. E. *floure-de-lice* (M.S. 2) ; O.Fr. *flor de lis* (Bartsch); Fr. *fleur de lis* ; *lis* = L. Lat. *lilius,* a form of Lat. *lilium,* a lily.

Foltring, i. 47, stammering. Gloss. 1.

Fond, vii. 14, foolish ; M. E. *fonned* (Wiclif). Gloss. 1.

Fone, viii. 21, x. 10 ; foen, iii. 13, foes ; M. E. *fon,* R. Gloucester (Mätzner) ; A. S. *fán,* pl. of *fáh* (*fá*), weak declension.

Food, i. 3, feud ; M. E. *fede* (a Northern form) ; A. S. *fæhð,* enmity (Sweet), from *fág* (*fáh*), see above. Cp. Skeat.

Fool-hardize, ii. 17 ; iv. 42, foolhardiness ; for exx. of *fool-hardy* see Richardson (s.v. *fool*) ; for the suffix -*ize* (-*ice,* -*ise*) formed on Lat. -*itia* see Earle, p. 323, Morris, p. 239.

Foot, iii. 3, to pace, to walk ; Shakespeare (Schmidt).

Forckhead, iv. 46, the barbed head of the dart.

Fordonne, i. 51, utterly undone ; pp. of *fordo* ; A. S. *fordón,* to ruin (Sweet) ; for the prefix *for-,* see Skeat, p. 728 (13 a).

Foreby, viii. 10, close by ; M. E. *forby* (Chaucer 2). Gloss. 1.

Forestall, iv. 39, '*forestalled* place,' taken previous possession of ; ix. 11, to be beforehand, hence, to prevent ; see Shakespeare's use of the word (Schmidt) ; M. E. *forstallen* (P. Plowman) ; orig. used as a marketing term, viz. to buy up goods *before* they had been

displayed at a *stall* in the market ; see Skeat.

Forgery, xii. 28, fiction, deceit ; from vb. to *forge,* M. E. *forgen,* see Wiclif, Ps. cxxviii. 3, ' synneris *forgeden* on my bak,' = supra dorsum meum *fabricaverunt* peccatores (Vulg.), from *forge* (Gower) ; O. Fr. *forge* ; Lat. *fabrica,* a workshop ; see Brachet. Diez, p. 145, Skeat.

Forlore, pp. iii. 31, lost (unawares) ; vi. 48, utterly lost, ruined (A. S. *forloren*) ; pret. xii. 52, (they) left, abandoned (A. S. *forluron*) ; see Sweet, lxxii. Gloss. 1. Forlorne.

Forthright, xi. 4, straightway ; A. S. *forðriht* (Leo).

Forthy, i. 14 ; vii. 65 ; xii. 8, therefore ; M. E. *forthy* (Chaucer) ; A. S. *for ðy,* therefore ; *ðy* is the instrumental case of the demonstrative neuter *ðæt* (that) ; see Sweet's glossary (s.v. *for*).

Fortilage, xii. 43, a little fort ; used by Spenser in his View of the State of Ireland, see Richardson ; cp. L. Lat. *fortilitium* (Ducange) ; It. *fortilizio* ; see Skeat (s.v. *fortalice*).

Fortuned (him), i. 5, it chanced to him ; for many exx. see Richardson.

Fouldring, ii. 20, thundering, thunderous, blasting with lightning ; Fr. '*fouldroyant,* darting thunderbolts' (Cotgrave), from *fouldroyer* (mod. *foudroyer*), from *fouldre,* O. Fr. *foldre* = Lat. *fulgurem,* a thunderbolt (Burguy) ; see Brachet (s.v. *foudre*).

Foy, x. 41, fealty, here tribute ; Fr. *foy* (Cotgrave) ; Lat. *fidem,* which in L. Lat. is used in sense of tax, tribute, see Ducange (s.v. *fides*).

Foyle, iii. 13, repulse, defeat ; cp. Shakespeare, 1 Hen. VI, iii. 3. 11, ' one sudden *foil* shall never

breed mistrust'; from the vb. to
foil, M. E. *foylen*, to trample under
foot; corrupted from O. Fr. *fouler*
(Bartsch), so in Cotgrave, '*fouler*,
to trample on, to presse, oppresse,
foyle'; L. Lat. *fullare, folare*, to
full cloth (by trampling or beating); from Lat. *fullo*, a fuller, one
who cleanses or bleaches clothes;
perhaps connected with Gr. φάλος,
white; see Skeat (*foil, full*).

Foyne, v. 9; viii. 47, to thrust or
lunge with a sword; so Shakespeare, see Schmidt; M. E. in
Chaucer, C. T. 1654; Fr. *fouine*,
an eel-spear (Cotgrave); Lat. *fus-
cina*, a three-pronged spear, a tri-
dent; so Skeat.

Frame, ii. 16, to prepare; M. E.
fremen (M. S. 1); A. S. (*ge*)*frem-
man*, to further, effect (Sweet);
see Skeat.

Franck, ii. 37, free, forward; O.
Fr. *franc* (Bartsch); L. Lat. *fran-
cus* (Ducange); O. H. G. *francho*,
a Frank, a free man; connected
with Go. -*friks*, G. *frech*, bold, insolent; so Weigand.

Franion, ii. 37, an idle, loose, licentious person; for exx. see
Nares.

Fray, xii. 40, to frighten; so in
Shakespeare, Troilus, iii. 2. 34,
'as if she were *frayed* with a
sprite'; shortened from vb. to
affray; Fr. '*effrayer*, to affright,
fray' (Cotgrave); O. Fr. *effreer*,
esfraër (Bartsch); Prov. *esfredar*;
L. Lat. *exfridare, exfrediare* (Ducange), from O. H. G. *fridu* (now
friede), peace, hence, 'to put out
of peace'; see note by H. Nicol,
in Skeat, p. 776.

Fret, ii. 34, to eat away; M. E.
freten (Chaucer 1); A. S. *fretan*
(Sweet); from *for*-intensive prefix,
and *etan*, to eat; cp. Germ. *fressen*
(= *ver-essen*).

Fret, ix. 37, to ornament, variegate;

M. E. *fretien* (Stratmann); A. S.
(*ge*)*frætwan* (Sweet); cp. O. S.
fratahon (Heliand).

Frigot, vi. 7; xii. 10, a little boat;
Fr. '*fregate*, a swift pinnace'
(Cotgrave); It. '*fregata*, a spiall
ship' (Florio); L. Lat. '*fregata*,
navis exploratoria A.D. 1362' (Ducange); for supposed etymology,
see Diez, p. 147, and Skeat.

Fro, i. 48, from; M. E. *fra, fro*;
O. N. *frá*; see Skeat.

Fry, xii. 45, to boil, foam; Fr.
'*frire*, to frie' (Cotgrave); Lat.
frigēre, to roast; cp. Gr. φρύγειν,
to parch.

Funerall, v. 25, death; so Lat.
funus, funeral, burial, occurs also
in the sense of 'death,' especially
violent death.

G.

Gaged, iii. 14, left as gages, or hostages; to *gage* = O. Fr. *gager*,
wager (Burguy); L. Lat. *wadiare*,
to pledge, from *wadius*, a pledge
(Ducange); see **Wage**.

Gainstrive, iv. 14, to strive *against*;
so F. Q. IV. vii. 12; the prefix
gain- is the A. S. *gegn*, against,
as in *gegncwide*, a speech against
anything (Grein).

Gan, i. 42 (and freq.), pret. of the
vb. to *gin*, M. E. *ginnen*, A. S.
ginnan, to begin'(only in compounds). Fick connects *ginnan*
with O. N. *gunnr*, war, as if the
orig. sense was 'to strike'; cp.
O. Slav. *žena*, I drive; see Skeat
(s.v. *gin*).

Garre, v. 19, to cause, make; common in Lowland Scotch, and see
P. Plowman, C. P.; a Scandinavian word, cp. the O. N. *göra*, to
make, pp. *görr*, ready = A.S. *gearu*
(*yare*); see Icel. Dict.

Gate, xii. 17, a way, path; a Scandinavian word, common in the
N. of Britain; O. N. *gata*; cp.

Go. *gatwo*, Ger. *gasse*. This *gate* = 'a way' should be distinguished from *gate*, 'a door, opening,' A. S. *geat* (Sweet), cognate with O. N. *gat*. Gloss. 1.

Gaze (at), ii. 5, staring; so Shakespeare, see Schmidt, and for other exx. cp. Richardson, Nares, and Halliwell; *gaze*, a vb. of Scandinavian origin, see Skeat.

Geare, iv. 26, dress; M. E. *gere* (Chaucer 1); A. S. *gearwe*, pl. fem. preparation, dress (Leo).

Geare, vi. 21, to jeer, mock, scoff; another form of *jeer*; Du. *scheeren*, to shear, to jeer, from the phrase *den gek scheeren*, to shear the fool, see Skeat (s.v. *jeer*).

Gent, i. 30, 'a ladie *gent*'; xi. 17, 'most *gent*' (of Arthur), gentle, i. e. having the manners of the well-born; O. Fr. *gent* (Bartsch); Lat. *genitum*, begotten, produced.

German, viii. 46; x. 22, brother; Lat. *germanus*, fully akin, said of brothers and sisters having the same father and mother; the word is from the same root as *germen*, a sprout, shoot, bud.

Gest, ii. 16; ix. 53, deed of arms, exploit; gestes, ix. 26, gestures; O. Fr. *geste*, an exploit (Burguy); L. Lat. *gesta*, lit. 'a thing performed,' but generally 'a history of exploits, donations, &c.' (Ducange). Gloss. 1.

Ghesse, i. 51, to guess; M. E. *gessen*. Gloss. 1.

Ghost, i. 42, spirit (of the living man); viii. 45, spirit (of a dead man); viii. 26, a dead body; M.E. goost, gost (Chaucer 1); A. S. *gâst*, a spirit; cp. O. S. *gêst*; Ger. *geist*.

Giambeux, vi. 29, leggings, greaves; M.E. *Iambeux* (Chaucer); Fr. '*Iambiere*, a greave, legharnesse' (Cotgrave), from *jambe*, the leg or shank; L. Lat. *gamba*, a hoof, a joint of the leg; O. Span. *camba*, the bend of the leg. The root is found in Lat. *camera*, a chamber, and in the Celtic *cam*, bent; see Rhŷs, p. 49, and Diez, p. 154.

Gibe, vi. 21, to mock, taunt; for exx. see Richardson; a Shakespearian word, see Schmidt. Etymology unknown; not from Icel. *geip*, idle talk.

Gift, vii. 28, quality; so Shakespeare often, see Schmidt.

Gin, iii. 13, snare; for M. E. *engin*, a contrivance; O. Fr. *engin, engien*, natural capacity, contrivance, engine of war (Bartsch); L. Lat. *ingenium* (Ducange).

Girlond, ii. 31, garland, wreath; cp. It. *ghirlanda*; Fr. *guirlande*; the mod. Eng. form *garland* comes to us from the O. Fr. *garlande*, see Ducange.

Glee, viii. 6, mirth, play; M. E. *gleo* (Stratmann); A. S. *gliw*, joy, music (Sweet).

Glistering, vii. 46, 54; xi. 24, shining, sparkling; occurs in the New Test. A. V., Luke ix. 29; to *glister* is also found often in Milton, as in *Comus*, 219, and in Shakespeare, see Schmidt; M. E. *glisteren* (Gower), see Skeat. *Glister* is in form a frequentative, cp. the *-er* in *stamm-er*, *stutt-er*, *falt-er*, see Morris, p. 221.

Glitterand, vii. 42; xi. 17, shining, sparkling; *-and*, the present participle form in Northern English, see Morris, p. 45.

Glory, iii. 4, vain-glory; cp. the frequent use of the vb. to *glory* = to boast in the New Test., see Concordance; Lat. *gloria*.

Gobbelines, x. 73, goblins; often referred to in Shakespeare; Fr. *gobelin* (Cotgrave); L. Lat. *gobelinus*, a demon (Ducange), a form of *cobalus*; Gr. κόβαλος, a rogue, a mischievous sprite, see Weigand (s. v. *Kobold*).

Gondelay, vi. 2, 11, gondola, a little pleasure-boat; It. *gondola,* a boat used at Venice (Florio); Low Lat. *gondola* from Gr. κόνδυ, a drinking-vessel, so Diez, p. 376.

Goodlihed, iii. 33, goodness, kindness; M. E. *goodlihede* in Gower, see Richardson; for the suffix *-hed,* see Earle, p. 308, and Gloss. 1. -hed.

Gore, xii. 52, to pierce; see **engore.**

Gore blood, i. 39, clotted blood; Shakespeare, Romeo, iii. 2. 56, 'all in *gore blood*'; M. E. *goreblod* (M. S. 1); A. S. *gor,* dirt, filth (Grein).

Goth, xii. 57, goeth.

Governall, xii. 48, management, lit. the helm; Fr. '*gouvernal, gouvernail,* the rudder or sterne of a ship' (Cotgrave); Lat. *gubernaculum,* from *gubernare,* to steer a ship; Gr. κυβερνᾶν; see Brachet.

Governaunce, i. 29; ii. 35, behaviour, self-control; *governance* in Shakespeare, 2 Henry VI, i. 3. 50.

Grace, vii. 59, favour, kindness; 'of *grace,*' cp. Fr. 'de grace, of courtesie, I pray you heartily, I beseech you, sir' (Cotgrave).

Gramercy, vii. 50; ix. 9, thanks! often in Shakespeare, see Schmidt, formerly *grand mercy* (Chaucer, C. T. 8964); Fr. *grand merci,* great thanks; see **Mercie.**

Graplement, xi. 29, grappling; the suffix *-ment* is Fr., as in *commencement*; Lat. *-mentum,* as in *vestimentum,* see Brachet, Introd. cxix, Earle, p. 315; Lat. *-mentum* = Sk. *-manta,* see Fick, i. 83.

Grate, i. 56, to weep, lament; Scot. *greit* (Jamieson); A. S. *grǽtan* (Sweet); cp. O. N. *gráta.*

Grayle, x. 53, 'the holy *grayle,*' the holy grail, the dish at the Last Supper, in which Joseph of Arimathea is said to have collected our Lord's blood, but in course of time the sense of *grail* was changed from 'dish' to 'cup,' namely, the Cup at the Last Supper; M. E. *grail* in Joseph of Arimathie; Fr. *greal* (Cotgrave); O. Fr. *graal, grasal,* a flat dish; L. Lat. *gradale, grasale*; supposed to be a corruption of L. Lat. *cratella,* dimin. of *crater,* a bowl; for *g* = *c,* cp. *grant* = L. Lat. *creantare* (Diez), and cp. **goblin**; see Skeat (s. v. *grail*).

Gree, iii. 5, favour; M. E. *gre,* see 'Halliwell; Fr. '*gré,* will, liking' (Cotgrave); O. Fr. *gred, gret, greit* (Bartsch); Lat. *gratum,* a favour, from *gratus,* pleasing.

Griesie, vi. 18, thick, sluggish (of a lake).

Griesly, xi. 29, grisly, hideous, horrible; so *grisly* in Shakespeare, see Schmidt; M. E. *grisiliche* (Stratmann); A.S. *gryslic* (Grein), *gryrelic* (Sweet).

Gronefull, xi. 42, full of groans.

Groome, iii. 32; iv. 24, a young man; M. E. *grom, grome* (Stratmann); a word often erroneously derived from M. E. *gome* (M.S. 1); A. S. *guma,* a man.

Groveling, i. 45; viii. 32; xi. 34, with face flat to the ground; so the M. E. *groveling, grovelings* is an adv., see Prompt. Parv.; Chaucer (C. T. 951) uses' *grof* (*gruf*) alone with exactly the same adverbial sense, cp. O. N. *á grúfu,* on one's face; for adverbs in *-ling* see Earle, p. 411.

Grudge, i. 42; xi. 32, to murmur; ii. 34, **grutch**; M. E. *grucchen, grochen* (Chaucer); Fr. '*gruger,* to grudge, repine' (Cotgrave);

O. Fr. *grouther*, *grocer* (Burguy);
see exx. of usage in Trench.

Gryde, viii. 36, to pierce, cut
through; Milton, P. L. vi. 329,
'*griding* sword'; M. E. *girden*,
Chaucer, C. T. 1012; lit. to strike
with a rod; from *gerde* (now
yard).

Gryphon, xi. 8, griffin (a fabulous
animal); Fr. '*griffon*, a gripe or
griffon' (Cotgrave); from L. Lat.
griffus (Ducange); Gr. γρύψ.

Grysie, xi. 12, horrible; cp. **griesly**.

Guerdon, i. 61; vi. 28, a reward;
occurs in Shakespeare, see Schmidt;
Fr. '*guerdon*, guerdon, recompence' (Cotgrave); see Gloss. 1.

Guifte, ii. 6, gift.

Guilt, ix. 45, gilded; cp. *guilty-*
cups, butter-cups (Halliwell).

Guize, ii. 14; vi. 25; xii. 21,
fashion, appearance, manner; Fr.
guise (Cotgrave); see **Wize**.

Guyler, vii. 64, deceiver; from
guile, deceit; Fr. '*guille*, *guile*,
craft' (Cotgrave); O. Fr. *guile*,
gile (Bartsch); cp. A. S. *wtl*, wile,
A. S. Chron. an. 1128.

Gyeld, vii. 43, guild, guild-house;
M. E. *gilde*; A. S. *gilde* = fra-
ternitas, Schmidt, p. 603, from
gild, a payment; see Skeat (s. v.
guild).

Gyre, v. 8, circle; Lat. *gyrus*;
Gr. γῦρος.

H.

Haberjeon, vi. 29, armour for the
neck and breast; M. E. *habergeon*
(Chaucer 1); Fr. '*haubergeon*,
a little coat of maile' (Cotgrave),
dimin. of O. Fr. *hauberc*, *halberc*
(Bartsch); see **Hauberk**.

Habiliments, i. 22, clothes; oft.
in Shakespeare; Fr. *habillement*
(Cotgrave). Gloss. 1.

Habitaunce, vii. 7, habitation.

Hable, iii. 22, able; so in More's
Utopia passim; O. Fr. *habile*, able;

Lat. *habilis*; see Skeat (s. v.
able).

Hacqueton, viii. 38, a jacket worn
under armour; M. E. *aketoun*
(Chaucer 2); Fr. *hocqueton*, *hoque-
ton* (Cotgrave); O. Fr. *auque-
ton*, *alquetun* (Bartsch); related
to Sp. *algodón*, cotton-plant (where
al is the Arab. def. art.); Arab.
qutun, cotton.

Hainous, iii. 14, heinous; M. E.
hainous, *heinous*; O. Fr. *haïnos*,
odious, from *haïne*, hate, from
haïr, to hate; of Teutonic origin,
see Brachet.

Hand (with easie), x. 61, at full
speed; cp. Fr. 'à la main, nimbly,
readily, actively' (Cotgrave).

Hardiment, i. 27; ii. 37, rashness,
boldness; a Shakesperian word,
see Schmidt; M. E. *hardement*
(Chaucer); O. Fr. *hardement*
(Bartsch); for suffix see *graplement*.

Harnesse, i. 5; xi. 43, armour;
M. E. *harneys* (Chaucer 1); O.
Fr. *harnois*, *harneis* (Bartsch);
supposed to be of Celtic origin;
see Diez (s. v. *arnese*), Weigand
(s. v. *harnisch*).

Harpy, xii. 36, a mythological
monster, half bird and half woman; Lat. *harpyia*; Gr. pl. ἅρπυιαι,
lit. the spoilers.

Harrow, vi. 49; viii. 46, '*harrow*
and well away'; vi. 43, '*harrow*
now out, and well away'; harrow! an exclamation of distress, a
call for help; M. E. *harrow*, *haro*
(Chaucer 1, 3); O. Fr. *haro*, *haré*,
hari (Bartsch). Cp. Cotgrave,
'*Haro*, ou *Harol*, crier *Haro* sur,
to crie out upon, or make huy and
crie after, used in Normandie by
such as are outraged, or in some
high degree wronged; in which
case those that are within the
hearing thereof must pursue the
malefactor, or else they pay a fine.'

Hartlesse, ii. 7, timid, wanting courage; so Shakespeare, see Schmidt.

Hartsore, i. 2, heart-sore; cp. Shakespeare (Schmidt); so in Milton, Samson Ag. 1339, 'heart grief.'

Hastly, x. 52, hastily.

Hauberk, viii. 44, a coat of mail; orig. armour for the neck; M. E. *hauberk* (Chaucer 1); O. Fr. *hauberc, halberc* (Bartsch); O. H. G. *halsberc, halsberge,* lit. the neck-protector; cp. O. Fr. *osbercs,* in the Chanson de Roland, It. *osbergo,* see Diez, p. 336, and **Haberjeon.**

Haviour, ii. 15, behaviour; so in Shakespeare often; see **Behave.**

Hayle, iv. 14, to drag, haul; M. E. *halien* (Mätzner); cp. O. S. *halón,* to bring (Héliand); allied to Gr. καλεῖν, see Skeat (s. v. *hale, haul*).

Hazardize, xii. 19, risk; M. E. *hasard* (Chaucer); O. Fr. *hasart* (Bartsch), orig. 'a game at dice'; Sp. *azar,* a die; Arab. *al zár,* the die; see Skeat (s. v. *hazard*). For the suffix *-ize* see Earle, p. 323.

Hazardry, v. 13, risk; for the romance suffix *-ry* (Fr. *-rie*), see Earle, p. 314, Morris, p. 233.

Heben, vii. 52; viii. 17, ebony, of ebony wood. Gloss. 1.

Hell, vii. 24, also **Hell-mouth,** the abode of evil spirits, and the entrance thereto; M. E. *helle;* A. S. *hell* (Sweet); the orig. sense is the hidden or unseen place; cp. A. S. *helan,* to hide, cognate with Lat. *celare.*

Hellebore, vii. 52, the name of a plant; Lat. *helleborus;* Gr. ἑλλέ-βορος.

Hent, ii. 1; iv. 12; xi. 17, took, seized; vi. 49, pp.; Shakespeare, Meas. for M. iv. 6. 14, 'citizens have *hent* the gates'; M. E. *henten,* to seize, pret. *hente,* pp. *hent*

(Chaucer 1); A. S. *hentan, gehentan,* A. S. Chron. an. 905.

Herbars, ix. 46, herbs; prob. peculiar to Spenser (Nares); from Lat. *herba;* O. Lat. *forbea,* food; Gr. φορβή, see Fick, i. 159.

Herce, viii. 16, a decorated funeral bier; M. E. *herse,* used by Chaucer, 'And doune I fel when that I saugh the *herse,*' Complaint to Pity, st. 3; Fr. '*herce,* a harrow, a portcullis full of outstanding iron pins' (Cotgrave). The changes of sense from the orig. one of 'harrow' are these: (1) a triangular frame for lights in church, and specially at funerals, (2) a funeral pageant, (3) a frame on which a body was laid. Fr. *herce* = Lat. *hirpicem,* a harrow. See Skeat, Trench (s. v. *hearse*).

Herried, xii. 13, honoured, praised; M. E. *herien* (Chaucer 3); A. S. *herian,* to praise (Sweet).

Hew, iii. 22; vii. 3, 23; ix. 3; xi. 13; xii. 24, appearance; ix. 52, face; xii. 31, shape; M. E. *hew, hewe* (Chaucer 2); A. S. *heó, hiw,* appearance; see Skeat (s. v. *hue*).

Hide, xi. 25, hied, hastened; M. E. *hien, hiʒen,* to hie; A. S. *higian* (Grein); see Skeat.

Hight, i. 18, 51; iv. 25, was called; ii. 17 (pp.) called. Gloss. 1.

Hippodame, ix. 50, a seahorse; M. E. *ypotamus,* Alexander and Dindimus, 157, also *ypotanos* (Coleridge); corrupted from Lat. *hippopotamus;* Gr. ἱπποπόταμος, the river horse of Egypt; see Skeat.

Hoars, xii. 8, hoarse, having a rough harsh voice; M. E. *horse* (Chaucer), *hos* (Skeat); A. S. *hás* (Grein).

Hogh (The westerne), x. 10, 'the *Hoe*' near Plymouth; called 'the *Haw*' in Camden's Britannia; *hoe* is a survival of M. E.

hogh, a hillock, also *houȝ* (Stratmann) ; cp. O. N. *haugr*, a mound (Icel. Dict.) ; see Skeat (s. v. *how*).

Hop, i. 43, to pulse (of blood in the veins) ; M. E. *hoppen*, to dance ; A. S. *hoppian* (Leo).

Hospitale, ix. 10, a place of rest, a building for receiving guests ; Fr. *hospital* (Cotgrave) ; L. Lat. *hospitale* (Ducange) ; hence *hostel*.

Hoye, x. 64, a small ship ; for early exx. see Richardson ; Du. *heu* ; Flem. *hui* ; whence Fr. *heu* ; Ger. *heu* (Hilpert).

Hurtle, v. 8 ; vii. 42, to jostle against, to rush confusedly ; occurs in Shakespeare ; M. E. *hurtlen* (Wiclif) ; a frequentative of *hurt* in the sense. 'to dash' ; M. E. *hurten, hirten*, to stumble, to dash the foot (Wiclif) ; O. Fr. *hurter*, to strike, dash (Bartsch) ; said to be of Celtic origin ; cp. Wel. *hwrdd*, a ram ; see Diez, p. 336, where *hurt* is supposed to have come to England as a tournament word.

Hyacine, xii. 54, jacinth, a precious stone, in colour dark purple ; M. E. *iacynt*, in Wiclif, Rev. ix. 17 ; Lat. *hyacinthus* (Vulgate) ; Gr. ὑάκινθος, jacinth (in N. T.), also the iris.

Hydre, xii. 23, hydra, a many-headed water-snake (in fable) ; Lat. *hydra* ; Gr. ὕδρα, also ὕδρος (in Homer), related to ὕδωρ, water.

I.

Idole, ii. 41, image, reflection ; Lat. *idolum* (Vulgate) ; Gr. εἴδωλον, an image, likeness.

Immeasured, xii. 23, that cannot be measured ; see Richardson.

Implore, v. 37, entreaty.

Importable, viii. 35, unbearable, irresistible ; for exx. see Richard-son ; used by Chaucer ; Lat. *importabilis* (Tertullian).

Importune, vi. 29 ; viii. 38 ; x. 15 ; xi. 7, violent, savage ; occurs in Chaucer ; Lat. *importunus*, troublesome, grievous, lit. difficult of approach, hard of access, hence unsuitable, etc., from *portus*, a harbour.

Importunely, with importunity.

Impresse, viii. 18, to make an impression ; so Shakespeare, see Schmidt.

In, i. 59 ; xii. 32, 'death . . . the common *In* of rest,' lodging, house of entertainment, lit. a place to which one turns *in* ; M. E. *in, inne* (Chaucer 1) ; A. S. *in, inne* (Leo). Gloss. 1.

Infant, viii. 56 ; xi. 25, used here for 'a young knight' (of Prince Arthur) ; see Nares ; cp. O. Fr. *enfant*, a young aspirant to knightly honours (Bartsch), and see especially Chanson de Roland, 3196, 'de bachelers que Carles cleimet *enfanz*' ; 'bacheliers que Charles appelle "*enfants*"' ; hence our 'infantry' = foot-soldiers ; Lat. *infans*, lit. 'one who cannot speak.' Cp. *childe*.

Ingowe, vii. 5, ingot, a mass of metal poured into a mould, a mass of unwrought metal ; M. E. *ingot* (Chaucer 3) ; A. S. *in + goten*, poured, pp. of *geótan* (Sweet) ; cp. Ger. *einguss*. From *ingot* comes Fr. *lingot* ; see Skeat (s. v. *ingot*).

Inquyre, x. 12, to call ; Lat. *inquirere*.

Intend, iv. 46, to stretch. Gloss. 1.

Irrenowmed, i. 23, inglorious. Gloss. 1. **Renowmed.**

J.

Jade, xi. 31, an old woman ; primarily, a sorry nag ; M. E. *iade*

(Chaucer 2); cp. Scottish *yade, yaud* (Jamieson); see Skeat.

Jarre, ii. 26, quarrel, discord; see Schmidt for Shakespearian uses; from the vb. to *jar* which stands for *char* (found in *charken*, to creak, Prompt. Parv.); cp. O. S. *karón*, to lament (Héliand); see Skeat (s. v. *jar*).

Jeoperdie, iv. 39, 43, jeopardy, risk, danger; only once in Shakespeare, K. John, iii. 1. 346; M. E. *jupartie* (Chaucer); the orig. sense was a game in which the chances are even, a game of chance, hence hazard, risk; O. Fr. *jeu parti* (Bartsch), lit. a divided game; L. Lat. *jocus partitus* (Ducange); see Skeat.

Jett, vii. 28, jet, a black mineral; M. E. *jet* (Chaucer); O. Fr. *jet, jaet, gagate*; Lat. *gagatem*, from Gr. γαγάτης, from Γάγας, a town in Lycia; see Skeat.

Joviall, xii. 51, propitious, kindly (of the heavens); Fr. '*jovial*, joviall, sanguine, born under the planet Jupiter' (Cotgrave), see Trench, Study of Words; Lat. *Jovialis*, pertaining to Jove; see Skeat.

Joy, vi. 6; x. 53, to enjoy; so Shakespeare often, see Schmidt. Gloss. 1.

K.

Keepe care, vi. 42, to take care; so Shakespeare, see Schmidt. Gloss. 1.

Ken, i. 3, to know; M. E. *kenne* (Chaucer); the sense 'to know' is Scandinavian, so O. N. *kenna*. The vb. is in *form* causal, meaning 'to make to know, to teach'; *kenna* is for *kannian*, cp. Go. *kannjan*, to make known, from *kunnan*, to know (base *kann*); the *e* is the regular substitute for *a*, when *i* follows in the next syllable; cp. **Feld, Drent.**

Kesars, vii. 5, Cæsars, emperors.

Kest, xi. 42, pret. cast; so Wiclif, Lu. xxiii. 35, 'thei *kesten* lottis,' they cast lots; O. N. *kasta*. Gloss. 1.

Kestrell kynd, iii. 4, base nature; '*kestrell*, the same as *castril* or *kastril*, a hawk of a base unserviceable breed, and therefore used by Spenser in the sense of base' (Nares); cp. Cotgrave, '*Quercerelle*, a *kestrell, kastrell* fleingall.' The corrupt form *coystrell* occurs in Dryden, Hind and Panther, iii. 1119, *kestrel* in Tennyson's Boadicea, 15.

Kight, viii. 16, kite, a bird of prey; A. S. *cýta*.

Kinred, x. 35, kindred; so Shakespeare *kinred* sometimes in old editions (Schmidt); M. E. *kinrede* (Wiclif N. T.); A. S. *cyn*, kin + suffix *-ræden*, condition, lit. law = Ger. *-rath* in *Heirath*, marriage, see Earle, p. 307.

Knife, v. 9, sword. Gloss. 1.

Kynd, ii. 36, nature; A. S. (*ge*)*cynd* (Sweet).

L.

Lap, iii. 30, to fold, entwine; M. E. *lappen*, cp. Wiclif, Matt. xxvii. 59, '*lappide* it' (in an earlier ed. '*wlappide* it'); *wlappen* = *wrappen*, to wrap.

Larum-bell, ix. 25, *alarum*-bell; *alarum* = *alarm*; Fr. *alarme*; It. *all' arme*, to arms!; see **Alarmes.**

Launch, i. 38, to pierce; O. Fr. *lanchier*. Gloss. 1.

Laver, xii. 62, basin; in A. V. Exod. xxxviii. 8; M. E. *lavour* (Chaucer); Fr. *lavoir* from *laver*, Lat. *lavare*, to wash.

Lay up, xii. 3, to throw up.

Lay, x. 42, law; M. E. *lay* (Chaucer 2); Norm. Fr. *lei* in William's Laws, see Schmid, p. 322; O. Fr. *lai, lei* (Bartsch); Lat. *legem*.

Lay, i. 35, cry ; prob. a poetical use of the word lay, a song ; Fr. *lay* (Cotgrave) ; O. Fr. *lais*, prob. of Celtic origin, a Breton word ; cp. Wel. *llais*, a voice, sound, cry ; see Diez, p. 623.

Leasing, ix. 51 ; xi. 10, a lie ; in Ps. iv. 2, v. 6 (A. V.) ; M. E. *lesynge* (Chaucer) ; A. S. *leásung* (Sweet), from *leás*, false, orig. empty ; see Skeat.

Leave, x. 31, to levy ; O. Fr. *lever*, to raise (Bartsch) ; Lat. *levare*, lit. to make light, from Lat. *levis*. With the form leave cp. the sb. *leaven* = Fr. *levain*, lit. that which raises.

Lefte, iii. 34, pret. of 'to *lift*' ; in the Bible of 1611 the two pret. forms *lift*, *lifted* were used indiscriminately, see Earle, p. 288 ; M. E. *liften*, pret. *lifte* (Stratmann) ; O. N. *lypta* (pronounced *lyfta*), to lift, from *lopt*, the air ; cp. Go. *luftus*, air.

Leman, v. 28 ; x. 18, a lover ; M. E. '*leman*, amasius, amasia' (Catholicon Anglicum), also *lemman*, *lefmon*, *leofmon* (M. S. 1). Gloss. 1.

Lenger, i. 13 ; viii. 46, longer ; M. E. *lenger* (Chaucer 2) ; A. S. *lengra*, comp. of *lang* (Sweet).

Lett, xi. 31, a hindrance ; M. E. *letten*, to cause delay (Chaucer 3) ; A. S. (*ge*)*lettan*, to hinder, from *læt*, late. Gloss. 1.

Lett, vi. 16, to leave, entrust ; M. E. *leten* ; A. S. *lǽtan* (Sweet), also *létan* ; see Skeat.

Level, xii. 34, 'their course they levelled,' directed ; M. E. *livel* ; O. Fr. *livel* ; Lat. *libella*, dimin. of *libra*, a balance ; see Skeat.

Lewd, i. 10, base, licentious ; for the successive stages in the meaning of this word see Skeat, and for exx. of usage cp. Trench ; A. S. *lǽwed*, prop. a pp. the weakened, enfeebled, as an adj. feeble ; from

lǽwan, to weaken, but more usually to betray, cognate with Go. *lewjan*, to betray, from *lew*, an occasion, opportunity, hence, opportunity to betray. From the sense of 'feeble' *lǽwed* came to mean 'ignorant, untaught,' hence 'the laity' as opposed to the clergy (Sweet). From this sense the word took a downward moral course, connoting gradually baseness, vileness, licentiousness. Note that the usual sense of M. E. *lewed* is 'ignorant.'

Libbard, iii. 28, leopard ; M. E. *lyberde* (Catholicon Anglicum) ; O. Fr. *liepart* (Bartsch). Gloss. 1.

Liefe, i. 16 ; ix. 4, dear ; A. S. *leóf*. Gloss. 1.

Liege, iii. 8 ; viii. 55 ; ix. 4, a free lord ; M. E. *lege* ; O. Fr. *lige*, cp. Chanson de Roland, 2421, 'lur *liges* seignurs' ; O. H. G. *ledec*, *lidic*, free from all obligations ; cp. Germ. *ledig* ; see Skeat, Weigand.

Liegeman, iii. 9 ; viii. 51, prop. a man connected with his lord by feudal tenure, and so *free* from all other obligations ; cp. Ducange, '*ligius* homo quod Teutonice dicitur *ledigman*.'

Light-foot, viii. 10, nimble in running ; cp. Shakespeare, Rich. III, iv. 4. 440, 'some light-foot friend.'

Like, vii. 27, 'thing that *likt* him,' that pleased him ; M. E. *liken*, to please, used impersonally (Chaucer 1) ; A. S. (*ge*)*lician* (Sweet).

List, vi. 26 ; x. 66, to desire ; vii. 18, 'if then *thee list*,' if it please thee, if thou wish ; A. S. *gelystan*, impers. (Sweet).

Lists, i. 6, the ground enclosed for a tournament ; used to translate O. Fr. *lices* (Burguy) ; cp. L. Lat. *liciæ duelli*, the lists (Ducange).

Livelyhead, ix. 3, liveliness ; for suffix see **Bountihed.**

Livelyhed, ii. 2, means of living, way of life; a corruption of M. E. *livelode, liflode,* also *lyfelade* (Catholicon Anglicum); A. S. *lif-lade,* way of life (Leo); see Earle, p. 309.

Loathly, viii. 44, hateful; A. S. *láðlic* (Sweet).

Logris, x. 14, cp. Wel. *Lloegr,* England.

Losell, iii. 4, a loose idle fellow; Shakespeare, Winter's Tale, ii. 3. 109, *lozel;* M. E. *losel,* also spelt *lorel* (Stratmann); see P. Plowman, p. 197.

Lothfull, xi. 46, unwilling; from M. E. *loth;* A. S. *láð,* hateful; see Skeat (s. v. *loath*).

Lott, vii. 19, apportionment; A. S. *hlot* (Sweet), usually *hlyt,* a lot; cp. O. N. *hlutr;* Go. *hlauts.*

Loup, ix. 10, a fastening.

Loute, iii. 13; ix. 26, to stoop, to bow; M. E. *louten* (Chaucer 2); A. S. *lútan* (Sweet); cp. O. N. *lúta.*

Lug, x. 11, a perch or rod of land; so in the Isle of Wight dialect; also spelt *log,* see Halliwell; M.E. *lugge,* a log (Coleridge); O. N. *lág,* a log, a felled tree, so called from its lying flat on the ground.

Lumpish, xi. 42, heavy, spiritless; so Shakespeare, Two G. of Verona, iii. 2. 62. Gloss. 1.

Lusty-hed, i. 41, youthful vigour; cp. Shakespeare, Much Ado, v. 1. 76, 'his May of youth and bloom of *lustihood.*'

Lyte, viii. 38, to light (of a stroke); M. E. *lihten;* see Skeat (s. v. *light* 3).

M.

Mace, x. 4, a sceptre; M. E. *mace* (Coleridge); O. Fr. *mace, make* (Bartsch); Lat. *matea;* see Skeat.

Magnes-stone, xii. 4, magnet, the loadstone; Lat. *magnes lapis* = Magnesian stone, from the country Magnesia.

Mahoune, viii. 33, Mahomet; M.E. *Mahoun,* also *Makomete* (Chaucer 3); O. Fr. *Mahum, Mahumet,* see Chanson de Roland; Arab. *Muhammed,* the praised, so E. Deutsch, Quarterly Rev. 1869, 'Islam.'

Maine, xii. 21, the ocean, the great sea; so in Shakespeare, see Schmidt.

Male, v. 9, steel net-work forming body-armour; M. E. *maille* (Chaucer 2); O. Fr. *maille* (Bartsch), a ring of metal, a mesh; Lat. *macula,* a spot, hole, mesh of a net.

Marke, iii. 34, to aim at; cp. in Shakespeare *mark* = butt, target, aim (Schmidt).

Marle, xi. 33, ground, soil; Milton, P.L.i. 296; M. E. *marle* (Chaucer, C. T. 3460); O. Fr. *marle* (still used in Normandy); L. Lat. *margila,* marl, from Lat. *marga,* used by Pliny, who considers it to be a word of Gaulish origin; see Brachet (s. v. *marne*).

Marshall, ix. 28, the official who places the guests in their proper order; the orig. sense is a ' horse-servant,' a farrier or groom; M. E. *marschal* (Stratmann); O. Fr. *mareschal;* O. H. G. *maraschalh* from *marah,* a battle-horse + *scalh,* a servant; see Skeat, also Weigand (s.v. *marschall*).

Matchable, x. 56, to be compared with; cognate with make, see Gloss. 1.

Maugre, v. 12, a curse on! The lit. sense of the word is 'ill-will' or 'displeasure'; O. Fr. *maugre, maulgre, malgre* (Bartsch); Lat. *malum* + *gratum;* see Skeat. Gloss. 1. Gree.

Mazer, xii. 49, 'a *mazer* bowle,' a large drinking bowl; *mazer* used still in this sense by itself, cp. Cotgrave, s.v. '*jadeau,* a bowle or *mazer,*' see also Halliwell (s.v.

maser)and Nares(s.v.*mazer*); M.E.
maser (Stratmann). *Mazers* were
so called because often made of
maple, which is a spotted wood,
the orig. sense of the word being
'a spot,' a knot in wood, cp. O.
Du. *maser*, a knot in a tree, O. N.
mösurr, a maple-tree, spot-wood;
an extension of the form which
appears in O. H. G. *másd*, a spot;
see Skeat. Cp. Fr. *madré*, spotted
(Brachet).

Medæwart, viii. 20, meadow-wort.

Medle, i. 61, to mix; M. E. *medlen*
(Stratmann); O. Fr. *medler* (Burguy), a corruption of *mesler*; for
intrusive *d* remaining after a
dropped out *s* see Brachet (s.v.
cidre), and Skeat (s.v. *medlar* =
O. Fr. *meslier*). *Mesler* = L. Lat.
misculare from Lat. *miscere*, to
mix. Cp. Gloss. 1. **Mell**.

Meed, iii. 10, 14; vii. 55; viii. 55,
reward; A. S. *méd* (Sweet), also
meard, Luke 6. 35, Lindisfarne
Gospels; the *r* stands for an old *s*,
cp. Go. *mizdo*; Gr. μισθός.

Menage, ii. 28; ix. 27; iv. i. 8, to
manage, to handle, wield arms, to
control a horse; to *manage* in
Shakespeare, see Schmidt; from
the sb. *manage*, control; Fr. *ma-
nege* (Cotgrave); It. *maneggio*,
a handling (Florio).

Mendes, i. 20, amends; *mendes* is
a mere corruption of *amends*; M.E.
amendes (Skeat); O. Fr. *amende*
(Bartsch), from *amender*; Lat.
emendare, to free from fault; *ex* +
menda, a blemish; for the unusual
change from *e* to *a* in the prefix
see Brachet, Hist. Gram. sect. 28,
and cp. **fray**.

Mercie, i. 27, grace, clemency; O.
Fr. *merci, mercid* (Bartsch); L.
Lat. *mercedem* (acc. of *merces*), a
gratuity, pity, mercy (Ducange);
in Lat. pay, reward.

Merimake, vi. 21, merry-making;

see Nares (s.v. *merry-make*); A. S.
myrig (Leo). **meriment**, vi. 3,
sport, a hybrid word with a French
suffix.

Mermaid, xii. 17, a siren (in English
Romance); M. E. *mere-maidens*,
Rom. of the Rose, 628, 'men
clepe hem sereyns in Fraunce,'
Chaucer vi. 21; A. S. *mere*, a
lake + *mægden* (Sweet). The
sense of *mere* was easily exchanged
for that of 'sea' under the influence of Fr. *mer*, a cognate word.

Mesprise, vii. 39, contempt;
Fr. '*mespris*, contempt, neglect'
(Cotgrave), mod. *mépris*; from
mespriser, to contemn; *mes* +
priser; the prefix *mes-* = Lat.
minus, used in a bad sense, see
Brachet, and cp. Gloss. 1. **Miscreant**. *Priser* is from O. Fr.
pris, preis (Bartsch); Lat. *pretium*.

Mesprize, xii. 19, mistake, mis-
understanding; O. Fr. *mespris*,
error (Bartsch), mod. *méprise*;
from *mesprendre*; Lat. *minus* +
prehendere.

Mew, v. 27; vii. 19, close confine-
ment, prison; orig. a cage for
hawks when *mewing* or moulting;
Fr. '*mue*, a change ... the *mewing*
of a hawk ... also, a hawk's *mue*
or coop' (Cotgrave), from '*muer*,
to change, to *mew*' (ib.); Lat.
mutare. iii. 34, to enclose, confine.
Gloss. 1.

Mickle, i. 6; x. 59, great; so Milton, Comus, 31; A. S. *micel*
(Sweet); cp. O. N. *mikill*. Gloss.
1. **Muchell**.

Middest, ii. 13, the middle one (of
three). Gloss. 1.

Mind, ii. 10, to call to mind; from
mind in the sense of memory, the
usual sense in M.E.; A.S. *gemynd*,
memory, thought (Sweet).

Mineon, ii. 37, a lover, with a
sinister sense; *minion*, often in
Shakespeare (Schmidt); see Trench

for exx. of usage in a good sense ;
Fr. '*mignon*, dainty, kind' (Cotgrave) ; cp. It. *mignone*, a darling.
The Fr. *-on* is a suffix; the base
is due to M. H. G. *minne*, O. H. G.
minna, memory, love ; see M.
Müller, Chips, iii. 58.

Miscall, xii. 86, to abuse, revile;
still common in many dialects in
North Britain, Oxfordshire, &c. ;
the prefix *mis-* is here Teutonic ;
see Skeat (s.v. *Mis-* 1).

Miscreant, viii. 31, unbeliever, in-
fidel, vile fellow ; for exx. see
Trench; O. Fr. *mescreant*(Bartsch);
for prefix *mes-* cp. **mesprize**.
From *miscreant* is formed **miscreaunce**, viii. 51, false belief ;
Fr. '*mescreance*, miscreancie, mis-
beleefe' (Cotgrave).

Miscreate, x. 38, illegitimate ; cp.
Shakespeare, Henry V, i. 2. 16.

Miser, i. 8, 9; iii. 8, a miserable
wretch; so Shakespeare, 1 Henry
VI, v. 4. 7; for different uses
of the word see Trench; Lat.
miser, wretched ; see Skeat.

Misseeming, ii. 31, unseemly;
from vb. to *seem* with Teutonic
suffix; M. E. *semen*, to be fitting
(Coleridge) ; A. S. (*ge*)*séman*, to
satisfy, reconcile (Sweet).

Misweene, Introd. 3, to ween,
think amiss ; M. E. *wenen* (Chaucer
1) ; A. S. *wénan*, to imagine, expect (Sweet); cp. Ger. *wähnen*.

Moe, vii. 63, more ; M. E. *mo, ma*
(M. S. 1); A.S. *má*, magis (Sweet).
Gloss. 1.

Molt, v. 8, melted; M. E. *malt*,
pret. of *melten* (M. S. i. p. lxxiii);
A.S. *mealt*, pret. of *meltan* (Sweet,
lxviii).

Moniment (for *monument*), x. 56,
memorial, anything by which a
thing is remembered ; xii. 80, used
of dints on a shield ; vii. 5, an inscription stamped on coin; Lat.
monumentum.

Monoceros, xii. 23, the sword-
fish; see quotation from Gesner
in Notes; Gr. μόνος alone + κέρας
a horn.

Monstruous, xii. 85, monster-like;
M. E. *monstruous* (Chaucer); Fr.
monstrüeux (Cotgrave); Lat. *mon-
struosus*, from *monstrum*, a monster, a divine omen, from *monere*,
to warn, to make to think ; see
Skeat.

Morands, x. 43, the Moriani (Holinshed); see Notes.

Mortall, ii. 22, 45 ; iv. 33 ; vii. 52,
deadly, fatal; so in Shakespeare
often, see Schmidt; Lat. *mortalis*,
only in the sense of 'liable to
death,' sharing the inevitable fate
of mankind.

Mote, i. 23, 29; ii. 12; viii. 25, 33;
ix. 42 ; xi. 17; xii. 23, 70, may,
must ; for M. E. exx. see M. S. 1 ;
A. S. *mót*, 1 pers. sing. ; *móst*, 2
pers. sing.; *móste*, pret. Gloss. 1.

Mould, iii. 41, to become mouldy,
- to rot ; *mould* is for *moul* = M. E.
moulen, as in Chaucer, ' Let us
not *moulen* thus in idlenesse,' C. T.
4452, also *muwlen* in Ancren Riwle;
O. N. *mygla* to grow musty, from
mugga, mugginess; see Skeat, p.
796.

Moytie, xii. 31, half; Fr. *moitié*
(Cotgrave); Lat. *medietatem*, from
medius, middle.

Munifience, x. 15 (ed. 1590), for-
tification ; cp. to *munifie*, to for-
tify, in Nares ; Lat. *mœnia*, walls +
facere, to make.

Muse, i. 19, to wonder ; M. E.
musen (Chaucer 3). Gloss. 1.

N.

Nathemoe, iv. 8 ; nathemore, v.
8; xi. 37, 38, none the more ;
M. E. *nathemo* (M. S. 2) ; see
Moe.

Nathlesse, i. 5, 20, 22 ; vi. 24;

vii. 45, none the less ; M. E. *natheles* (M. S. 2).

Ne, i. 15, nor ; M. E. *ne* (M.S. 1); A. S. *ne . . . ne,* neither . . . nor (Sweet).

Needes, x. 1, 'spirit *needes* me,' is wanting to me, I need more ample spirit.

Needes, xii. 3, 'we *needes* must passe'; M. E. *needes, nedes,* adv. (Chaucer) ; the final *-es* is an adverbial ending, orig. due to A. S. gen. cases in *-es,* see Earle, p. 410; but in this case *nedes* is for an older *nede* (M. S. 1) = A. S. *nýde,* gen. case of *nýd* ; see Skeat.

Nephewe, viii. 29; x. 45, grand-child; so in 1 Tim. v. 4 ; O. Fr. *neveu,* a nephew (Bartsch) ; Lat. *nepotem,* a grandson, nephew ; see Skeat. Gloss. 1.

Nill, vii. 33, will not. Gloss. 1.

Nimble, viii. 8, active; the *b* is intrusive ; M. E. *nimel* ; formed from A. S. *niman,* to take, with the A. S. suffix *-ol* ; see **wench.** Gloss. 1. **Griple.**

Nobilesse, viii. 18; nobleness ; O. Fr. *noblesse, noblece* (Bartsch). Gloss. 1.

Noriture, iii. 2, nurture, bringing up ; O. Fr. *noriture* (Burguy) ; Lat. *nutritura* ; on the suffix *-tura* see Brachet, cxxiv.

Note, iv. 4, 13 ; vii. 39, wot not, know not ; M. E. *noot, not* (M. S. 1) ; A. S. *nát = ne wát* (Sweet).

Nould, iv. 12; viii. 30, would not ; M. E. and A. S. *nolde = ne wolde* (Sweet).

Noyous, ix. 16, 32, harmful ; M. E. *noyous* (Wiclif, N. T.).

O.

Oberon, i. 6; x. 75, the fairy king; Fr. *Auberon, Auberich* ; M. H. G. *Albrich,* in the Nibelungenlied. Gloss. 1. **Elfe.**

Obsequy, i. 60, funeral rite; Mil-ton, Samson, 1732 ; L. Lat. '*ob-sequium,* officium ecclesiasticum, praesertim pro mortuis'(Ducange); instead of the classical *exsequiae,* a funeral, from *exsequor,* to follow or accompany to the grave. In classical Latin *obsequium* = compliance, obedience.

Offáll, iii. 8, worthless refuse ; for exx. of usage see Trench ; e. g. it was once used of chips of wood falling from a cut log ; a compound of *off + fall.*

Offend, i. 3 ; viii. 8, 21 ; xi. 16, to harm ; M. E. *offenden* (Chaucer 1) ; Fr. '*offendre,* to hurt' (Cotgrave); Lat. *offendere,* lit. to strike against.

Ofspring, ix. 60 ; x. 69, origin ; so in Fairfax, Tasso, vii. 18. Gloss. 1.

Onely, i. 2, chief, especial ; *only* often in this sense in Shakespeare, see Schmidt ; A. S. *ánlíc* (Grein).

Order, ix. 15, rank of army ; M. E. *order* (Coleridge) ; O. Fr. *ordre, ordene* (Bartsch) ; Lat. *ordinem*; for change of *n* to *r* cp. Fr. *coffre, diacre, Londres* (Brachet); ix. 28, to arrange.

Ordinaunce, ix. 30, arrangement ; xi. 14, ordnance, artillery ; with this latter meaning it orig. meant the *bore* or *size* of the cannon, and was thence transferred to the cannon itself; cp. Cotgrave, 'engin de telle *ordonnance,* of such a bulke, size, or bore'; L. Lat. *ordinantia,* a regulation (Ducange).

Organ, i. 33, instrument; Gr. ὄργανον.

Otherwhere, xii. 45, elsewhere.

Otherwhiles, xii. 45, at other times.

Outráge, ii. 38; vi. 29, excess, violent conduct; O. Fr. *outrage, oltrage* (Bartsch), from *oltre (ultre)* = Lat. *ultra,* beyond. Gloss. 1.

Outwrought, vii. 65, passed, completed.

Overhent, x. 18, overtook; see **Hent.**

Oversee, ix. 44, to overlook, to fail to see.

Owre, vii. 5, 36, ore; A. S. *ár,* brass (Leo); cp. M. Müller, ii. 256.

Oystrige, xi. 12, ostrich; M. E. *oystryche,* also *ostrice,* in Ancren Riwle; O. Fr. *ostrusce, austruce;* Lat. *avis struthio,* i. e. the bird struthio; *struthio =* Gr. στρουθίων, the struthio camelus of Pliny (Liddell and Scott), from στρουθός, a bird, particularly of the sparrow kind. See Skeat, also Brachet (s. v. *autruche*).

P.

Pace, i. 26; viii. 10, 17, to step, walk ; so in Shakespeare often, see Schmidt. Gloss. 1.

Pagan, viii. 32; x. 62, a heathen, one not believing in Christ; so L. Lat. *paganus* (Ducange); Lat. a peasant, villager, a civilian, as opp. to a soldier, hence rustic, unlearned. Gloss. 1. **Paynim.**

Page, viii. 10, a servant; M. E. *page* (Stratmann); O. Fr. *page* (Bartsch) ; L. Lat. *pagium,* acc. of *pagius,* famulus, cp. *paganus, pagensis* (Ducange). The word therefore orig. meant a peasant, rustic, hence a serf, a servant.

Pageant, i. 33, 36, exhibition, spectacle ; it orig. meant a moveable scaffold, such as was used in the representation of the old mysteries; M.E. *pagent* (Prompt. Parv.), also *pagyn,* Wiclif, see Skeat, p. 796 ; L. Lat. *pagina,* a scaffold, stage, in Lat. a plank of wood, from *pag,* base of *pangere,* to fasten, fix.

Pall, ix. 37, a long garment with skirt ; cp. Milton, Il Pens. 98 ; Lat. *palla,* a mantle, loose dress.

Palmer, i. 7; viii. 26, a pilgrim, lit. one who bears a palm-branch in token of having been to the Holy Land ; M.E. *palmere,* Chaucer, C. T. 13 ; L. Lat. *palmarius* (Ducange).

Pap, ii. 6, teat, breast ; M. E. *pappe* (M. S. 1) ; see Skeat (s.v. *pap,* 2).

Paramour, ii. 35 ; vi. 16 ; ix. 34, a lover. Gloss. 1.

Parentage, x. 27, parent; Fr. '*parentage,* kindred' (Cotgrave).

Partake, iv. 20, to make to share.

Pas, ii. 17, to surpass, to go beyond; Fr. *passer* from Lat. *passus,* a step, a pace.

Passioned, ix. 41, deeply affected ; in Shakespeare *passion* often occurs in the sense of '*deep sorrow.*'

Patronage, viii. 26, defence ; Fr. *patronnage* (Cotgrave) from *patron,* Lat. *patronum,* acc. of *patronus,* lit. one in place of a father.

Paynim, viii. 10, 18, heathen. Gloss. 1.

Payse, x. 5, to poise, balance; M. E. *peisen* (Prompt. Parv.) ; O. Fr. *peiser,* to weigh (Bartsch) ; Lat. *pensare* from *pendĕre,* to weigh. Gloss. 1. **Poyse.**

Peece, a structure, xi. 14, a fortress; xii. 44, used in connexion with 'the wondered Argo,' so Morris. Gloss. 1.

Pelfe, vii. 7, booty; cp. O. Fr. *pelfre* (Burguy).

Pendragon, x. 68, title borne by Uther, see Notes, quotation from Hardyng; Shakespeare, 1 Henry VI, iii. 2. 95 ; cp. Gibbon, Decl. & Fall, ch. xxxi; Wel. *pendragon,* i. e. the head or chief dragon, see Rhŷs, Celtic Britain, p. 133.

Perdie, iii. 18 and freq., a common oath; M. E. *pardee, pardé* (Chaucer 2) ; O. Fr. *par deu = per Deum.*

Pere, iii. 39 ; x. 33, an equal ; iv. 18, a companion ; x. 62, 'Commons and *Peares,*' i. e. the nobles ; O. Fr. *per =* Lat. *parem,* equal. Gloss. 1.

**Perlous, v., 9, perilous; in most modern edd. of Shakespeare *parlous*; from *peril* (Fr.) = Lat. *periclum, periculum*, danger, lit. a trial, proof.

Persant, iii. 23, piercing; Fr. *perçant*; see **Thrillant**.

Person, xi. 40, the outward appearance; Lat. *persona*, the mask worn by the actors of antiquity, then the part or *rôle* in the play, cp. use of Gr. πρόσωπον. In L. Lat. *persona* means dignity, rank, a parson, man, person (Ducange); see Skeat (s. v. *parson*).

Personage, iii. 5, dignity, importance; see above. O. F. *personnage* (Bartsch).

Pesaunt, iii. 43, peasant; O. Fr. *paisant* (Bartsch), and *paisan* (cp. It. *paisano*) from *païs*, a country; L. Lat. *pagense* adj. neut. pertaining to a village; see **Pagan, Page**.

Picturale, ix. 53, pictures.

Pight, vii. 35; xii. 4, fixed; M.E. *piht*, pp. of *picchen*; see Skeat (s. v. *Pitch*, 2). Gloss. I.

Pitteous, x. 44, compassionate; so Shakespeare often, see Schmidt (s. v. *piteous*); M. E. *pitous* (Chaucer); O. Fr. *piteus*, merciful (Bartsch); L. Lat. *pietosus* (Ducange), from Lat. *pietas*.

Pitthy, ii. 28, pithy, forcible, impressive; Shakespeare, T. of Shrew, iii. 1. 68; *pith* occurs in Shakespeare in the sense of marrow, strength, force, the essential part of a thing, see Schmidt; M. E. *pithe*, Chaucer, C. T. 6057; A. S. *piða*, medulla arborum (Leo); see Skeat.

Plate, v. 9, plate armour; lit. a thin piece of metal; O. Fr. *plate*; cp. L. Lat. *plata* (Ducange).

Playn, i. 30, to complain; Shakespeare, K. Lear, iii. 1. 39; M. E. *pleyne* (Chaucer 3); O. Fr. *plain-*

dre (Bartsch); Lat. *plangere*, to strike, beat, esp. to beat the breast as a sign of grief; see Brachet.

Pleasaunce, vi. 11; **pleasauns**, xii. 50, pleasantness; M. E. *plesaunce* (Chaucer 1); O. Fr. *plaisance* (Bartsch).

Plesh, viii. 36, a shallow pool; *plash* in Shakespeare, T. of Shrew, i. 1. 23; M. E. '*plasche* or flasche, where rain water standeth' (Prompt. Parv.); cp. O. Du. *plasch*; see Skeat.

Plight, vi. 7, to plait or pleat, to weave; ix. 40, a fold; Milton, Comus, 301; Shakespeare has '*plighted* cunning,' K. Lear, i. 1. 283 (in quartos *pleated*). The word is misspelt, and should be *plite* = M. E. *pliten*, to fold, a variant of *plait*; see Skeat.

Pollicie, ix. 48, 53; x. 39, statecraft; M. E. *policie*, Chaucer, C. T. 12534; Fr. '*police*, policie' (Cotgrave), Lat. *politïa*; Gr. πολιτεία, citizenship.

Portaunce, iii. 5, 21; vii. 41, bearing; so *portance*, Shakespeare (Schmidt); cp. Nares.

Portcullis, ix. 24, a sliding door pointed with iron, let down to protect a gateway; M. E. *portcullise*; Fr. *porte coulisse* (Cotgrave), in O. Fr. *porte coleïce*; *coleïce* = L. Lat. *colaticius**, sliding, flowing, from *colatus*, p.p of *colare*, to flow (through a sieve); see Skeat.

Pourtraict, i. 39, viii. 43, portrait; Fr. *pourtraict* (Cotgrave); L. Lat. *protractum*, p. p. of *protrahere*, to paint, depict; orig. to drag forward, reveal.

Poynant, viii. 36, piercing; now spelt *poignant*; M. E. *poynant* (Chaucer); O. Fr. *poignant*, pres. part. of *poindre*, to prick (Bartsch); Lat. *pungere*.

Practick, i. 3; iii. 9, deceitful,

treacherous; cp. L. Lat. *practicus*, skilful, and *practica*, a plotting, a piece of treachery (Ducange); from Gr. πρακτικός, able to do, practical. Gloss. 1.

Prancke, ii. 36, iii. 6, to display, to adorn gaudily; M. E. *pranken* (Prompt. Parv.); see Skeat.

Preace, vii. 44, 46, to press, throng (x. 25, as a subst.); M. E. *presen*; O. Fr. *presser*; Lat. *pressare*. Gloss. 1.

Prejudize, ix. 49, forethought; Lat. *praejudicium*.

Pretend, xi. 15, to attempt; cp. Shakespeare, 1 Henry VI, iv. 1. 16; Fr. '*pretendre*, to aim at, intend' (Cotgrave), Lat. *praetendere*.

Pricke, i. 50; v. 2, to spur on quickly. Gloss. 1.

Pricke, xii. 1, point, centre of target; see Shakespeare's use in Schmidt, and cp. Nares.

Prickling, v. 29, having prickles.

Priefe, i. 48; iv. 28; vi. 51, proof, probe; M. E. *preef*, *preoue*; O. Fr. *prueve*; L. Lat. *proba*.

Prime, ix. 25, morning; x. 58; xii. 75, springtide of prosperity or life; cp. Fr. *prime*, the first hour of the day, *printemps*, the spring (Cotgrave). Gloss. 1.

Privitie, iv. 20, private life; Fr. '*privoité*, private friendship' (Cotgrave), mod. *privauté*, O. Fr. *privalté*; L. Lat. *privalitatem**; see Brachet.

Procure, ii. 32, to arrange; see L. Lat. *procurare*.

Proper, iv. 28; x. 57, (one's) own; so Shakespeare (Schmidt); O. Fr. *propre*; Lat. *proprium*, acc. of *proprius*.

Prowesse, ii. 25, bravery; O. Fr. *proëce* (Bartsch); see Skeat. Gloss. 1.

Prowest, iii. 15; v. 36; viii. 18; xi. 30, bravest; see Bartsch, s. v.

preu, prudent, brave, for French forms. Gloss. 1.

Prune, iii. 36, to pick out damaged feathers and arrange the plumage with the bill; in Shakespeare (Schmidt); M. E.*proine*(Chaucer); prob. from Fr. *provigner* (Cotgrave), a dialectic form of which was *progner* (Littré), meaning to plant a slip, from *provin*, O. Fr. *provain*, a slip or sucker planted (Brachet); Lat. *propaginem*, a layer, sucker. So the M. E. *proinen* seems to have meant (1) to take cuttings in order to plant them out, (2) to cut away superfluous shoots, to prune trees, (3) to prune feathers (of birds), as in this passage; see Skeat.

Puissant, iii. 1, powerful; O. Fr. *puissant* (Bartsch).

Pumy, v. 30, '*pumy* stones,' pumice stones; A. S. *pumic-stán*; Lat. *pumic*, base of *pumex*; see Skeat.

Purchase, iii. 18; v. 26, to obtain; O. Fr. *purchaser*. Gloss. 1.

Purfled, iii. 26, embroidered on the edge; Milton, Comus, 995; M. E. *purfilen*; O. Fr. *porfiler*, from *filer* to twist threads, from *fil*, a thread; Lat. *filum*. Gloss. 1.

Purge, iv. 31, to cleanse; Fr. *purger*; Lat. *purgare* from *purus* + *agere*.

Purloyne, iii. 4, to steal; lit. to put far away; Milton, P. L. ii. 946; M. E. *purlongen* (Prompt. Parv.); O. Fr. *purloignier, porloignier*, to prolong (Burguy); Lat. *prolongare*.

Purpose, ii. 45; vi. 6; viii. 56, conversation, discourse; xii. 16, to converse; Fr. *pourpos*, a variant of Fr. '*propos*, talk, speech, discourse' (Cotgrave); Lat. *propositum*, a thing put forward, see Brachet. This word is distinct in origin from to *purpose*, to intend =

Fr. *proposer*, Lat. *pro + pausare*. Gloss. 1.

Pursuivant, viii. 2, herald; Fr. '*poursuivant d'armes*, a herald extraordinary, or young herald, a bachelor in the art of heraldry' (Cotgrave), *poursuivant*, pursuing, following; see Skeat (s. v. *pursue*).

Purvay, iii. 15, to provide; M. E. *purveien, porveien*; O. Fr. *porveier*; Lat. *providere*; see Skeat.

Puttocke, xi. 11, a kite; in Shakespeare (Schmidt); M. E. *puttok*, miluus (Prompt. Parv.).

Pyonings, x. 63, diggings, work of the *pioneer* = Fr. *pionnier* (Cotgrave), O. Fr. *peonier* (Burguy), an extension of *peon*, a footsoldier, then one who works at digging; L. Lat. *pedonem* a footsoldier; cp. It. *pedone*.

Q.

Quaile, viii. 35, to shrink, to fail in spirit; the old meaning of the word was 'to suffer torment, to die'; the spelling *quail* is not quite exact, but it must stand for M. E. *quelan*, to die; A. S. *cwelan* (Sweet); cp. O. H. G. *quelan*, to suffer torment (Tatian). iii. 16, to defeat, discomfit, a misspelling for **quell.** Gloss. 1.

Qualifyde, vi. 51, abated, soothed; for exx. of this use of *qualify* see Shakespeare (Schmidt); Fr. *qualifier*; L. Lat. *qualificare* (Ducange).

Quarrel, xi. 24, 33, a square-headed crossbow bolt; M. E. *quarelle* (M. S. 2); O. Fr. *quarrel*, Chanson de Roland, 2265 (mod. *carreau*); L. Lat. *quadrellum*, acc. of *quadrellus* (Ducange), from Lat. *quadrus*, square.

Quarrey, xi. 43, the animal slain in hunting &c.; M. E. *querré* (Skeat); O. Fr. *cuiree*, formed (with suffix *-ee* = Lat. *-ata*) from *cuir*, skin, hide = Lat. *corium* (Scheler). The *quarry* as given to the dogs was wrapped up in the *skin* of the slain animal; see Skeat, ed. 2, p. 824.

Quart, x. 14, quarter.

Quarter, i. 18, (heraldic term) to divide the field of the shield into four parts, see Clark's Heraldry, p. 179; O. Fr. *quartier* (de l'écu), see Chanson de Roland, 3867.

Queene, i. 1, 'soveraine Elfin Queene'; A. S. *cwén*, A. S. Chron. an. 672; cp. Go. *kwens*, a woman, wife, cognate with Gr. γυνή.

Queint, v. 11, quenched; M. E. *queint*, p. p. of *cwenchen* (Stratmann); A. S. *cwencan* in compounds, a causal of *cwincan*, to be extinguished; see Skeat (s. v. *quench*).

Quell, ii. 20; vii. 40; x. 11, to crush, subdue; M. E. *quellen*, to kill; A. S. *cwellan*, causal of *cwelan*, to suffer torment, see **Quaile.** With A. S. *cwellan*, cp. O. N. *kvelja*, to torment; see Skeat.

Quick, i. 39; x. 26, 71, living; A. S. *cwic*; cp. Lat. *vivus*, see Curtius, p. 469.

Quight, v. 4; viii. 9, quite, entirely; lit. freely; O. Fr. *quite*, discharged, freed, released; Lat. *quietum*, acc. of *quietus*, at rest, free (said of the debtor).

Quilted, v. 4, stuffed with wool or cotton; the vb. from **quilt,** a bed-cover; M. E. *quylte* (Prompt. Parv.); O. Fr. *cuilte*; Lat. *culcita*, a mattress, pillow; see Skeat.

Quoth (passim), he said; M. E. *quoð, quað*, pret. of *queðen* to speak = (M. S. 1). Gloss. 1.

R.

Rablement, xi. 8, 12, 17, a rabble, a disorderly crowd; Shakespeare,

Jul. Cæs., i. 2. 245, 'the *rabble-ment* shouted.' Gloss. 1.

Race, xii. 83, to raze, to level with the ground; M. E. *rasen,* to scrape (Prompt. Parv.); Fr. *raser* (Cotgrave); L. Lat. *rasare* (Ducange), frequentative of Lat. *radere,* to scrape.

Ranck, iii. 6, 'to ride *ranck,*' to ride furiously; for exx. see Nares; M. E. *rank, ronk,* strong; A. S. *ranc,* strong, proud; see Skeat.

Randon, iv. 7, 'at *randon,*' with rushing force, left without guidance; so in Spenser's Sheph. Cal. May, 46; O. Fr. *randon,* force, impetuosity (Bartsch), whence aller à grand *randon,* to go very fast (Cotgrave). *Randon* is the swiftness of a brimming river, from Germ. *rand,* a rim, brim; see Skeat (s. v. *random*).

Ransacke, vii. 32, x. 23, to pillage, plunder; lit. to search a house. A Scandinavian word, O. N. *rannsaka,* from *rann,* a house + *sak,* base of *sækja,* to seek; *rann* is for *rasn* (Icel. Dict.); cp. Go. *razn,* a house.

Rash, iii. 30, quick; M. E. *rasch* (Stratmann); a Scandinavian word, cp. Dan. and Swed. *rask,* brisk, quick; Germ. *rasch.*

Raskall, ix. 15; xi. 19, mean, base (always used before a subst.); prop. a subst.; for Shakespeare's use see Schmidt (s. v. *rascal*); '*rascall,* refuse beast' (Palsgrave); O. Fr. *rascaille* * = mod. '*racaille,* the base and *rascall* sort' (Cotgrave). Gloss. 1.

Raught, iii. 2; iv. 5; xi. 20, 25, reached; so Shakespeare (Schmidt); M. E. *raughte,* pret. of *rechen,* to reach (Chaucer 2); A. S. *ráhte,* pret. of *ræcan* (Sweet). Gloss. 1.

Ray, i. 40, to soil, dirty; for exx. see Nares; 'I *araye* or fyle with myer, j'emboue' (Palsgrave).

Rayle, viii. 37, to flow; M. E. *reilen,* used by Chaucer, see Stratmann.

Rayne, vii. 21, kingdom; so Milton, P. L. i. 543, 'the *reign* of Chaos and old Night'; M. E. *regne* (Chaucer 2); Fr. *regne,* a realm (Cotgrave); Lat. *regnum.*

Read, Reede, xii. 70, to interpret, discern; i. 18; iv. 36; vii. 2; viii. 54, to declare; i. 17; vii. 7, 12, to consider, hold; viii. 12, to advise; ix. 2, to experience; M. E. *reden;* A. S. *rædan,* to discern, advise, read; see Skeat.

Reædifye, x. 46, to rebuild; L. Lat. *reaedificare* (Andrews).

Reare, i. 61; ii. 11; xii. 22, to raise; A. S. *ræran,* Deut. 28. 30; *ræran = ræsan = raisian,* causal of *risan,* to rise; see Skeat.

Reave, i. 17; viii. 15; xi. 19, to take away by violence; M. E. *reven* (Chaucer 3); A. S. *reáfian.* Gloss. 1.

Recke, viii. 15, to care, heed; M. E. *rekken, recchen* (Chaucer 3); A. S. *récan = rócian;* cp. O. S. *rókian* (Héliand).

Recoyle, xii. 19, to get a stranded ship off from a quicksand; M. E. *recoilen,* to drive back; O. Fr. *reculer* (Bartsch). Gloss. 1.

Recreaunt, vi. 28, base, cowardly; O. Fr. *recrëant,* pres. part. of *recroire* to desist, to give up (Bartsch); L. Lat. *se recredere* to own oneself beaten in a duel or judicial combat (Ducange). Gloss. 1.

Recure, i. 54; iv. 16; x. 23; xi. 21, to restore to health, to cure; L. Lat. *recurare* (Ducange).

Recure, xii. 12, 19, to recover; M. E. *recoueren;* O. Fr. *recuvrer* (Bartsch); Lat. *recuperare;* see Skeat (s.v. *recover*).

Red, i. 30, declared; pret. of **read.**

Redeemer, v. 20, deliverer; from

redeem, Lat. *redimere*, to buy or take back.

Redoubted, iv. 38; v. 26; viii. 25, dread, feared; *redoubt*, to fear (Minsheu); O. Fr. *redoubter*, to fear (Bartsch), mod. *redouter*; Lat. *re + dubitare*. Gloss. 1.

Reft, iv. 13, taken by violence; p.p. of **reave**; Milton, Lycidas, 107.

Regalitie, i. 57, rights of royalty; cp. L. Lat. *regalitates* (Ducange).

Regardes, vii. 33, subjects for consideration or attention; cp. Shakespeare, Lear i. 1. 242, 'love's not love when it is mingled with *regards* that stand aloof from the entire point'; Fr. '*regard*, a regard, respect, consideration of (Cotgrave), from *regarder*, to look, *re- + garder*, O. Fr. *guarder*, in Chanson de Roland, *warder* (Bartsch) = O. S. *wardôn* (Héliand); cp. Eng. *ward*.

Regester, i. 32, a record of names; Fr. *registre* (Cotgrave); L. Lat. *registrum*, more correctly *regestum* (Ducange), lit. something brought back, recorded.

Regiment, ix. 59; x. 30, government; cp. Shakespeare, Ant. & Cl. iii. 6. 95; O. Fr. *regiment*, sway (Littré); Lat. *regimentum*.

Relent, xi. 1, 27, to give way, to slacken; Fr. *ralentir*; Lat. *re + ad + lentus*, slack, slow, aiso tenacious, pliant.

Remercie, xi. 16, to thank; O. Fr. *remerciier* (Bartsch); see **Mercie**.

Rencounter, i. 26, to meet in combat; Fr. *rencontrer* (Cotgrave), for *reëncontrer* from *re + en + contre* (Brachet).

Renfierst, viii. 45, made more *fierce*.

Renforst, iv. 14, he recovered strength; x. 48, pp. enforced again.

Renowmed, iv. 41; vi. 35, renowned, famous; cp. More's Uto-

pia, p. 166, 'the *renowmed* travailer Ulysses'; O. Fr. *renommé*, *renomé* (Bartsch), from *nom* = Lat. *nomen*, a name. Gloss. 1.

Repaire, xii. 52, to resort to; M.E. *repairen* (Chaucer 3); O. Fr. *repairier*, *repadrer* (Bartsch); L. Lat. *repatriare*, to return to one's country (*patria*). Gloss. 1.

Report, x. 3, to carry off; Lat. *reportare*.

Repriefe, iv. 28, reproof; see **Priefe**.

Reprive, i. 55, to release, set free; *reprive = reprieve*, cp. F. Q. iv. 12. 31; M. E. *repreven*, Wiclif, Lu. 20. 17; see **Priefe**.

Reprize, xi. 44, to take again; see Nares; cp. **Mesprize** 2.

Reseized, x. 45, reinstated, repossessed; O. Fr. *saisir*, *seisir*, to put one in possession of, also to take possession of (Bartsch); O. H. G. *sazzan*, *sezzan* = *sazjan*, to set, place, hence to *put* in possession of; cognate with Germ. *setzen*; see Skeat (s.v. *seize*).

Respondence, xii. 71, correspondence (in music).

Respyre, iv. 16; vi. 44, to breathe again, to breathe; Fr. *respirer*; L. Lat. *respirare*.

Retourne, iii. 19, to turn back (the eye).

Retraitt, ix. 4, picture, portrait; It. *ritrátto*, a picture, lit. drawn out (Baretti); iii. 25, 'graces working belgards and amorous *retrate*'; *retrate* prob. = *retraitt*, and is used in the sense of 'look, cast of countenance'; so Nares.

Revest, i. 22, to dress again.

Revilement, iv. 12, reviling; M.E. *revilen*; *re- + Fr. *aviler*, to make *vile* (Bartsch); see Skeat (s.v. *revile*).

Rew, i. 25; x. 66, to *rue*, to be sorry, to pity; M. E. *rewen* (Chaucer 1); A. S. *hreówan*, to

grieve, from *hreów*, sad (Sweet);
see Skeat.

Ribauld, i. 10, a low, licentious
person; M. E. *ribald, ribaud* (P.
Plowman); O. Fr. *ribaut, ribault*
(Bartsch); cp. It. *ribáldo, ribaudo*, ·
a rascal (Florio); L. Lat. *ribaldus*
(Ducange). The origin of the
word appears to be lost.

Richesse, vii. 24, 31, wealth; M.
E. *richesse* (Chaucer 1); O. Fr.
richesse, richece, power, wealth
(Bartsch). ii. 41, *richesse* is
treated as a plural; for Shakespeare's use in this respect see
Skeat (s.v. *riches*). Gloss. 1.

Rife, v. 9, excessively; M. E. *rif*,
adv. *rive*; O. N. *rífr*, munificent,
abundant. Gloss. 1.

Rifte, vii. 23, pp. riven, rent; M. E.
riven (Coleridge); O. N. *rífa*, to
tear, to rend; cp. Germ. *reiben*,
to grate (Weigand).

Rime, x. 50, verse, poetry; A. S.
rim, number, reckoning (Sweet),
then in M. E. *rime* (Chaucer 2).
The word is used of verse, from
the numerical regularity of verses
as to syllables and accents; lastly
it is used to denote a particular
accident of modern verse, viz. the
consonance of final syllables; see
Skeat. Gloss. 1.

Rosiere, ix. 19, a rose-bush; O. Fr.
rosier (Bartsch); L. Lat. *rosa-
rium*.

Rosmarine, xii. 24, a *sea*-monster
that was supposed to feed on the ·
dew on the tops of the rocks, so
Morris in Glossary to Spenser.

Rote, x. 3, lyre (of Apollo); the
name of an old musical instrument;
in fact there appear to have been
two kinds of *rotes*, one a sort of
psaltery or harp played with a
plectrum or quill, the other much
the same as the fiddle; M. E. *rote*,
Chaucer, C. T. 236; O. Fr. *rote*,
rotta (Bartsch); O. H. G. *rota*,

hrota; L. Lat. '*chrotta* Britanna,'
a word of Celtic origin, the proto-
type in point of form of Wel.
croth, the womb, the calf of the
leg, and in point of meaning of
crwth, a crowd or *rote*; cp. Ir.
cruit, a fiddle, also a hump on the
back (O'Reilly). The *crwth* was
so called from its curved shape;
cp. Gr. κυρτός; see Rhŷs, p. 114,
and Skeat. From the Wel. *crwth*
came M. E. *croude*, 'he herde a
symfonye and a *croude*,' Wiclif,
Luke 15. 25, see also Catholicon
Anglicum (s.v. *crowde*).

Routs, ix. 15, crowds, troops; M.
E. *route*, a number of people,
troop (Chaucer 1); Fr. '*route*,
(1) a *rout*, overthrow, (2) a *rowt*,
troop, company, multitude of men
or beasts; (3) a *rut*, way, path,
street' (Cotgrave); L. Lat. *rupta*,
(1) a defeat, (2) a troop of men,
(3) a way cut through a forest
(Ducange). The different senses
of *rupta*, 'broken,' may be thus
explained:—(1) a *broken* mass of
flying men, a defeat; (2) a company in *broken* ranks, a· disorderly
array; (3) a way *broken* or cut
through a wood, a route; see
Skeat.

Rubine, iii. 24; xii. 54, ruby; It.
rubino; L. Lat. *rubinum*, acc. of
rubinus, from the stem of *rubere*,
to be red; cp. Sp. *rubin*.

Ruinate, xii. 7, 'to *ruinate* itself'
(of a rock), to fall down; for
exx. of *ruinate* in Shakespeare,
. see Schmidt; formed from L. Lat.
ruinare (Ducange).

Ruth, ii. 1, 45; iii. 2; v. 24; x.
62, pity, sorrow; M. E. *rewthe*
(Chaucer 2); see Rew. Gloss. 1.

S.

Sacred, xii. 37, accursed; cp. Fr.
sacrer, to consecrate, also to ex-
communicate (Cotgrave), mod.

sacré, cursed (in oaths); cp. also Lat. *sacer*, devoted to a divinity for destruction, accursed; *sacred* is the pp. of M. E. *sacren*, to consecrate (M. S. 1); Lat. *sacrare*, to consecrate, to doom to destruction.

Sad, i. 45; viii. 30, heavy; ii. 14, 28; vi. 19, 37, grave, serious; xi. 3, sober, dark-coloured (of attire); M. E. *sad*, with various meanings, see Halliwell; the oldest sense is 'sated'; A. S. *sæd*, sated, filled (Leo, p. 53); cp. O. S. *sad*, satisfied, filled (Héliand), Goth. *saths*, Germ. *satt*, full, weary; see Skeat.

Saliaunce, i. 29, onslaught; from the vb. **salie**, vi. 38, to *sally*, to rush out suddenly; O. Fr. *salir*, to leap (Bartsch); Lat. *salire*.

Salvage, vi. 39; viii. 42, wild; lit. living in the woods; O. Fr. *salvage* (Bartsch); L. Lat. *salvaticus*, in Reichenau Glosses 8th cent. (cp. It. *salvático*), for Lat. *silvaticus* (Pliny); see Brachet.

Salue, viii. 23, to salute; spelt *salew*, F. Q. iv. 6. 25; Fr. '*saluer*, to salute, greet, give the time of day unto' (Cotgrave); O. Fr. *saluder* (Bartsch); Lat. *salutare*.

Salve, x. 21, to remedy; whence **salving**, i. 20, the making clear and fair; in Shakespeare, to *salve* occurs in sense of 'to remedy, to palliate,' see Schmidt; from the subst. **salve**, xi. 21, medicinal substance applied to wounds and sores; A. S. *sealf*, ointment, Mk. 14. 5; cp. Ger. *salbe*.

Sanguine, i. 39, blood-colour; M. E. *sanguin*, Chaucer, C. T. 335, 'of his complexion he was *sanguin*'; Fr. *sanguin*; Lat. *sanguineum*, from *sanguin-*, stem of *sanguis*, blood; cp. Fr. *sang*; see Skeat.

Sarazin, viii. 49; **Sar'zin**, viii.

18, Saracen, a pagan; M. E. *sarezin*, *saracen* (Skeat); O. Fr. *sarrazin*, *sarrasin* (Bartsch); L. Lat. *saraceni*, a people of Arabia Felix, in Ammianus, A.D. 380, and Pliny; Gr. σαρακηνός, Ptolemy, A.D. 160. Etymology unknown; for the various guesses see Gibbon's learned note, Decl. and Fall, ch. 50.

Saufgard, v. 8, guard in fencing, defence; for Shakespeare's use of *safeguard*, subst. and vb., see Schmidt; Fr. '*sauve garde*, safeguard, protection' (Cotgrave); hence L. Lat. *salvagardia* (Ducange).

Scarmoge, vi. 34, skirmish, a slight battle; *scaramouch* is another form, see Halliwell; O. Fr. *escarmouche* (Bartsch); It. *scaramúccia*, a skirmish, also, a scaramouch, an actor, posture-master (Florio), from O. H. G. *skerman*, to defend, fight; see Diez, p. 284, Skeat (s.v. *skirmish*).

Scath, v. 18, hurt, harm; in Shakespeare, Rich. III, i. 3. 317; M.E. *scathe* (M. S. 1); A. S. *sceaðe* (Leo). Gloss. 1.

Scattered, ii. 2, let drop; A. S. *scateran*, to squander, A.S. Chron. an. 1137; the suffix *-er* is frequentative, see Morris, p. 221.

Scatterlings, x. 63, persons scattered about; cp. 'losells and *scatterlings*,' in View of Ireland, Spenser, p. 624; *-ling* is an A.S. suffix, see Sweet, lxxxv; for its widespread Teutonic use, and for its analysis *l + ing*, see Weigand (s. v. *-ling*).

Sclave, vii. 33, slave, one under the power of another; O. Fr. *esclave* (Bartsch); L. Lat. *sclavus*, captivus, servus (whence Ger. *sclave*); Gr. Σκλάβος, a Slav; the L. Lat. *sclavus* was orig. applied by the Germans to Slavonian prisoners. The old name for the Slav, *Slovéne*, is connected with Old Slavonic *slovo,* 'a word,' meaning 'the intelligibly speaking people,' the Slavs thus distinguishing themselves from foreigners whom they called *Némci,* i. e. 'the mute, dumb.' See Weigand (s. v. *sclave*).

Scolopendra, xii. 23, a fish resembling a centipede; Lat. *scolopendra,* a kind of sea-fish (Pliny) Gr. σκολόπενδρα in Aristotle, see Liddell and Scott.

Scorse, ix. 55, exchange; to *scorse,* to exchange, see F. Q. iii. 9. 16, and Jonson's Tale of a Tub, i. 2, and Bartholomew Fair, iii. 1; cp. Cotgrave s. v. 'courtier, a broker, horse-*scourser,* messenger,' and 'courratage, brokage, *scoursing,* horse-*scoursing*'; to *scorse,* to exchange, is still in use in Devonshire and East Cornwall, and occurs in Pegge's Kenticisms.

Scoule, ii. 35, to look angry or gloomy; M. E. *scoulen, seowle* (Prompt. Parv.). A Scandinavian word, cp. Dan. *skule,* to scowl; see Skeat.

Scrine, ix. 56, a case or chest for keeping books or documents; Lat. *scrinium,* a chest, box, case; *shrine* is the same word; cp. Ger. *schrein.* Gloss. 1.

Scruze, xi. 46; xii. 56, to squeeze, crush; for exx. see Richardson; *scrouge* in various dialects (Halliwell).

Sea-satyre, xii. 24; see Notes.

Seele up, i. 38, '(a hind) up her eyes doth *seele,*' doth close; Fr. *siller, ciller* (Cotgrave). Gloss. 1.

Seely, iii. 6, harmless. Gloss. 1.

Seeth, x. 26, to *seethe,* to boil; M. E. *sethen* (Chaucer 1); A S. *seóðan* (Leo); cp. Go. *sauths,* a burnt-offering.

Sell, ii. 11; iii. 12; v. 4; viii. 31, a saddle; Fr. '*selle,* a saddle' (Cotgrave); O. Fr. in the Chanson

de Roland; Lat. *sella,* a seat, also a saddle in the Theodosian code; see Brachet.

Semblaunt, i. 21; ix. 2, 39, appearance, likeness.

Semblants, xii. 48, 49, appearances. Gloss. 1.

Serve, x. 55, to bring to bear upon; cp. the phrase 'to *serve* a writ'; viii. 1, 'to *serve to* wicked men, to *serve* his wicked foe,' '*to serve to*' is Shakespearian, see Schmidt; the second *serve* = to do with, to deal with, i. e. to subdue and punish.

Sew, ii. 17; vii. 9, to follow; spelt *sewe* in Palsgrave; M. E. *suen,* Wiclif, Mt. 8. 19, 22; O. Fr. *suir,* one of the forms of *sivre* (Bartsch), mod. *suivre*; L. Lat. *seqvere* for Lat. *sequi*; see Brachet.

Shame, i. 30; xii. 23, to be ashamed; so M. E. *shamie, samie* (M. S. 1); A. S. *sceamian,* to be ashamed, to blush (Grein).

Shamefast, ix. 43, modest; so Shakespeare (in the quarto ed.), Rich. III, i. 3. 142, see Schmidt; M. E. *schamefast* (Chaucer 1); A. S. *scamfæst*; see Skeat (s. v. *shamefaced*). Gloss. 1.

Shard, vi. 38, division, boundary; A. S. *sceard,* adj. broken (Grein). Spenser appears to use *shard* actively of that which divides, namely 'a channel.'

Shayre, x. 37, a part, division; A. S. *scearu,* as in *land-scearu,* a share in land (Grein).

Sheares, viii. 5, *shears,* used of wings wherewith to 'cut' the air; A. S. *sceara* (sing.) = Lat. *forfex*; see Skeat; from A. S. *sceran,* to cut; see **Shere.**

Shed, vii. 30, 'lives were *shed,*' with reference to spilling life-blood; A. S. *sceádan,* to part (Leo).

Shee, xi. 49, she; so spelt in Morris'

ed.; for M.E. forms of A.S. *seó*
see Stratmann (s. v. *scheo*). *Seó*
is fem. of *se*, used as def. art., but
orig. a demonstrative pronoun,
meaning 'that'; see Skeat.

Sheene, i. 10; ii. 40; x. 8, bright,
clear, beautiful; M. E. *schene*, fair,
beautiful (Chaucer 1); A. S. *scéne*,
sceóne, fair; cp. O. S. *scóni*, Ger.
schön.

Shend, vi. 35; viii. 12, to disgrace,
abuse; *shent*, v. 5 (pret.); i. 11,
27 (pp.); M. E. *schenden*, Wiclif,
Ps. 119. 31; A. S. (*ge*)*scendan*
(Sweet); cp. O. H. G. (*gi*)*skenten*,
Tatian, p. 437.

Shere, vi. 5, to *shear*, cut; A. S.
sceran; see **Sheares.**

Shop, i. 43, the body is said to be
the 'shop' of life; M. E. *schoppe*,
Chaucer, C. T. 4420, cp. Fr.
eschoppe (Cotgrave); A.S. *sceoppa*,
a stall or booth, used to translate
Lat. *gazophilacium*, the treasury,
Lu. 21. 1.

Shrightes, vii. 57, subst. pl. shrieks;
for *shright*, pret. of *shriek*, see
Nares; M. E. *shríghte*, pret. of
shriken, see Stratmann, p. 431.

Shrub, vii. 3, a low tree; M. E.
schrub, shrob (Skeat); A. S. *scrob*,
in *Scrob-scir*, 'Shropshire, A. S.
Chron., an. 1094, and in *Scrobbes-
byrig*, Shrewsbury, ib. an. 1016.

Siege, ii. 39; vii. 44, a seat; xi. 1,
a sitting down, with an army,
before a fortified place; *siege* =
seat in Shakespeare, cp. Meas. for
M. iv. 2. 101; M. E. *sege*, a seat,
Wiclif, Mt. 25. 31; O. Fr. *sege*,
later *siege*; from a vb. *sieger** =
L. Lat. *sediare** (as in *assediare*),
from *sedium** (as in *assedium*),
from Lat. *sedere*, to sit.

Sight, i. 47, sighed; so in ed.
1590; M. E. *siȝte*, pret. of *siȝen*,
to sigh; A. S. *sícan*, pret. *sác*;
see Skeat.

Sightes, v. 27, appearances, forms;

M. E. *sigte, cyhte* (M. S. 1); A. S.
(*ge*)*siht*; see Skeat. For substantival forms in -*t* see Earle,
p. 299.

Sith, i. 2 (and *passim*), since; M. E.
sith, sippe, seppe (M. S. 2); A. S.
siððān, since (Sweet); vi. 48,
sithens, since; M. E. *sithens,
sithenes* (Stratmann); the -*s* or
-*es* is due to the old adverbial
ending, as in **needes**, *twi-es, thri-
es*, really a genitival form, see Earle,
p. 431. A. S. *siððān* = *sið ðám*,
after that; A. S. *sið* was orig. an
adv. with the force of a comparative, meaning 'later'; cp. Go.
seithus, late; see Skeat (s. v.
since).

Skie, viii. 10, cloud; M. E. *skie*
(Stratmann); O. N. *ský*, a cloud;
cp. A. S. *scúa*, a shade.

Skill, i. 54, reason, prop. discern-
ment; M. E. *skile*, reason (Chaucer
2); O. N. *skil*, a distinction, cp.
skilja, to separate, from root
SKAL, orig. to cleave; see Skeat.

Skippet, xii. 14, a little boat; the
stem *skip* = *ship*, cp. O. N. *skip*,
and Du. *schip*, a pronunciation
preserved in *skipper* = Du. *schip-
per*; -*et* is a French diminutive
form, as in *bosquet, bouquet*; see
Earle, p. 317.

Sleight, i. 3; xii. 81; **slight**, i. 4,
contrivance, trick; M. E. *sleighte*
(Chaucer 1); O. N. *slægð*, sly-
ness; see **Sly.** Gloss. 1.

Slug, i. 23, to be inactive; *slogge* in
Palsgrave; M. E. *sluggen* (Prompt.
Parv.); a Scandinavian word, cp
Dan. *slug*, drooping; see Skeat.

Sly, viii. 47; ix. 46, clever, ingenious; xii. 49, cleverly; M. E.
slie (Chaucer); O. N. *slægr* (for
slœgr), sly, cunning. The word
is from the Teutonic base SLAG,
to strike, which appears in the vb.
to *slay*; smith's work—striking
with the hammer being taken as

the type of clever handicraft; see
Skeat.

Smouldring, v. 3, suffocating (of
dust); there may perhaps be also
an idea of *mouldering*, crumbling
in Spenser's use of the word here;
M. E. *smolder*, a stifling smoke
(P. Plowman); see Skeat.

Snag, xi. 23, a lump on a tree
where a branch has been cut off.
Gloss. 1.

Sold, ix. 6, pay, remuneration;
O. Fr. *solde*; L. Lat. *soldum*, pay,
from L. Lat. *solidus*, a piece of
money, lit. 'solid' money, from
Lat. *solidus*. We still use £ *s. d.*
to signify *libræ*, *solidi*, and *denarii*.
From O. Fr. *solde* come *soldeier*,
in the Chanson de Roland, our
soldier, ix. 5.

Sooth-sayes, ix. 51, foretellings;
A. S. *sóð*, true; see Skeat. Gloss. 1.

Souse, xi. 36, the swoop (of a
hawk); cp. Shakespeare, K. John,
v. 2. 150, 'like an eagle ... to
souse annoyance that comes near
his nest'; see Halliwell.

Sovenaunce, vi. 8; viii. 51, remembrance; Fr. '*souvenance*, memorie,
remembrance, also a ring with
many hoopes, whereof a man lets
one hang downe when he would
be put in mind of a thing' (Cotgrave), from *souvenir*; Lat. *sub-
venire*; see Brachet.

Soveraine, vi. 17, supreme; O. Fr.
souverain (Bartsch); L. Lat.
superanum from Lat. *super*,
above.

Sowne, v. 30; vi. 47, sound; M.E.
soun (Chaucer 3); O. Fr. *son*;
Lat. *sonum*, acc. of *sonus*. Gloss. 1.

Spalles, vi. 29, the shoulders;
Scotch *spauls*, see Jamieson (s.v.
spald); O. Fr. *espalle*, *espalde*
(Bartsch), mod. *épaule*; cp. It.
spálla, a shoulder; Lat. *spatula*,
a broad-bladed knife for spreading
plasters.

Spel, vi. 51, a form of magic words;
so in Shakespeare (Schmidt, s.v.
spell); A. S. *spel*, a saying.

Spight, i. 3; ii. 23, spite; the *gh*
employed carelessly or arbitrarily,
see Earle, p. 150; cp. Gloss. 1,
Despight.

Spill, ix. 37, to destroy; cp. Shakespeare, Hamlet, iv. 5. 20, '(guilt)
spills itself in fearing to be *spilt*';
M. E. *spillen* (Chaucer); A. S.
spillan for *spildan* (Leo). Gloss. 1.

Spoile, vii. 25, to plunder, pillage;
Fr. *spolier* (Cotgrave); Lat. *spo-
liare*, to strip of spoil, from *spolium*,
orig. the skin or hide of an animal
stripped off, hence the armour of
a slain warrior.

Sprent, xii. 45, sprinkled; M. E.
spreynd (Chaucer 3), pp. of *sprengen*, to scatter (Stratmann); A. S.
sprengan, Mt. 25. 24, lit. to make
to *spring* or leap abroad, being
the causal of A. S. *springan*, to
spring, regularly formed by the
change of *a* (in the pret. *sprang*)
to *e*, as if from *sprangian**; cp.
O. N. *sprengja* (Icel. Dict.); M. E.
sprenkelen (our *sprinkle*) is the
frequentative form of *sprengen*.

Spright, iv. 7; vii. 10; ix. 36; xi.
38, spirit; for spelling cp. **Spight.**

Spring-headed, xii. 23, having
heads that spring afresh.

Spyal, i. 4, a spy; so Shakespeare,
1 Henry VI, i. 4. 8, *spial*=*espial*,
see Schmidt; cp. Cotgrave, s.v.
'*espie*, a spie, scowt, *espiall*';
M. E. *espial*; from O. Fr. *espier*;
O. H. G. *spehón*, to observe closely;
cp. Lat. *spec-ere*; see Skeat (s.v.
espy).

Squadrons, viii. 2, used of angelic
hosts; the word occurs in Shakespeare, see Schmidt; It. '*squadrone*, a squadrone, a troupe or
band of men' (Florio), from
squadra, a square, a part of a
company of soldiers, formed from

a L. Lat. *exquadrare**, intensive of Lat. *quadrare.*

Squire, i. 58, a square, a carpenter's rule; 'by the *squire*' occurs three times in Shakespeare, see Schmidt; M. E. *squire* (Stratmann); Fr. *esquierre* (Cotgrave), another form of *esquarre* = It. *squadra*, see above.

Squire, i. 13, 17; xi. 48, an attendant on a knight; O. Fr. *esquier*, Chanson de Roland, 2437. Gloss. 1.

Stale, i. 4, a decoy, a snare; Shakespeare, T. of Shrew, iii. 1. 90, 'to cast thy wandering eyes on every *stale*'; M. E. *stale*, theft (M. S. 1), hence stealth, deceit or a trap; A. S. *stalu*, theft (Sweet); cp. A. S. *stælhrán*, a decoy reindeer; see Skeat.

Starke, i. 42, rigid; see Skeat. Gloss. 1.

Stayne, iv. 26, to spoil the colour of, to dim; M. E. *steinen* for *disteinen*; Fr. '*desteindre*, to distain, to dead or take away the colour of' (Cotgrave); Lat. *dis-*away + *tingere*, to dye; see Skeat (s. v. *stain*).

Stead, ii. 21; iv. 42; xii. 1, a place; M. E. *stede* (Chaucer 2); A. S. *stede* (Sweet). Gloss. 1.

Stead, ix. 9, to help, avail; so in Shakespeare (Schmidt).

Steare, ix. 13, a *steer*, a young ox; A. S. *steór*; cp. Lat. *taurus*, Gr. ταῦρος; see Skeat.

Steme, vi. 27, to steam. See Notes.

Stent, iv. 12; stint, v. 8, to cease; M. E. *stenten*, *stinten*, to shorten, to pause; see Skeat.

Sterve, vi. 34; viii. 58, to die; M. E. *sterven* (Chaucer 1); A. S. *steorfan*, A. S. Chron. an. 1124; cp. Germ. *sterben.*

Steward, one who has charge of a household; M. E. *stiward* (M. S.

1); A. S. *stiward*, Chron. an. 1093. Gloss. 1.

Stile, viii. 12, cognisance; a heraldic term, cp. quotation from Burke in Webster-Mahn); Fr. *stile*; Lat. *stilus*, an iron-pointed peg used for writing on wax tablets, also, a manner of writing.

Stire, i. 7, to direct, guide; A. S. *stýran*, to steer (Grein).

Stire, v. 2; ix. 30, to stir, spur on; A. S. *styrian*, to stir (Sweet).

Stomacke, vii. 41, pride, arrogance; Shakespeare, Henry VIII, iv. 2. 34, 'a man of an unbounded *stomach*' (of Wolsey); cp. Fr. '*s'estomaquer*, to take the pet, or pepper in the nose, at' (Cotgrave); Lat. *stomachus*, the stomach, also chagrin, vexation; Gr. στόμαχος stomach, in oldest Gr. the throat, gullet, strictly, a mouth, dimin. of στόμα, the mouth.

Stownd, viii. 32; xi. 25, 'the bitter *stownd*,' the moment of peril; M. E. *stounde*, time, instant (Chaucer 2); A. S. *stund*, short space of time (Sweet); cp. Germ. *stunde*, an hour. Gloss. 1.

Stowre, v. 10, battle; viii. 35, 48, onset; vi. 16, conflict; iii. 34; viii. 43, peril; M. E. *stoure*, battle (Chaucer 2); O. Fr. *estour*, *estur*, combat (Bartsch); O. N. *styrr*, the tumult of battle. Gloss. 1.

Strakes, iv. 15, streaks; cp. Gen. 30. 37 (A. V.); M. E. *streke* (Prompt. Parv.); cp. Swed. *strek*, a dash, stroke, line.

Strayne, vii. 21, to grasp tightly; M. E. *streinen*; O. Fr. *estreindre* (Bartsch); Lat. *stringere.*

Strayt, vii. 40, street; M. E. *strete*, Wiclif, Mt. 12. 19; A. S. *strǽt* (Sweet); Lat. *strata* (via), a paved way.

Streight, xi. 32, *strait*, close, narrow, contracted; for the spelling with *gh* cp. Spight; M. E. *streit*

(Chaucer 1); O. Fr. *estreit* (Bartsch), mod. *étroit*; Lat. *strictum*, pp. of *stringere*.

Stressed, x. 37, distressed; the word here is doubtless a short form for the pp. of to *distress*; cp. O. Fr. *destresse* (Bartsch); see Skeat.

Strich, xii. 36, the screech-owl; Lat. *strĭgem*, acc. of *strix*; Gr. στρίγξ.

Strond, viii. 10, a shore; M. E. *strond* (Chaucer 1); A. S. *strand*, Mt. 13. 48.

Stryful, ii. 13, *strife-full*, contentious; O. Fr. *estrif* (Bartsch); O. N. *striŏ*, strife; cp. O. S. *strid* (Héliand), Ger. *streit*. For *f = ŏ* cp. Eng. *stiff* = A. S. *stiŏ* (Sweet).

Sty, vii. 46, to ascend, to mount; M. E. *steʒen* (M.S. 2) A.S. *stigan* (Sweet); cp. Ger. *steigen*, Gr. στείχειν. Gloss. 1.

Suborned, i. 1, procured privately; Lat. *subornare,* = *sub*, under, secretly, + *ornare*, to furnish, adorn.

Surbet, ii. 22, (a traveller) with feet *surbet*, bruised, as the feet by travel; for exx. see Nares, and cp. Webster-Mahn (s. v. *surbate*); cp. Fr. 'surbatture, a surbating' (Cotgrave), see also *soubatture*, ib.

Sure, iii. 14, assuredly; Shakespeare, Henry V, i. 2. 8, '*sure*, we thank you'; for other exx. see Schmidt.

Surquedry, xii. 31, 39, presumption, petulance; for exx. see Nares; M. E. *surquidrye*, presumption, see definition in the Persones Tale, Chaucer, iii. 295; O. Fr. *surcuiderie* (Roquefort); cp. *seurcuidé* petulant (Bartsch), from *sur* = Lat. *super* + O. Fr. *cuider* (in the Chanson de Roland *quider*) = Lat. *cogitare*, to think; see Brachet (s. v. *cuider*); hence Fr. *outrecuidance*. See Diez, p. 103.

Surview, ix. 45, to survey; *view* = O. Fr. *vëue* (Bartsch), prop. the fem. of *veu*, seen, pp. of *vëoir* = Lat. *videre*.

Swart, x. 15, dark (of visage); Milton, Comus, 436, 'no goblin, or *swart* faery of the mine'; M. E. *swart* (M. S. 1); A. S. *sweart*, black (Leo); cp. Germ. *schwarz*.

Sway, x. 49, to move with force; M. E. *sweʒen*, to go, walk, come (Skeat); O. N. *sveigja*, to bend.

Swayne, viii. 40; ix. 14; xi. 28; xii. 79, a youth; *swein* a Scandinavian word found in A. S. Chron. an. 1128; O. N. *sveinn*, a boy, servant. Gloss. 1.

Swinck, vii. 8, 36, 58, to toil; Milton, Comus, 293, '*swink'd* hedger,' hedger overcome with toil; M. E. *swinken* (Chaucer 3); A. S. *swincan* (Sweet).

Symbole, ii. 10, a token, memorial; Fr. '*symbole* a token' (Cotgrave); Lat. *symbolum* (Plautus); Gr. σύμβολον, a sign by which one calls to mind a thing; from the base of συμβάλλειν to throw together, compare. See Trench.

T.

Table, iii. 24, a smooth surface for a picture; see Trench. Gloss. 1.

Tand, vii. 3, tanned; M. E. *tannen* (Skeat), to tan, from *tan* = Fr. *tan*, oak-bark (Cotgrave). Origin unknown.

Targe, v. 6, shield; O. Fr. *targe* in Chanson de Roland; *targe* occurs in an A. S. charter an. 970, but it is prob. a borrowed word; cp. O. H. G. *zarga*, a frame, a side, wall; see Fick, vii. 119, Skeat (s. v. *target*).

Teene (1), i. 59, 'both alike . . . religious reverence doth burial *teene*,' query, misprint for *leene* = give (M. S. i. s. v. *lene*)?

Teene (2), i. 15, 21, 58, trouble, sorrow; M. E. *tene* (M. S. 1); A. S. *teóna*, injury, insult (Sweet); cp. O. S. *tiono*, facinus (Héliand); see **Tine** (2).

Termagaunt, viii. 30, an imaginary God of the Mahometans; cp. Shakespeare, Hamlet, iii. 2. 15; M. E. *Termagaunt* (Chaucer 2, p. 157); O. Fr. *Tervagan*, in Chanson de Roland one of the three supposed Gods of the Saracens, the other two being Mahum (see **Mahoune**) and Apollin; cp. It. *Trivigante*, Ariosto, O. F. xii. 59. Derivation uncertain, see Skeat.

Tetra, vii. 52, deadly nightshade; see Notes.

Thee, i. 33, xi. 17, 'Well mote yee *thee*,' 'fayre mote he *thee*,' cp. M. E. 'so mote I *thee*' (Chaucer 2); M. E. *thee*, to thrive, prosper; A. S. *þeón, þíhan* (Sweet); cp. Germ. *gedeihen*, Go. *gaþeihan*.

Then, iv. 7 (and often), than; *then = than* common in Shakespeare (1st folio) see Schmidt; M. E. *thanne, thenne*; A. S. *ðonne*; see Skeat. Gloss. 1.

Thewes, i. 33; x. 59, manners, good qualities; M. E. *þeawes*, habits, practices; A. S. *þeáw*, habit, in pl., manners, morals (M. S. 1). The original sense of the word was sinew or strength; see Skeat. Hence **thewed**, vi. 26, mannered.

Thicke, iii. 21, thicket, a close wood or copse; M. E. *þikke* (adj.); A. S. *þicce* (Leo); cp. Germ. *dick*.

Tho, iii. 13 (and passim), then; M. E. *þo* (M. S. 1); A. S. *þá*; cp. O. S. *thó* (Héliand).

Thorough, ix. 23; xii. 45, through; M. E. *þoru* (M. S. 1); A. S. *þorh, þurh, þuruh*. Gloss. 1.

Thrall, iii. 8; iv. 16; v. 18; vi. 17, a slave; M. E. *þral* (M. S. 1);

O. N. *þræll*; *ðrǽl =* servus occurs in the Lindisfarne Gospels, Luke 7. 3, not an A. S. word, but borrowed from Norse; *þræll* prob. meant orig. 'a runner,' representing a Teutonic type THRAGILA; cp. Go. *thragjan*, to run, Gr. τρέχειν; see Skeat. Hence to **thrall**, i. 54; vi. 17, to enslave.

Threasury, viii. 4, treasury; cp. Cotgrave, '*thresorerie*, a *threasurie*, the place wherein *threasure* is kept'; from Lat. *thesaurus*; Gr. θησαυρός, a treasure.

Threat, iv. 44, 'rancour *threats* his rusty knife,' brandishes in a threatening manner; M. E. *þreten*; A. S. *(ge)þreátian*, to threaten (Sweet), from *þreát*, a throng of people (Leo), also, a great pressure, trouble, a threat. The orig. sense was 'pressure'; see Skeat. Hence *threatfull*, xii. 5, threatening.

Thrillant, iv. 46, piercing; to *thrill =* M. E. *þirlen*; A. S. *þyrlian* for *þyrel-ian*, to make a hole (*þyrel*); see Skeat. For the Fr. pres. part. form in *-ant* cp. Earle, p. 378. See **Persant**.

Thrist, vi. 17, thirst; M. E. *þrist* (M.S. 1). Gloss. 1. Hence **thristy**, v. 30, thirsty; see **Thrust**.

Throwes, v. 9; viii. 41, attacks causing pain, lit. pangs; M. E. *þrowes*, pangs; A. S. *þreá* (Sweet), for *þreáw*, a rebuke, pain; see Skeat (s. v. *throe*).

Thrust, ii. 29, to thirst; M. E. *thrusten*, Troylus and Cryseyde, 1406 (Chaucer); cp. **Thrist**.

Thunder-light, vi. 50, lightning.

Till, i. 16, to; M. E. *til, till*, to (M. S. 1); *til* is a mark of the Northumbrian dialect, cp. Mt. 26. 31 (Lindisfarne Gospels); O. N. *til*, to, till, too, see Icel. Dict. *Till =* to is still a note of the Scottish language.

Tine (1), viii. 11, to kindle, to light; so in various dialects (Halliwell); prop. spelt *tind*,—in Minsheu, ed. 1627, *tinde*; M.E. *tenden*, Wiclif, Luke 11. 33; A. S. *tendan* (in compounds), see Leo; cp. Go. *tandjan*.

Tine (2), xi. 21, to feel pain; from *tine* = teene (2); cp. F. Q. iv. 12. 34, 'cruell winter's *tine*,' and iii. 11. 1, 'bitter milke of *tine*.'

Tire, i. 57; ii. 36; ix. 19, 40, attire, a head-dress; an abbreviation for *attire*; M. E. '*tyre* or *a-tyre*' (Prompt. Parv.), *atiren*, to dress; O. Fr. *atirier*, to dispose, adorn, from *a tire*, in order; *tire* = O. H. G. *ziari*, Germ, *zier*, ornament; A. S. *tiér*, a row, order.

Told, vii. 4, counted; pret. of to *tell*; M. E. *tolde*, pret. of *tellen*, often in the sense 'to count' (Stratmann); A. S. *tellan*, pret. *tealde*; cp. Germ. *zählen*.

Tomb-blacke, viii. 16, epithet of a steed.

Toole, iii. 37, weapon; so in Shakespeare, Rom. & Jul. i. 1. 37, 'draw thy *tool*'; A. S. *tól*; see Skeat.

Tort, v. 17, wrong; so in F. Q. iii. 2. 12; prop. a legal term, cp. extract from Blackstone's Com. in Richardson; O. Fr. *tort* (Bartsch); L. Lat. *tortum* (Ducange) from Lat. *tortus*, twisted; see Brachet. Hence **tortious**, ii. 18, injurious, wrongful.

Tourney, i. 6, to joust, lit. to turn about; Shakespeare, Pericles, ii. 1. 116, 150; O. Fr. *tournoier*, to joust (Bartsch), from *tornoi*, a wheeling about.

Touze, xi. 33, to pull about, to worry; Shakespeare, Meas. for M. v. 1. 313; M. E. *tosen* (Stratmann); cp. Ger. *zausen*.

Toward, iv. 22, approaching, future; A. S. *tóweard* as in 'on *tóweardre worulde*,' in the future world, in

the life to come, Mk. 10. 30; see Skeat.

Toyes, vi. 7; xii. 60, sports; toy, vi. 11, 21; ix. 35, to play; Palsgrave, '*Toy*, a tryfell,' also 'I *toye* or tryfell with one'; Du. *tuig*, tools, stuff, trash; cp. Ger. *zeug*.

Trace, viii. 10, to walk; O. Fr. *tracer*, to follow (Bartsch); see Brachet. Gloss. 1.

Tract, vi. 39, to trace; L. Lat. *tractiare**; see Skeat (s. v. *trace*).

Trade, vi. 39, a path; cp. Surrey's Virgil, Æn. ii. 593, 'a common *trade* to passe through Priam's house'; from A. S. *tredan*, to tread (Sweet); xii. 30, frequent resort; see Trench.

Tramels, ii. 15, nets for the hair; cp. Cotgrave, '*tramail*, a tramell, or a net for partridges'; cp. It. *tramaglio*, a drag-net; L. Lat. *tramacula*, *tramagula*, in the Lex Salica; see Skeat, and note in Prompt. Parv. (s. v. *tramayle*).

Transmew, iii. 37, to transmute; Fr. *transmuër* (Cotgrave). Gloss. 1.

Travell, xi. 44, the same word as *travail*, labour. The two forms are used indiscriminately in old editions of Shakespeare (Schmidt); cp. Cotgrave, '*travail*, travell, toile.' The Fr. *travail* is from a L. Lat. *travare**, to build with beams, to pen, shackle, hence to cause embarrassment and trouble; for traces of *travare** see Skeat (s. v. *travail*); it is from Lat. *trabem*, a beam, acc. of *trabs*.

Trayle, xii. 61, a trailing tangle (of ivy); from Lat. *trahere*, to draw or drag along; see Skeat (s. v. *trail*).

Trayne, i. 4, a snare; Fr. *traine*, a drag-net (Cotgrave). Gloss. 1.

Trayne, iii. 27, to drag, trail; Fr. '*trainer*, to traile, drag' (Cotgrave); L. Lat. *trahinare* (Ducange), from Lat. *trahere*.

Treachour, i. 12; iv. 27, a traitor; M. E. *trechoure,* a trickster, cheat (Chaucer), spelt *trychor* earlier; cp. Prov. *trichaire,* a traitor, from O. Fr. *trichier, trecher,* to trick (Bartsch); M. H. G. *trechen,* to push, pull, also to entice; see Diez, p. 326 (s. v. *treccare*), and Skeat (s. v. *trick*).

Treachetour, x. 51, a traitor; so F. Q. vi. 8. 7; Nares suggests that this Spenserian word may be a corrupt form of Chaucer's *tregetour,* a juggler, who also uses *tregetrie,* a piece of trickery; *treget,* guile, trickery, see Morris' Glossary, and cp. Halliwell, and Prompt. Parv. *Tregetour* = O. Fr. *tresgettere,* a magician (Roquefort), from *tresgeter, trasgeter, to* form (Bartsch); Lat. *trans* + *jactare*; see Burguy.

Treague, ii. 33, a temporary cessation of hostilities; Sp. It. *trégua,* a truce; cp. L. Lat. *treuga,* as in the historical '*Treuga* Dei,' la *Trève* de Dieu. Cp. Ducange, '*Treuga,* securitas praestita rebus et personis, discordia nondum finita'; *tregua, treuga,* from O.H.G. *triwa, triuwa,* faith, a covenant; cp. Go. *triggwa,* a covenant; see Diez, p. 326.

Treble, xii. 33, the highest part in music; = *triple,* cp. Fairfax, Tasso, xviii. 24; O. Fr. *treble,* triple (Burguy); Lat. *triplus*; for *b* = *p* cp. Fr. *double* = Lat. *duplus.*

Trespass, viii. 28, crime; M. E. *trespas,* so O. Fr.; Lat. *trans,* across, over + *passus,* a step.

Troth, i. 11; ii. 34, a variant of *truth*; M. E. *trewthe, trouthe* (Chaucer); A. S. *treowð* (Sweet) from A. S. *treowe,* true (Grein).

Trow, v. 13, to think, suppose to be *true*; M. E. *trowen* (Chaucer 1); A. S. *treowan* (Grein), from

A. S. *treowa,* trust, Mk. 11. 52, from *treowe,* true; see above.

Troynovant, x. 46, London, the capital of the British tribe, the *Trinobantes,* according to Caesar; by popular etymology however *Troynovant* was connected with '*Troia nova,*' and supposed to mean 'new Troy,' cp. legend taken from Nennius by Geoffrey of Monmouth, Bk. i. (near end).

Truncked, v. 4, decapitated, truncated; from Fr. '*tronc,* a headlesse body' (Cotgrave); Lat. *truncum,* acc. of *truncus,* a piece cut off, from *truncus,* maimed.

Tway, vi. 31, 'in *tway,*' in two; M. E. *tweie* (M. S. 1).

U.

Unbrace, iv. 9, to loosen; so Shakespeare (Schmidt); from *brace,* a firm hold; O. Fr. *brace,* the two arms (Bartsch); Lat. *brachia,* pl. of *brachium,* the arm.

Uncivile, vii. 3, wild, uncivilised.

Uncouth, i. 8, 24, 29, strange; in Shakespeare (Schmidt), and see Trench; M. E. *uncouth* (Chaucer 1); A.S. *uncúð,* unknown (Sweet); from *cúð,* pp. of *cunnan,* to know; cp. Scot. *unco'.* Gloss. 1.

Undight, xii. 15, undressed; see **Dight.**

Uneath, i. 27, 49, 56; x. 8, with difficulty; also *uneathes,* vi. 1. Gloss. 1.

Unkindly, x. 9, unnatural; see Trench (s. v. *kindly*).

Unmannurd, x. 5, not cultivated; the old sense of to *manure* was 'to work at with the hand,' being a contracted form of *manœuvre,* see Trench, Skeat; Fr. *manœuvre*; L. Lat. *manuopera* (Ducange).

Unreproved, vii. 16, blameless; Milton, L'Allegro, 40, 'in *unreproved* pleasures free.'

Unware, iv. 17, not aware; A. S. *unwær* (Leo).

Unwares, i. 4; iii. 31; iv. 17; ix. 38, unawares, unexpectedly; A. S. *unwares,* A. S. Chron. an. 1004; from *wær,* cautious; cp. Ger. *gewahr.*

Unweeting, iv. 17; xii. 11, 22, not knowing, unconscious; M. E. *unwytyng* (Chaucer); see **Weet,** Gloss. 1.

Upbray, iv. 45, to reproach; a Spenserian form for the sake of the rhyme, cp. F. Q. iii. 6. 50; iv. 1. 42; M. E. *upbreiden* (M. S. 1); A. S. *upp + bredan, bregdan,* to braid, also, to lay hold of; the orig. sense of *upbraid* was prob. to lay hands on; hence, to attack, lay to one's charge; so Skeat. Gloss. 1, **Upbrayd.**

Upstaring, xii. 39, 'rearing their *upstaring* crests,' i. e. standing on end; cp. Shakespeare, Tempest, i. 2. 213 'with hair *upstaring,*' Jul. Cæs. iv. 3. 280 'makest my hair to *stare,*' i. e. to be stiff; see Skeat (s. v. *stare*).

Urchin, xi. 13, a hedgehog; so in Shakespeare (Schmidt); M. E. *urchone* (Prompt. Parv.), also spelt *irchone* (M. S. 2); O. Fr. *ireçon, heriçon* (Burguy), mod. *hérisson*; from Lat. *ericius* with dimin. suffix *-on. Ericius* is a lengthened form from *ēr = hēr =* Gr. χήρ, a hedgehog, lit. the stiff, bristly animal; see Skeat.

Usaunce, vii. 7, use; *usance* in Shakespeare (Schmidt); O. Fr. *usance* (Bartsch).

Use, v. 19, habit, practice; so in Shakespeare often (Schmidt); O.Fr. *us,* usage (Burguy); Lat. *usus.*

Utter, ii. 34, outer; A. S. *uttor,* see Grein (s. v. *útor*).

V.

Valew, vi. 29, worth, valour; for exx. of this use see Nares; Fr. *valuë* (Cotgrave), fem. of *valu,* pp. of *valoir,* to be worth; Lat. *valere.*

Valiaunce, iii. 14; viii. 51; ix. 5; x. 38, bravery; O. Fr. *vaillance* (Bartsch).

Varlet, iv. 37, 40, 45; v. 2, 25, servant to a knight; see Shakespeare (Schmidt); in Berners' Froissart, see Richardson; O. Fr. *varlet* (Bartsch), used as a title of honour, the *r* is intrusive, cp. *hurler,* from Lat. *ululare* (Littré); other forms are *valet, vallet, vadlez, vaslet,* dimin. of O. Fr. *vassal,* a brave man, a dependent, see note in Chanson de Roland (glossary); L. Lat. *vassallus,* a feudal tenant (Ducange), also *vassus, vasus,* a servant, a word of Celtic origin; cp. Wel. *gwas,* a youth, a servant, see Rhŷs, p. 146.

Vassall, iii. 7, servant (figuratively); see above.

Vauntage, i. 4, vantage (Fr. *vantager* in Palsgrave); a headless form of Fr. *avantage.*

Vaut, vii. 28, an arched roof; O. Fr. *vaute, voute, volte* (Burguy), from Lat. *voluta,* fem. pp. of *vol- .vere,* to roll.

Vellenage, xi. 1, servitude; see **Villein.**

Vengeable, iv. 30, 46, '*vengeable* despight,' revengeful; see Nares, Richardson for exx.

Vermeill, iii. 22; vermell, x. 24; xii. 45, vermilion; O. Fr. *vermeil* (Bartsch); L. Lat. *vermiculus,* a little worm, in Vulgate, Ex. 35. 25 as a rendering of the Heb. *tóla'ath,* a worm, esp. that insect which produces the scarlet dye, the coccus insect. See **Cremosin.**

Verse, i. 55, a magic formula, a spell; cp. the use of Lat. *carmen,* a song, then, a charm.

Vertuous, viii. 22; xii. 86, 'v.

steele,' 'v. staffe,' possessing virtue or power; so in Shakespeare (Schmidt); Fr. *vertuëux* (Cotgrave); L.Lat.*virtuosus* (Ducange).

Villein, iv. 9, 17 (used of Furor); ix. 13; xi. 26, a base-born, low fellow, a clown, a scoundrel; M. E. *vilein* (Stratmann); O. Fr. *vilein*, *vilain*, a low person, a rustic (Bartsch); L. Lat. *villanus*, a farm-servant, a serf (Ducange), from Lat. *villa*, a farm. Gloss. I.

Virginall, i. 10; ix. 20, maidenly; in Shakespeare (Schmidt); Fr. *virginal* (Cotgrave); Lat. *virginalis*.

Vitall, i. 12, life-giving; Lat. *vitalis*.

Voyage, i. 34; v. 25, journey; Fr. *voyage* (Cotgrave); O. Fr. *veiage*, in Chanson de Roland; L. Lat. *viaticum*, from *via*, a way, journey. Gloss. I.

W.

Wage, vii. 18, to barter, exchange; from M. E. *wage*, pay (Prompt. Parv.); O. Fr. *wage* (also *guage*, *gage*), see Bartsch; from *wager*, to pledge; L. Lat. *wadiare*, from *wadius*, a pledge; cp. Goth. *wadi*, a pledge; see Skeat; cp. gaged.

Walke, iv. 5 (of the tongue), to roll about, wag; A. S. *wealcan*, to roll (Sweet).

Wan, iv. 34; vi. 32; vii. 65, weak, pale; M. E. *wan*, pale (Chaucer 3); A. S. *wann*, *wonn*, dark, black, an epithet of the raven, of night; see Skeat.

Wanton, xii. 53, 76, unrestrained, playful; M. E. *wantoun* (Chaucer 1), *wantowen* (P. Plowman) = *wan-*, lacking, wanting, + *towen*, A. S. *togen*, pp. of *teón*, to draw, educate, bring up, so that *wanton* meant orig. ill-bred; cp. Ger. *ungezogen*, ill-bred.

War-hable, x. 62, fit for war; see Hable.

Warke, i. 32, work; a northern form, see Jamieson.

Warne, i. 36, to keep off; from a Teutonic root WAR, to defend; see Skeat.

Warray, x. 50, 72, to harass with war; x. 21, 'Ebranck *warreyd* on Brunchild,' made war on; M. E. *werreien* (Chaucer 2); O. Fr. *werreier**, *guerroier* (Bartsch), from O. Fr. *werre*, war (Burguy); O. H. G. *werra*, strife; cp. Eng. *war*; see Skeat. Gloss. I.

Wasserman, xii. 24, a sea-monster; Ger. *wassermann*, homo marinus.

Waste, ix. 9, 'to *waste* much way,' i. e. to travel some distance; cp. the Lat. *viam terere*. Gloss. I.

Wastful, vii. 2; xii. 35, uncultivated, wild. Gloss. I.

Wawes, xii. 4, waves; M. E. *wawe* (Wiclif, N. T.), see also Chaucer 3, from *wawen*=A. S. *wagian*, to move to and fro (Grein); cp. O. N. *vágr*, Dan. *vove*, Ger. *voge*, a wave. Our *wave* is late, and not the same word as *wawe*, as it comes from A. S. *wafian*; see Skeat.

Wayment, i. 16, to lament; M. E. *waymenten* (Chaucer 1); O. Fr. *se guaimenter*, *gaimenter*, *waimenter* (Burguy), cp. also note in Prompt. Parv. (s. v. *wamentyn*).

Weede, i. 52; iv. 35, herb; A. S. *weód*; cp. O. S. *wiod* (Héliand).

Weede, iii. 21, 27; iv. 29; viii. 16; xii. 55, dress; A. S. *wǽde* also *wǽd*, a garment; cp. O. S. *wádi*, *giwádi* (Héliand).

Weeke, x. 30, wick; M. E. *wueke*; A. S. *weoca*; cp. O. Du. 'wiecke, a *weeke* of a lampe' (Hexham); lit. the soft or *weak* part; see Skeat.

Weene, iii. 3; iii. 13; vi. 45; vii. 30, 34, to think, suppose, intend; M. E. *wenen* (Chaucer 1); A. S. *wénan* (Sweet). Gloss. I.

Weet, i. 4, 29 and often, to know; M. E. *witen,* to know (M. S. 1); A. S. *witan* (Sweet). Gloss. 1.

Weetlesse, v. 36, ignorant of; from A.S. *wit,* knowledge (Grein).

Wefte, vi. 18, was wafted; a Spenserian pret. of the vb. to *wave,* to be moved about.

Weld, vii. 40; ix. 56, to wield, govern; M. E. *welden,* to govern, possess (Wiclif, N. T.); A. S. (*ge*)*weldan* from *wealdan*; see Skeat.

Well away, vi. 32, 43; viii. 46, an exclamation of great sorrow; M. E. *weilawei* for *wa la wa!* A. S. *wá lá wá,* lit. woe! lo! woe! (Sweet). Hence *welladay!* which occurs in Shakespeare, Merry Wives, iii. 3. 106.

Wench, vi. 8, girl; used in a sense between tenderness and contempt, as in Shakespeare (Schmidt); M.E. *wenche,* Mt. 9. 24, Wiclif, ed. 1380; earlier *wenchell,* in Ormulum 3356, where it is used of a male infant, viz. in the account of the annunciation of Christ's birth to the shepherds; A. S. *winclo,* children, allied to *wencel,* weak, *wancol,* tottery; cp. Ger. *wanken,* to totter; see Skeat. For A. S. suffix *-ol,* see Sweet lxxxvi, and **nimble.**

Wend, i. 51; vi. 10, to go, take one's way; M. E. *wenden* (Chaucer 1); A. S. *wendan,* to turn anything, to go; lit. 'to make to *wind,*' formed by change of *a* to *e* from *wand,* pret. of *windan,* to wind.

Wexe, i. 42; iii. 9; v. 20, to grow; M.E. *wexen* (Chaucer 2); cp. A.S. *weaxan* (Sweet); cp. Ger. *wachsen,* Go. *wahsjan.*

Whelm, ii. 43; iv. 17, to overturn, submerge; Shakespeare, Merry Wives, ii. 2. 143; M. E. *whelmen,* to turn over, Chaucer, Troilus, i.

139, related to *whelven, hwelfen* (Skeat), a vb. related to Swed. *hvalf,* an arch; thus the orig. sense of *whelm* (=*hwelf-m*) was to arch over, hence to turn a hollow dish over, hence to upset, overturn. The final *-m* is due to the fact that the vb. *whelm* is formed from a sb. *whelm* (=*whelf-m*); for this suffix cp. the word *qualm.*

Whenas, iv. 16, as soon as; often in Shakespeare (Schmidt).

Whereas, vi. 2; vii. 3; xii. 30, where; so in Shakespeare (Schmidt).

Where-so, i. 18; iii. 20, 38, wheresoever.

Whiles, ii. 5; vi. 11, while; so in Shakespeare often (Schmidt), cp. Mt. 5. 25, A. V. an. 1611, and Revision, an. 1881'; M. E. *whiles,* Chaucer, C. T. 35 (Harleian MS.), from A.S. *hwil, hwile,* time, space, *ðá hwile ðe,* while (Sweet); the *-s* is due to the old adverbial ending in *-es,* which was orig. a gen. case, as in *ned-es,* needs, *elles,* else (but note that the A. S. gen. of *hwil* is *hwile,* the sb. being fem.), see Sweet lxxxix. Hence **whilst,** ii. 16, with added *t*; see **emongst.**

Whirlpoole, xii. 23, a large fish, so named from the commotion which it makes; *whirlpole,* in Palsgrave; cp. Job 41. 1 in A.V. margin, 'a whale or a *whirlpool,*' the explanation of the Heb. 'leviathan'; see Davies (s. v. *whirl whale*), and Richardson (s. v. *whirl*).

Whistler, xii. 36, 'the *whistler* shrill,' some bird of ill omen; cp. A. S. *hwistlere,* Mt. 9. 23.

Whott, i. 58; iv. 37; ix. 29, 39, hot; for the initial *w* (once pronounced) cp. *whole*=M. E. *hol,* A.S. *hál,* and *whoop*=M. E. *houpen,* also *wun* the pronunciation of *one,* A.S. *án;* the vowel of *hot* was formerly long, M. E. *hote, hoot*; A. S. *hát.*

Whyleare, ii. 11 ; viii. 3 ; xi. 25, a while before. Gloss. 1.

Whylome, ii. 13 ; vii. 30 ; x. 16 ; xii. 13, 41, 85, in time past, formerly ; Milton, Comus, 827, Death of an Infant, 24 ; A. S. *hwilum,* sometimes, dat. plur. of *hwil,* time (Sweet). Gloss. 1.

Wield, i. 18, 'to *wield* a steed,' to manage ; see **Weld.**

Wight, i. 36 ; ix. 39 ; xi. 8, a being, creature ; A. S. *wiht,* a person, thing (Grein). The orig. sense is 'something moving,' prob. used for something seen at a distance, which might be a man, child, animal, or a supernatural being, so Skeat ; cp. O. N. *vættr,* Dan. *vætte,* an elf, also Scot. *seely wights,* a term applied to the fairies (Jamieson).

Wild, x. 32, willed.

Wisard, ix. 53, a wise man, M. E. *wysard* (Prompt. Parv.) ; O. Fr. *wisc-hard,* the older form of *guisc-hart, guisc-art,* prudent, clever (Burguy), cp. *Guiscard,* the surname of the famous Norman soldier, see Gibbon, Decl. and Fall, ch. 56 ; from O. N. *vizk-r,* clever, with Fr. suffix *-hard, -ard* due to O. H. G. *-hart* ; see Brachet, cxi, M. Müller, Chips, iv. 9. The O. N. *vizkr* is for *vit-skr* ; from *vita,* to know, with suffix *-sk* = A. S. *-isc* ('-ish'), see Sweet, lxxxvi ; and Skeat (s.v. *wizard*).

Wist, ii. 46 ; vi. 22 ; vii. 34, knew ; A. S. *wiste,* pret. of *witan* (Sweet) ; see **Weet.**

Witch, i. 54, a woman having magical power ; M. E. *wicche,* formerly used also of a man ; A. S. *wicca,* a wizard, *wicce,* a witch ; *wicca = witga* for *witiga,* a soothsayer, from *witan,* to see ; cp. Skeat.

Witch, vii. 10, to bewitch ; A. S. *wiccian* (Leo).

Wite, xii. 16, to blame ; M. E. *witen,* to blame (M. S. 1) ; A.S. *witan,* videre, imputare (Grein) ; cp. our *twit,* which = *æt-witan,* to reproach ; see Skeat (s.v. *twit*).

Withhault (pret.), xi. 9, withheld ; M. E. *held, heold* (M. S. 1) ; A. S. *heóld* pret. of *healdan,* to hold (Sweet).

Witt, vi. 13 ; ix. 49, mind ; xii. 44, intellectual power ; A. S. *wit,* mind, intellect (Grein), from *witan,* to know.

Wize, i. 35 (and often), manner. Gloss. 1.

Woe, viii. 53, sorrowful ; see Nares ; M. E. *wa* (M. S. 1) ; A. S. *wá, weá,* woe (Sweet).

Wondred, xii. 44, marvellous ; Shakespeare, Tempest, iv. 123, 'so rare a *wondered* father.'

Wonne, i. 51 ; iii. 18 ; vii. 49 ; ix. 52 ; xii. 69, to dwell ; M. E. *wonen, wonien,* to dwell (M.S. 1) ; A. S. *(ge)wunian* (Sweet). Hence *wonne,* vii. 20 ; xii. 11, dwelling. Gloss. 1.

Wont, i. 50 ; ii. 42 ; iii. 41 ; vii. 59, to be accustomed ; so in Shakespeare (Schmidt) ; Milton, Comus, 332 ; *wont* is a vb. formed from the pp. *woned (wont)* of the vb. *wonen,* see **wonne,** and cp. Skeat (s. v.).

Wood, iv. 11 ; v. 20 ; viii. 40, furious ; M.E. *wood,* mad (Chaucer 2) ; A.S. *wód* (Sweet). Gloss. 1.

Worship, i. 6; honour ; M. E. *worshipe* (Chaucer 2) ; A.S. *weorðscipe,* i. e. *worth-ship,* honour (Grein) ; for suffix *-scipe,* meaning 'shape, condition,' see Sweet, lxxxvi. Gloss. 1.

Worth, vi. 32, 'wo *worth* the man,' evil be to the man ; cp. Ezek. 30. 2, 'woe *worth* the day' (A.V.) = 'væ, væ diei' (Vulgate) ; M. E. *worþen,* to become (P. Plowman) ;

A. S. *weorðan, wyrðan* (Grein);
cp. Ger. *werden.*

Wote, i. 18; iii. 16; vii. 50; viii.
14, pres. t., know; **wott,** iv. 45;
M. E. pres. t., sing. 1st and 3rd,
wat (*woot, wot*), 2nd *wost,* from
witen, see M. S. 1, p. lxxxii; A. S.
wát, wást, a preterite-present of
witan, to know (Sweet); see
weet.

Woxe, vi. 13; viii. 9; x. 17; xii.
22, grew; A. S. *wóx, weóx,* pret.
of *weaxan,* to grow, Sweet, lxxiii;
see **Wexe.**

Wreak, iii. 13, to avenge, punish;
M. E. *wreken* (Chaucer 2); A. S.
wrecan, to wreak, orig. to urge
(Grein); cp. Germ. *rächen;* cognate with Lat. *urgere;* see Fick.

Wreath, i. 56, to turn, to twist;
spelt *wrethe,* in Palsgrave; M. E.
writhen (Coleridge); A.S. *wriðan,*
to twist (Grein).

Wrest, xii. 81, to wrench, twist;
A. S. *wrǽstan,* to twist forcibly
(Grein); see Skeat.

Wroke, v. 21, avenged; pp. of
wreak.

Y.

Y-. In this book this prefix represents three distinct particles:—

(1) *Y-* stands for the A. S. *ge-,* an
extremely common prefix, both in
sbs. and vbs.; in sbs. *ge-* has often
the meaning of partnership, com-
panionship, as *ge-sið,* a companion
(on a journey), from *sið,* a journey;
with vbs. it sometimes denotes
success or attainment, as *gefrig-
nan,* to hear of, learn, from *frignan,*
to ask; but is often prefixed to
various parts of a vb. without ap-
preciably affecting the sense; in
M. E. as in mod. Germ. it is usually
prefixed to the pp., the forms in
M.E. being *i- y-.* Hence the *y-* in
   yblent, vii. 1, confused, obscured; see **Blent.**

yclad, iii. 26, clad; used in
Shakespeare (Schmidt); pp. of
M. E. *clothen,* from A. S. *cláð.*

ydred, xii. 38, afraid; from A.S.
drǽdan (in compounds), to dread.

ylincked, vii. 46, linked; from
A. S. *gehlencian,* from *hlence;* cp.
Ger. *gelenk,* see Skeat.

ymett, i. 26, met; from A.S. *mé-
tan,* to meet, from *mót,* also *gemót,*
a public assembly.

yplight, iii. 1; vii. 50, plighted;
from A. S. *plihtan,* to risk, to
pledge (Leo).

ywritt, xii. 44, written; from
A. S. *writan.*

In **ybuilt,** ix. 29, and **yglaunst,**
vi. 31 (pret.), this Teutonic prefix
is put before vbs. of Scandinavian
origin; no trace however of *ge-* as
a tense or participle formative remains even in the earliest Icelandic
writers.

One word more remains to be
noted:—

   ywis, i. 19, certainly; M.E. *ywis,
iwis;* A. S. *gewis,* certain; cp.
Germ. *gewiss,* certainly.

(2) *Y* = A. S. *á-,* forth, away; so
   ygoe, i. 2; viii. 53, ago; A. S.
á-gán, gone away, past, cp. Mk.
16. 1, 'ða sæternes dæg wæs
ágán = cum transivisset sabbatum'
(Vulgate); *ágán,* pp. of *ágán,* to
go away, to pass.

(3) *Y* = A. S. *in;* so **yfere,** i. 35;
ix. 2, in company, together; M. E.
iferen (M. S. 1), *i fére,* Laȝamon,
27435, *in fére,* see Stratmann, p.
166, from A. S. *féra, geféra,* a
companion. Gloss. 1, **Fere.**

Yeed. iv. 2, to go; cp. Gloss. 1,
Yede; prop. a pret., cp. M. E.
yede, ȝede, in Mt. 8. 32, 'thei
ȝeden out,' i. e. they went out
(Wiclif); A. S. *eóde,* the weak
pret. of a lost vb., which serves as
a pret. to *gán,* to go; from this
eóde comes also **yode,** vii. 2;

xi. 20, went; M. E. *yode, ʒeode* (M.S. 1, p. lxxxi). Etymology of *eóde* unknown.

Yeoman, ix. 28, an officer in a noble household; M. E. *yeman* (Chaucer 1), also *ʒoman*; the word does not occur in A. S. texts, but it prob. represents an older *geá-man**. The sense of the prefix is probably 'district' or 'village,' cp. O. Friesic *ga, go,* whence *gaman,* a villager; see Skeat (Principles of English Etymology, p. 429).

Yond, viii. 40, fierce (of a lion); F. Q. iii. 7. 26, cp. Fairfax, Tasso, i. 55, 'Lombards fierce and *yond* '; M. E. *yond, ʒond, ʒeond* (Strat-mann); A. S. *geond,* at a distance, cp. O. Fr. *oultrageux,* outrageous, from *oultre,* Lat. *ultra,* beyond; so Webster-Mahn; see Nares.

Youthly, iii. 38, youthful. Gloss.1.

Yron-braced, v. 7, sinewed like iron (of the arm); cp. the Fr. *Fier-a-bras,* name of a hero of romance.

Z.

Zephyrus, xii. 33, the west wind; Lat.; Gr. ζέφυρος.

Zifflus, xii. 24, a sea-monster; prob. for *xiphias,* a sword-fish (Pliny); Gr. ξιφίας (Aristotle), also ξιφιός (Liddell and Scott), from ξίφος, a sword.

THE END.

The plan of the poem wa
contrived in Eng. and carried ou
in Ireland. It was to represent a
the moral virtues, assigning to
every virtue a knight to be th
patron and defender of the sam
in whose actions and feat
of arms and chivalry the o
ations of that virtue whereof
he is the protector, are to Ib
expressed, and the vices and
unruly appetites that oppos
themselves against the sam
to be beaten down and overcome.

In designing it he felt that i
must not only interest but in-
struct; it must be a work on
both moral and political phi-
osophy.

It was cloudily enwrapped in
allegorical devices. At that
those readers were supposed to
look everywhere for a moral
to be drawn, or a lesson to b
inculcated, or some practical
rule to be deduced. The scene
of trouble and danger in which
the F.Q. drew us afflicted it.

This may possibly account for the looseness of texture. His life in Ireland added to it force and vividness. In Ireland were found wilderness, outlaw ruffian, an bushes treacheries, deceits and frauds against righteousness, but between error and religion, betw justice and selfishness.

These realities of Irish wars an social and political life gave body and form to the allegory. It bodies forth the trials wh. beset the life of man in all c ditions and at all times.

Note:
1. The wild wanderings of its personage
2. Its daily chances of battle.
3. Its hairbreadth escapes.
4. Its strange encounters.
5. Its prevailing anarchy & violence
6. Its normal absence of order & la

Spencer's aim —

To fashion a gentleman in vir tuous and gentle disposition. It is colored with historical fiction because men like variety of matter. He followed the an- tique poets: Homer, Virgil, Ar- isto.

Clarendon Press Series.

— ❖ —

Greek School-books.

GRAMMARS, LEXICONS, etc.

Chandler. *The Elements of Greek Accentuation* (for Schools). By H. W. CHANDLER, M.A. *Second Edition.* . . [Extra fcap. 8vo. 2s. 6d.

Jerram. *Graece Reddenda.* By C. S. JERRAM, M.A. [„ 2s. 6d.

—— *Reddenda Minora.* . . . . [Extra fcap. 8vo. 1s. 6d.

—— *Anglice Reddenda.* First Series. . [Extra fcap. 8vo. 2s. 6d.

—— —— Second Series. . . . . [Extra fcap. 8vo. 3s.

Liddell and **Scott.** *A Greek-English Lexicon.* . . [4to. 36s.

—— *An Intermediate Greek-English Lexicon,* abridged from LIDDELL and SCOTT's Seventh Edition. . . . . . [Small 4to. 12s. 6d

—— *A Greek-English Lexicon,* abridged from LIDDELL and SCOTT's 4to. edition, chiefly for the use of Schools. . . . [Square 12mo. 7s. 6d.

Sargent. *Passages for Translation into Greek Prose.* By J. YOUNG SARGENT, M.A. . . . . [Extra fcap. 8vo. 3s.

Wordsworth. *A Greek Primer.* By the Right Rev. CHARLES WORDSWORTH, D.C.L. *Seventh Edition.* . . [Extra fcap. 8vo. 1s. 6d

—— *Graecae Grammaticae Rudimenta in usum Scholarum.* Auctore CAROLO WORDSWORTH, D.C.L. *Nineteenth Edition.* . . . [12mo. 4s.

King and **Cookson.** The Principles of Sound and Inflexion, as illustrated in the Greek and Latin Languages. By J. E. KING, M.A., and CHRISTOPHER COOKSON, M.A. . . . . [8vo. 18s.

Papillon. *A Manual of Comparative Philology.* By T. L. PAPILLON, M.A. . . . . [Crown 8vo. 6s.

A COURSE OF GREEK READERS.

Easy Greek Reader. By EVELYN ABBOTT, M.A. *In one or two Parts.* . . . . [Extra fcap. 8vo. 3s.

First Greek Reader. By W. G. RUSHBROOKE, M.L. *Second Edition.* [Extra fcap. 8vo. 2s. 6d.

Second Greek Reader. By A. M. BELL, M.A. [Extra fcap. 8vo. 3s. 6d.

Specimens of Greek Dialects; being *a Fourth Greek Reader.* With Introductions and Notes. By W. W. MERRY, D.D. [Extra fcap. 8vo. 4s. 6d.

Selections from Homer and the Greek Dramatists; being *a Fifth Greek Reader.* By EVELYN ABBOTT, M.A. . . [Extra fcap. 8vo. 4s. 6d.

[B]

Wright.   *The Golden Treasury of Ancient Greek Poetry.*   By R. S.
WRIGHT, M.A.   .   .   .   .   [*New edition in the Press.*

Wright and Shadwell.   *A Golden Treasury of Greek Prose.*   By
R. S. WRIGHT, M.A., and J. E. L. SHADWELL, M.A.   [Extra fcap. 8vo. 4*s.* 6*d.*

THE GREEK TESTAMENT.

A Greek Testament Primer.   By E. MILLER, M.A.
[Extra fcap. 8vo. 3*s.* 6*d.*

Evangelia Sacra Graece.   .   .   .   [Fcap. 8vo. *limp*, 1*s.* 6*d.*

Novum Testamentum Graece juxta Exemplar Millianum.
[18mo. 2*s.* 6*d.*; or on writing paper, with large margin, 9*s.*

Novum Testamentum Graece.   Accedunt parallela S. Scripturae
loca, necnon vetus capitulorum notatio et canones Eusebii.   Edidit CAROLUS
LLOYD, S.T.P.R., necnon Episcopus Oxoniensis.
[18mo. 3*s.*; or on writing paper, with large margin, 10*s.* 6*d.*

Appendices ad Novum Testamentum Stephanicum, curante
GULMO. SANDAY, A.M. , ...   [*In the Press.*

The Greek Testament, with the Readings adopted by the Revisers of
the Authorised Version.
[Fcap. 8vo. 4*s.* 6*d.*; or on writing paper, with wide margin, 15*s.*

Outlines of Textual Criticism applied to the New Testament.
By C. E. HAMMOND, M.A.   *Fourth Edition.*   .   [Extra fcap. 8vo. 3*s.* 6*d.*

GREEK CLASSICS FOR SCHOOLS.

Aeschylus.   *Agamemnon.*   With Introduction and Notes, by ARTHUR
SIDGWICK, M.A.   *Third Edition.   In one or two Parts.*   [Extra fcap. 8vo. 3*s.*

—— *Choephoroi.*   With Introduction and Notes, by the same Editor.
[Extra fcap. 8vo. 3*s.*

—— *Eumenides.*   With Introduction and Notes, by the same Editor.
In one or two Parts.   .   .   .   .   [Extra fcap. 8vo. 3*s.*

—— *Prometheus Bound.*   With Introduction and Notes, by A. O.
PRICKARD, M.A.   *Second Edition.*   .   .   .   [Extra fcap. 8vo. 2*s.*

Aristophanes.   *The Acharnians.*   With Introduction and Notes,
by W. W. MERRY, D.D.   *Third Edition.*   .   .   [Extra fcap. 8vo. 3*s.*

—— *The Birds.*   By the same Editor.   .   .   .   [*In the Press.*

—— *The Clouds.*   By the same Editor.   *Third Edition.*
[Extra fcap. 8vo. 3*s.*

—— *The Frogs.*   By the same Editor.   *New Edition.   In one or two
Parts.*   .   .   .   .   [Extra fcap. 8vo. 3*s.*

—— *The Knights.*   By the same Editor.   .   [Extra fcap. 8vo. 3*s.*

Cebes. *Tabula.* With Introduction and Notes, by C. S. JERRAM, M.A.
[Extra fcap. 8vo. *2s. 6d.*

Demosthenes. *Orations against Philip.* With Introduction and Notes.
By EVELYN ABBOTT, M.A., and P. E. MATHESON, M.A.

Vol. I. *Philippic I* and *Olynthiacs I—III. In one or two Parts.*
[Extra fcap. 8vo. *3s.*

Vol. II. *De Pace, Philippic II, De Chersoneso, Philippic III.* [*In the Press.*

Euripides. *Alcestis.* By C. S. JERRAM, M.A. [Extra fcap. 8vo. *2s. 6d.*

—— *Hecuba.* By C. H. RUSSELL, M.A. *Immediately.*

—— *Helena.* With Introduction and Notes, etc., for Upper and
Middle Forms. By C. S. JERRAM, M.A. . . . [Extra fcap. 8vo. *3s.*

—— *Heracleidae.* By the same Editor. . [Extra fcap. 8vo. *3s.*

—— *Iphigenia in Tauris.* With Introduction and Notes. By the
same Editor. . . . . [Extra fcap. 8vo. *3s.*

—— *Medea.* With Introduction, Notes, and Appendices. By C. B.
HEBERDEN, M.A. *In one or two Parts.* . . . [Extra fcap. 8vo. *2s.*

Herodotus. Book IX. Edited, with Notes, by EVELYN ABBOTT,
M.A. *In one or two Parts.* . . . . . [Extra fcap. 8vo. *3s.*

—— *Selections.* Edited, with Introduction, Notes, and a Map, by
W. W. MERRY, D.D. . . . . . . [Extra fcap. 8vo. *2s. 6d.*

Homer. *Iliad,* Books I–XII. With an Introduction, a brief Homeric
Grammar, and Notes. By D. B. MONRO, M.A. *Second Edition.*
[Extra fcap. 8vo. *6s.*

—— *Iliad,* Books XIII–XXIV. By the same Editor.
[Extra fcap. 8vo. *6s.*

—— *Iliad,* Book I. By the same Editor. *Third Edition.*
[Extra fcap. 8vo. *2s.*

—— *Iliad,* Books VI and XXI. With Notes, etc. By HERBERT
HAILSTONE, M.A. . . . . . . [Extra fcap. 8vo., each *1s. 6d.*

—— *Odyssey,* Books I–XII. By W. W. MERRY, D.D. *New Edition.*
In one or two Parts. . . . . . [Extra fcap. 8vo. *5s.*

—— *Odyssey,* Books XIII–XXIV. By the same Editor. *Second
Edition.* . . . . [Extra fcap. 8vo. *5s.*

—— *Odyssey,* Books I and II. By the same Editor.
[Extra fcap. 8vo., each *1s. 6d.*

Lucian. *Vera Historia.* By C. S. JERRAM, M.A. *Second Edition.*
[Extra fcap. 8vo. *1s. 6d.*

Lysias. *Epitaphios.* Edited, with Introduction and Notes, by F. J.
SNELL, B.A. . . . . [Extra fcap. 8vo. *2s.*

Plato. *The Apology.* With Introduction and Notes. By ST. GEORGE
STOCK, M.A. *In one or two Parts.* . . . [Extra fcap. 8vo. *2s. 6d.*

—— *Meno.* With Introduction and Notes. By the same Editor.
In one or two Parts. . . . . . . [Extra fcap. 8vo. *2s. 6d.*

Sophocles. (For the use of Schools.) Edited, with Introductions and English Notes, by Lewis Campbell, M.A., and Evelyn Abbott, M.A. New and Revised Edition. 2 Vols. . . . . [Extra fcap. 8vo. 10s. 6d.
Sold separately, Vol. I. Text, 4s. 6d. Vol. II. Notes, 6s.

☞ *Also in single Plays.* *Extra fcap.* 8vo. *limp* :—

Oedipus Tyrannus, Philoctetes. New and Revised Edition, 2s. each.

Oedipus Coloneus, Antigone. 1s. 9d. each.

Ajax, *Electra,* *Trachiniae.* 2s. each.

—— *Oedipus Rex:* Dindorf's Text, with Notes by W. Basil Jones, D.D., Lord Bishop of St. David's. . . . [Extra fcap. 8vo. *limp,* 1s. 6d.

Theocritus. Edited, with Notes, by H. Kynaston, D.D. (late Snow). *Fourth Edition.* . . . . . [Extra fcap. 8vo. 4s. 6d.

Xenophon. *Easy Selections* (for Junior Classes). With a Vocabulary, Notes, and Map. By J. S. Phillpotts, B.C.L., Head Master of Bedford School, and C. S. Jerram, M.A. *Third Edition.* . [Extra fcap. 8vo. 3s. 6d.

—— *Selections* (for Schools). With Notes and Maps. By J. S. Phillpotts, B.C.L. *Fourth Edition.* . . . [Extra fcap. 8vo. 3s. 6d.

—— *Anabasis,* Book I. Edited for the use of Junior Classes and Private Students. With Introduction, Notes, and Map. By J. Marshall, M.A., Rector of the High School, Edinburgh. . . . [Extra fcap. 8vo. 2s. 6d.

—— *Anabasis,* Book II. With Notes and Map. By C. S. Jerram, M.A. . . . . [Extra fcap. 8vo. 2s.

—— *Anabasis,* Book III. With Introduction, Analysis, Notes, etc. By J. Marshall, M.A. . . . . . . [Extra fcap. 8vo. 2s. 6d.

—— *Vocabulary to the Anabasis.* By J. Marshall, M.A. [Extra fcap. 8vo. 1s. 6d.

—— *Cyropaedia,* Book I. With Introduction and Notes. By C. Bigg, D.D. . . . . [Extra fcap. 8vo. 2s.

—— *Cyropaedia,* Books IV, V. With Introduction and Notes. By the same Editor. . . . . [Extra fcap. 8vo. 2s. 6d.

—— *Hellenica,* Books I, II. With Introduction and Notes. By G. E. Underhill, M.A. . . . . [Extra fcap. 8vo. 3s.

London: HENRY FROWDE,

Oxford University Press Warehouse, Amen Corner.

Edinburgh: 6 Queen Street.

Oxford: Clarendon Press Depository,

116 High Street.